Praise for K. G. Dunca
I'm Only Dreaming of Dragons

"Educator and first-time author K. G. Duncan takes us on a road trip through time... With his command of storytelling, combined with his love affair with language, Duncan serves up a delicious feast seen through the eyes of a twelve-year-old, mind-reading shapeshifter named Aurora Borealis Rubideaux."
—DREW VAUPEN, Writer/Producer and Co-Creator
of Good Luck Charlie, a family sitcom for the Disney Channel

"A fascinating and practical immersion into the concept of non-linear time. In Abby, K.G. Duncan creates a character whose worldview of the "multi-verse" and theme of "discovering your life's purpose" is a neat, thought-provoking tip of the iceberg for young readers... This is not only a unique adventure, but also a learning... I absolutely ate up K.G. Duncan's words and phraseology. Can't wait for Book Two!"
—ROBERTA KAY, Singer/dancer/actress and
Emmy award winner and nominee for her work on PBS SoCal/KOCE

"Compelling reading from start to the exciting finish... K.G. Duncan's young heroine A.B. Rubideaux is smart and sassy... full of insights that many of us admittedly older readers could use as a refresher... Abby's adventures are a fast-paced backdrop for some important life lessons. I look forward to more from Abby and K.G. Duncan, but for now I will just have to be content with a re-read of this one!"
—KELLY RYAN, Author, lawyer, punk rocker. Author of
Science Classroom Safety and the Law - A Handbook for Teachers

"I'm Only Dreaming of Dragons takes readers on a wild ride through different worlds and times, following an 11-year-old girl's journey of not only self-discovery but of the age-old battle between the forces of light and dark. The first book of the series by debut author K.G. Duncan is a mind-bending and eye-opening peek of what's to come for the young Aurora Borealis Rubideaux and for all of humanity!"
—LIZ MOORE, author, blogger, and editor for
Bryant Street Publishing

AWAKENED

I'M ONLY DREAMING OF DRAGONS
BOOK I

K.G. DUNCAN

I'm Only Dreaming of Dragons—Book One: Awakened.
Copyright © 2021 by K. G. Duncan.

Library of Congress Cataloging-in-Publication Data
Names: Duncan, K. G., Author
Title: I'm Only Dreaming of Dragons – Book One: Awakened.

Library of Congress Control Number: 2021907530

ISBN 978-1-7370561-0-2 | ISBN 978-1-70561-1-9 (ebook)

Books > Teen & Young Adult > Science Fiction & Fantasy
Books > Teen & Young Adult > Literature & Fiction > Loners & Outcasts
Books > Teen & Young Adult > Literature & Fiction > Girls & Women

Chapter Illustration by K.M. Bornhoft
Cover Design: 100 Covers
Interior Design: Formatted Books
Editor: Erik Seversen

Under the Sun Press
Los Angeles

Under the Sun
Press

ACKNOWLEDGEMENTS

Thank you for reading this book. It was a long time coming, and left to my own devices, the first manuscripts may very well have sat, collecting dust in a box, never to be read by anyone. (Note to all of you creative people out there: You are worthy! Get your work out there and make it happen. Do it! Do it! Do it!)

First and foremost, thank you to my family. You were the first readers and the primary force that kept me going. Qing, you are my anchor in this fleeting and ethereal existence on the planet earth. I feel grateful for you every day. Megan and Josh—you are the light that inspires me, and you make me feel happy and proud to be your father. Josh, it was your influence that got me into the whole YA thing—thank you for bringing those books home to me way back in middle school—they were the first pebbles that made the first few ripples that led to my writing this book.

To my editor and primary lighter of fires, Erik Seversen, I owe a huge debt of gratitude. Thank you for navigating me—from beginning to end—through the murky waters of the publishing business. I can see clearly now, and there are no more obstacles in my way. Erik, you truly inspire me. Thank you also for your unswerving support and optimism. I would also like to give a very boisterous shout-out to all of my early readers: Sister Laurie, Blake, Grant, and my UCLA Crew, Shelley and Eleanor. Your thoughtful feedback and encouragement were instrumental in the shaping and growing of this book. I feel lucky to have your support.

A special thank you to my sister, Marilyn, who, when I was a young lad, gave me two books that shaped my future as a writer. Watership Down, by Richard Adams (Wow! A story told from the point of view of wild rabbits!) and The Hobbit, by J.R.R. Tolkein. That hard bound edition in the green box with gilded runes... I still have it and cherish it. I love the chapter illustrations that the reader comes across unexpectedly. You turn the page and OOH! There it is. It is magical and inspired me to do the same here in my first book.

And speaking of illustrations, thanks to Phyllis and Lan and the whole design team at 100 Covers! Also, a very special thank you to Kat. Your chapter drawing is simply stunning and beautiful—the perfect complement to make this novel into everything I envisioned it to be. I am so happy that we reconnected after so many years. Let's do it again!

I would be remiss if I neglected to mention some of the inspirations I found in the research for this book. If you, dear reader, are interested in the scientific and spiritual concepts that served as catalysts for the bolder and more speculative elements contained in this novel, here are some books and authors to check out: Jeremy Narby's The Cosmic Serpent—DNA and the Origins of Knowledge; Terrance McKenna's classic Food of the Gods—the Search for the Original Tree of Knowledge; The Holographic Universe by Michael Talbot; and The Ascent of Humanity, by Charles Eisenstein. I could go on... Just read and do your research, good people! Of course, I am indebted to many other authors who have inspired me over the years: J.R.R. Tolkien, Orson Scott Card, Frank Herbert, and Philip K. Dick, just to name a few. Among YA authors, I am especially indebted to Michael Smith for his amazing series The Secrets of the Immortal Nicholas Flamel, to Brandon Mull for his many book series, and to Clare Vanderpool for her amazing Newberry Gold Medal book Moon Over Manifest. I can still hear the small town, country voice that helped to inspire the many ramblings of Abby and Olivia in this novel!

Last, but not least, thank you, dad. Although you are no longer with us here on this earth, you took me out to the garage when I was seven, climbed up into the rafters and got down that dusty, old box of books. "Here. Read these," you said, handing me a book. I held in my hands an original hardback edition of Tarzan, Lord of the Apes, by Edgar Rice Burroughs. Over the years, the original artwork on the paper sleeves got rubbed away by my excessive handling, but I've still got those books. Oh yeah. I've been reading ever since.

To Qing, Megan and Joshua,
who keep me smiling,
and who make the world beautiful.

I

***

TORNADO

From the Audio transcripts of Dr. Joanna Kinsey
Chief Psychiatrist, CHNOLA Northshore Center,
New Orleans, LA

Audio File Transcript #AR10089-17

June 07, 2022

Subject: A. B. Rubideaux. Female. Age: 11

Transcript of recording begins: 11:09 AM EST.

Kinsey: *In our last session, we discussed the visual and audio distortions as well as the frequency and duration of the change. Today I want you to describe the specific physical aspects of the transformation—how your body changes, from beginning to end. Are you ready to begin?*

A.B.: *(Inaudible murmuring.)*

Kinsey: *I'm sorry, A.B.? Shall I repeat my question?*

A.B.: *We've talked about this before. Do that thing you always do. Please.*

Kinsey: *Of course. (Clears throat.) This is audio file number seventeen, May 22, 2022. Dr. Joanna Kinsey interviewing Subject number AR10089: Miss Aurora Borealis Rubideaux. Female. 11 years old. Miss Rubideaux, are you aware that this conversation is being recorded?*

A.B.: *Yes.*

Kinsey: *Do I have your permission to record this conversation?*

A.B.: *Yes.*

Kinsey: *Shall we begin?*

A.B.: *(Laughter.) I think we can now, yes. Thank you, doctor. (Long pause.) I'm sorry, could you repeat the question?*

SEVEN YEARS EARLIER, JUNE 2, 2015

Well, even a five-year-old girl knows that something ain't right with the world when the sky has turned green.

A somewhat anxious Abby Rubideaux, stood on the porch of their dilapidated wood-planked house, clutching the railing and staring up at the swirling sky. Storm clouds roiled and spun away. The wind was blowing hard—real hard—the tops of the trees bending over at impossible angles, and the dust and debris in the air made her eyes squint.

Green. Definitely green. Not even close to normal. Not one trifling bit.

There was that Voice in her head again—the deep rumbling one that she never told anyone about. Hearing it in that moment made her feel instantly calm. Even though the Voice usually wasn't very talkative, it was more like she could *feel* it.

Abby wasn't sure if the Voice was a he or a she, but either way it was very cool and spoke to her in an adult way, using words like "trifling" because somehow, some way, she could always understand. The Voice was her constant companion. She never really thought about it too much because that was the way it had always been—it was just there—the Voice in her head. But the Voice had always been with her, and it was her secret friend.

Abby took a deep breath and felt the fear slip away, even when icy hail stones the size of golf balls started hammering down, making a terrible racket on the roof of the porch and house.

Boom. Boom. Boom. Do we have your attention now? Are you ready to come out and play?

Abby grinned. On most ordinary days in Mandeville Louisiana at 3 O'clock in the afternoon, Abby could go for a swing, play hop-scotch in the driveway, or look for tadpoles down by the creek. On an ordinary day if she went outside to play, she wouldn't have to dodge killer ice balls or use a rope to tie herself down just to keep from flying off all helter-skelter into the bayou.

Precisely! Ordinary days are overrated, don't you think?

Abby's smile widened. Well, on an *ordinary* day her mother wouldn't be acting so funny, either. Abby's newfound confidence suddenly crumbled. Her momma was scared, and that's why she was feeling scared, too.

As if it could hear her thoughts, a gust of wind sent the door banging behind her. Her long, wavy black hair whipped around her round face, and the coppery-brown skin of her unusually high cheek bones shone in the eerie green light, which matched the intensity of her wide set, deep green eyes.

Abby thought to herself, and not for the first time, that there were extraordinary things in the world, and she was about to discover some of those things today.

"A.B.…. A.B.…." Abby thought she heard the name her mother always called her, but it was distant, floating and muffled on the wind. Her Mother— that would be Beatriz Roy, or "Momma Bea" as Abby always referred to her— was the reason why she was standing on the porch in the first place. Now, Momma Bea was not her real, biological mother, but her adoptive mother, and this was how things got a little complicated, especially when it came to Abby's name. Her mother always called her "A. B." for short, just like the first two letters of the alphabet. A. B., and that's because her actual, full given name was Aurora Borealis Rubideaux, which is a mouthful. And for most folks, A. B. somehow became "Abby," and that's what most folks called her. A.B., Abby. It's an honest mistake, and one the little girl didn't really mind.

Abby generally kept her full name to herself—for experience had taught her that other children could be cruel and unrelenting when it came to the proper naming of persons and things—but she secretly liked it when her Sunday school teacher, Ms. Pettijean called her by her full name, Aurora Borealis Rubideaux, which, the young girl had also known for quite some time, was the name that her birth or "biological" momma had given her when she was born. She was given that name because during the winter of her pregnancy, her birth mother was living up in Alaska, where the northern lights would dance in a colorful, magical and most wonderful way. And her birth momma loved them northern lights about as much as anything in the whole wide world. At least that's what Momma Bea always told Abby when she asked about it, so that's why she liked it so much.

Whew! Now you know what's in a name!

So Abby—and let's stick to Abby for the duration of this story—was standing on the porch in this whale of a storm, looking up at an unnaturally green sky, hearing (or just imagining) that the storm was carrying her name in the wind, and trying to ignore the lethal hail stones raining down upon the earth, and you might be wondering why Momma Bea had dragged her outside in the middle of a hellacious storm! Well, there wasn't much to it, really, and very little in the way of explanation. But it is how all of this got started, so let's go back and tell it proper from beginning to end.

They had been watching the news on TV, and all the news commentators were apprehensive, talking about a tornado, and how the situation had been upgraded from a "Tornado Watch" to a "Tornado Warning." And Abby was just about to ask Momma Bea what that meant, when the screen on the television went dead. And it was at that precise moment that Momma Bea had turned to the form of her boyfriend/husband/life partner (sort of), Henry, who was passed out in the recliner amidst a pile of beer cans and a box of Cheez-its, clucked her tongue, grabbed her purse, and said in a very matter-of-fact tone of voice, "Well, A. B., I believe there is no better time than the present to do what must be done."

Momma Bea then grabbed Abby, lifted her up from the sofa, told her to put on her shoes and grab whatever she could grab in the next 30 seconds.

"We're leaving, darling." Momma Bea had said. "We got to get to New Orleans."

New Orleans! Now Abby just loved driving over Lake Pontchartrain and heading into the city. It usually meant new shoes or dresses or shopping of some sort. Sometimes it meant street performers, folks walking around in costumes and all sorts of music. It always meant good food. This was different however, and Momma Bea was in a completely frazzled and manic state that Abby had never seen before.

Exactly 34 seconds later, Abby appeared back in the family room. She had only had time to grab her panda bear, Ling-Ling, snap on the golden cross necklace that had belonged to her real mother, slip into her crocs, and toss two of her *Magic Tree House* mystery books into her school bag before Momma Bea yanked her out the bedroom door to scurry past the dozing Henry.

"Careful not to kick those cans," momma had whispered as they tiptoed over the pile around his chair. "Last thing we wanna do is wake him!"

"We leaving pa?" Abby asked quietly as they reached the front door. Just before the door shut behind her, she looked back and caught a glimpse of the sleeping Henry, his slack-jawed mouth hanging open, and it seemed like for no reason at all she felt a thrill of fear shoot through her entire body.

"We're leaving your pa, and that's a fact." Momma Bea scanned the sky and her stern demeanor wavered into worry as she clutched at Abby. The wind was whistling and hissing through the writhing big elm tree in the front yard. A neighbor's lawn chair shot across the yard, tumbling and clattering in the powerful wind. The pine trees that lined the driveway were bending over at their tops, black and purple thunderhead clouds roiling above their agitated limbs. And yes. The sky was most assuredly green.

"You stay here and wait while I go get the car!" Beatriz needed to shout over the howl of the wind. "It's too dangerous. Don't come out till I pull up with the car!"

Abby nodded, scared out of her wits, and then her mother darted across the driveway to the garage. Abby was standing on the porch, the screen door banging behind her, and she was scolding herself for feeling so afraid.

"Well, what am I? Still a baby?" Abby whispered, then glanced up at the sky again. "Nothing but a stupid little storm. But why are we going out if it's so dangerous, Momma Bea?" Abby caught her breath then yelped as a wood shingle ripped off the porch roof above her, then hurtled across the lawn.

Come fly, little sister.

The Voice inside her head soothed her, and she began to breathe more easily. Abby clutched Ling-Ling to her chest and rubbed the well-worn spot where the panda's left eye had fallen out. She watched as Beatriz struggled to open the garage door, then dashed inside, the wind howling even louder. Abby found a strange, almost clinical place of calm in the question that suddenly popped into her head:

Where do birds go when there's a storm? She glanced at the flailing elm tree in the front yard. *Lord knows I wouldn't want to hunker down in a flimsy old tree or try to fly in the sky right about now.*

And that's just about where we were at when Abby had decided that something wasn't quite right with the world when the sky had turned green.

No ma'am. Not one trifling bit.

Abby smiled, and just like that, everything was okay.

Her mom's old, weather-worn blue Hyundai came roaring to a stop right in front of the porch, its wheels spinning ferociously and kicking up gravel and rocks, which flew like bullets pelting the porch. Abby covered her face in the shower of tiny rocks and flinched as she felt a sting rap sharply against her bare leg.

"Get in!" Momma Bea was screaming as she reached across the seat and struggled to hold open the door.

Abby darted down the steps and dove into the front seat as the door slammed shut behind her, narrowly missing her feet. She could barely breathe as she glanced down and saw that she was missing one of her crocs.

"Momma, I lost my shoe!" She shouted, looking back as the car sped away. Her pink croc was lying on the gravel, trembling beneath the force of the wind.

"Leave it!" Momma shouted as she struggled to straighten out the car, which was fish-tailing down the driveway. "Get yourself in the back seat and keep your head down!"

Abby obeyed automatically, and quick as a cat she leapt into the back. Still looking behind the car, she watched breathlessly as the wind snatched her sandal away, a tumbling blur of pink, and then it was gone. The engine of the Hyundai roared to life as they picked up speed, and her house grew smaller behind.

"Momma! The wind took my shoe!" Abby screeched, more excited than scared. But then she felt her momma's hand firmly pressing down on her head.

"Get down, A.B.!" Momma was yelling. "I told you to stay down, Jiminy Christmas!" Momma Bea swerved, then put both hands on the wheel as she made the turn from the gravel driveway onto the smoother surface of the road. Abby threw herself down on the floor boards of the back seat, and the car picked up speed. From her vantage point down on the floor, Abby could still look out the windows and see the green sky above the bending trees. She yelped as something hard smacked against the side of the car, but Momma Bea kept driving, speeding up even faster.

Keep calm, little sister. This is our storm!

That Voice in her head buoyed her spirit, and Abby dared to lift her head up slightly so she could see the front windshield in the space between the front seats. They careened around a corner, and now they were racing down highway 190 through her hometown of Mandeville. The whine of the car's engine was discordant against the howl of the wind outside, and she could feel her heart pounding inside of her breast. She watched a large branch of some unlucky tree fly horizontally across the road in front of them. Momma Bea's knuckles whitened, tightly gripping the steering wheel, and she stepped down on the accelerator.

"Got to get to New Orleans…Got to get to New Orleans…" Momma Bea was muttering, over and over under her breath. The Walmart and the video depot whizzed by. They raced down empty gray streets; the only souls foolhardy enough to venture out into the storm. Abby stared at her momma's lips, repeating the mantra, and she could sense the fear in her mother almost turning into panic. Abby's gut suddenly all wrenched up inside and her pulse was pounding with a pressure that felt like it would burst right outside her ears.

Breathe, little sister. Breathe.

Abby obeyed and took deep breaths. She managed to keep calm even as the skies whirled above, and hail stones started raining down again, rapping against the car like a drum.

"Momma?" Abby lifted herself up from the floor and leaned in between the seats. "Why you drivin' so fast?"

"Hush now!" Beatriz glanced back distractedly. "Get back and buckle that seat belt," she snapped as the car hurtled onto the East Causeway Approach.

Abby slid on back and complied, her mind oddly empty and detached, like her spirit was separating from her body. What an odd feeling! A part of her felt no safer, even after the buckle clicked. The other part of her just kept breathing, slow and deep. She pulled the adjuster tighter and clutched her panda, Ling Ling to her chest.

The curve of the road, slick as it was, proved perilous as the car slid alarmingly across the lanes of the highway before her mother straightened it out and accelerated once again down the straightway. Abby lifted herself up slightly and peered out the window—she could just make out the Waffle House and the Sesame Inn Chinese restaurant on the right, before they whizzed by and there was nothing but angry sky, the swaying trees of the bayou giving way to open wetlands. Up ahead and approaching quickly, the vast expanse of Lake Pontchartrain came into view, a boiling whirl of grey water and frothing white caps.

Abby's eyes grew big as she spotted the bridge in front of them. The causeway jutted out on top of the water like two grey fingers, nearly 24 miles of concrete that spanned the entire lake. From north to south, it connected Mandeville in St. Tammany Parish to Jefferson Parish and the city of New Orleans. On an ordinary day, Abby loved driving across the water because the bridge was so low and sat right on top of the lake—she would roll down her window and let the wind hit her face, and she could fancy herself like some great water bird gliding free and easy across the water. A blue heron or an egret. Momma Bea would laugh and call her a puppy, like some golden retriever whose favorite thing was to hang her head out a window and just grin in the wind with her jowls flapping. Today, however, the normally smooth and glassy surface of the lake was a churning, heaving force of nature, and the causeway ahead looked ominous and uninviting. Wind-whipped waves slapped across the railings of the bridge, the water threatening to swamp the road at any moment. No other cars were on the bridge.

"Momma?" Abby's voice was barely a squeak as they bolted toward the bridge. Beatriz ignored her and sped on, blowing by the state trooper car, parked near the entrance to the bridge. A lone officer, plastic blue parka splattered wetly against his body, emerged from a small concrete hut next to the road and ran towards their car, arms waving madly in the air above his head. The Hyundai streaked past him, not slowing at all, and Abby was just able to catch a glimpse of a thick mustache and the eyes of the shocked trooper's face before it was gone.

The car blasted through a makeshift barricade and blinking wooden hazard signs shattered off the front fender. "Gotta get you to New Orleans!" Abby's momma shouted above the storm.

"But why, momma! Why?" Abby squeaked as they sped out over the bridge. Her eyes got bigger as she spotted the roiling clouds straight ahead, a mad swirling cluster of black, purple and blue. Waves dashed across the road in front of them as far as the eye could see, but the wind whipped the water away before it could form any hazard on the road.

"Hush, A.B." Momma's voice was oddly calm and quiet. "This is our storm. It's calling to us. Can't you hear?"

Abby found her momma's question oddly reassuring. Maybe she could feel it, too? There *was* someone or something out there, calling to them. Maybe Abby wasn't imagining things that were just in her head.

She tried listening real hard to find the voices of whomever might be calling, but all she could hear was the raging wind and the hail stones clacking off the car. The Voice in her head was silent. She leaned back and pressed herself tightly against the seat back and just felt the roar of the engine beneath her as the wind, water and ice pelted them.

Up ahead the roiling mass of clouds took on form and shape, and Abby's heart nearly stopped as she saw it: the swirling vortex of a cyclone. Just off the right side of the bridge, about one third the way across, the spinning finger touched down on the lake and drew the water up into its hungry, whirling maw. The needle-like nose of the twister darted erratically, touching down at random.

And they were racing straight towards it.

Abby knew right there and then that she couldn't watch, so she clamped her eyes shut, covered her face in her hands, and turned away.

"Got to get to New Orleans…" Momma Bea was still muttering, over and over, and Abby latched on to the words just so she could hold on to something, anything.

A few deep breaths, and she felt the calm returning, the deep rumble of the Voice within soothed her, reminding her that she was not alone. Her courage returned, Abby opened her eyes once again and peered out between her fingers. She could see the top of the lake looking west outside her window where more dark clouds pressed down upon the middle of the lake.

Unfortunately, she did not find any signs of encouragement; in fact, she found the opposite. There was another cyclone there—bigger and badder—swirling and sucking water into its spinning, snaking cylinder. The green of the sky seemed brighter and glowing there above the waterspout, and Abby watched in horrific fascination as it looked as if the entire lake would be sucked up into the sky.

She snapped her head back and screamed as her momma suddenly slammed on the brakes and the car spun around in circles before coming to a lurching halt. The engine stalled. Now the car was sitting in the middle of the causeway, having spun perpendicular to the road. The ice had stopped falling, but rain and wind continued to pelt and buffet the stationary car. Abby's window looked out directly down the causeway in the direction they had been driving. The railings of the bridge ahead of them were being yanked out, one by one, pulled ferociously into the first cyclone, which was no more than a thousand feet away, directly over the bridge, and barreling straight down on them.

"Momma! Turn back! Turn back!" Abby shrieked and banged on the seat in front of her. Momma Bea glanced back at Abby, her mouth a perfect gaping "O." She clumsily put the car back into park, and desperately turned the ignition over. The car roared to life, and Momma Bea popped the engine into drive. The tires spun in place for several moments before squealing to a sudden, jolting start. They shot forward like a rock from a sling, hurtling back down the way they had come. Abby's heart was pounding, and just when she thought she could bear no more, a wall of grey swallowed them, and the road below and everything ahead of them disappeared. They were weightless, and they were flying.

Now, at the time something like this occurs, the brain doesn't always let it register, but that is exactly what Abby thought as the car was lifted. She felt just like when your insides get all fluttery all of a sudden when you're riding on a rollercoaster and the bottom just drops out. Like that. But what she couldn't grasp at that moment was the unimaginable. They were caught in a fifteen-foot wall of water that had rolled unseen across the surface of the lake, and the wave had crested the bridge and swallowed them. There was a moment or two of profound silence. Then her stomach felt like it was suddenly being pushed through the top of her head as the car suddenly dipped, rolled over once, and slammed back down on the road. In less than a second the car smashed against the side railing, and the back window shattered into a million fractals of spinning light.

Abby screamed on impact as her head was painfully jerked to the right and then left. Everything seemed to wobble and rock before settling into a stunned and silent center of stillness. The raging storm all around was replaced by ringing in her ears.

Abby opened her eyes and saw broken glass covering her blouse and Ling Ling, her stuffed animal still clutched tightly in her arm. "Momma!" Her voice seemed distant and muted, but she knew she was shouting. "Momma!" She could see her mom's head resting against the steering wheel, the cracked front windshield beyond her. She fumbled to unbuckle her seat belt and then flung herself forward, reaching for her mother. There was a trickle of blood seeping down her mother's temple, but then her eyes fluttered open as Abby's hand stroked her hair and face.

"We're alive momma! We're alive!" Abby was yelling and then laughing, and it all sounded weird and remote with the ringing still in her ears. But Abby felt fine. She felt fine. And her mother also smiled.

Come fly, little sister.

The Voice was different this time, like it was just outside her head, almost like somebody was sitting right next to her, whispering in her ear.

Then mother sat upright and stared down at her hands. Hundreds of little shards of glass were trembling and hovering in the air above them. Momma Bea turned and looked back at Abby, who gasped and froze as the shards of broken glass that moments before were on and all around her lifted and quivered, suspended like snowflakes in the air. She glanced down at her own hands, the one still holding Ling Ling, the other reaching out towards her mom. Her curly black hair and the golden cross that hung by a chain around her neck were also lifted up as if by invisible hands.

That was when the ringing in her ears became a roar.

Instantly, the car trembled then groaned and lifted. Beatriz screamed, "NOOOOO!" a long wailing note that was sucked away as the force of the cyclone descended upon them. She had to cover her eyes as the glass suddenly streaked outside the shattered rear window. Then Abby's school bag, and the twisted-up papers and the gum wrappers and stale peanuts that were under the seats—everything was sucked away in a flash.

And then there was Abby.

Beatriz locked unto her daughter's incongruently calm grey-green eyes. Abby seemed to be mouthing the words, "It's okay, momma…" And then she was gone, ripped from the back seat, through the back window, and into the screaming purple-black void above.

2

NO TIME FOR DREAMTIME

What we have forgotten can be found in the tears of the stars.
It is from such things that we have come.
The threads from Great Mother spin and spiral downwards to the earth.
But we can climb back up again.
This, we have forgotten.

—*from **The Book of Sayings**, "Bo M'ba Nesh Speaks"*

ANOTHER TIME, ANOTHER PLACE – THE SEASON OF THE ISHWI VINE

The forest was quiet and still. Abby walked silently, her bare feet making no sound on the soft jungle floor. Through the canopy of trees ahead she could see blue slits of sky. She approached closer, wanting to have one more look. As she brushed past the lush foliage, she could hear the sound of rushing water. She slowed her steps as she came up to the rim of a steep gorge.

Pushing purple and pink blooming vines aside, she stopped with her toes gripping the lip of the cliff. She caught her breath as she looked out over the river valley. Giant boulders dotted the mountain side across the gorge—they hovered in the air like giant heads, defying gravity, their gray faces glowing with the pink of the sinking sun. Abby knew this meant that the elders were still at their looms weaving. As long as they worked the tapestries, the rocks would slowly lift and move up the mountain. It was how the *Sihanaka* people got the giant slabs up the mountain. "Dream Engineering," the elders called it. Abby smiled to herself as a single word bubbled up from somewhere deep inside of her. Magic. But that was a voice from somewhere far away and unreachable. It was a voice that she had heard before. A voice that was hers but wasn't hers. A sneaky voice that whispered things like "magic."

Abby shook herself and the thought that was not her voice fluttered away and was gone. Just like that. Such a slippery thing. Once her mind tried to fix on it, it squirted away like a wet bangku seed between her fingers. She took a deep breath and her eyes swept up the side of the mountain. Yes, there, like tiny ants, she could see the builders moving on the terraced top, guiding the stones into their proper position where the temple was being erected. Once on the ground, the stones would be cut and polished, then placed.

Abby looked down the cliff's edge below her feet. Water fell noisily over rocks and down for hundreds of feet. The spray misted all around creating rainbow arcs of light. Not much longer and the sun would dip below the western mountains, and the long semi-darkness of mountain twilight would settle in. With another deep breath, Abby turned and slipped back into the forest.

She quickened her pace, counting her breaths as she sped down the path. Sixty-four breaths later, the sound of wood chopping and muffled voices came to her in soft, intermittent waves. The village was getting closer. As she neared the edge of the jungle, Abby could make out the thatched roofs of houses built into the side of a hill. She could smell the cooking fires and beneath the smoke, the sweet scents of fried plantains and taro; she could hear the distant laughter of children, their voices much clearer now. No doubt they were playing alongside the river, a robust game of *Adawa i Kek-chirri*, or Stones and Frog.

The village, surrounded by jungle and mountains on all sides, was built on terraces carved into a hillside that overlooked a lush and fertile river valley. Abby was approaching from the north along a stream, one of many rivulets that wound its way circuitously down from the mountain top. Up there were fresh springs, where water bubbled up from deep within the mountain. At the source, the water was clean and full of minerals—perfect for the late afternoon bath from which Abby was returning.

She was near the weaving hut now, a larger structure raised on a wooden platform supported by thick stilts above the stone bluff. Abby knew at this time of the day the old woman would be there. She squatted in the brush and watched.

Through fern fronds and wild orchids, she caught a glimpse of the women moving about below the hut. Large baskets and bundles were strapped to their heads or to their hips. They were bringing in the *ishwi* vines and the branches of the *bangku* tree, unloading their daily haul from the heart of the jungle. The vines would be shredded and picked clean, the bark of the *bangku* would be stripped and soaked overnight, then later hung out to be dried. Eventually all would be sorted and recombined by color and used for dying and weaving.

Abby watched the women from her hidden spot at the forest edge. Their movements were measured and graceful, nothing wasted or overexerted as they flowed in and out of the shady confines beneath the weaving hut, their soft voices rippling amongst them, occasionally punctuated with a burst of laughter.

Abby smiled when she saw the elder. Sitting in her usual spot near the edge of the stone bluff but still beneath the shade of the house above. It was the perfect spot to watch the children who played down by the river below. She had her loom with her, and her fingers nimbly danced as they worked the colorful threads pulled tautly between the reed and the heald shaft. Abby waited at the edge of the jungle wall for the other women to move away. She wanted to sneak up on the elder and surprise her—it was an old game, one which she never succeeded at. Somehow the old woman always knew she was there.

The last of the other women had unloaded their baskets and were moving away. Abby seized the opportunity and pounced. She slipped silently between the ferns and the bamboo reeds and stalked catlike towards the old woman. One last stalk snagged on her leg and whipped back with a snap. A bird startled and flew away noisily, squawking in protest. Abby froze in mid-crouch.

"Avy aiza kaka vanao? Ona leshilahy afaka entiko mandihi, ve iano?" (Who is making such a racket? Did you come to dance with me, little monkey?)

The old woman spoke, then turned and smiled at Abby. Her fingers still deftly moving along the shuttle of the loom, not missing a beat. Not for the first time, Abby caught her breath as she gazed upon the woman; the dark skin of her entire face crisscrossed with the white and pinkish latticework of scars.

Like a spider's web.

It was the mark of the honored elders, and Abby felt her heart tremble and beat a little faster when she found herself in the presence of this one, so old and wise. The elder clicked her tongue then laughed.

"You will not catch me today, little monkey. How does such a small one move like a rutting elephant?" The language of the old woman was a mellifluous purr, and without asking why, Abby could understand and speak it.

Suddenly the fingers of the woman stopped, and she put the loom to the side and turned to look directly at Abby.

"The work on the mountain top has stopped for the day. It will be time for the evening meal soon," the old woman continued, "but first we need to talk, alone, without the others." The smile left the lips of the woman.

"Yes, Bo M'ba," Abby replied as she uncoiled herself from her prowling stance and strode over quickly to stand before the elder. A sudden twinge of dread filled her.

The old wise one regarded Abby soberly, her eyes glittering like deep black pools beneath her protruding, web-scarred brow. Several moments of silence followed before she spoke.

"Oh, little wanderer, why do you waste my time? Once again, you are not really here." The old woman smiled slightly then sighed. Abby thought she might fall into the elder's eyes if she stared back too long. She looked down and fixed her stare on the gnarled and bony fingers folded in the old woman's lap.

Abby suddenly gasped when the words of the old woman finally sunk in. She whipped her head up and found ancient eyes that pinned her like a trembling branch to the sky. She took a step and stumbled; her mind suddenly dizzy. She gasped as her knee scraped hard against the stone pavers that circled the weaving hearth. She frowned at the small trickle of blood that seeped forth and tickled its way down her shin.

The Elder named Bo M'ba Nesh sighed again. Her body wavered and flickered and then began to disappear in front of Abby's eyes. "Come to me when you are not so busy dreaming," her voice was loud and clear even as her body faded into blurry light. "We need to talk and perform the rites. It is the only way to stop your brother, before it is too late."

Abby's eyes drifted down to a smooth and polished black bear claw hanging by a necklace around the old woman's neck. It shimmered and quivered as the old woman's shape wavered and faded and the blurry light overwhelmed everything.

And then the elder named Bo M'ba Nesh winked into nothingness.

3

MANY RETURNS

From the Audio transcripts of Dr. Joanna Kinsey
Chief Psychiatrist, CHNOLA Northshore Center,
New Orleans, LA

Audio File Transcript #AR10089-17

June 07, 2022

Subject: A. B. Rubideaux. Female. Age: 12

Transcript of recording begins: 11:11 AM EST.

Kinsey: *Fine. Let's pick up where we left off last time. Miss Rubideaux, can you describe—and please, in as much specific detail as you can—the physical changes to your body? What are the earliest outward signs that the transformation is about to begin?*

A.B.: *It always begins in the extremities. The physical aspect that is. Always in the extremities. About six or seven days before the change, you'll find a scaly patch of skin on your elbow or on the small nub of bone just behind your ear... a build-up of plaque beneath the finger and toenails. A hardening of the skin on the fingertips or on the heels of your feet. Within a day, the hardened skin will start to spread. Those are the early signs. The physical signs.*

Kinsey: *Are there any other physical or psychological symptoms besides these changes in your physical extremities. Any discomfort or pain? Any change in mood or emotion? Things like that.*

A.B.: *Why yes, doctor. Let me run those down for you, in my most clinically summative manner. (Chuckling.) I'm sorry, doctor. But I really do enjoy our conversations.*

Kinsey: *I know, A.B. As do I. And I've told you, please, call me Joanna.*

A.B.: *Yes, thank you. Joanna. The physical changes are accompanied by an acute loss of appetite, intermittent nausea. There are body aches, muscle cramps, and involuntary, extreme muscle spasms. (Pause) Is this what you want?*

Kinsey: *Yes. You're doing fine, A.B. Please continue.*

A.B.: *(Giggling.) Okay. I also experience a dull, throbbing headache, which accompanies the blurred distortions of color and light, but nothing severe in the beginning. Just enough to distract and irritate. The headaches will grow incrementally, both in strength and length, lasting up to several hours—this is usually about the time that my visual and audio perceptions warp and bend dramatically and the whole world starts to swirl and go blurry.*

Kinsey: *Yes, we've talked about your visual distortions before, and we can return to it later. Right now, I want you to describe only the visible, physical changes to your body, as well as your internal changes.*

A.B.: *It's hard to separate those things. They are all connected. Ok—What I've been describing to you—That's just the physical change. You asked me to describe the psychological component as well, yes? Whether I had any mood or emotional swings. Well, I was about to get to the interesting part. The juicy bits. The scaling of my skin and the vertigo and the pain that comes with it? That's not really what the change is all about. The best part—the part where I get all tingly inside—now, that's the main thing. (Giggling.) You ever get all tingly inside, Joanna?*

Kinsey: *Well, I'm not sure what you mean. Please, tell me about the interesting "tingly" part.*

A.B.: *(Laughs and snorts.) Okay, so, there is so much more that goes beyond my ability to put into words! I can't even begin to describe... (An audible gasp.) Underlying all of it—everything from the beginning of the first itching in my fingertips right up to the sudden, cataclysmic and bone-splitting transformation itself—underlying all of it is the feeling... of... elation.*

Kinsey: *Elation?*

A.B.: *Yes. Elation. Pure and unadulterated bliss. That's what it feels like when I change—when I take my true form. That's what it feels like to be everywhere and nowhere all at once. It's what makes me tingle.*

Kinsey: Well, I must confess, what you have described to me doesn't sound very much like elation. It sounds… excruciating… and terrifying. I'll have to dig a little deeper to understand it.

A.B.: (Laughter.) Dig a little deeper, Doctor Kinsey. Joanna. But I have a question for you. Have you ever turned into a dragon before?

Kinsey: No, I can't say that I have.

A.B.: Then truly, you don't have any idea of what I'm talking about.

FOUR MONTHS EARLIER: FEB 4, 2022.

Ain't no big thing. Any child could do it. It happened every day. All the time. It's just imagination. You know, how your thoughts can kind of just slip out the back door, jump off the stoop, and run off all willy-nilly? You could go anywhere you want. Other worlds, even. Other times. There was no limit. The little voice in her head just told her to go. Sometimes Abby didn't listen, but most of the time, she did.

Because when you have a dragon inside of you, it is usually wise to listen.

On this day, at this moment, Abby was trying her best *not* to listen to her dragon. She was lazing in the window bench just off the dining room. It was her favorite spot in the house. The cushions were just the right mix of firm and soft. She could lean back against the recessed edge of the alcove on the big pillow with blue butterflies stitched on it and read a book. It was the brightest spot in the house, with sunlight all day. She could also stare out the window for hours at the garden below, watching her Momma Bea working in the planter boxes where fresh vegetables and flowers grew. Or she could gaze beyond the garden, where trees draped with Spanish moss marked the boundary of the property line, and beyond that was the shimmering glint of bayou water. Miles and miles of it.

The sight of that water made the dragon stir deeply within her. Abby wasn't in the mood to listen to that stirring today. It took every ounce of her will to resist the dragon and not go flying off to plunge into that water and maybe catch a few fish. She'd learned in her few short years that there was a proper time and place for the dragon. Like when she was alone. And in the dark. Yeah, always better to ride with the dragon alone and in the dark!

Abby brought her focus back to her little window perch. She sighed deeply. It had been a sleepy afternoon, and Abby's book lay unopened in her lap. She had been watching a plump, yellow and black orb weaver spider spin its web all day. It was a beautiful web—spun meticulously with the grace and perfection of some intergalactic geometry. The spider had been building her web all morning, from beginning to end. Just a little bit of magic here on this earth. And something about watching the spider at work stirred feelings deep inside of her. A sense of somewhere other, where all she had to do was close her eyes and she could be there. She could almost smell it and taste it, for that's how close it was. If she could just hold on to the thought a little bit longer, then she could vanish and be there. Instead, it was the thought that vanished.

That's how it was—how it always had been. Just when things were about to get interesting, she ended up back here... with Momma Bea and Henry. And any thoughts that might transport her somewhere far away and utterly, completely different—well, they just had a habit of disappearing all at once.

She had once talked to Momma Bea about it. Abby had asked her if she ever had the kind of thought that as soon as she thought of it, it would slip away like wet seeds slipping between your fingers, and some other thought would replace it. Then, before she knew it, she would be brushing her teeth or getting ready for school, or helping Momma Bea in the kitchen, and all of it would be entirely gone and forgotten.

Just like a dream. But Abby's dreams were real. And dreams didn't leave scars.

Abby looked down at a scab on her knee that she had been absently picking at. She scrunched up her forehead and closed her eyes. There was something very important that she needed to remember, but she couldn't quite get a hold of it. She rubbed at the scab when she realized that she had picked it open again, and it was starting to bleed. She also realized that she couldn't remember where she got that scab.

Somewhere deep within her the Voice rumbled, stirring and growing restless. Abby quickly quelled that rumbling and sent it back down into a still and sleepy place. She sighed again and sank deeper into the pillows of the alcove window. It was quiet, and that was the best thing about Abby's spot in the window. Its location was placed perfectly by some trick of acoustical engineering as the one and only spot in the house where she could not hear the din of the TV, which her ne'er-do-well stepdad, Henry, always had on. Constant, loud, and blaring, the television could not penetrate her island of calm and silence. It was her sanctuary.

But Henry didn't need a blaring TV to find his way into her thoughts and dreams.

Abby felt that familiar finger of trepidation tracing down the back of her neck. Henry was growing restless and bored. Abby sensed the change in frequency all at once. His reptilian mind was starting to wander and seek out its familiar target.

Out of sight, out of mind. He'll think about her less if he doesn't see her.

Too late for that. Momma Bea was already there with him. He was already working her. Same old thing. Same sad story. But this time Abby was going to put an end to it. She just needed to let the dragon into Henry's mind and work on him from the inside. She had to do it. She had to make him stop.

Henry's mind was not Abby's favorite place to be. In fact, she spent a considerable amount of effort every day trying to avoid Henry's mind. Some things are better left untouched. She could resist the pull into his mind by finding distractions—occupying her mind with various pursuits and entertainment. But he was always there... lurking, like a miserable old, cold-blooded toad that could never feel the warmth of others. He just sat there stewing in bitterness and bringing forth ugliness to the world. He was an energy-sucking toad, and other people were like flies that he would just swallow, sucking down their terrible fly juices. Maybe that was what made him so cantankerous.

But even with all of that, Abby didn't hate him—she just felt sorry for him.

She smiled, and she realized at that very moment that she would never be afraid of papa Henry again. She also smiled because she had decided that it was time to put an end to Henry's abuse of Momma Bea. Never again. It would end today.

Now, it wasn't in Abby's nature to go prying or to invade others, but when you have a dragon inside of you, well then you don't have the normal boundaries that keep people's minds separate from each other. For Abby, it was always the touch of another person that connected her mind to theirs. Skin on skin—feeling the pulse and the vital energy of another. Then the flood gates would open. But in this case, no touch was necessary. For folks like Henry and Momma Bea, it was constant proximity and, in the case of Henry, unfortunate familiarity.

So, deep breath. Find a place of calm. A quiet mind. Abby began reaching out. It came almost immediately. Henry's frequency always felt to Abby like a violation of what was normal and natural. It slammed into her like a fist to her belly. Like so many people, his mind, not conscious of itself, was like a greedy, little child, grasping and desperately seeking the attention he longed for.

Now, what happened next is difficult to explain in real time. Let's just say that it was like a slide show of Henry's life—his vivid memories, buried deep but still informing him on a daily basis—also his aspirations, his fears, his obsessions. Everything real or imagined that had happened or could have happened or might not have happened yet—an entire life actually lived or merely made up in a matter of seconds. Abby could process it all in a few moments.

Slide number one began with Henry's birth. Maybe this was the way it actually went down. Or maybe it was just a version of the story, endlessly recounted, refined and edited for those to whom it was being told. Regardless, it was the one that was stuck in Henry's mind. It was the one he held on to, so it was the version Abby could know.

Flick. Henry Thierrey came into this world butt-first. The appropriate medical term for that is "breach baby," but "butt-first" seems more appropriate here because Henry was indeed a butthead of the first degree. He was just plain mean. Normally, folks don't put much stock in the prophetic nature of these kinds of things, but when Henry's slippery and pink baby behind came squishing and squeezing unapologetically into this world, it was an omen of profound proportion, way beyond the domain of chance or mere pedestrian coincidence. Although there was no official documentation, it seemed clear that Doc must have pulled Henry Thierrey out by his baby cheeks and slapped him upside the head because he had been angry and taking exception ever since.

Ah, Abby could hear Henry's mother's voice. This was the family joke. She was fond of telling this story at family gatherings. It was a strong theme that Henry took a sort of twisted pride in. He didn't mind that it made his other family members laugh—mostly at his expense. He didn't mind because it was acknowledgement. It was all about him, it was most likely the truth, and he totally owned it.

AWAKENED

Abby flicked past the temptation to linger—There were too many rabbit holes to go down. She was looking for something else and needed to move on. And so, the kaleidoscope reel began:

Flick. His daddy, an ornery and spite-filled drunk, lifting his hand and striking his mother. Then daddy just gone—a door closing, floorboards creaking, and him never coming back.

Flick. The corner of a blanket hanging down from the table-top. It was a cream-colored fleece with yellow edging and a pastel green and yellow lamb print. His brother lying on top, gurgling, cooing, and making happy baby sounds. Henry's hands moving toward the blanket… hands tugging on the corner… consuming, burning thoughts of jealousy and rage. Henry could feel the weight of his brother on top of the blanket. The blanket slowly moving. Thoughts of making little brother go away… Thoughts of murder. If he could just pull on it a little more before his momma came back into the room… Woosh! Too late. A whirl of skirts. Momma pushing him out into the hallway. The door closing. The hardwood floor, so cold on his little bare feet.

Flick. Abby moving on, delving, searching… Little brother Chucky, older now—maybe four or five—rough-housing with Henry. The bigger, stronger Henry holding him down, pinning his arms back, awkwardly, painfully. Henry laughing, then muttering in Chucky's ear, "Say it. Say it, you wussy! Little pussy! Say uncle!"

Flick. Chucky, a few years later, his face squeamish, being held at knife point, being forced to watch as 10-year old big brother Henry nails the still living fish to a tree. "Don't you turn away!" Henry barks, pointing the knife at Chucky's face before he turns back to the fish and begins to peel and scrape off the scales of the wriggling fish. The sharp boning knife slitting into the belly of the fish. The careful, meticulous cleaning and gutting of the fish. Henry stepping back to admire the way the still-moving fish twitched, the way the light of the sun glinted and danced on the glistening flesh, making patterns that Henry could connect all together. An ever-changing dance of geometric shapes. Henry's joy. Chucky's horror. Perfect.

Flick. Henry captivated by shapes and patterns in nature: the perfect triangle made by a darting martin as it flew down to the ground, across the grass, then back up to its perch again. The spiraling eddies in the water of the bayou, which matched the pattern of hair at the crown of Chucky's head. And yes, in the wriggling flips and flops of the fish he had nailed to the tree—all points connecting. All shapes dancing.

It was in those times that Henry felt a sense of wonder and joy. It was in those moments that Henry transcended his sociopathy and found beauty. It was in those moments that Abby could love him.

Flick. Fast forward through the muddling and awkward teenage years—the first fumbling sexual encounter—and afterwards, the laughter of the girl that made Henry's cheeks burn with shame. Abby cringed. A stronger man would get over it and not spend the rest of his life taking it out on other women. Like Momma Bea.

Flick. The rush of adrenalin when committing petty crimes… Beneath the glare of a back room green light, drugs bought and sold… a daily meth habit developed… a young girl looking for a fix. Henry explaining the price… His hand moving up the girl's leg, slipping under her skirt.

Flick. Enter Momma Bea. Take it up to the present moment. Abby had access to it all: the total blur and mostly mindless existence that was Henry's life. If Henry had his druthers, he'd just stay at home all day drinking beer and watching football on the TV. Then he'd sneak away when Momma Bea was out or too busy to notice, and Henry would do some of those other things. Bad things. Loathsome things. Abby knew about it all. Too many images to count.

Oh, Momma Bea! Why don't you have the strength or resolve to just leave him? Kick him out!

Snap! Abby sat up. She was fully back in her own mind, her mind clear. She knew what she needed to do.

Abby got up from her little window seat and wandered over near the hallway leading into the small and cluttered family room. She could see Henry sitting in his recliner chair—his back to her—and Beatriz sitting on the sofa with a basket full of laundry. He was scoffing, like he always did, at Beatriz, who was holding an open letter in her hand, while he pointed the remote control at the television and systematically flipped through the channels.

"Finally get some peace and quiet," Henry was needling her between gulps of a Miller High Life. "You know I missed the games on Saturday cuz of all the circus show you got going on 'round here."

Beatriz was quiet, reading the words on the paper in front of her.

"Criminal negligence." Henry's nasally drawl was the rather unpleasant string that drew Abby deeper into the room. He had been at her momma for a few minutes. She went and sat next to Momma Bea on the sofa and took her hand. Momma squeezed it tight. Abby glanced at the letter. It was some kind of notice from the county.

Henry was still cutting into her from his recliner, and damned if he didn't seem to be enjoying himself. "Isn't that what the lady-boss said? That woman from the county? Criminal negligence. Ha!" He chortled and nearly choked on his glee. "Once you get the letter, likely as not, they gonna put you away." He took another swig of his beer and grinned. "And if you ask me, I think they should put you away. Not a modicum of sense or adult responsibility. At the very least, it would get you away from me, and I'd have one less mouth to feed. No wait," he turned and looked directly into Beatriz's grief-stricken face. "Make that *two* less mouths to feed!"

His smile widened. "I keep forgettin' that Protective Services is most likely gonna take baby girl away now, too. My, oh my... And it's not like I would miss her. Don't know why you carry on so much about her. It's not like she's even yours. Or did you forget that?" Henry belched then chortled.

He continued, "The way I look at it, everything can now return to normal. It's high time for some peace and quiet 'round here, and everything back to normal. Yes ma'am."

Momma Bea got up, set the notice down, and walked over to the window and peeked out through the shutters.

"Oh, they ain't comin' yet," Henry twanged, almost like he was reading her mind. "But when they do, I'll be sure to hold the door open for them."

She sighed heavily. Henry was probably right. Beatriz had never really "officially" adopted Abby. Abby's birth mother had simply shown up one day with an infant in her arms and said, "Keep an eye on my baby for a little while." Then she had left and never returned. No further correspondence. No further explanations. That was over eleven years ago.

"I have half a mind to give 'em a call today," Henry continued, eyes fixed on the ever-changing television screen as he flipped through the cable channels. "Maybe there's a finder's fee or... or a reward for turning folks like you in. You know they paid me two hundred dollars back there in Mandeville when Baby girl went a missing in that tornado. Yes ma'am. Channel five paid me two hundred dollars to let them set up in the driveway." He glanced over at Beatriz and belched again. "Maybe I just give them television folks another call and update the story. Headline: "Whatever Happened to the Miracle of Mandeville?" "Mother of the Miracle Child Found Negligent in Houma."

Henry turned and looked back at Momma Bea. "How much you think baby girl is worth today?"

"You are a vile human being, Henry Thierrey!" Beatriz spoke in a soft, monotone hush.

But Henry's words had cut deep. A helpless feeling settled over Beatriz like a black caul, slowly tightening, constricting her entire body and soul. She hadn't felt this much despair since that fateful day six years ago, when Abby had been ripped out of the back of the car by a monster tornado.

It's okay, momma.

The memory came back again, stronger and more vivid than ever. Abby's calm and controlled eyes in the face of the whirling, screaming vortex. Her eyes were the same grey-green color of the sky. Beatriz just couldn't shake the image from her head. Something had compelled her to go out into that storm, directly into harm's way, and she had nearly lost A.B. for good.

"Guess that makes me a vile human being…" Henry's relentless, droning attack continued. "I don't know how vile you think two hundred dollars is. That was easy, good money, darlin'. Easy good money." He snickered and belched again before turning back to the TV.

Beatriz shuddered as she reflected, taking a long, hard look at herself.

It's me that is the vile human being.

Yes, a little self-loathing ought to balance out her despair. Take all the blame inside and just hold it there without mercy. No forgiveness. No absolution. Just what the doctor ordered.

Abby was nearly torn in two by the grief and despair that flowed through Momma Bea. Now was the time she had to help her. Now was the time to act!

As if she knew what Abby was thinking, Momma Bea looked at Abby, sobbed, then turned and left the room. Abby heard the front screen door open and bang shut.

Abby turned back to look at Henry who glanced over at her and smirked.

"She gonna go water her garden now," he quipped. "That's how your momma cries." He chuckled again before turning back to the TV.

Yes. Do it now. He won't know what hit him!

"You know," Abby began slowly, "I used to like the way you would help me with my school work. That was nice."

"What you going on about, baby girl?" Henry continued to flip through the channels.

"Do you remember helping me out with geometry?" Abby asked softly. "With all the shapes?"

Henry paused the remote and cocked his head slightly. He took a swig of his beer, but Abby could tell she got his attention.

"There was that one time," she continued, "Oh when was it? The third grade? Second maybe? You know, when you helped me find things all around the house with different shapes? That was the assignment. Find things and name their shapes. You remember? The Kleenex box was a rectangle. The stop sign out on the street was an octagon. The batteries were cylinder spheres..."

"And my coke can," Henry perked up. "Don't forget the coke can. That was a cylinder, too!"

"Sure. The coke can, too." Abby smiled and walked over to stand in front of Henry, who looked up at her and grinned.

"The thing is, Henry," Abby continued, and their eyes locked. "I remember that and more. I remember it all. Your love of shapes and patterns. How you genuinely enjoyed working with me on that assignment. You took me all around the house, out in the yard... the shed house. It was amazing to discover all of those things... through your eyes. It was enough to make me love you."

"Oh!" Henry scoffed and leaned back in his recliner, started switching through the TV channels again. "What you going on about? You think you can weasel some money outta me today? What? How much you gonna ask for today?"

"The thing is," Abby continued, ignoring his question, "I remember all the other things, too." She stepped over and in front of Henry, blocking his view of the television, forcing him to look up and meet her eye.

Abby continued. "How you pick your moments to torment Momma Bea— bring her down just when she's about to find something happy. How you creep out at night and piss in her garden bed, which kills her herbs and her vegetables. How you snicker when you watch her dismay as she fusses over the spoiled shoots and greens, trying to figure out what went wrong."

Henry barked out a laugh. "You little sneak. You been spying on me?"

Abby didn't blink and continued, "How you take her money from her little stash in the hidden coffee can on the top shelf of the kitchen cabinet—yeah, you know it. The one behind the bags of flour? You take that money and sneak out to go get high. How you justify your theft by thinking that you'll replace the money later, and she'll never be the wiser, now will she?"

"Hey now!" Henry sat up and snarled at Abby. "Don't you go poking your pretty little nose in other people's business!" He set his beer down, raised a fist and spat, "Don't you think I won't teach you what it means to go prying into my affairs."

"Thing is," Abby continued, ignoring his threat. "you never do pay that money back, do ya? But that ain't even the half of it," Abby paused, took a breath, and stepped in closer to Henry. His eyes widened and started to dart about. He lowered his hand.

"I can see more than that. Go deeper." Abby was almost whispering now. "I can go back further. I can see how you are so full of bitterness. How you blame your mother for loving your brother Chucky more and not loving you enough. How your little mind was full of murder. How you enjoyed hurting your brother. How you used his humiliation and fear to fill up that empty hole inside of yourself. How you do the same thing to Momma Bea now that little bro grew up, got smarter, and had the good sense to move away."

"Hold on now..." Henry protested and sputtered, but his sneer had been replaced by a look of uncertainty and doubt. "You the Devil himself... How... how you know these things?"

"How old is Caroline?" Abby abruptly changed the topic, and Henry's eyes widened and betrayed a look of recognition.

He stammered and replied weakly, "C-C-Caroline? Who?"

"Maybe fifteen? If that?" Abby leaned in closer, and Henry recoiled. Abby could see the fear and panic taking over in his eyes. "Why, that's not much older than me, now, is it? She's a pretty little thing with a meth habit. The things you make her do..."

"W-what? What?" Henry stumbled over his tongue, casting his glance all about. He started to twist away and attempted to rise up, but Abby firmly placed both hands on his shoulders and pushed him back down. Stunned, Henry fell back hard in the recliner and gazed up at her, open-mouthed.

"I'm not finished yet," She said, calmly, behind clenched teeth. "That's statutory rape, Henry. With a minor? Do you know that?" Abby paused, and she could swear those were tears welling up in Henry's eyes.

"Yes, I believe you do," Abby continued, softly. "Poor Henry. Is it hard to hear the truth now? Well, let me tell you a little more about the truth—about what is going to happen next." Abby leaned down just inches away from Henry's face. She could smell the beer on his breath.

"If you ever... *ever* start in on Momma Bea like that again... if you *ever* do anything to hurt her and cause her to feel pain of any sort, then so help me God, I will bring all of your pathetic, dark little secrets out into the open. I will turn *you* in to the authorities, and I will tell them everything—everything that you've done to that poor girl. Not to mention the drugs and all the other criminal activities. How much time do you think you'd do for all of that?"

"You...you been following me around?" Henry was dazed and confused. "You been watching me?"

"You will go to prison, Henry." Abby pulled back and raised her finger right in front of his nose. "A weak little weed, like you? Well, I shudder to think what your life would be."

"How you...how...how did you...?" Henry had gone completely limp. He was spent, diminished and muttering more to himself than to anyone else. "Nobody gets hurt. No harm done, right? She... she tells me it's all right. How... why you doin' this to me? Oh, sweet Jesus... I'm sorry... I'm sorry."

Abby slowly lifted herself up and stood above him. Henry was crying and blubbering all over himself. His body wracked with each shuddering breath. She turned and walked away. She headed out the front door in search of Momma Bea.

She would find her in the gardens, then, and she would hold her. She would tell her that everything was going to be all right.

4

A FLIGHT OF FOREVER

Tiamat cried out in distress, fuming within herself,
"How can we destroy what we have given birth to?"

—From *The Enuma Elish*

Air.

A warm draft.

Electricity.

Flex and extend.

Lifting up.

A slight turn of the wing, a sudden plunge.

Dip. Tuck. Roll.

Speed. Exhilaration.

In the distance, a metallic screeching roar.

The company of another.

Answer the call.

Turning. Yearning. Rumble deep inside.

Below. Coolness. Fetid reek. Methane.

Water. Swamp.

Silver glint of fish.

Feed. Later.

Climbing now. Night sky. Wisp of cloud. Stars.

Roar of triumph.

Shuddering release.

Calling me home.

I am free.

5

DANS LA NATURE

From the Audio transcripts of Dr. Joanna Kinsey
Chief Psychiatrist, CHNOLA Northshore Center,
New Orleans, LA

Excerpt of Audio File Transcript #AR10089-31

June 19, 2022

Subject: A. B. Rubideaux. Female. Age: 11

Transcript of recording begins: 10:17 AM EST.

Kinsey: *You are in a particularly playful mood today, A.B.*

A.B.: *Well, it's just my truer nature. You should try smiling more often, Joanna. You're pretty when you smile, and you get all those crinkles in your cheeks, and your forehead goes completely smooth. It's a complete crinkle transformation from forehead to cheeks. (Giggling.) Quite remarkable actually. Are you sure you've never made the change yourself?*

Kinsey: *(Laughing.) Well, no, I'm quite sure. And thank you, A.B., I think… for the compliment. But I'd say there's quite a bit about you that is remarkable. Some very significant people are starting to take an interest in such a precocious young lady. How old did you say you were?*

A.B.: *This body is 11 years, 10 months, 15 days, 10 hours and 26 seconds old. 28, 29, 30…*

Kinsey: *(Chuckling.) Okay, I get the picture. But that's not what I meant. I have the school records of one Aurora Borealis Rubideaux. We have your false birth certificate but no medical records, and I'll take it for close enough to the truth that you were born in or about September of 2010. Right? I'm asking you about the dragon inside of you. Your truer self. How old is the dragon?*

A.B.: *Hmmm, now that's tricky. We don't measure time the same way that humans do.*

Kinsey: We? You mean there are more of you?

A.B.: Oh yes, of course. There are any number of us anywhere at any one time. What, did you think that I alone existed?

Kinsey: I never really thought to ask about it before. But let's go there in a moment. How old are you, really, A.B.?

A.B.: (Giggling.) Well, "really," now that's the thing. You see, I do not exist in the linear scheme of things. Time itself, as you measure it, is a linear progression, yes? The past to the present and into the future… It's a very convincing experience: I know that in this human body the week-to-week, day-to-day, hour-to-hour progression of time seems indisputable. Even comforting in its simplicity. A child is born, discovers awareness, experiences youth, journeys through the middle stages, then eventually, inevitably, grows old and dies—all in the course of a clearly defined and linear time. But this concept of time is a focused and localized construct. And I'm sorry to say it's a limitation of most intelligent beings. To more completely understand time, you must "defocalize" your perception and experience in the space-time continuum, and you must come to terms with a "non-local" viewpoint. Some of your physicists and molecular biologists are beginning to understand this. Quantum physics. Field theory. Shamans in the rainforests have always understood this. We've been talking to them for thousands of years.

Kinsey: You've been talking to shamans for thousands of years? Help me understand this.

A.B: Oh yes, not just shamans, but priests, prophets, seers, and many a good king and queen of old. Simple farmers and peasant folk, too—rank and station never matter—if you are open and connected enough to the world around you, then you can find us. You can slip through the fold.

Kinsey: The fold?

A.B.: That's my term. Call it the multiverse? Infinite dimensions? Our conscious reality is like a piece of holographic film… We live in one piece containing all of the others through time and space. One point bursting forth into infinite others. Or infinite points converging into one? I'm actually not sure which one is the truer…

Maybe both are correct? (Giggles.) At any rate, you make choices in the infinite possibilities of the multiverse. And life unveils itself. I call it "the fold." Simple, but fitting.

Kinsey: *I see... but that doesn't explain why you come to us in the form of a dragon.*

A.B.: *The form and shape we take is purely incidental. When Abby first encountered me, she chose the figure of the dragon. It was the form and expression that came from her mind—I'm so glad it wasn't a unicorn or Tinkerbell. Too girly. (Giggles.) No, she chose the dragon, and it's been a long time since I have been a dragon. Let's see, the ancient Babylonians called me "Tiamat," and that was one of the few times I've come to humans in the shape of a dragon. I do so love being a dragon...Usually I'm just a snake, and sometimes even just a vine or a rope or a ladder made of hemp. Dragons and serpents are so much more intriguing! Look to the strands of DNA. In their shape you will find some answers.*

Kinsey: *Hang on... How do we get from strands of DNA to Tiamat? You're talking folklore and mythology, now. I'm very skeptical, A.B..*

A.B.: *Yes, and your skepticism is precisely one of your greatest strengths as well as your primary weakness. At least when it comes to phenomena such as myself and the improbability of the way I manifest in your perception. (Giggles.) Okay, let's try this: One of the great flaws of the scientific, empirical process is the very fact that you believe that you must separate yourself from that which you are studying or observing in order to objectively understand it. But we never fully understand something unless we are a part of it. Your PhD's and scientists have forgotten this. But you, Joanne, as a medical psychiatrist, know, reluctantly perhaps, that this is true. Even though you pride yourself on whatever code of ethics stipulates that in your practice you are to remain personally or intimately separate from your patients, you still have to wonder about those moments of insight when you have a breakthrough and come to a better understanding of your patient. It wasn't your objectivity but your inevitable **connection** to the subject that made your insight or the revelation of truth possible.*

Kinsey: *Maybe I will concede your point, Abby, but we aren't here to talk about me or the nature of my insights. You changed the subject and redirected the focus* *of our conversation. We were talking about the nature of the dragon inside of you and the dimension beyond time that you call "the Fold."*

A.B.: *Well, we're going to need more than the remaining 15 minutes of our session today, Joanna. Much more than that! Shall we make it a working lunch? (Giggling.)*

TWO MONTHS EARLIER: APRIL 18, 2022.

"Dancine Willoughby needed to have a tumor removed." The woman who spoke glanced nervously at the young girls, Abby and Olivia, who were sitting in front of the TV watching an episode of Spongebob Squarepants.

"Yeah, right!" That would be Olivia's mom talking now. "And that tumor just had to travel across the county line and turned out later to be a seven-pound baby boy!"

"Oh, you hush, Georgina!" Momma Bea laughed and then turned towards the girls. "Abby?" She called out to them. "Why don't you and Olivia go outside and play?"

Abby switched off the TV and turned toward her mom and her two friends. They were sitting at the kitchen table having coffee. Pat, the woman who spoke first, was nervously fiddling with her shirt collar and glancing down at her coffee, which she was slowly stirring. She had one of those tight-lipped smiles that was used to hide secrets. Only some secrets couldn't be hidden so well. Georgina, Olivia's mom, was staring right at her and grinning from ear to ear. She looked just like an older version of her friend—the same frizzy hair bordering an impish, round face. Momma Bea was sipping her coffee and peering over the rim of her cup expectantly at Abby.

"Can we go down to the crick?" Abby replied and stood up, pulling a reluctant Olivia to her feet.

"Don't go too far into the bayou," her momma answered. "Be back before dark. We're gonna have supper early tonight."

"Early supper?" Olivia asked, suddenly perking up. "The best kind!" She turned toward the front door, and now she was the one tugging on Abby. "C'mon, let's go!"

The two girls exploded out the screen door and raced down the stoop. It was a glorious day, with blue skies streaking between ragged grey clouds and sunlight dancing through the trees and warm on the grass. It wasn't too humid—a perfect Spring day to get outdoors and away from the women and their talk.

"Hold up!" Olivia stopped and crouched down to tie her shoe. She looked up at Abby and smiled.

Olivia Fist. Abby looked down and grinned back at her. It had been over five years since the tornado incident where Abby had earned her fame. Of all the kids that Abby knew, Olivia was the only person that never seemed to pay that no nevermind. She got all of that out of the way the very first time their paths had crossed.

She thought back to that day over two years ago when she and Olivia had first met. It was the first day of fourth grade at her new school, just after Momma Bea had moved them to Houma, and Abby was sitting alone at lunch, having quietly endured the taunting catcalls of the other children, with their cruel looks of scorn and their ceaseless, vicious whispering. Olivia had approached Abby and plopped down across from her, and in a direct and frank demeanor without hesitation (which Abby soon learned was a consistent characteristic of Olivia Fist), she said, "You're that girl who got sucked up into that twister out on Lake Ponchertrain, ain't ya?"

Abby, sat quietly and looked back into the freckled, pale face of a nine-year-old girl with wild and frizzy auburn curls shooting out every which way. The girl had a look of such earnestness that it left Abby quite speechless.

Olivia studied Abby's face for several moments before continuing, "Well, shoot a biscuit. I think that must be the coolest thing that ever happened this side of Kathmandu." Then Olivia grinned, showing her missing front tooth. "And listen," she gestured over at some of the other kids who were nearby and watching, "Any of them turd balls give you a hard time, well, you just let them know that Olivia Fist is your friend, and they gonna have to come through me if they got anything to say about it." She held up her clenched fist, still grinning. "Yeah, my last name is Fist. I kind of like it, and it gives me license to knock a few heads from time to time." She stopped suddenly, pulled up her brown lunch bag and set it down next to Abby's dinged up tin lunch pail. "So, what you got in there, Miss Rubideaux? Are you in the trading business?"

And from that moment on, Abby had found her best friend. And for the past two years, Olivia had never mentioned the tornado incident again, but she sure could talk about everything and anything that was known to man upon the face of this earth.

So, on this day, back on the driveway of Abby's house, Abby waited while her friend tied her shoe. Olivia had that look in her eye, and Abby just knew that she was about to launch into one of her verbal tirades bemoaning some perceived injustice or stupidity that was the plague of mankind, or more specifically, a direct assault to the very refined sensibilities of one Olivia Fist.

"Why do old people even talk at all?" She growled and then harrumphed back to her feet. The two of them began quickly walking toward the line of cypress trees that was down at the end of the driveway and marked the beginning of the bayou.

"What do you mean?" Abby asked, knowing that in her friend's following response she would be lucky if she could get a word in edgewise.

"Well, what I mean, dear Abby, is why do they think they can talk around us, the children, like we're not even there, and then suddenly remember that we are in fact there! "Dancine Willoughby's tumor. "Whatever." Olivia snorted and barked out a laugh.

"Well," Abby began slowly. "I find it kind of colorful and creative. I mean, it's not every day that a seven-pound tumor can become a living and breathing baby boy."

Olivia snorted again and laughed for real. "Well, you got that right," she snickered and continued. "But I don't think you've thought this one all the way through. There's much more to it!'

"Oh, do tell," Abby replied drily. "I am simply all a'twitter with anticipation."

"You sure do talk funny," Olivia looked both ways as they reached the end of the driveway, then they crossed the road and into the woods. "How can you be some kind of Mensa smart and yet at the same time be such a dummy?" Olivia paused to leer at her, but she was just warming up.

"What all of that really means can be explained," Olivia continued rubbing her hands together. She bent over to pick up a fallen tree branch and peeled off a few leaves. "D'you ever stop to think why Dancine Willoughby had to go clear across the county line to see a doctor about birthing some baby?"

She paused as she extended the stick out in front of her and peered down its edge, admiring its firm line. It was a perfect walking stick. She didn't really wait for Abby to respond, and she continued, "Well it's as clear as the nose on your face! Our dear Dancine doesn't have a husband."

Abby let in a dramatic breath and turned to the smug grin on Olivia's face. "No! You don't say."

Olivia chuckled. "That's right. Dear Dancine Willoughby was living in sin." Olivia continued with a gleeful glint in her eye. "But that's not all."

Abby paused to grab Olivia's stick that was being waved in a slicing and dicing manner in front of them, and they watched a blue jay squawk and hop across a water-logged ditch.

"There's much more," Olivia continued in a hushed tone. "Dancine Willoughby probably has a demon child, now. A child not born of this world."

The two girls continued on as the trees thickened around them, shutting out the sounds of the cars on the highway behind them. Soon the shimmer of the bayou appeared in front of them. The day was brightening, and the gray clouds that had been there moments before all seemed to have magically streaked away. The skies were clear and blue above the tops of moss-strewn cypress and tupelo trees—here and there a lone pine or oak tree stood out taller, spreading limbs majestically. The sunlight glittered on the water. They took a trail that paralleled a small waterway and continued on.

"Well," Abby replied with a smile. She was used to her friend's wild flights of fancy. Buried somewhere within the imaginary embellishments was usually a pearl of wisdom—or an outrageous fabrication—and it was always a pleasure to get to the bottom of these things with Olivia.

Abby went on, "Have you met or even seen this child not born of this world? I must endeavor to admonish you for unsupported speculation! Be careful if you know not of what you speak. Stranger things are known to this earth."

"Ha," Olivia snorted. "That's why I like you so much, Abby-liscious. You are so delicious!" She suddenly straightened up and spoke in an excellent imitation of her friend: "I must endeavor to add relish to your what...what... what? You know not of what you speak." Olivia slapped her knee and snorted again. "Bless your heart."

Abby peeked over at Olivia and smiled herself. "That's what they always say. "Bless your heart" or "Bless her heart." You know? When they talk about someone but can't say what they really want to. Cuz, it's like that person is right in front of them, and maybe the person has some kind of deadly disease or is like a cripple or something..."

"Or a retarded person!" Olivia interrupted enthusiastically.

"Or just a simple innocent child," Abby added with a giggle. "Maybe someone who is too dim-witted to understand."

"That's exactly right!" Oliva stabbed her stick into the ground for punctuation. "That is talk for just plain stupid people. "Well, bless your heart..." Makes me just wanna roll over and die!"

Abby laughed at her friend's sudden and vehement disdain. She added, "They say it like it's an expression of compassion or sympathy..."

Now it was Olivia's turn to laugh and interrupt. "Yeah, but what it really means is that folks are just too chicken to speak the truth about what's really on their minds." She paused, then glanced sideways over at Abby before continuing in a more serious tone. "Abby, you can never let them know that you are paying attention. You should just play dumb. Like we never think about things. That's what they are counting on. Us not listening or thinking about things. Never let them know that you can be a little meta-spherical, too."

"Meta-spherical?" Abby piped in because it was polite to let folks know that you were in fact paying attention.

"Yeah, meta-spherical," Olivia turned towards Abby and scrunched up her face in earnestness. "You know, like you was just sayin', when you're not supposed to say things directly so all you can do is talk in circles. It's like you're avoiding something that you can't talk about, so you just dance around it and try not to hurt people's feelings.

Abby piped in, "So you just talk in circles. Meta-spherical! Huh. I guess that makes perfect sense!"

"Of course it does!" Olivia was so passionate and full of zeal that she nearly tripped over a tree root that snaked across their path. Abby reached out to hold her friend up and prevent her from falling.

"Watch out, rambling Sally! It's not so easy to talk and walk at the same time, bless your heart."

"That's exactly right!" Olivia nearly screamed. "I rest my case!"

They both laughed and Olivia snorted, and then they both laughed harder.

Abby cherished her friend Olivia—really her only friend. Abby was happy to have someone like Olivia to whom she could tell all of her secrets. Well, most of her secrets—she hadn't told anybody, not even Olivia, about her dragon. That was a secret she would keep a while longer.

Abby glanced over at Olivia striding beside her with a slight bounce in her step. She would occasionally lunge with her stick or whack at the bushes and tree branches they passed. It was a playful action, but there was a feel of aggression in the intensity of her sweeps and jabs. Abby knew it was a rough spell that Olivia was going through with her ma and pa getting a divorce, and she wouldn't talk about it unless Olivia wanted to. But Abby was there for her in any way that Olivia wanted her to be. She never pried, and she didn't gossip. When it came to personal issues, she and Olivia always played it straight with each other. And for now, she would let Olivia destroy the surrounding foliage without comment.

Abby just wished that other folks would treat them the same way. Unfortunately, most people rarely applied the same rules of engagement that they so often touted in public. It wouldn't have been so bad if folks were more genuine, but one thing the dragon had given Abby was the ability to cut through all the talking and fussing that people made and see right through to their level of intent. She could see through to their hearts, as it were, and most of the time folks were prevaricating, so full of lies that they were even lying to themselves. Most other people weren't even aware of how convoluted and complicated the pathways of their own minds were.

Other people. Well, that's the down-side of growing up in a small town in the country. Even though they appear to be minding their own business, the gossip mill was always churning. Whether it was moms having coffee in the kitchen, old men on the back stoop, or church ladies in their fancy hats at a social. There wasn't much else happening in and around town. So, people loved to talk about each other.

Abby's thoughts were interrupted by the manic chirping of a woodpecker somewhere nearby. It was actually louder than Olivia who was still jabbering beside her.

It brought another thought to Abby's mind: When you remove other people from the equation, there are particular advantages to growing up country, particularly if there are woods and bayou nearby.

And particularly particular if you had dragon senses.

Abby reached out with her mind to really feel the earth beneath her feet. The ground was thrumming with the pulse and energy of nature. Critters tucked away in their burrows. Water moved underground, speaking the secret language of river, mountain, and stone. Yes, the whole world was alive and talking! You just had to recalibrate your mind and be open to hear it.

Abby breathed in deeply and smelled the cypress nettles and the wet, boggy scents of the bayou. She focused on her feet and imagined that each step she and Olivia were taking were like little hammers on the strings of a dulcimer, adding to the rhythm and the vibrational song of the earth.

Olivia, of course, was still yammering on and on beside her, a chatterbox of the first and highest order, oblivious to the language of the earth. "Oblivia" as others sometimes called her. She decided to interrupt her friend, who was currently breaking down the snorts and laughs of her extended family members, as well as their propensities for flatulence, trying to figure out which ones were most like her own.

"Hey fart-knocker. I want to show you something," Abby suddenly announced when Olivia finally paused to catch her breath.

"You what?" Olivia replied as she used her stick to whack some unlucky rushes that were growing alongside their trail.

Abby breathed in once before responding with great articulation and precision, "I said that I wanted to show you something. Here, let's sit for a bit." Abby gestured at a large log off to their right which lay across a sandy patch of soil. It was broad and sturdy, recently fallen, and yet to be overgrown with weeds or moss or fungi.

Olivia eyed their impromptu bench with suspicion. "Looks like the home to all manner of creepy-crawlies. You ever get a chigger up under your drawers? Not a pleasant experience." Olivia grimaced and rubbed her thighs with comedic intensity.

Abby laughed, then replied, "Relax. I think we're fine with this one. It hasn't been down long enough to fester." She sat down and patted the surface of the log next to her. Olivia followed, slowly and reluctantly, finally sitting after a lengthy inspection.

"Now, what I want to show you requires your silence," Abby began. "Is it possible for you to stop yapping for a few minutes?"

"Yapping? I'm yapping?" Olivia scowled in mock indignation. "So, I'm just one of those annoying little froo-froo dogs, now, all yapping and carrying on? Is that what you think of me?"

"Actually," Abby continued calmly, "It is the human being who is the primary violator of nature's balance. And you, my friend, are a human being! Now, let's do a little experiment." Abby scooched around so that she was straddling the log and facing Olivia, crossed her legs and rested her hands, open-palmed like a buddha across her knees. "Strike the pose!"

Olivia snickered and followed suit. A few moments passed as Abby watched Olivia squirm and shift her leg alignment three times before settling on the right ankle on top of her left. She imitated Abby's pose then looked back at her in expectation.

"Now," Abby began. "I want you to breathe deeply and close your eyes." Olivia complied. "Good… Continue to breathe deeply. In through your nose and out through your mouth." Abby closed her eyes and demonstrated. Then she peeked her left eye open and asked, "You must be silent for a bit while I talk and guide you through this. Can you do that for me?"

Olivia opened her eyes and replied, "Yes!" Then she stuck her tongue out before closing her eyes again. Abby chuckled, and together, they started breathing.

As they breathed, Abby gathered her thoughts for a few moments. Another thing the dragon inside of her had given her was the ability to think very deeply and to articulate her thoughts, which anyone who spent a lot of time around Abby could tell you. You may have already noticed this, but Abby didn't speak like an ordinary 11-year-old child. She used words and sentence structures that most adults with college degrees might not be able to put together. And she had been doing this for years. Her momma thought she was touched by angels and the divine. Her friend, Olivia thought she was cool. Other kids at school and around the neighborhood just thought she was a freak. But some of her teachers had started to notice. There had even been talk of accelerating her and skipping a grade or two. When asked about it by a school counselor, Abby simply said, "I like to read," to which the counselor had actually replied, "Well, bless your heart." Really. She did!

Abby smiled at the memory, then took a few more deep breaths on her log before peeking open her eye one more time to make sure that Olivia was in a proper meditative position. Her friend was sitting erect, eyes closed, and grinning like the Mona Lisa. Abby nodded and then continued.

"Let us talk to the Mother, who is this Earth. First and foremost, we must find in our minds a place of solitude, which is not so easy to find in the electric hubbub of the city or in a small town like Houma, or even out here in the bayou. But it's easier out here, and that's because there are not so many *other people*. Yes, that's the main thing. It's all those other people that carry on with all sorts of activity and industry that, when you put it all together, it adds up to an ever-present and veritable din."

"Veritable din," Olivia repeated in an awed voice. "I want to name my next cat Vera Tippleton." She snickered and snorted.

"You hush!" Abby scolded with a smile. "My point is that there's always too much noise, and you, my dear, are proving the point. Now, don't interrupt! Please."

"Yes ma'am," Olivia responded, still smiling.

Abby breathed in deeply a few more times before continuing. "Out here in the bayou, it is peaceful. Back in town it's all noise. Oh, you can forget it's there, all right, when you live in and among the noise all your life, and I guess you can just get used to it. But it's there, even when you think it's quiet. You might not ever even know the difference between city quiet and deep country quiet until you find yourself out here, in the wilderness—away from all those other people with their chatterbox children, their machines and vehicles and their humming current—it's not until you find a true deep country woods that you realize its absence. And that is solitude."

"Excuse me?" Olivia opened her eyes and interrupted. "Is this the lecture series? I only signed up for the three-minute session."

Abby ignored her and continued. "Now solitude comes in two types: there is *physical* or *geographical* solitude, which is a rather easy thing to understand. You're alone—nobody else around—and that's a fine thing to discover by walking out the screen door, stepping off the back stoop and just walking into the woods, or the swamp, or the fields."

"Yes, indeed," Olivia murmured.

"Yes, indeed," Abby echoed, "For we are indeed blessed to have our homes so close to nature. One can find such solitude within moments and just a few steps away. I am often so inclined to find such aloneness because with that there also comes *unique state-of-mind* kind of solitude. This is the second kind of solitude, one which is often feared or misunderstood by those not accustomed to its benefits. So, a point of clarification might be in order: Wanting to be alone doesn't mean you are lonely—that's just a simple conflation or mixing up of two very different concepts."

"They are not the same thing!" Olivia interrupted. "I like being alone sometimes—Yes, ma'am. It helps me think about things and clear my mind without distraction. I like being alone. And that's not the same thing as being lonely. Now, my momma is lonely—ever since my pa went away. She's just sad."

Olivia stopped talking suddenly, and there was an awkward silence. She and Abby opened their eyes and stared at each other. After a while, Olivia smiled, and Abby smiled back, letting out a deep breath.

"That's exactly right," Abby said softly. "Loneliness is a feeling of sadness—when you feel that you are not loved. And you can be in a room full of people or a city filled with millions and still feel lonely. But you would definitely not be alone. Yes, being alone means physical separation and isolation—which is not everybody's preference, admittedly, but being alone like that doesn't mean you feel lonely. I kind of like my quiet self."

Abby reached over and brushed a stray auburn curl from Olivia's face.

Olivia grinned back at Abby, then spoke teasingly, "You're not gonna try to kiss me, or anything like that, are ya? I mean, I like you, but it's not like that…"

She laughed suddenly, a deep, unapologetic chortle—well, more like a donkey's braying, and Abby had to join in too until tears were streaming down both their cheeks. Olivia was like that. There wasn't another person in this world that could make Abby laugh like Olivia.

They wiped away the tears, resumed their meditative positions, and Olivia finally managed to speak again.

"Now let's get on with this holy nature sermon. You had something that you wanted to show me, right?"

"Right!" Abby replied eagerly. "You are the master of side-tracking distraction. Which is precisely why I want to show you this. Now, try to relax yourself." Abby closed her eyes and took several deep breaths. "Breathe in through your nose and exhale through your mouth, slowly."

Olivia followed suit, her inhalations and exhalations audible and strong.

"That's it," Abby said quietly. "With the breath comes clarity and focus. It is into such a state of clarity and focus that I would now like to bring you. Breathe deeply in… and slowly let it out. Breathe in… and out. Breathe in… and out. There is nothing else." Both girls sat quietly facing each other, cross-legged in Buddha pose, completely still but for their breath.

After a minute or so, it was only their breathing that moved like ripples on water between them. They had returned to the quiet *state-of-mind* kind of solitude.

Clarity and focus. Abby found herself in a deeply meditative state, accompanied by a heightened awareness throughout all of her senses. Now, the dragon inside of Abby knew this intimately, for it was permanently in a heightened state of awareness. Abby was only beginning to understand this, for the human mind was always so busy and full of clutter.

State-of-the-mind solitude. The dragon inside knew that it could open you up to the myriad of mysterious things that existed just below the surface, where nature's equilibrium was restored to balance.

After some time had passed, Abby spoke again, softly, "Do you feel it? The breath has guided us to a place of quiet. We are far from our iPhones and high frequency devices. Far from the constant buzzing and the great electronic hum. We are sitting here, and we are just breathing."

Abby sat quietly for a moment; she could hear Olivia breathing deeply, in sync with her own in-and-out rhythm. "Now," she continued, "I want you to reach out with your senses. Extend them beyond your body, beyond your mind."

"Can you hear the trees moan and creak at each other?" Abby asked in barely a whisper. "Right here, right now. Can you smell the rain coming? Reach out, slowly. Feel the rabbit squatting still and unseen amongst the briars…"

"Yes, he's there," Olivia said in a hushed voice filled with awe. "I feel him."

"We are not alone. Ever." Abby spoke in a soft but clear voice. "Right now, where everything is alive and all-around-you so weird and wonderful. Olivia… open your eyes."

Olivia did so, and she blinked back at Abby, who was pointing down and looking at the path beside them. Olivia slowly turned to see a blue-bellied lizard that had scampered on to a warm sandy patch in the sun. Then the most curious of things—the lizard began to do push-ups. Up down. Up down. Up down. Quick little bursts of movement that were like magic, for each time he went up, the blue of his belly would flash in the sun, and his push-ups became a strobe effect.

Up down. Up down. Flash! Flash! Flash!

Within a few moments, another lizard, this one grey and mottled brown, scurried out of the brush and cozied up to the flasher. The two touched noses then, as if some silent accord had been reached, they turned together and scampered away, side by side.

Olivia chortled and exclaimed, "What in tarnation?"

Abby laughed then said, "Didn't you know? That's how the little fella calls his lady friend. They've gone off to make little baby lizards, no doubt."

"Well, I've never seen such a thing," Olivia replied in wonder.

"One of the benefits of *State-of-the-mind* solitude," Abby said happily. "There's all manner of things that can come to you unbidden, free and easy. I like to savor them and hold on to them."

"Like butterscotch on top of vanilla ice cream!" Olivia joyfully proclaimed. "I like to eat it real slow." She paused as Abby eyed her suspiciously. "What? It's what come to me, unbidden," she continued somewhat unconvincingly.

Abby leaned in, almost touching foreheads, and they both laughed.

"Exactly, I guess!" Abby said. "Just like that."

Olivia frowned at her then spoke very briskly, "Well, all I'm saying is that if that is not one of your favorite things, then it most certainly should be!"

"Indubitably!" Abby announced with a smile.

"In doubly dubitably!" Olivia replied, and they both shrieked with laughter.

When their fits had subsided, Olivia suddenly grabbed Abby's arm and pulled her up standing. "Oh, what else? What else?" She asked, closing her eyes and breathing in deeply. "Let's be still again and see what happens."

Olivia was facing Abby and held firmly on to her hands—too long for Abby's comfort. Olivia popped open her eyes when Abby slipped her hands away from Olivia's.

There was an awkward tense moment as the two sat staring at each other, Abby slowly rubbing her arms.

"I'm so sorry," Olivia began. "I…I forgot that you don't like to be touched."

Abby's heart was beating quickly, fluttering, actually. There it was again. The unbearable weight of her dragon secret. Abby so desperately wanted to tell someone like Olivia everything that was going on with her. Here she was, five years after the tornado, on a path in the bayou with her best friend, and she didn't even know how to begin.

While Olivia had been holding her hands, Abby caught glimpses of her friend's stream of thought. *Spaghetti and meatballs sounded real good for dinner… kickball a few days ago with the head of Ms. Tully, their sixth grade math teacher, in place of the ball—it felt so good to kick it hard… a memory from when*

Olivia was much younger, of lying in bed at night, listening to her mom sobbing quietly in the next room, then suddenly her father' face through the window of his pick-up truck, the vehicle slowly backing away... and of course, *hot butterscotch dripping from a spoon of vanilla ice cream...*

These thought streams always came to Abby unbidden, raw and all jumbled up like a thousand bits of different stories. Olivia's thoughts were usually about food or downright funny, but lately there was always something sad. These latest bits were no different.

How could any person focus on a conscious thought with so much racing around in their heads? Abby found it immensely disorienting and disturbing to the rational mind. But to the dragon inside, this was just what it meant to be open and in tune with the world around her. And, if she dared, what it was like to touch someone else's mind. The dragon didn't think it strange or unusual in the least bit. The problem was that the little girl part of Abby had no idea how to control it when it happened. And nobody, especially the dragon, ever told her where certain boundaries might be or just how extraordinary it all was.

Abby stared deeply back into the concerned eyes of her best friend. How do you tell someone like that that there is nothing you already don't know about them? How do you explain the things you have already seen, the things that you know are coming but have yet to happen? Should she tell Olivia—whom she already knew was the purest soul and the most loyal friend that she would ever know—that she would live to be over 100 years old and have dozens of glorious grandchildren and great grandchildren (Well, in most of the futures she had caught a glimpse of)? Should she tell her that she loved and admired her so much because she was a person who would always come to the aid of the weak, the marginalized, the bullied, the wronged, the fallen and the frightened, because that was who she was and who she would always be in this lifetime and countless others? How do you tell someone all of that? How would you explain it to them and also convince them that you weren't crazy?

"It's okay," Abby finally said, smiling and then picking up Olivia's walking stick and handing it back to her. "Don't you worry about it. It's just my thing. One of these days I will tell you everything." Abby closed her eyes, and yes, of this she was certain. Olivia would remain her friend even if she told her everything—all of her secrets. There was no pathway where Olivia would not understand or accept her for what she was.

Abby opened her eyes and Olivia was smiling at her.

"You promise?" Olivia asked half teasing.

"I promise." Abby nodded and let out a deep breath. "One day I will tell you all about the dragon."

"The dragon?" Olivia asked all scrunchy-faced once again.

Abby chuckled, then responded, "It's part of my secret. My spirit animal. It will explain a lot... well, everything. I will tell you all about my dragon."

Olivia piped in, "So you've got a dragon spirit animal, like a totem? Does it live inside of you?"

"That's right," Abby answered. And I will tell you everything. But not today. I will find the right time... and it will be soon."

"That's cool," Olivia said smiling slightly. "I know you will."

Abby raised an eyebrow and quipped, "And I know you know that I will."

"And now I know that you know I know that you know that I know you will." Olivia and Abby both laughed at that.

Abby closed her eyes and tilted back her head. "Too many knows... Now, where were we?"

Olivia closed her eyes and did the same, rocking gently back and forth, smiling. "We were about to explore the wonders of solitude."

"Ah, yes," Abby whispered as they both grew still and silent. The wind hushed through the cypress trees. Something plopped out in the middle of the water. The two breathed in deeply, nerves alive with anticipation.

Then the spell was broken, shattered by the hum of a motor boat off in the distance. This was soon followed by a loud chorus of voices emerging on the other side of the lake, a troop of hikers stomping down the trail, gabbing and guffawing like a band of drunken gypsies.

The girls opened their eyes and stared back at each other.

"Other people," Olivia muttered sadly.

"Human beings," Abby nodded. "The worst violators of nature's equilibrium."

The two girls watched as the troop slowly merged into the trees and the hanging Spanish moss of the bayou. Their clamor slowly faded.

"No blue-bellied lizard dance for them," Olivia muttered, slowly shaking her head.

"Afraid not," Abby agreed as they watched the hikers disappear. "Hey!" She slapped Olivia on the back. "That gives me an idea. I think we're ready for this." She grabbed Olivia's shirt and pulled her friend along the path. "There's a fork in the trail right up ahead."

She jogged down the path and came to a stop in front of a halfway submerged tupelo tree. There was a small lake beyond it, and the trail split left and right bordered by nettles and river rushes and more cypress trees.

Abby smiled at Olivia before pointing with her hand, "The trail forks here and goes all the way around the lake. Now, you go left, and I'll go right. We'll meet on the other side of the lake mid-way... there's an old stone bench there looking out over the water. It's under the biggest oak tree you've ever seen. You can't miss it." She turned back at Olivia and leered like the devil.

"Here's the catch, though," she said, eyebrows dancing. "Along the way, see what you can find to disguise yourself. Anything goes. No limitations. We will meet on the other side in nature's costume. You up for that?"

"Sure thing," Olivia replied, grinning. "How long we got to make our costumes?"

"It's only about a five-minute walk to go all around the lake, Abby said. "But I'll give you an extra ten minutes for foraging and preparation."

Olivia rubbed her hands together. "Ooh, I got the *state-of mind-kind of solitude* and sensibilities, now. There is no way you will ever guess what I will become!"

Abby high-fived her and grinned. "Fifteen minutes," she said. "See you on the other side."

But Olivia was already gone, darting down the path to the left. Abby laughed then peeled off to the right. She was walking quickly, surveying the land left and right. She found a clump of horse-feather nettles and plucked two, sticking them in her hair like two antennae ears. She was humming to herself, and found her mind was just racing with a million different thoughts. Her sense of solitude was filled with a clamor of different things, so she breathed deeply and tried to empty her mind.

She kept walking but found her search for costuming accessories was distracted. Her mind was still occupied by thoughts of her hidden abilities. She very much wanted—no, she needed to tell Olivia everything. Soon. Everything.

She picked up her pace and was now half jogging along the trail. She was feeling electric and full of energy, her mind still racing, fueling her along. She found herself thinking about Dancine Willoughby and her "tumor." The thought of Olivia's snorting analysis of that whole situation brought a smile to her lips. It actually made her think more deeply about the behavior of her mother and the other ladies. She doubted any of them ever knew the benefits of *state-of-the-mind* solitude. Here, all by herself in the bayou, Abby thought that the trees and the blue-bellied lizard tended to be more honest than most people. Abby had returned to her earlier observations: Folks are nosy by nature, and even though most human neighbors seem to highly value their own sense of privacy and their peculiar territorial claims, this is quickly forgotten when it comes to the business and scandalous affairs of others.

Abby was always taught to follow the Golden Rule, but it seemed to her that folks found it easier to follow this rule when it was others who were doing it unto them rather than when it was them who were doing it unto others. Now, most folks didn't seem too keen to acknowledge the obvious double-standard of this position, but for Abby, and those like her who found themselves living in the remote countryside, where neighbors, by design, tended to be few and far between, well, they seemed to understand this and respect it more than most. *You mind your business, and I'll mind mine.* And when there aren't a lot of other folks around, well it's a lot easier to follow this advice.

This is particularly true if you have a habit of changing into a dragon. Abby giggled to herself as she raced along. *No sir*, she thought to herself. *You don't want folks coming around when you are making the change.*

The dragon inside of Abby rumbled in agreement.

Abby came to a sudden stop along the path. Unaware that she had picked up her pace, she found herself standing by the old stone bench. It sat, slightly tilted, beneath a very large oak tree. The limbs of the oak were gnarled and massive, and they spread out above her. She gazed up at them and found herself feeling some butterflies inside of her belly. As she looked up into the leaves of the tree, her vision began to blur slightly. It began as a fuzzy distortion that moved from the right of her peripheral vision and across her line of sight. It looked like a force field of energy, a sort of blotchiness, like the air itself were made of plastic bubble wrap that was expanding and contracting, distorting shapes and colors.

Like the whole world is breathing.

The dragon voice rippled up from somewhere inside of her. Abby drew in her breath sharply. These physical and visual sensations were a sign that the dragon change was imminent. She looked down at her fingertips but could not see any scaling or feel any itching. She looked up at sunlight coming down through the oak tree, and it was dancing, full of color and different intensities of light. The limbs of the tree seemed to merge and melt together, then the leaves themselves started to spin and spiral, left and right, as they filled with light. They were glowing geometric shapes that were transforming into fractals of light. Back and forth. Back and forth.

Shoot! Abby almost panicked as she thought of Olivia, who would be arriving a mere matter of minutes from now. Abby didn't think that a full-on dragon was the kind of "costume" that Olivia would be expecting. And it wasn't fair, either. Olivia would probably accuse her of cheating and rigging their little game in her own favor.

The blurry field of vision in front of her, cleared momentarily, and the rainbow patterns of color returned to the greens and browns of oak tree. High above her, one solid limb looked particularly inviting.

Safe. Up high.

The dragon's voice rumbled again. Abby turned to study the tree, and as she examined more closely, the blurry vision returned. Somewhere not so far away, a bird, (or maybe Olivia?) called out in song, its melodic notes warping and blending into sustained echoes and vibrations of tintinnabulation—like bells ringing in slow motion. Abby focused on the trunk of the tree and the lowest limbs, and like a 3-D map of color and light, a pathway up the tree appeared before her. One step there on that knot, where a footprint glowed indigo, then faded quickly, winking out. Next a violet hand-print flashed on and off not far above it, an easy reach to that first branch, then up the trunk with this now shimmering branch then that one—more hands and feet winking so blue and hot pink, then indigo again, now green! A trace of light remained where each print appeared—the pathway up was so clear!

It was no time for thinking.

She reached out with her hand and grabbed the trunk of the tree. It seemed to coil and slither as she stepped up, and *whoosh!* She was climbing. Hopping, then grabbing, then lightly criss-crossing, now swinging, one step, two steps, now leaping—all the while she was following the multi-colored pathway that appeared again in sequence in front of her. A flash of indigo, then violet. Now pink… Her body moved sure and easily, a quick wrap around the trunk and a shimmy, then two little hops, one more swing, one more step, a little drop and finally, a sliding butt scooch to the left. And *plop!*

She had made it. Her little perch amidst the rainbow hum of the majestic oak. Her safe haven engulfed by fractals of geometry and light. She was hardly breathing, not even one little gasp for breath. The climb had been effortless.

"AAH-WOOO!" she bellowed from the depths of her belly core, elated and feeling very much alive. From her new vantagepoint she could look out over a huge section of the bayou. She could see all around the little lake—the glowing hues of all the cypress and tupelo trees, their erect trunks seeming to shiver and hum with blue and red sparks bursting from their tops. There was a blue and red vein of light, like that of a leaf, spread out and over everything. Abby reached out with her hand and she could see it flowing to and from her fingertips. It was the energy of the earth. Mother Gaia's qi had gone electric. It was dragon vision at its best!

Abby waved her hands in front of her and the threads of blue and red light wove tracer patterns like spirals in the wake of her fingers. In and out. In and out.

Yes. Like the whole world is breathing.

Abby turned toward the sound of the Voice. It hadn't come from inside herself but seemed to be coming from inside the tree. She stared at the trunk of the oak to her right and watched in fascination as the mottled bark of the tree shifted and writhed. The trunk itself seemed to be coiling and sliding, slithering up and clockwise like a strange vine or rope that had suddenly come to life. She watched as the brown of the tree seemed to merge into the blue and red veins of the light. The coiling rope twisted and turned going up, then it slowly came to a stop.

Now it began to spin counter-clockwise and down, slowly at first, then speeding up till it was a blur of red and blue light. Abby gasped as the coiling trunk slowed, at last coming to a stop. Now it was pulsing, expanding, then constricting as if with a breath of its own.

Slowly, what Abby at first thought to be a stubby limb extending from the trunk of the tree, began to emerge and transform its shape before her. The limb turned toward her then the leaves of the limb rippled and gleamed, filling out like the crest of some magnificent bird all red and glowing with indigo and purple light. A face emerged beneath the crest, all glistening scales and serpent like. It was the eyes that first struck her—deep and bottomless black diamonds framed in golden amber light.

A dragon head now peered back at her, mere inches from her face. Its nostrils flared then contracted. Was it smiling at her?

Hello, little Sister!

This time the Voice came simultaneously from both within and without her, moving over her like soft ripples. Warm breath wafted across her face. It smelled vaguely like cinnamon.

Abby closed her eyes and breathed in deeply, smiling.

And then it was gone. Suddenly and without warning. Completely gone. Abby opened her eyes. She was just staring at a stubby limb on an oak tree. She looked around. It was a sunny afternoon and the green water of the bayou shimmered beneath her.

"No! Come back!" She cried, darting her eyes all around the limbs and branches of the tree. It was just a tree. Green leaves trembling in the soft breeze. No dragon.

"What in the world?" A voice sounded below.

Abby looked down. Olivia was standing some 20 feet below her, shading her eyes and looking up at her with a scrunchy face. Her auburn-haired friend had adorned her head and entire body with strands of Spanish Moss. Water cress and yellow flowers hung in random bits from her hair. She had streaked some kind of yellowish-ochre brown shade of clay or slime across both cheeks of her face with two fingers. There was an animal skin or bark wrapped around the tip of her stick, which she still carried. She looked like a swamp princess gone terribly, demonically wrong.

"How'd you get up there?" Olivia asked, now smiling at her. "And you call that a costume?"

Still somewhat shaken, Abby looked down at herself. She was naked, sitting cross-legged in the tree. She didn't remember taking off her clothes and couldn't quite put together how she had gotten up the tree. There was just a vague recollection of something—a pathway of glowing color?

She reached up behind her ears and felt the two horsetail reeds that were still there. She did remember putting those in her hair.

Nothing else to see here.

This time the dragon's voice was familiar and deep within.

"Why, I'll be..." Abby muttered under her breath. In a flash it all came back to her. A blurring distortion of shapes and light. Waves of pulsing red and blue vein-like patterns of light. Swirling spirals. The whole world breathing.

A tree trunk that contained a hidden map of colored light and that somehow turned into a dragon.

She smiled despite herself. "Are my clothes down there?" She called down to Olivia.

Olivia looked around her feet and then around the base of the tree.

"Eureka!" She cried, then she dropped her walking stick and scrambled under the tree out of Abby's sight. A few moments later she reappeared holding up a pair of pants, a badly torn shirt, and one wet sock. "I found these," she shouted up. She glanced at the shirt which was shredded like a tiger had ripped through it. She added more quietly, "You were in a hurry to get out of this, I guess."

"I'm comin' down!" Abby yelled. "Do me a favor and don't look. Make yourself useful and see if you can find the rest of my clothes. And my shoes!"

Olivia dropped Abby's clothes in a pile at her feet and saluted like a very erect soldier, then marched back under the tree.

Abby waited a few moments, listening to Olivia scrabble around in the brush below, muttering to herself. Abby groaned to her feet and then surveyed her most likely pathways down. It wasn't going to be easy, but she made her choice.

With much less confidence, and a whole lot more hesitation, she began to shimmy, scooch and hop her way down. The climb down was not nearly so nimble and graceful. By the time she was close enough to drop down to the ground, she was scratched up, scuffed and ornery.

Abby quickly went over to the pile of her clothes, picked up her pants and quickly slipped into them, wriggling and grimacing as the blue jeans scraped against her abrasions. She buttoned them up and reached for her shirt—or what remained of it. She held it up and spread it out with both hands. There was a clean single rip right down the middle of the shirt-back, and a few of the buttons were missing. Still, it would work if she tucked it in.

She was just sitting to put on her wet sock when Olivia reappeared with both shoes and the other sock.

"These," she announced, holding up both shoes, "I found perfectly stacked side by side behind the tree," Olivia paused to blow a stray strand of Spanish Moss from between her eyes. "Which usually I wouldn't find so peculiar." She held up the sock in her other hand and said, "This one was floating in the water, nowhere near where I found the other one." She squeezed the sock and water gushed and dribbled out for emphasis. "Sorry, no panties could be located. I think a little squirrel ran off with them. It's a thing, you know. For some squirrels."

She walked up to Abby and handed her the rest of her clothes. She pressed her lips together and rolled her eyes, then walked over to pick up her stick.

Abby watched her and said as she wrung out the last few drop from the sock and pulled it on, "Well, I don't usually wear them anyways. Panties that is." She stood up and grimaced with discomfort. "But I don't recommend shimmying down a tree without them, actually, for reals." She turned and the two girls faced each other. "I think I got splinters where I've never had any before!" Abby finished with a tight-lipped smile.

"Oh lordy," Olivia murmured and shook her head.

Abby studied Olivia's "costume" closely for the first time and snickered. "You look ridiculous," she said still smiling. She sniffed and wrinkled her nose recoiling slightly. "What is that you smeared across your cheeks?"

"Don't you make fun of my war paint!" Olivia folded her arms then continued at pace, "Oh, and little miss I'll-just-rip-off-my-clothes-and -sit-completely-naked-up-in-a-tree. That is anything but a little bit peculiar." Olivia scoffed, and turned away muttering. "Ridiculous...yeah ridiculous, all right..."

She turned suddenly back to Abby and snarled. "Damn it! Yeah, okay. You win." She threw up her hands and wobbled her head, mouth gaping in disgust. "But I want to cry foul! You didn't explain all the rules clearly to me." Olivia turned and started striding away.

Abby gasped and hopped-stepped next to Olivia as she struggled to put her shoes on and keep up.

"Rules?" Abby cried. "Now, hold on Miss Fist! I distinctly remember saying "Anything goes. No limitations." How clear is that? Rules... You want rules?"

"Well, all I'm saying," Olivia replied somewhat sheepishly, "is that you didn't add in any part about climbing up trees all naked like a cherub." Olivia caught herself, then turned to eyeball Abby next to her. "How in tarnation did you get up there? You were likely to break your neck, you crazy girl. You crazy." Olivia smiled reluctantly.

"Oh, you just a jealous Julie! You mad that you didn't think of it first!"

Olivia snorted at that and then they both were laughing. They went on jawing at each other and laughing like loons all the way back home.

At the end of Abby's driveway, the two girls stood looking up at the house. Olivia's mom was talking to Momma Bea on the porch, and it looked like they were wrapping up their visit.

Abby turned and laughed one more time at the besmirched face of Olivia. "Here," she said, holding up the one wet sock that she still held in her hand. "Now you know why I got 'em all wet." She reached over and started wiping off Olivia's "war paint."

"Yeah, right," Olivia said, rolling her eyes again. She winced as Abby had to scrub harder because it had dried and was caked on something fierce.

As she continued to work at it, Abby said softly, "Now, promise me. You don't tell nobody about what happened today, all right?"

"Oh, like they would believe me anyway!" Olivia replied, then snorted again. That made Abby smile. "You are crazier than me," Olivia added after a few moments, "and that's saying a lot." Olivia's eyes sparkled as she smiled back at her friend.

Olivia then held up two fingers and stood at attention. "Your secret is safe with me, Miss A. B. Rubideaux. I promise!"

Abby held up two fingers opposite Olivia's, then they both started miming the snipping of scissors. They moved their fingers in a circle counter-clockwise, then pointed them at each other like a gun, thumbs up, and they made "poof-ing" noises as their hands recoiled. Each girl staggered around in circles saying, "My oh my oh my," and then they were facing each other again and laughing.

Right about then, Olivia's mom came and told them it was time to go.

"See you in school tomorrow," Abby said.

"Not if I see you first!" Olivia replied as she walked away with her mother.

Abby stood and watched them go. She had to suppress a laugh when she heard Olivia's mom exclaim, "Good lord, child. What is that all over your face? And in your hair? You look like the cat just drugged you up out the river!"

They got in their car and drove away, Olivia waving out the back window like a spastic robot. It was only then that Abby heard her mom call her in, and she turned to walk up the driveway.

She told her momma that she wanted to take a bath, and her momma, after taking one look at her, wholeheartedly agreed.

Later, she floated in the hot water of the tub after several minutes of sting-ing agony as the objections from her cuts and scratches subsided. She was just beginning to relax when she felt the rumble of the dragon stir once again deep inside of her.

Only this time, rather than settling into the peaceful, comfortable feeling that usually accompanied the dragon presence, she was all aflutter and nervous inside.

This time, she was thinking thoughts that she had never thought before, and her mind wouldn't stop racing with each thought colliding into the others. This time, there was no relaxing because she had made a new and very important discovery that day.

She wasn't sure who or what she had seen up in that tree. But one thing was for sure: The dragon voice was not just in her head. There were others like her out there.

She was not alone.

6

SCHOOL

From the Audio transcripts of Dr. Joanna Kinsey
Chief Psychiatrist, CHNOLA Northshore Center,
New Orleans, LA

Audio File Transcript #AR10089-27

June 23, 2022

Subject: A. B. Rubideaux. Female. Age: 11

Transcript of recording begins: 8:25 P M EST.

Kinsey: *Audio file number twenty-seven, subject A. B. Rubideaux not present. Blood and Lab work has been completed for A.B.. MRI's and cat scans of her brain reveal hypomanic activity in prefrontal cortex and in the basal ganglia. EEG tests, however, reveal abnormally low levels of beta brain activity with unusually high delta brain waves. A.B. appears to have the brain activity of a person in a deeply meditative state of mind, although she was conscious and conversing throughout the process. Very unusual given the stress usually associated with these types of tests and procedures, and also the fact that such brain wave activity is nearly impossible without a subject going into a deep sleep or a trance-like state. Chemical tests reveal increased production of dopamine in the basal ganglia. Abnormal brain chemistry also noted in the limbic system. Both of these regions show altered connectivity with the prefrontal cortex. All consistent with signs of schizophrenia. Possible dementia. A.B.'s description of her response to intense light and colors, however, are not consistent with symptoms of schizophrenia. A.B.'s active seeking of the company of others and heightened but non-hostile emotional states also run counter to traditional measures of schizophrenic behavior. And her blood work, well, the blood work results are remarkable. Blood samples repeated three times: all come back as type A positive with traces of an unknown blood type. There's never been any blood type like A.B.'s. Ever. She is unique. A possible mutation. With the evidence in front of me, I do not hesitate in my assertion that A.B. Rubideaux is a scientific anomaly that prior to these tests I would have insisted to be an impossibility.*

45 DAYS EARLIER. MAY 2, 2022

Abby, as was her usual habit, was sitting alone at a bench-table in the middle school yard, some distance away from the other kids. Julia De Champlain, a "princess" of the first order, was holding court with her minions across the way, and lucky for Abby, their attention did not seem to be directed at her—a good thing, as Abby was tightly gripping the bench of her lunch table, breathing deeply and just trying to keep it together by tuning out all of the school yard sounds, closing her eyes, and focusing on the slight breeze that gently caressed her face.

Lunch time was not her favorite time, especially when she was having vivid dreams again. Maybe it had something to do with that dragon she saw up in that tree, but in any case, the flood gates sure seemed to be open now. Most of the time, the dreams came to her while she was sleeping. And those were okay—she didn't have to worry about losing control while she was all alone in the middle of the night and in her own bed. But sometimes, they would come to her while she was awake, and most unfortunately when she was at school. Like she was right now, in this moment. Clear and powerful visions. Knock you down to the floor kind of visions—which were not very convenient when you were just trying to be a normal kid who wanted to fit in.

Normal kid. Right. Who was Abby fooling? There wasn't anything normal about any of her dreams. Especially since most of them seemed to be coming from other people and one person in particular: Balthazar Luster.

Now Balt—and that's what everybody called him, and woe be onto anyone who dared to call him Balthazar—was a classic bully, so full of rage and hurt that it took Abby's breath away. In the normal scheme of school yard universals, Abby wouldn't pay a bully much never mind. It would be a waste of time and effort for Abby to go into any depth with someone who was just plain mean and stupid. Like the way you would figure most bullies were. Only with Balt, it wasn't that simple, you see, first of all because it's wrong to think of all bullies as stupid—and Balt certainly was no dummy. And secondly, and more importantly, it was because Abby had been connected to him ever since her first day in the fourth grade, two years earlier.

Now this connection might not be what you expect it to be. Most people know a bully when they see one—especially eight and nine-year-old fourth graders. Abby, having lived her entire life with Henry—and being in the possession of an ancient dragon's soul, knew quite a bit about bullies. But that knowledge did not make her immune to the depredations of one bully in particular. She knew, for instance, that among your garden variety bully, you will find an individual, male or female, who acts strong on the outside but is weak on the inside. She also knew that the bully has often been deeply traumatized by some scarring event or regular and persistent abuse, usually at the hands of a relative (like a parent or an older sibling). The bully is not necessarily stupid, for abuse does not discriminate for intelligence, but he or she is definitely full of anger and hurt, and it was Abby's observation that there is a classic outward projection of this anger and hurt onto others around them, especially those who are perceived as weaker.

Of course, projecting your own anger and hurt on to the innocent may seem like a senseless thing to you, or at the very least, it is an unfair thing to do. But you must understand, the bully is not motivated by a desire to be liked or accepted by others, nor does he think logically. He is an emotional being who is motivated by acquiring the power and sense of self-worth that has been lost or taken from him by his abuser. It's about self-esteem, or rather the lack of self-esteem! It's like a reaction to every wrongful action that the bully has himself endured. And anyone who is a top-notch, brainiac solver of mathematical equations, or a phenomenal athlete, or an expert at fixing machines, or at building things with their hands, or someone who is just a lazy couch potato that plays video games all day—any one of these individuals and countless others yet to be described here—are subject to this same reaction. They hold on to their hurt, and the emotional memory of what caused that hurt, and that is what informs and shapes their actions.

And yes, then eight-year-old and now eleven-year-old Abby, was in the habit of making these types of clinical observations.

Now, anyone who understands the nature of school children will not be a stranger to the concept of classroom universals. And certainly, as a dragon who exists simultaneously in multiple dimensions of space and time, Abby had certain insights into these universal archetypes. By the time she was eleven years old and in middle school, where everything is hormonally amplified by one thousand, she might as well have had a PhD in the subject, for she was a master.

The fact of the matter is that humans are all very much alike, and we are connected together in ways that can only be explained by sequences of DNA, mundane planetary experiences, predictable patterns and habits, and the fact that most folks are afflicted with a somewhat limited imagination. But children are wide open and more susceptible to their environment, and they haven't developed the internal resources or had enough life experience to overcome the flaws of their predisposed natures. In other words, and just to keep it easier to understand, let's just say that there are certain types of children that you can always count on when dealing with the classroom and, perhaps even more to the point, the relatively unsupervised schoolyard.

While there are a few individuals who defy stereotypes and archetypal typecasting, the truth of the matter is that most human beings fall somewhere within the spectrum of particular classifications. In school, these classifications include spoiled Princesses, like Julia, and a whole array of others: dorks, gamer-geeks, science nerds, jocks, clowns, stoners, goth chicks, cheerleaders and bullies. And Balt Luster was no exception. He was the classic bully.

And Abby loved him.

Now, why would anyone love a bully? It doesn't make much sense to those of us on the outside looking in. For Abby, however, it wasn't complicated at all. Most bullies, and Balt was no exception, are unaware of their motivation—of what makes them do the things they do. For some bullies, they could be made aware of it when placed into the proper hands of certain wise souls who know how to empathize and reach out to people like them. And a bully who becomes self-aware is usually no longer a bully.

Abby was in a position to help Balt Luster. When she opened herself to him, she could find out exactly what it was that made him act the way he did. Be forewarned, however: some bullies are sociopathic—that means they are incapable of feeling the normal range of emotions that most people extend to others when monitoring their own behavior. Maybe they were born that way—like Henry; or maybe they were traumatized. The point is, most people know what it means to be hurt, and most people don't like to hurt others. But for bullies, it is different. Sometimes a bully is so damaged or maybe their internal wires are so crossed up that they lack the fundamental awareness and compassion that most of us use to inform ourselves and become better human beings. Bullies can't help it, in other words. That may give you grounds for feeling compassion toward them. But that doesn't make them any less danger-ous until they find help or get medication.

Medication was something Balt Luster never had. And his meth-addict parents—who just happened to be clients of Henry the Toad—were not the kind to go find help, so Balt was kind of on his own. Except for Abby. Only he didn't know it. Abby never let on to what she was truly capable of. All it took was that one time she came into physical contact with him—that first day of school back in the fourth grade.

That was when it happened.

Now, Balt had already established a reputation by the time he had reached the fourth grade. Most of the children had known Balt since preschool, and experience had taught them that Balt Luster was a person to avoid. He was that odd mixture of mean and calculated cunning that made him a bully to be extra wary of. But Abby was new to school and didn't know about any of that. On the first day of class, Abby had made the mistake of saying "hello" to him.

In return, Balt had reached over and pinched the skin of her arm, holding on like a vice grip and drawing her in close so that Abby could look up into his hard, cruel blue eyes. "You don't talk to me, freak." Those were the words he spat at her, twisting his pinch real hard before letting go. It had left a welt and a bruise that painfully persisted for days.

What Abby didn't tell Balt, or anyone else, was that in those few painful pinching moments of contact, she had access to all of Balt's life—his horrible evenings at home, as he lay awake in bed at night as his father would start in on his mother, loud voices followed by the smack of hands on flesh. The one time he would try to stand up to him and defend his mother—that was the time his father turned on him, and his balled-up fist struck Balt quickly, without warning. Abby knew that was how he would lose his front tooth and miss a good week of school because the shame of his broken face was too much to bear before others.

That was just one thing she knew about Balt. That thing just stuck in her mind because of the little details that accompanied it. Like the fact that despite the bone-crunching hurt of the punch, which made him see stars and ring his bell, he still managed to hear the tiny tick-tacking sound of the tooth as it fell and bounced on the linoleum kitchen floor. Later, Balt would crawl under the table to retrieve his tooth and cry when everyone else had gone to bed.

Yeah, she remembered that one—it was hard to forget. But she was able to see dozens of the myriad pathways of his current and future possibilities, most of them leading to a life of addiction (like his parents), dysfunctional and abusive relationships (ditto), and in most cases, prison (ditto again). But there were also moments of humanity and gratitude. There was the little puppy he had hid away out in the barn before his father took it away. Balt loved that dog more than anything. Had it already happened or was it going to happen? Oh, Abby would get so confused when she tried to focus on any one thing, any one detail, for the visions and the memories all came so fast and spilled together in such a flurry.

What wasn't confusing at all, however, were Balt's future pathways that burned brighter than all the others. In those pathways, Abby was together with him—she was older and living out west somewhere in California, and they were together, and she was loving him like no other. In those pathways there was a life of hope and immeasurable joy. It was possible, yes! In that vivid and vibrant lifetime, Balt was a wise and gentle man. He was a builder—a maker of things. He had a workshop that he just loved. He was an architect and a designer and a craftsman that built things with his hands. Beautiful things that sometimes came to Abby in the form of gifts—little carved animals, a wooden birdhouse, an exact and highly detailed model replica of the town they lived. In that lifetime, with all of its myriad visions of realized potential and unrelenting happiness, in that future possibility of what could be, every one of those moments led back to one seemingly insignificant incident that occurred between Abby and Balt, which if followed up with action and intention, would lead to a life of success, fulfillment and happiness. For both of them. And in that lifetime, Balthazar Luster burned so brightly, and he was so beautiful that it brought Abby to tears.

Of course, Balt and the other kids in school watching at the time just thought it was the brutal pinch that caused Abby to cry, but in that moment, Abby had fallen in love with the "Balt-to-be," and she had resolved herself to finding the right time to tell Balt about this wonderful, shining, life that could be his. This was the nature of the dragon inside of her. This was her true calling in life—to help others find their way to happiness and to their higher self. And, yes, well, what would it matter if it could also bring just a little bit of happiness to herself, too?

In the case of Balt, however, finding the right time to tell him proved difficult beyond what she imagined. She always knew that the time would present itself, and that she would instantly know when that time had arrived, but Balt, two years later, was sure as heck making it seem like that time might never come. It didn't help that Balt's uncle was a gator tour operator who just happened to discover Abby one morning a few years back out in the Bayou.

Now, wandering around without one's clothes in the bayou may not be a big deal from a dragon's point of view, or even for someone like Olivia, who was true to her word and told nobody about the sitting-up-in-the-tree incident, but for most two-legged human denizens of the swamp lands, it was notable behavior, to say the least. Secrets are hard to keep in a small town like Houma. Things happen. People talk. And folks have very long memories. And Balthazar Luster's uncle sure liked to talk. A lot.

After the tornado, the "Miracle of Mandeville" clamor persisted, and it was only a matter of time before Abby's odd behavior would be discovered in Houma and add fuel to the fire. Now, there was that time a few years back when Sug Messier claimed to have seen a dragon flying over the swamp waters, but he was an old Cajun swamp rat and the town drunk, so nobody believed him. But this other time when Abby had first arrived in town… well that one had a little more staying power. And folks knew all about it. When Abby was seven, she was found early one morning wandering stark naked in the bayou by uncle Luster's gator tour group. Why he was giving gator tours at the crack of dawn on that day remains a mystery to Abby. From her perspective, it was just one of those unearthly and divine dawns, with the sun swimming up over the lip of the bayou, spreading yellows and oranges across the purple skies. It was beautiful. But then Abby came across the tour group and everyone was so anxious that the beautiful moment got lost in all these strangers' wild speculations.

And wild speculation is the polite way to characterize it. The way Abby saw it, folks' minds were wandering every which way, and some of those turns that people made in their minds were not worthy of being repeated. It was a whole lot of fuss that young Abby just couldn't understand.

Well, needless to say, the police got involved, and they had to call Momma Bea early in the morning. The general consensus was that something evil had befallen this naked little girl, and everybody around Abby sure seemed intent on making a big fuss. Well, long story short, it turned out that the doctor couldn't find any signs of trauma or physical abuse, and Momma Bea kind of made up a white lie about Abby often going a sleep walking in the night, and as it turns out, this happened not too much after the incident with the tornado, so the authorities and just about everyone in town, actually, had it in their minds that there was something kind of "off" and even downright strange about Abby and her Momma Bea.

In the end, the authorities and the grown-ups who deal with these kinds of matters just went back home and returned to the normality of their every-day mundane lives. Oh, people around town still talked about it, for sure. It was the kind of thing that followed you. And those folks on the tour boat had themselves a story that they could tell that would entertain their friends and families for generations to come. Stupid gator tourists.

Now, Momma Bea, maybe she knew more than she let on, because when they got back home, she just put Abby back to bed without saying even a word. For the next few days, though, Abby would catch Momma staring at her when she thought Abby wasn't looking. A few nights after that, Momma Bea asked her about the incident in the most direct way possible. She looked Abby right in the eye when she was tucking her in for the night, and then she said, "I know what you were doing, A.B., the other night? You were flying with the dragon, and you didn't want no one to know, not even me. Isn't that right, Peaches?"

Now, Abby, being an honest sort of little girl, and quite frankly somewhat caught off guard, could only respond in one way.

"Yes, momma," she said truthfully, and she smiled.

Then Momma Bea just smiled right back at her, a sweet and true smile, and she quietly said, "I know you like to wander off all by your lonesome. You take to them woods just about every day, I reckon. And I understand. It's okay to tell me or leave some sort of sign when you're gonna go off like that. But just so you know, when you get done with all that wandering, after you go flying, you always come back here to me, you hear?"

"Yes momma," little Abby replied.

"And lan' sakes, Peaches, don't go wanderin' around stark naked! It's not like folks around here got a lot to talk about!" Then Momma Bea and Abby both burst out laughing. Momma Bea kissed her on the forehead, still chuckling and said good night. As she slipped out the door, Abby turned on her side and went straight to sleep, still grinning such a sweet grin.

Before Olivia, that was the closest Abby ever came to telling another soul about her dragon. The problem was that the dragon had other ways of letting the world find her. Like the fact that any time other people spent any sort of time around Abby, they would invariably start to notice things. It was one thing to find solitude in the bayou—around the town of Houma, the bayou was much thicker and other people were much more scarce, which is exactly the way the dragon liked it—but it was another thing entirely to spend all day every day at school surrounded by other people.

School. A confined and heavily supervised space crammed full of children. Not an ideal place for a dragon to be hiding in plain sight. And to add to her woes, Abby had a reputation that preceded her. It was her grave misfortune that Balt's uncle was the one giving *that* gator tour, and he made sure that Balt knew everything about Abby's little naked incident from a few years back. It was the kind of story that followed you around like an unwanted, starving mongrel dog. And it was a story that a bully like Balt relished. That type of information gave Balt leverage, an advantage over Abby that he never missed an opportunity to exploit.

In school, Balt had immediately dubbed her "the Swamp Thing." Of course, because she was found that morning in the bayou without a stitch of clothing, his list of pet names for her quickly grew, both in absurdity and in their salacious aspects. At various times she had been hailed as "Jay Bird" (as in "Naked as…"), "Ruby-No-clothes-Rubideaux," "Nature Girl" (which seemed to Abby relatively benign, compared to some of the others), "Rosy Butt Cheeks," "the Mighty Butt Cracker," and "A. B. R.," which was an abbreviation for "All Beaver Revue." Balt seemed particularly fond of that last one, and predictably, the other kids, particularly Princess Julia and her entourage, picked up on these names, and of course they stuck. Like it's been said, kids are cruel. All Abby could do was wear her names proudly. And even though most kids would say them to hurt Abby, truth be told, they didn't really bother her. But that was something she kept to herself as well as a few other things.

But not everything could be kept in the shadows, away from the light. Mean-spirited nicknames are one thing, but needless to say, Abby soon got a reputation as a weirdo who didn't like to be touched. This was a feature of her life that soon became a regular source of conflict and cruelty, for in the hierarchy of school children, there is no mercy for the freaks and the feckless few, better known as the outsiders. For most of her elementary school life, Abby would find herself the victim of the various and sundry school yard predators. But most of the time, she was left alone, and that meant that she had most of her time to herself—most of her time to watch and learn what made others do what they do.

Now it was the voice of a particularly accomplished predator, miss Julia DeChamplain, who brought Abby out of her reverie. She had been clutching the bench seat of her lunch table with white-knuckled intensity as she tried to block out a slightly older and particularly dreamy image of Balt Luster kneeling down with her on the sand of some beach, laughing, and showing her how to make drip castles with wet sand—it was just one of many chapters of her hopeless love affair with him through all time.

She was back in the present moment now, and in the center table of the lunch court, well-shaded by one of the few serviceable light blue awnings, Miss Julia DeChamplain was holding court surrounded by her minions. And "court" is absolutely the correct word to use, for Julia was by all accounts a "Little Miss Princess." Sitting there in her fine expensive dress with silk ribbons in her perfectly curled hair, which had been styled and set in such a way usually associated with a much older girl—not an eleven-year old sixth grader. Julia was in the middle of an elaborate recounting of last weekend's party in which her Bichon Frise doggie, a most vile beast by the name of "Bon-Bon" grabbed uncle William's sausage from his plate and proceeded to race around the garden, sausage in mouth, and unmistakably grinning from ear to ear as only a Bichon Frise can. The other family members and guests were simply "appalled," but of course "Bon-Bon was simply too cute for anyone to remain upset or cross with for any length of time." The other girls at her table—and there were only girls, for boys were and are a completely separate matter all together—laughed and giggled obligingly at the proper cues, and Miss Julia DeChamplain reveled in their attention.

Abby watched her from her corner table, and luckily today was one of those days when Julia's attention would not be turned towards her, so Abby could watch her uninterrupted. A classic princess, or sometimes referred to as "Daddy's Girl," Julia is the one who always gets what she wants through false charm and an unparalleled skill in artful manipulation. The princess is often the teacher's pet, and this was something that Abby stopped trying to figure out because it absolutely made no sense that grown up teachers couldn't see right through a little eleven-year old princess's charade, but Julia was no exception, for she was no novice when it came to jockeying for power among the class hierarchy and outwardly pleasing those who hold authority or power. A princess is usually smart, which is its own form of irony, but she almost always lacks emotional intelligence and self-awareness. Sometimes she grows up to be a decent person, but almost never if she comes from money, nor if she marries one who will worship her and continue to enable her. She is quick to betray others when it comes to her self-interest. She is spoiled, of course, and this is often not her fault but the permissive parents who allow her to hold court every day with her demanding demeanor and unchallenged sense of superiority. For the princess, other people are servants, and woe be the individuals who dare to challenge their proper station in the life of the imperious princess. She is often accompanied by minions—other girls who suffer from inferiority complexes, are aspiring princesses themselves, and like to bully. Super-secret fact: beware of the princess when adults are not around—she is ruthless and capable of extreme cruelty when she feels that you are a rival, or, in many other cases, when you are perceived to be weak and disenfranchised with no allies. Sabotage or direct assault are both possibilities. She will destroy you to get what she wants or when there is a real or imagined slight to her reputation.

The lunch table bench suddenly sagged with the weight of another individual who had plopped down, jarring Abby out of her thoughts. She turned to see the freckled face of Olivia Fist smiling next to her, her chin resting across folded finger tops. Abby grinned back at her as a loud burst of laughter and girlish giggles caused Olivia to shift her gaze over to Julia's table. She and Abby watched together as the girls squeaked and giggled over some private joke. Julia, at the center of the table, sitting erect and by all appearances gracefully in her element, glanced over at the two of them. She stared right back at Abby, a knowing, slightly triumphant glint in her eye, and suddenly Abby knew beyond a shadow of a doubt that the royal princess and her court were indeed talking about her. Julia squinted ever so slightly, a brief cold and cruel acknowledgement that didn't match the smile that remained on her lips.

"Oh, look out," Olivia murmured under her breath. "Queen Julia and her killer bees are gonna be gunning for you later, sunshine." Olivia turned and smiled wickedly back at Abby. "Don't you worry about a thing. I'll make them soil their panties if they start in on you."

Abby chuckled and tore her gaze away from Julia. She glanced appreciatively at Olivia, who had crossed her eyes and scrunched her face into a painful grimace. Abby laughed uninhibitedly now and slid her lunch over for Olivia to peruse.

To the other children in her class, Olivia was known as the "Class Clown." This is usually a manic individual who vacillates between extreme introversion and extreme extroversion. Sometimes they are "off," and sometimes they are "on." In other words, they are usually a jumbled up, neurotic mess, but they can be so much fun to be around when you catch them when they are "on." Overtly fearless and affable, the class clown usually holds very close to the chest some deeper issues involving low self-esteem and hyper-sensitivity. They want to be liked and fear rejection more than anything else. Sometimes the Class Clown may contain the deeper archetype of the classic "Fool," who is a very wise but tragically sad soul. Classic fools are quick to wit and the first to easy laughter, but the Fool is also an expert observer and judge of human character. The secret of the "Fool" is that nobody really takes them seriously or perceives them as a threat, and thus are they free to speak to truth and to point out things that no one else would dare for fear of repercussions. The Fool gets a free pass and is not held to the same standard of justice as most others; unfortunately, they are doomed to be ignored when it matters most. "Class Clowns" and "Fools" usually grow up to be psychiatrists or twinkly-eyed grandparents, and they are often the owners of several cats.

For Abby, though, it wasn't fair to put Olivia—or "Oblivia," which was the nickname everyone called her—into a single category. She defied all labels, and quite simply, she was the most genuine person that Abby had ever met. Oh sure, Olivia had her issues and hidden weaknesses, but Abby knew that the clown act was just a way for Olivia to work out a few things that would otherwise remain repressed and, if left unattended to, would probably end up doing some real damage as she grew older.

Olivia was also Abby's personal champion and protector, as alluded to before. She fit into the archetype of the "Hero," who is a person, male or female, who has a divine calling to protect the weak, the defenseless, and the powerless. Not that Abby was any of those things, but Olivia had come to her aid on more than a few occasions and bloodied a lip or two. Olivia would come to her rescue because it was something deep within the nature of a hero. They are unselfish, righteous warriors, who come to the aid of others when no one else will, overcoming all stigmas and often, placing their own reputation and certainly their own physical well-being at risk. They do it because they are driven by a moral compulsion—there is something inside of them, the very essence of their karmic DNA, that they cannot ignore, and this thing always drives them to defend what is right, to defy the dishonest, the deceitful, the unprincipled, and the corrupt. And they are always the one who stands up to a bully. Olivia Fist. That was who she was. A person, who at this moment, just happened to be busy fishing through Abby's lunch box and muttering about an equal exchange of her peanut butter sandwich for Abby's cheese and apple slices.

"Dork!" A boy's hand slammed down Abby's lunch box lid, and Olivia's fingers barely missed being crushed. The hulking figure of Balt Luster was striding away from their table, shoulders shaking with laughter.

Abby watched him walk away, and it was all she could do to keep the flood of his pathways from overwhelming her once again—she didn't even have to touch him to be susceptible to an incursion—all she had to do was think of him. She gripped the bench tightly once again and took a few deep breaths to settle herself.

Olivia's voice brought her back to the one-sided conversation at the lunch table. "Ain't that right?"

"Huh?" Abby turned to look at her friend who was now busy spreading peanut butter on to Abby's apple slices with her index finger. Olivia looked up at her and feigned exasperation.

"I said," and Olivia blew off a thick stray curl that was hanging down in front of her face, "I said that you once told me you didn't think old Balthazar was as mean as everyone made him out to be. That deep inside he was a good and beautiful person." She paused as she artfully spread the last bit of peanut butter onto the edge of the last apple slice. She licked her finger and quickly popped a slice into her mouth, crunching with joyous abandon. "Well, you could've fooled me!" She exclaimed in a garbled peanut butter and apple filled mouth.

Olivia proceeded to pop slice after slice into her mouth, carefully licking her fingers between each slice, and somehow managing to speak between bites as if it were not an impossible thing to do. "That boy is meaner than a hissing goose. And what I really want to know, by the way, is why you look at him the way you do. After all the horrible things he's done to you, why do you love him so, Miss Aurora Borealis Rubideaux?" Olivia proceeded to smack the last bit of apple and peanut butter down, then loudly lick her fingertips and raise her eyebrows inquiringly at Abby.

Abby just stared back at Olivia, trying not to smile, and trying her best to sound indignant. "Well Miss Fist, I do declare. My personal affections for vile creatures and horrible, reptilian monstrosities otherwise known as human boys, is none of your business." She watched as Olivia began to lick what remained of the peanut butter off the bread that used to be her sandwich. "And if I didn't know any better, I'd say you had a bit of dragon inside of you too. So perceptive. Don't let it swell your head."

At the mention of the word "dragon," Olivia squealed and pounded the tabletop ecstatically. "Ooh, you promised. You promised now. When you gonna take me out into the bayou and show me your dragon? When, oh when, oh whensy, when, when?" Olivia clutched her hands together in mock prayer and fluttered her eyes at Abby.

Abby just laughed and said, "Tomorrow is Friday, right? Let's do it after school."

Olivia sprung up to her feet and danced around in circles like a banshee. Abby just laughed, stood up herself, and then said, "Oh, and miss Fist? Need I remind you?"

They both turned to each other, leaned in towards each other, heads almost touching, and pantomimed with their right hands over their lips like they were quickly zipping them shut.

"Damn straight," Olivia declared.

"You better believe it," Abby responded.

The school bell rang and they both smiled. "Gotta go," Olivia exclaimed breathily. "Why do we have P.E. right after lunch? It's downright inconsiderate. I think I'm gonna barf all over Miss Trudy's gym shoes today."

Abby laughed and said she had to put her books away. "I'll catch up with you later."

As they parted ways, Abby's mind returned to her earlier thoughts. Of course, for every bully, there is usually a hero or warrior to balance things out, for such is the nature of the natural world; it might even be a cosmic law that applies to all of the universe. No light without dark. No attraction without repulsion. No Ying without the Yang. No Bully without a Hero—you get the picture? Only now she was wondering if a bully like Balt could also, some day, be a hero.

"Most assuredly yes," she muttered and smiled to herself as she ran up the steps and into the classroom building.

As she made her way through the hallway, like a lone salmon against the stream of kids rushing out the other way, she let the flow of all the others wash over and through her. All of the students in school were, of course, individuals, and each had a unique signature. Even so, there were patterns and habits of mental and emotional energy that shaped them and informed who they were.

These patterns also shaped how others saw them and how those perceptions and beliefs in turn further shaped how the individual perceived him or herself. It was a wild dance of back and forth, but it was consistent and true for every one of them. It was all about those universals.

Abby played a familiar game with herself as she passed the surging streams of other children in the hall. She called it her universals game, and it also helped to occupy her mind and screen out the unwanted intrusions of others.

A boy in thick-framed glasses, a hand-me-down plaid shirt and blue jeans whose waistline rode halfway up his belly awkwardly scurried past Abby, his hands full of notebooks and papers. That was Bobbie Penske.

"Nerd." She quickly categorized him. Only that didn't seem to do justice at all to what Bobby was or could be. "Nerd" seemed somewhat one-dimensional. In Bobbie, you've got the Nerd, which we are all familiar with, and this unfortunate child, like most nerds, was pretty good on the academic side of things, but Bobbie lacked social skills and had yet to master the elusive wiles of the popular clique of students (cheerleaders, football quarterbacks, ASB presidents and school annual editors). Bobbie wasn't helped by his choice of wardrobe (mom-bought and at least two generations behind the times), and he was doomed to a life that must suffer the aspersions and ridicule of others.

Abby took a deep breath as another sudden image of Balt and sand came into her mind—only this one involved Balt holding down Bobbie in the schoolyard sand box and funneling sand into the squealing Bobbie's open mouth. She had to quickly repress that image and force it out of her head. She had to think of Bobbie and his future pathways.

Bobbie would not be considered as "cool," nor would he be invited to join in any reindeer games until that magical moment, sometime near the end of high school or later in college, when the Nerd label suddenly didn't matter anymore, and somehow, some way, he would manage to rise above his nerd-like demeanor and suddenly be considered as "cool." This of course would be accompanied by the fact that a nerd like Bobbie actually belonged to a subset of nerds known as "the Brainiacs." He would be accepted to an Ivy League school and is clearly on the path to becoming an engineer (MIT), attorney (Harvard) or doctor (Harvard again—all three of these were high probabilities—Abby just wasn't sure which path would be the one he would follow). Ka-ching! Money has a way of smoothing out things and obscuring clearly defined labels.

Or at least make it so they don't seem to matter that much anymore. Bobbie would be set for his life, and he would get it all together sooner than most.

But 11-year-old Bobbie was a big hot mess. Like most Brainiacs, being super smart in middle school doesn't release you from the legions of nerds, and in this case, Bobbie is prone to suffer from a lack of emotional and/or interpersonal intelligence—he's just not very good around other people. But he more than makes up for this with mathematical, logical, and linguistic intelligence. Still, he was not a really well-adjusted human being, for the most part, and he was at some risk of falling into the sociopathic sphere. The pathways don't lie, however. Wait for the end of high school. Hello Harvard, M.I.T, and Stanford. It wasn't his choice, exactly, but being the nerd was his habit and weirdly enough, it was his own sense of order and fulfillment to provide others with the satisfaction of meeting their expectations of him. So, to the point at hand: We all strive to belong—well most of us anyway—and that is true even for a complicated nerd like Bobby Penske. There was a certain order beneath the chaotic dance of life. That's what the universe seemed to be telling us. Julia was the Princess, Olivia the Clown, and Balt was the Bully.

But what category did Abby belong too?

She quickly moved on as others filed past. Billy Dawes. "Dork." This was another one of the nerdy subsets. The dork, unfortunately, is just a nerd without any smarts. Billy was pretty good at video and computer games, however, and by middle school he had crossed over into the "Gamer" category. Good for his street cred, anyway. More students brushed past her. Jenna Baptiste: musically talented, but struggling with low self-esteem, so she had joined the "band geeks." Arianna Denard, god forbid, another "Thespian." She was very annoying and narcissistic. The entire world was a stage for her to work out her issues. Very high maintenance.

Abby stepped aside as a whole phalanx of rowdy, cocky boys made their way noisily down the hall. In the vanguard was Rudy Massey, who walked with the quiet confidence and grace of a powerful athlete. "Jocks," of course, were omnipresent in every school, for it was the one archetype that allowed alpha-males to keep acting out in physically aggressive ways that the teachers and adults around them continued to praise and encourage. Rudy strode past Abby and smiled at her. It wasn't a mean smile, just one that told her that she was insignificant in his world, but she should count herself lucky that he chose to acknowledge her. Maybe she could do something useful for him down the line. At any rate, such a smile was totally ego-driven and brimming with a type of smug, self-satisfaction (what most other girls inexplicably considered "adorable" and "cute.") that for all effective purposes was telling the rest of the world: "Here I am, your elite special person. Don't you want to have me as your friend? How would you like to accommodate me?" He was a star, and it was hard not to like him.

Now, Rudy could have easily been a bully, but he wasn't really scarred or emotionally unstable. Quite the opposite, actually: he had the world on his own little silver platter. Most Jocks do, at least until they finish school. But Rudy also happened to be gracious and nice, even to someone like Abby. Perhaps that was a little bit of humility (good job to Rudy's mom and dad). But on the field of play, watch out! Between the lines, he was a beast, and he played to win at all costs, which might include knocking your block off. Well, that was Rudy anyway. The Jock is the individual who excels at sports and all things athletic. They are not necessarily poor academic students, but most jocks quickly learn how to leverage their superior physical prowess into popularity (like ASB office and homecoming King or the Princesses Court), and most definitely they discover that they have special status among the aforementioned crooning adults. Jocks are tribal and hierarchical, and that simply means that loyalty to the group is tantamount to one's identity, and there is a tight-knit pecking order, and everyone knows their place in it. It's kind of like the army—a regimented and all disciplined routine. And because they are afforded special status among the adults who surround them, they tend to coast through school and make everything look easy. Do not cross the alpha male jock. He is bigger, faster, and stronger than you, and he usually has minions to carry out lower order deeds and dirty work. And, as mentioned before, they are often exempt from punishment because they are elite members of the team. Don't ask Abby to explain it—it's just the way it is. Unfortunately, if they have an ultra-competitive nature, or—to simplify it—a mean streak, they can also become bullies, especially if they're not up to snuff in their academics or when things are tough at home. However, and this seems to be connected to the aforementioned special status among adults, Jocks seem to get a free pass when they violate the policies and the regulations—transgressions that would carry significant repercussions for the rest of us. Call it unfair, call it favoritism or call it a double standard—you can call it whatever you want. But because Rudy can catch and throw a ball, he gets a free pass. And he knows it.

The boys loudly moved on, leaving the hallway nearly empty. Abby drifted over to her locker. Beside her was Delores Multaney, who awkwardly fiddled with her lock while nervously casting her glance around. She spotted Abby and grinned a grin that quickly transformed into a grimace as she continued to struggle to open the locker. She had on braces, which didn't help her overcome her natural shyness or sense of lower self-worth. She was pretty but didn't know it. She was a "Wallflower." "Wallflowers" are worthy of mention because they feature prominently in Abby's first year of middle school. Wallflowers are those sad individuals who lack assertiveness and imagination, who always linger in the background or in the shadows watching others. The "Wallflower" is usually a term reserved for girls in this gender-discriminating world of ours, for flowers are forever metaphorically an aspect of the feminine. A male wallflower is usually referred to as a "beta" as opposed to the "alpha," for boys are often gender-discriminated in terms of a hierarchy of power and status; therefore, we are more likely to turn to Latin words and more scientific sounding nomenclature when describing the world of boys, for didn't you know that the male half of the species is infinitely more rational and linear than their female counterparts? (And yes, that is sarcasm.)

Experience will bust that myth sooner or later, even for the most ardent creator of stereotypes, but one of the benefits of being a dragon is that by entering other people's dreams and seeing their past, present, and all possible future paths, well, one soon realizes that we are all constructed of the same neuroses. And insecurity and neurosis are the human condition. Hence, the preponderance of "Wallflowers" like Delores. Sadly, many people fall into this category, for they do indeed suffer from low self-esteem, which seems to be a very common human condition. But trust me—it is one that can and should be overcome, and it is the only way to reach one's full potential as a human being. Delores would figure it out one day. Abby was sure of this as she saw all the multiple ways that her life burned brightly and happily. More than most, in fact.

Abby leaned over and gave Delores' locker a sharp tap with the flat of her hand, and the door swung open. "Mine does it, too," she said. "I have the touch!" Abby displayed her hand, turning it slowly, majestically, and then she grinned.

Delores returned her smile and murmured her thanks, before cramming her books into the locker, grabbing her PE clothes and darting off.

Abby watched her go. There were many sub-categories of Wallflowers. Booger-eaters, Goths, and Automatons just to name a few…luckily, for her sake, Delores was none of them. She, like thousands and thousands of other kids, just hadn't found any purpose in her life, so she muddled through as best she could, trying not to be noticed.

"Look sharp, Miss Rubideaux!" The big voice of Ms. Trudy Greenwood startled Abby. "Class resumes at 1:00 PM, sharp! On the hop, now, on the hop!" Abby watched as Ms. Trudy (as all the children called her) filed by, leading a line of the "special ed" kids. Ms. Trudy Greenwood was the remedial education teacher who handled all the children with learning disabilities of one sort or the other. She was also the PE instructor and, by virtue of her reputation and consistent daily demeanor, part-time Nazi drill sergeant. A large, muscular woman with thick lips, thick bones, and basically thick everything, Ms. Trudy was not to be trifled with. Abby watched as she rounded the corner, leading the line of five students along to their afternoon "therapy session" with the school counselor. Abby would see Ms. Trudy in just a few minutes out in the field, whistle and sharp voice ready for any stragglers or mischief-makers. Tardy students would be punished by being made to run laps. Abby needed to hurry up and change into her gym clothes—or maybe not, running laps as punishment was often more pleasurable than the silly games they played which passed for "sport."

As she rushed to put her books in order and grab her gym clothes, she heard a meek squeak, and then a flurry of books thumping on the floor.

"March of the Retards!" That would be the unmistakable voice of Balt the Bully, once again making his presence known.

Abby was able to catch a glimpse of him as he sauntered off down the hall, disappearing amid the sea of scurrying children, unflappably leaving the scene of his crime.

The last special ed girl in the line was Fina Lee Bentley, and she was a large girl who was probably a few years older and should have been in high school by now, but she was somewhere pretty high up on the autism spectrum, which meant her brain was organized differently from most folks, so she didn't learn or relate to others the same way as most people do. The rumor was that her momma named her "Fina Lee" because she had wanted a baby for many years before her daughter was "finally" born, and well, you get the picture. Not exactly the kind of name you would want to give your child if you knew what other children would do with it. Abby had heard Princess Julia once loudly proclaiming to her entourage as Fina Lee walked by that some folks had better be careful what they wish for, cuz Fina Lee's momma sure got a bad bargain for all of her hopes and dreams. Abby thought that was just a cruel thing to say, but it got the desired giggles from the other girls. And not for the first time, Abby wondered why people took such delight in being mean to those less fortunate than themselves.

Well, anyway, Fina Lee was autistic, but Abby had heard Ms. Trudy explaining to another adult that she was "still functional," and "capable of sophisticated and meaningful conversations," of which Abby had engaged her in a few, but it was Abby's observation that Fina Lee was emotionally in no way, shape, or form cut out to handle the unexpected terrains and hidden pitfalls of middle school. And she was certainly not capable of dealing with the targeted malice of Balthazar Luster.

Abby could see Fina Lee standing in the hallway, her right hand held motionless above her as her papers fluttered all down around her, her books and heavier objects already on the floor. She looked as if her face were about to contort into a wild visage of horror mixed with the saddest empty-eyed stare of incomprehension. Abby figured out what had happened in an instant. Balt had been waiting for Ms. Trudy to round the corner and go out of sight before he knocked all of Fina Lee's books and school supplies out of her hands. Then he disappeared quickly, leaving Fina Lee all alone. Mission accomplished.

Abby closed her locker as Fina Lee was starting to whimper, a frightened mewling sound like a terrified kitten, and Abby had to act quickly or this would turn into a major scene.

"Here let me help you with that, Fina Lee!" Abby rushed over and began to scoop up books, and school supplies, quickly and deftly putting them back inside of Fina Lee's backpack. "What a mess!" She said gently, as Fina Lee continued to whimper. "Some people are just full of piss and vinegar, I guess. Old Balt Luster ain't worth a darn to think about." She gently took Fina Lee's still raised hand, and the stunned girl started in surprise, but she stopped mewling as Abby slowly lowered her hand. Abby was one of the few people who actually bothered to touch Fina Lee, which might have been the case because Fina Lee didn't like to be touched by just about everyone, and physical contact of any kind often brought about wild tantrums and histrionic fits. But Abby was different, somehow. Ms. Trudy called her "the Fina Lee Whisperer."

Abby pointed at all of the papers on the ground.

"Here Fina Lee, let's get these all in order." That seemed to do the trick, for Fina Lee clutched Abby's hand tighter, and they both went down on their knees. Order. If there was one thing Abby knew about Fina Lee and her special mind, then it was certainly that all things must be done in their proper place and in their proper order. It wasn't so strange after all, it seemed to Abby, to want all things done in a certain way. But unfortunately, Fina Lee couldn't control all things around her all the time, and it must have been very frustrating indeed to constantly be at odds with the inherent chaos of the middle school universe. In any case, Abby could always find the right frequency for someone like Fina Lee, and they got along just fine. You just needed to "tap in" and be fully present. There wasn't any special trick. It was called being nice.

With her left hand, Abby picked up the papers one by one, and there were a lot of them. After a few moments, Fina Lee began to pick up the remaining papers as well, and Abby passed them over to her. As she looked down at them, Abby could see that they were some sort of written journal, with neat and precise handwriting. Actually, there was beautifully scripted handwriting filling each page. Abby caught her breath as suddenly a wave of images swept through her. Images of an illuminated manuscript leapt into her mind like the one she had seen on some school field trip to the museum in New Orleans. That's what these pages reminded her of, for the words were so carefully and perfectly sculpted in a tiny script. Fina Lee must have spent hours of painstaking work on this.

As she passed the pages over, another wave washed over Abby, and this time it was coming from Fina Lee. Like a jolt of electricity thrilling through her entire being, Abby recognized the flood of mind and dream images that filled her mind. These were the jumbled pieces of Fina Lee's life—her past, present, and potential futures. It was happening again. She had learned to put up a continual screen of sorts to keep it blocked out—otherwise the clamor of voices and images would overwhelm her. But this time, it happened so fast and so powerfully, that Abby just let it come. She released all resistance.

Immediately, like magic, there was clarity and purpose. The illuminated manuscript pages were memories from Fina Lee's childhood—a trip to the Smithsonian when she was eight, to be precise. She had made her mother return to the Museum three days in a row, for she had been so enraptured by the pages of the manuscripts. A flicker of light, and some tingling vibration shot through Abby's body. The manuscript images were gone, and it was replaced by a muted, shadowy image: Fina Lee sitting in a dark room as voices raised in anger argued in the next room—her mother and father talking about her again. The scene merged and revolved, turning into another dark room, but this time her father, whose foul whiskey-soaked breath was now muttering things in Fina Lee's ear, was standing above her bed. In the dark room, his voice was amplified and clear, only this time Fina Lee was pretending to be asleep as he hoarsely sputtered words of her uselessness, how she had become such a heavy burden, the futility of her existence…

With a jolt, the dark images were gone. Fina Lee was now walking down the school hallway, painful tension in her slumped shoulders, as she stutter-stepped awkwardly in the line of children. A quick blur of images flash by in a sequence: Fina Lee's gaze locked on to the red and black sport shoes of the child walking in front of her; Balt's leering face among the gallery of countless other children, and their voices, repeating over and over: "Retard!" "Retard!" "Retard!" Sudden silence, and a feeling of calm delight, as Ms. Trudy's smiling face replaces the sea of taunting faces. Fina Lee peeks over the dark reddish-brown leather-bound notebook as Ms. Trudy extends it, a cherished gift of words yet to be written; then, amazingly, flashes of brilliant light as page after page of neatly written script zip by, one after another. Abby clutches tightly on to Fina Lee as she is nearly lost in a swirl of vertigo. Another image: An adult, Fina Lee, maybe twenty years from now, standing on a stage beneath bright lights—there is a thunder of applause as a woman at the microphone intones proudly, "…in recognition for literary excellence for the field of Adult Fiction, the Pulitzer prize goes to…" Last, there is only silence and an immense feeling of warmth, as a much older Fina Lee, maybe in her eighties, sits by a window, watching several grandchildren play in the garden outside the window near her writing desk. Somewhere in the house, a bird softly twitters. Future Grandma Fina Lee smiles as she flexes the stiffness out of her fingers and picks up the pen and resumes writing in her journal.

And just like that, Abby is back in the hallway, on her hands and knees, Fina Lee beside her gazing intensely into her eyes. Abby flexes the fingers of her right hand, still stiff from the powerful picture in her mind—no, Fina Lee's mind—no, the multi-verse "Fold" of time that was a future reality yet to be that had just washed over her. Oh, but it could be! It could be true; it burned so bright within her.

Abby took a deep, shuddering breath and passed a paper over to Fina Lee, aware now of the cold school hallway linoleum pressing against her bare knees. But the memory of that thunderous applause, the warmth of contentment that filled her after a lifetime of struggle and misperception, of cruelty and shame… There was one path that burned so brightly above all the others. It could be true, if only she stayed true to the path. It could be true!

Abby turned and suddenly took both of Fina Lee's hands in her own, blurting out as fast as she could a tumble of words.

"Fina Lee! No matter what happens in this life, now and forever more, no matter what, promise me… promise me that you will always keep writing, that you will put down in words what nobody else could ever know or understand, and…and that you will keep following that voice inside of you that shines with light and love so powerful… so beautiful. And, please, please, don't forget… that… that there will come a time to let others see it, and you will know it when you are ready for it. Oh, you will know it! Promise me, that, Fina Lee. Promise me!"

Fina Lee just stared back at Abby, her eyes suddenly watery and larger like liquid silver dollars. She glanced down at the stack of papers, now crushed in her hands, and she smiled. "Yes," she said quietly, as she unclasped her hands from Abby's grip. She looked momentarily into Abby's eyes, flirted briefly with the feintest of smiles, then darted her gaze back down to her hands and the papers. "Got to put these in order."

"That's right, Fina Lee." Abby let out a deep tense breath that she didn't realize she had been holding in. "Put it all in order. Beautiful and proper order."

Abby sat back and watched as Fina Lee sifted through the papers, shuffling and resorting them in a sequence only she could fathom. Abby reached over and picked up Fina Lee's school bag and began putting its spilled content back inside. She could not get out of her mind that last image of grandchildren playing just outside the glass window next to the writing desk. The cool metal of the fountain pen, perfectly balanced in her fingers… A feeling of love and contentment that she had never felt so acutely before…

"Ms. Rubideaux!" The voice of Ms. Trudy snapped her back to the here and now. "What is the meaning of this?" Abby looked up at the thick legs of Ms. Trudy and followed them up past hands on hips, past thick, broad shoulders, over fleshy, grimacing lips to the hard stare of Ms. Trudy's brown almost black eyes, which currently were squinting with suspicion.

"Just a little accident here," Abby said as she quickly stuffed the last few things back in the school bag and handed it over to Fina Lee. "I'm just helping Fina Lee put everything back in order."

"Everything back in order," Fina Lee echoed. They both stood up and Ms. Trudy helped Abby put the straps of Fina Lee's bag over her shoulders and securely on her back. The sheaf of papers was still clutched tightly in Fina Lee's hands.

Ms. Trudy quickly soothed the wrinkles and twisted bunches of the blouse sleeves that had gone askew around Fina Lee's arms. She hemmed and clucked, before patting Fina Lee on her shoulder, "All right, Ms. Bentley. On the hop! We don't won't to be any later for our afternoon session."

As Fina Lee quickly marched off, Ms. Trudy looked over her shoulder and smiled back at Abby, and it was the exact same smile from Fina Lee's memories, a smile that Abby had never seen (nor ever see again) pass over that stern Ms. Trudy countenance. It was a smile of gratitude and love.

"Well done, Ms. Rubideaux." Ms. Trudy said just a little too loudly. "Now, on the hop! Laps three times around the field for all tardy students. No excuses!"

Abby watched as Ms. Trudy turned and strode away, and she found herself breathing deeply and appreciatively of the stale hallway air, a faint lemony scent rising from the polished floor. She needed a few more moments to clear her mind and consider the miracle of what had just happened. Gym class and Ms. Trudy's impending laps could wait a while longer.

7

HALABE

Look, but don't look.
Sometimes that is the only way to see.
Use the corners of your eyeballs—do not move your eyeballs.
Do not turn your head!
Keep your eyes fixed on whatever it is you were doing.
There. You see?
A flash. A flicker of movement on the side? Just at the edges of your vision?
If you move your head and try to look at it directly, it will be gone.
That is the nature of some beings.
They live on the edges, so it is only with the edges of your eyes that you may see them.
*—from **The Book of Sayings**, "Bo M'ba Nesh Speaks"*

ΛNOTHER TIME, ΛNOTHER PLACE – THE CEREMONY OF THE BINDINGS

Everyone from the village was there. They had all gathered down by the river where the rushing waters splashed over rocks, and the misty spray brought welcomed relief from the searing heat. The sun was high in a cloudless blue sky, and the last of the coolness of morning had finally seeped away. Only the humans were foolish enough to be out at this time of the day.

Abby had linked arms tightly with the elder, Bo M'ba Nesh, who stood to her left, regal and erect. The old woman's finest blue headdress, adorned with bright feathers and gleaming stones, sparkled under the sun. The elder was smiling. Abby turned to focus her attention once more on the younger mothers and the teenage girls. The mothers sat in a circle on stone chairs beneath the spray of the river. Next to them knelt the teenage girls. All of the women were humming and swaying in sync with each other. In fact, the entire village of onlookers, who formed a semi-circle against the edge of the river, were swaying and humming and rhythmically stomping their feet. Abby was swept up in the movement, and she and the old woman rocked their bodies from left to right.

On each of the seated woman's laps a baby sat, propped up and swaddled by the teens, while the humming mothers were busily wrapping thin cords around the heads of the babies. There were nine babies in all. A good number that promised good fortune and providence for the generation to come. Abby watched as the mothers' fingers moved across the faces and around the head of each baby. The cords were laid down in criss-crossing lines—no two patterns exactly the same, as each mother created her own design.

The cords were made from durable vines that grew on the *Ishwi* tree, and these vines could grow as long as fifty feet in length. Once they had been cut from the tree, their leaves were thoroughly stripped, then the 1/8th-inch vines were boiled in water and left to soak for several days. The soaking leeched out the reddish-pink hues of pigment in the vines, creating a pale-white, flexible cord that could be used as a strong rope that would last for years: bundling twigs and other workloads, fastening poles together for frames, the weaving of fishing nets, and countless other things.

In this case, the cords were reserved for the most sacred of tasks: they had been set aside for the *Halabe* ritual: the Ceremony of the Spider. Among the *Sihanaka*, the forest people of Bo M'ba Nesh's tribe, on the third day of the third moon in the Year of the Spider, one third of the newborn babies in each clan were selected by the elders to be marked to follow the path of the Sacred *Halabe*, the Great Mother Spider. It was said that in the beginning, Great Mother Spider came from the stars, climbing down her great silver threads to create and shape the Earth and give birth to the first people. All of the *Sihanaka* people held Mother Spider in the greatest of reverence, and to be marked by the vines was the greatest honor that the people of the forest could bestow to an individual.

These children were the preordained spiritual leaders and future members of the Council of Elders. They had been carefully observed and evaluated since birth. They were chosen by the elders if they exhibited any of the ancestral signs—the genetic and behavioral markers that linked them to great leaders of the past. The vines that would leave their marks upon the faces of the children were the literal representation of that link to the past and all of those who came before.

Abby watched as a mother's hand carefully laid the cord across her baby's face, she pulled the cord tightly around to the back of the baby's head. With each tug, Abby could see the skin beneath the cord blanch as the line was pulled taut. Abby knew that as the child grew, the cords would cut deeper as they tightened. The cords would not be removed until the child turned 12-years old, and at that time the removal would reveal the pink latticework of scars that would mark their face for a lifetime.

One of the babies started crying, and the old woman standing next to Abby chuckled and said in a low, soft voice, "Oh, that one will be the leader of the council one day. Big voice! Not afraid to speak her mind!" She chuckled again.

Abby turned to glance at the elder standing beside her. The scars across her face did indeed resemble a spider's web. Abby tried to imagine Bo M'ba Nesh as an infant, her head being wrapped with the still-wet vines. Did she cry out, too?

"Did the vines hurt you when you were a child, Bo M'ba?" Abby asked quietly. She returned her eyes to watch the women and their babies. The wrapping of the baby heads was nearing the end.

"Oh no dear," the old woman answered. "There may have been a few itches I could not scratch. But no pain. You get used to it, and after a while you don't even notice that they are there."

The crying baby flailed and howled even louder, and the young girl kneeling next to her had to hold the baby's head tightly as the mother nimbly continued to wrap.

"It seems cruel to me," Abby muttered. "The child did not ask for this, nor did she choose it."

The elder named Bo M'ba Nesh glanced down at Abby, she was still smiling, and her large black eyes were like pools of water. "Cruel? Is it cruel to be honored by the gods? These children will grow to be schooled in the ways of the Spirit. The ancestors and Great *Halabe* herself have chosen them. It is their birthright. They will one day soon be revered above all others and accorded privileges unknown to those of lesser rank. They are the chosen ones and will soon learn how to be intricate players in the divine dance of creation. They will learn wisdom and leadership. They will have great powers. They will be directly connected to and bathe in the light of the stars."

Here, the old woman paused, and she turned back to watch the binding ritual. Her eyes filled with tears. "They will have been touched by the hands of the gods," she murmured in awe. She glanced back at Abby and patted the young girl's head.

Bo M'ba Nesh continued more heartily, "But, as in all great gifts, there is a price to be paid, to remind us of our humility and to restore the balance. We must all sacrifice. Theirs is a sacrifice that each of us would make a thousand times over. There is no higher honor. This you will understand one day."

Elder and youth both turned back to watch as suddenly drums beat loudly behind the gathered women. The warrior men of the tribe had come along the river, each banging a cone-shaped drum, dancing, and slapping down their feet. They grunted and hooted in time to the rhythms that pounded from their drums. The onlookers of the village parted to allow the men through, then each of the women began to sing—a counter melody that was the perfect complement to the deeper voices of the men. As the men entered, they slowly danced, twirled, and stomped around the sitting women and their babies.

The women's voices rose—a single, long note that hovered in the air before cascading down, then rising again. The notes of their song wavered beautifully on the edge of the mist and the tiny droplets of water that rose from the river. The shimmering spray suddenly burst with rainbow colors as the wind turned slightly and the light of the sun was reflected in prisms. Abby felt the water patter on her face as if each drop were a musical note in the women's song.

She was enraptured by the beauty and the harmony of the moment as the deep, throaty voice of Bo M'ba Nesh joined in the song beside her. The elder's face was kindled with pure joy, a light and a happiness that was contagious, and Abby could not but laugh and begin dancing and singing herself.

8

MISCHIEF

From the Audio transcripts of Dr. Joanna Kinsey
Chief Psychiatrist, CHNOLA Northshore Center,
New Orleans, LA

Excerpt of Audio File Transcript #AR10089-31

June 29, 2022

Subject: A. B. Rubideaux. Female. Age: 11

Transcript of recording begins: 10:02 AM EST.

Kinsey: *You have spoken before of severe alterations in your visual and audio senses.*

A.B. *Why, yes, doctor. I'm sorry. Joanna. Dr. Kinsey, ma'am. When my visual and audio senses begin to alter, the transformation is imminent. Significant changes in the visual spectrum always occur a few hours before the metamorphosis is complete. These are drastic distortions of sound and spectral light waves. There is a distinct blurring, usually coming from the right side of my field of vision. It's like a force field of energy… expanding and contracting. (Giggling.) It's like the whole world is breathing.*

Kinsey: *And these contractions—are they sustained or intermittent?*

A.B.: *Sustained. With each contortion of this distortion comes a dancing of light and colors. Like fireworks. Light kind of goes fractal and spiral, and all shapes and colors shift into geometric patterns. Patterns that merge and melt together. Back and forth. Back and forth. In a spinning vortex. I do not recommend looking into another person's face while this is occurring. That can be most unsettling.*

Kinsey: *I imagine so. But if you don't mind, I'd like for you to describe in greater detail the changes in your audio perceptions only—we haven't gone very deeply into that yet. You have stated that these visual changes are usually accompanied by sound distortions as well?*

A.B.: *You are correct, doctor. I'm sorry, Joanna. Sound travels in waves and frequencies, much like light. All sounds—people's voices, the hum of machinery,* *the hush of a passing bus, the mewling of a cat, the clacking of a woman's heels in the hallway—everything. They distort and bend, too. Like reverb on an amplifier. (More giggling) A giant wa-wa pedal takes over the planet. Only it's not a cacophony of sound. There's an underlying pattern and beauty to it. A base wavelength. It kind of reminds me of thousands and thousands of whales and their mating calls, happening all together at the same time. I imagine it is like that. Beautiful, to say the least, and virtually beyond anything you can experience in this human form.*

Kinsey: Well, in this "human form" of yours, have you ever heard the mating calls of thousands and thousands of whales happening at the same time?

A.B.: Well, naw. Come to think of it. (Chuckling.) But that's what I imagine it is like.

Kinsey: That's quite an imagination you have there, A.B.

47 DAYS EARLIER: MAY 11, 2022.

Two things happened within a very short time of the Fina Lee incident that would change everything. And Abby didn't see them coming.

Even though the week that flew by was deceptively calm and pleasant, Abby couldn't foresee what would befall her—her gift applied to others, and she never saw herself in all the manifold loops and patterns of realized and unrealized moments of the present, or in the myriad streams of possible futures—unless it was through the experience of another, like what had been recently happening with Balt. Her dragon powers were inconveniently stingy when it came to her own journey.

Anyway, these two events were coming, and both things involved her friend, Olivia. Neither thing was really anyone's fault—Like it has been said before: folks have a certain nature to which they, for the most part, remain true. Olivia, remember, was part Class Clown, but she was also a Hero, or more to the point: She was Abby's personal champion. She didn't mean to put into action the series of consequences that would change Abby's life forever, and at the time that it happened, it seemed justified and the right thing to do. But we get ahead of ourselves. Let's go back to a few days after the hallway incident with Fina Lee. It's important to know the irony of how these two events came unexpectedly and on the heels of a personal breakthrough for Abby.

After the incident, Abby was feeling more focused than ever before on the growing power of the dragon inside of her. The voice inside of her head was bubbling up to the surface more often, more persistent now. She knew that the itchiness on the ends of her fingers and all across her scalp meant that a transformation would be coming soon, maybe in about a week. The dragon needed to manifest and be free.

Fly little sister.

Yes. She was eager to fly, for sure. The build up to the dragon change was usually not so palpable and electric. What was different this week was that Abby was also in a place of inner calm and confidence. She was enjoying a peaceful tranquility that was not usual for her school life experience. She was so full of gratitude and kindness toward others. Well, the kindness and gratitude toward others was usual—what was new was the inner calmness that anchored her amidst the usual relentless turmoil of her daily existence. Frankly, Abby welcomed it like an old friend who had been away too long. Unfortunately, it was this relaxed state of mind that was, in part, what lulled her into the predicament.

She felt good. Her anxiety and natural, defensive alertness around others had receded. This led to a bold experiment for her: "Operation integrate with others." For the next few days, she played hop-scotch and kick ball with her classmates. She sat at the table of other girls at lunch and laughed and carried on like the previous three years of separation never existed. She raised her hand and participated in class. She was *almost* accepted as one of them.

Almost, but not quite, because the other children were leery of the sudden changes in her behavior. This was the kicker: although Abby was obviously so very different and awkwardly removed among her school peers—for it is in the nature of dragons to stand out among a crowd—she had always been just so awfully nice and gracious that the other kids were now wondering what her sudden interest in normal schoolyard fraternization was all about. Most of the other kids had accepted Abby for what she was, and if they had taken part in cruelty and targeted acts of bullying against her, they had long since abandoned such activity. This had been true since kindergarten, anyway. Abby was too sincere and humble and wise for anyone to keep dishing out such ill-conceived and malicious behavior toward her. Acts of cruelty lost their appeal for most when the intended target returned such acts with unconditional kindness and consistent acts of generosity. She was by nature, kind and considerate. It was hard not to like Abby once you shortened the distance created by her innate separateness. Oh, there were a few who persisted—Balt Luster and Princess Julia, to be precise—but for the most part, after the initial "otherness" of Abby wore off, kids actually liked her or even better for Abby, they ignored her.

But the new Abby—the loquacious and participatory Abby—was regarded with cautious reserve and suspicion by most or her school mates. Abby could perceive all of this, of course, but in her heart, she just figured that as usual, these kinds of things took time. And patience, which is something Abby had a lot of.

So, the week flew by, and in this new state of inner peace and heightened self-confidence, Abby broke out of her customary shell. Oh, she heard it for sure from some of the other school children, who whispered rude remarks that were just loud enough to overhear. Children, when given license, can be remarkably creative in their cruelty. Most of it didn't bother Abby at all. In fact, she had a little private laugh with Olivia over "concerns" that she had come down with something contagious or that her doctor had prescribed some new form of medication that made Abby all giddy and garrulous.

For her part, Olivia was in fine form, helping to keep things light and making everybody laugh with her antics. She was in her element when all eyes were drawn to her, and if Abby was "gonna act plum crazy," well, how could she miss an opportunity to "get her digs in?" So, the sociable, newfangled Abby was able to integrate with the others, but the watchful eyes of Olivia Fist were always there to oversee, and, if necessary, her quick fists and even quicker wit were there to protect Abby if things got out of hand.

At least that's the way Olivia had it all worked out in her mind. Unfortunately for her and Abby, a few days of the "new" Abby was not enough to erase away a lifetime of aloofness and shunning. That took time and a certain willingness on the part of other children, who, aside from Olivia, were not inclined to invest any effort in getting to know Abby or changing their attitudes toward her.

The truth of the matter was that Abby might as well join the line with Fina Lee and the other special ed kids, for even though she was not mentally ill or suffering from a learning disability, most of the other kids viewed her as an "other," and the resulting ostracization had, over the years, created a lasting and devastating effect on Abby. I suppose if Abby didn't know any better, she would just accept the "other" category and get on with her freak life. But on the inside, it hurt Abby. She wanted to be sociable and friendly with others. She wanted to be normal. But she couldn't touch the other kids without the intrusions into her mind happening, and that made everything all whopper-jawed and every which way so that she couldn't keep anything straight. It was easier just to simply not let anyone else touch her. But how could she explain that to anybody? How could she make them understand?

It's why she sometimes felt like she should just get in line with Fina Lee.

Friday rolled around, which meant the weekend without any school. For Abby, that also meant long walks or kayaking in the bayou. She hadn't forgotten her promise to Olivia, either, and she was determined that her best friend know the truth of who or what she really was. And this was when the first incident happened.

Abby had agreed to take Olivia along with her for a Friday afternoon walk through her favorite trail in the bayou. Olivia was eager to accompany her, so as soon as school was over, Abby found her best friend waiting at her locker, grinning like a loon.

"You ready for this?" Abby asked with a smirk.

"Does the pope wear funny hats?"

"Blasphemous."

"Scandalous."

Then together, with hands extended and raised toward each other in their secret, finger-wiggling salute, they both chimed in, "We're gonna burn in Hell together!"

Through a bark of laughter, and after a complicated set of final finger wiggles, Olivia snorted, then exclaimed, "I've got sandwiches… for second breakfast!" She patted her backpack and hoisted it on to her shoulders.

"Well," Abby giggled, "Peanut butter in the bayou sounds like a good supper to me!"

"Baloney." Olivia announced. "I've got real Oscar Meyer baloney this time. And it ain't supper. It's second breakfast."

"At three in the afternoon?"

"Whatever." Olivia and Abby laughed.

So, with schoolbooks stashed in lockers, sleeves rolled up, and bicycles ready to roll, the two girls set off for the Bayou. Houma was swamp land, and if you were looking for the bayou, well, you could pretty much head out in any direction and you'd find it within a few blocks or so. Abby knew of a trail that led down to her neighbor's launch not far from the Mandalay Wildlife Refuge. It was private property, but they had a boat down there, and the way Abby figured, nobody seemed to mind if she used it because her neighbor was like, eighty gazillion Jurassic Park years old and never used the boat anyways. And it was only by boat that a person could get to where Abby wanted to go.

"Are you kidding me?" Olivia was scowling down at the rickety old kayak that was hauled up beneath a dilapidated, old, wooden dock. She swiped at cloud of gnats that hovered around her head. Their bikes were laid down beside the dock, and Abby was busy covering them with a nasty green tarp that she had taken from the boat.

"Relax, Pochahontas. Grab the oars and let's get her out on the water." Abby was excited and breathless, pointing at the end of the kayak. "Ain't no bugs out there."

Olivia crouched down and dug out the oars, brushed off the cobwebs, and handed one over to Abby. Like the kayak, they were made of some kind of hard plastic, thankfully, and thus immune to the wood rot and insects that seemed to be having their way with the wooden planks of the dock. Together, they slid the craft down to the water. Abby had slipped out of her shoes and was already wading out into the water getting ready to hop in.

"Hold it, Abby!" Olivia was kicking off her shoes and looking around. She walked over and carefully placed them under the tarp with the bicycles. "Did you check for spiders? That old thing is filthy. And snakes? What about snakes?"

Abby smiled mischievously back at Olivia, then she dropped her oar and pressed down with both her hands, submerging the kayak. She groaned and strained as she flipped the boat over and over until it lay bottom up on the water. She walked around to the far end and lifted it up. "There, clean as a whistle!" She laughed and lifted her end of the boat up over her head, water dripping. "Now, come on over here and lift your end. Let's give it a good shake, unless you want soggy drawers!"

"Soggy drawers are not an option, Bayou Becky," Olivia snickered as she complied by lifting her end of the kayak. She moaned loudly as she struggled to separate the boat from the water. Finally, with kayak raised above both heads, the girls laughed as they shook the boat, getting a good soaking for their efforts.

"Jiminy Christmas!" Olivia spat the water from her face. They placed the kayak back on the water, and Abby grabbed her oar and jumped in. Somewhat more reluctantly, Olivia followed, plopping down heavily then grabbing the edges of the craft as it rocked with her weight.

"Whoah! Hold 'er newt." She breathed out heavily and glanced up at the still smiling face of Abby. Little rivulets of water streamed down her friend's face. "Are you sure this thing is even sea-worthy?"

"Sea-worthy, I know not!" Abby responded. "But this here little boat is 100 percent bayou-proof, guaranteed!" Abby had affected a thick Cajun accent for that last word, then flipped herself around and began to paddle.

With an audible "harrumph," Olivia followed suit. "If I die out here today and become some lucky gator's dinner, A.B. Rubideaux, it is entirely on you!" And with an eruption of raucous laughter, the girls shot out into the water, paddling in symmetry like experienced Indian braves.

The majority of their kayak journey was spent with Abby prattling on and on about their classmates, and schoolyard universals, and how everything fit into one single moment in time because each moment in time contained all the others, and that meant that just about anything was possible if you could just open your mind to it. Olivia could barely get a word in edgewise, and the only time Abby would pause to catch her breath was when she would suddenly change course, and paddle through what looked to Olivia like a solid wall of water rushes until it wasn't solid anymore, and they were clear and through to the other side following a course that only Abby knew.

"Aha! Land ho!" Abby interrupted her monologue, in which she was talking about Fina Lee Bentley and how her life was going to take a turn that no one in Houma would ever have suspected, and they began to row with renewed purpose toward an island in the middle of a small lake. A large willow tree majestically drooped down over the center of the island, but there were flowers and mossy logs scattered across a large, sandy clearing where the edge of the island touched water.

"But I don't understand one thing," Olivia interjected as the kayak slid up on the shore and they both jumped out. "How does all of this stuff you know about all these folks have anything to do with dragons?"

Abby grasped the edge of the kayak and hauled it up well above the water line. She absently brushed the wavy strands of her black hair from her face and turned back to face Olivia. "That's what I've been trying to tell you, numb-skull!" She held out her hand as Olivia passed her the oar, which she dropped into the kayak with a clatter.

"All of these things I know come to me through the dragon. The dragon lives inside of me and is always there. It's like a little voice, only she speaks to me in pictures."

"She? Your dragon is female? Well, thank God for that!" Olivia placed her hands on her hips and winked at Abby. "I wouldn't want you to turn into no boy dragon—that just wouldn't be right."

"The dragon is me, silly. Of course I'm a female, and so is she. At least I think so. I'm not really sure. But whatever he or she is, we are part of each other, and we can't be separated. But no matter what, I'm still a girl." Abby wringed her hands together as she could see Olivia purse her lips and scrunch up her face with suspicion.

"Okay," Abby continued. "Let's try this: I'm a girl just like you, except I have this other part of me that's the dragon part of me. And the dragon talks to me and helps me see things. It's like I have dragon vision. Like a dream, only it's not. It's all real. I can feel the truth of it. The dragon voice and the pictures she sends me inside my head. It's my secret superpower."

"Go on now!" Olivia scoffed and chuckled. "You got some secret super-powers that you call Dragon Vision? Girl, sign me up for a subscription, cuz I got to see the next episode on Netflix, and I don't know what all."

Abby sighed and tried to find her composure. "I know it's hard to believe. I will try to explain it to you so that everything makes sense." Abby rolled her neck around and shook out the cramping muscles in her hand. She then sat down suddenly, cross-legged, and gestured for Olivia to follow suit.

"Guess my drawers are gonna be soggy after all," Olivia complained as she looked around before plopping down on the wet, sandy shore.

Abby was looking directly, and earnestly at Olivia. No more smiles. She took another deep breath and began, "Now, I never told no one about this, not even Momma Bea. So, you're the first." Abby paused and Olivia nodded her head.

Abby continued, "When I meet people for the first time or when I touch them, I get these visions, you know? Pictures of their life from a long time ago, like when they was just little kids or even babies. I can see things that happened to them, like memories that they been holding on to and won't let go. Sometimes it comes just in flashes, but other times the details are crystal clear and so… powerful, like I am there experiencing these things for myself."

"You can see people's memories?" Olivia was all serious, no more grinning.

"Yes, I suppose that's what it is." Abby pressed her lips together and looked up into the sky, thinking, trying to gather her thoughts. "But it's more than that. I can see and feel everything that is happening to them right now, in the present, and it's like this little light turns on… I call it their soul-fire, and this little light can go anywhere and show me anything—everything that's happening in their lives, and everything that might happen in their lives. I can follow their soul-fire like on a path, a path that leads to all the countless possibilities of the future."

"Go on, now!" Olivia scoffed. "How is that possible? You see things in the future? How do you know they gonna happen if they ain't even happened yet? Don't make no sense to me."

Abby smiled and rubbed her legs excitedly before continuing. "But it does make sense, Olivia. The little soul-fire light shows me the pathways, and everything is connected to this moment, right now. It's like the soul-fire knows what it wants, and it knows how to find its way to make it so. Or not… I mean, not everything I see in the future comes true. Sometimes there are forces or other people in your life that make it almost impossible to follow your soul-fire. Sometimes you get beat down so hard that you can't find it, but it's still there, buried deep. Only then, it's more like a soulful yearning… but it's incomplete or hindered by some deeper emotion, like a fear, or maybe it's caught in a pattern that shapes and forms a life. And it's real hard to break those patterns. Not everyone knows how to follow their soul-fire. In fact, most don't without some help. And that's why I'm here, I think."

Abby paused and stopped rubbing her legs. She leaned over to stare directly into Olivia's eyes. Olivia flipped her frizzy red hair out of her face and stared back. Abby noticed that Olivia's green eyes had yellow suns around their pupils. Olivia was beautiful. And Olivia was staring back at her, completely open and unintimidated. A flash of blurry light erupted around the two of them for a few moments, and then Olivia's face changed. She was old, a grandma in her eighties, maybe older. Her face was wrinkled, and her hair was dyed a ludicrous shade of orangey-red, but her eyes were the same. And she was laughing and slapping her knee, rocking her body back and forth in front of some of the ugliest gold and brown patterned wallpaper Abby had ever seen. Then the image was gone. It had happened just like that. A future flash forward to a time that was somehow connected to this moment. Abby knew right then and there that they were going to be friends for life.

Slowly, Abby refocused on the face of her twelve-year old friend. Olivia was now staring at her suspiciously, her lips pressed tightly together.

"What are you grinning about?" Olivia asked.

"Nothin'," Abby grinned wider and shrugged her shoulders.

"Horse turds!" Olivia broke into a big smile and slapped her knees. "Something just happened! Tell me!"

Abby just smiled, still seeing a ghost of the wrinkled granny superimposed over her friend's face. Abby giggled and shook her head. "No, no, no. It's nothing. I'll tell you later." She stilled herself and took a deep breath. "I don't want a distraction right now. I was about to tell you something." She took another deep breath, exhaling noisily through her mouth.

Slowly, Abby began to articulate her belief. "I think I am here to help people follow their soul-fire. That is what my Dragon Vision is all about. I can help them find it. I can show them the path that their soul-fire most wants to follow. I can help them find their bliss. Their greatest happiness. Yes, that's it. That which fulfills them the most and helps them... evolve. To become the most incredible person that they can be."

Abby paused and grinned, glancing away from Olivia, who was now scrunching up her nose with the intensity of her gaze. She continued, "I saw everything just the other day, with Fina Lee Bentley..."

"The retard?" Olivia blurted out.

"Please don't call her that!" Abby scolded Olivia. "She's autistic, but she's not stupid. In fact, she's super smart!" Abby closed her eyes so that she could remember, and then she spoke in a sudden rush. "But...but her pa does terrible things to her. Unspeakable things. And she can't communicate that to anyone... she can't find the words because none of it has any rhyme or reason. Oh, she's so full of hurt, Olivia, but she has this gift inside of her. One day she will figure it out, she will find the words... if she just keeps to the path... She's already started it. She keeps a journal, and it's amazing—filled with stories and pictures and poems... it's the most beautiful thing I've ever seen. And, I know—I know beyond a shadow of a doubt that that journal—what she writes and what she draws in it—that's her soul-fire trying to get out. That's the reason why she is here. And that will be her salvation."

Abby finished, opened her eyes, and felt the blood flush all the way up through her cheeks. Olivia was intensely staring back at her, her lips quivering and her eyes watering like she was about to burst into tears. Suddenly Olivia smiled, and thrust both her hands forward.

"Do me! Oh, do me now! I wanna see what you do. Do it to me! I wanna see how it feels."

Abby brushed her hands aside as Olivia reached over trying to grab her arms. "Wait! It don't work like that."

Olivia, still smiling, rolled up the sleeves of her blouse, and reached out again. "What do you mean, it don't work like that? You said all you need to do is touch someone, right?" She paused and placed her hand on her hip. "C'mon! Cuz if I'm not mistaken, you were doing something with me just a moment ago… Right? Right?" She leaned over saucily, forcing Abby to giggle and turn away. "C'mon! Let's do this. Skin to skin."

Abby stared up at her friend, standing there in front of her with both arms extended in over-the-top supplication. She couldn't help but grin at Olivia's infectious enthusiasm. She glanced sideways, then back at Olivia. "Well, I have a confession to make," she said coyly. "I've already seen what you are. And what you are gonna do in this life. After my Momma Bea, you were one of the first people that I ever felt their soul-fire with."

"What?" Olivia nearly exploded as she plopped down with an audible squish. "If that isn't the coolest thing this side of a witch's tit." She was grinning unabashedly as she tucked her legs in under her Indian style. But then she looked over at Abby and frowned dramatically, pointing a finger. "But why would you keep something like that from me? Oh, my best, bestiest friend, and you're keeping the secrets of my whole life from me?" She rolled her shoulders back and slowly raised her arms like a preacher in a sermon. "Oh, lord, please forgive her. She is so grievously unaware of the dire consequences of withholding her knowledge and her insights into the truer pathways of one particular person, her one and only best friend—namely, that would be me, Olivia Felicita Fist!" She clenched her raised hands into tight fists as she rose to her feet like an enraptured spirit. "She knows not the harm she has done, but there is still time for redemption!"

Olivia finished her speech and beamed down at Abby, who was giggling uncontrollably, before she managed to squeeze out an intelligible sentence.

"Felicita? Your middle name is Felicita?" She asked, still giggling.

Olivia lowered her fists and with great care and dignity, she began to soothe out the wrinkles of her blouse. "Yes," she said testily. "It means "happiness," kind of… I think… can't you tell?" She shrugged and smiled down at Abby, but then she put her finger in Abby's face. "Don't you dare tell a single soul, you ol' giggle farts. You know you owe me! And there is a cost!"

Olivia glanced around the little island briefly. She returned her stare to the now composed face of Abby. "Oh yes, you owe me. With interest. And you're gonna tell me every last bit of my soul-fire's story. Past, present and future! All this time, and I didn't even know that I had my own little fortune-teller right here beside me!"

"Well, it's a little more than that, actually." Abby interrupted.

"Of course! Of course, but you are gonna have to explain it all to me again. You promise?"

Abby held Olivia's gaze for just a few moments, then smiled. "Promise."

Olivia beamed, hooted and cracked her knuckles, before turning to look around again. "But after I take a pee! Any recommendations for a desperate girl on this island?"

Abby chuckled again and pointed at the enormous willow tree in the center of the island. "Over there, behind old man Willow, and beyond just a bit. Follow your nose. You can't miss it."

"How delightful," Olivia murmured with disgust before trotting off.

Abby sat quietly, enjoying a cool breeze that lit up from across the bayou. She closed her eyes and listened to the sounds of birds, the splash of water behind her and out in the middle of the lake—some creature stirring—then, the distant hum of a motor boat somewhere far away, and of course, to the noisy mutterings of Olivia as she scrabbled about in the brush to relieve herself.

"Old man Willow, my ass!" Olivia's monologue was in full swing. "Is that a hornet's nest up in that tree? Jeez-uz… this is disgusting back here… You wouldn't happen to have any toilet paper? How on earth did you find this island? Are we in unchartered lands? Did you fly here in your dragon form? I think we are completely off the grid… Does anybody else even know that this is here? Why you never take me here before? This is so cool! Keeping a secret like this from me is a capital offense. I bet your momma don't even know about…"

Olivia cut herself off mid-sentence as she rounded the trunk of the tree. Abby opened her eyes to see her friend standing beneath the Willow tree staring directly at her, slack-jawed and open-mouthed, a look of horror on her face.

Abby was sitting on the shore of the island, her back to the water, with three rather large alligators coiled up around her. Abby was smiling and absently stroking one of the gators under its chin as two more even bigger gators emerged from the water and slowly padded up to Abby. They jostled with the other gators a bit before settling in and around Abby. All five gators wrapped themselves around Abby more tightly, almost protectively, as Abby continued to sit there completely unalarmed, like she didn't have a care in the world. Just sunbathing on the sandy beach—nothing strange to see here.

"Um, I don't want to alarm you," Olivia began, "but I do believe we have some visitors?"

Abby glanced down at the gators, happily knotted around her, and then she smiled. "Well, now! Where did y'all come from?" She glanced back at Olivia and had to laugh at the shocked expression on her face.

"Don't worry," Abby purred as she glanced down and stroked another gator on its belly. The reptile opened its mouth and moaned in what appeared to be alligator rapture. "This is all part of what I need to show you. I have met these fellas before. They would never hurt me. Come on down, I will introduce you!"

"You've got to be kidding!" Olivia exclaimed not budging from her spot.

"Well, actually, they might take a liking to you in a way that may not end too well for you."

"Yeah, like maybe I wind up as their supper?" Olivia did not look amused.

Abby sighed and breathed in deeply. She gave one of the gators one last stroke before suddenly rising and clapping her hands. "Off! Off you go!" She pointed to the water, and the gators immediately roused from their stupor and quickly waddled away, splashing loudly into the green water, submerging and within a few moments completely disappearing. Several moments went by, and the two girls watched as the surface of the water rippled, then slowly returned to stillness.

Olivia still hadn't moved from her spot as Abby turned and walked up beside her, smiling. "You know," Olivia murmured, "a normal person would just get some puppies or a kitten." She glanced briefly at Abby before exhaling loudly through pursed lips. "I do believe I have seen it all, now. Would you care to explain what just happened?"

"Reptilian mind," Abby began somewhat sardonically. "You need to access the older part of your brain, the stem of your medulla oblongata," Abby pointed at the back of her neck, "which is the only part of your brain old enough to speak alligator." She grinned at Olivia. "It's a base frequency thing. I can't really explain how it works other than it's the dragon part of me that does it, kind of, automatically."

"Yeah, ri-i-i-i-ight," Olivia walked over to the side of the boat and began looking around, searching the ground. "I think maybe we should head back. It's getting late, and my fortune can wait for another time." Olivia stopped and put her hands on her hips in exasperation. "I can't seem to find my shoes."

Abby chortled. "We left them back at the launch, dummy. With the spiders and the snakes." She walked down to the boat and grabbed it firmly, turning it around and then towing it out into the water.

Olivia stood on the shore, casting her eyes about apprehensively at what, at least in her mind, was only deceptively calm water.

"Oh, lan' sakes, Olivia!" Abby exclaimed as she shook the boat and laughed. "You are the bravest person I know. I always believed you weren't afraid of anything." She paused to smile sympathetically at Olivia, who scowled back at her. "The gators are gone. I promise."

"I ain't afraid of no gators," Olivia muttered indignantly. "I just gotta wrap my head around the fact that my best friend is a dragon fortune-teller who communes with primordial reptiles." She glared back at Abby before cracking a begrudging smile. "A love fest with gators was not a planned part of my fortune telling session. You gotta give a girl time for things to sink in." She strode out into the water and clambered awkwardly but very quickly into the boat. Abby followed much more nimbly and sat at the back where she pushed off the shore with her paddle.

They began to row, Olivia with a sense of purpose that had been lacking before. Abby dug in her feet and endeavored to keep up the pace. Quietly she guided the small craft through the wall of river rushes and back out into the main course way of the bayou. After a few minutes, and in between strokes, Olivia spoke.

"Okay. Just to let you know. You aren't off the hook. We're coming back to your island, were gonna sit down under that willow tree, and you're gonna tell me my fortune. You absolutely cannot keep something like this from me! Only no gators this time! Deal?"

Abby laughed, and answered sincerely, "Deal!" They rowed silently all the way back to the dock and their bicycles and their soggy, sand-filled shoes.

Of course, there are children who don't fit neatly into any of the universal categories that Abby had exhaustively and breathlessly been explaining to Olivia on the day of their little trip through the bayou. They are the outliers, the human anomalies. And for the rest of the weekend and into the next week, Olivia was thinking to herself that Abby did indeed belong to this last group. Her friend was an outlier, a rare individual that you don't meet just any old day. And she was a true friend. Olivia realized that now, more than ever, she was going to fiercely protect Abby from the harm and enmity of others. That was and always had been her role, and she was more inclined than ever before to pursue her purpose with an even deeper resolve.

She wouldn't have to wait long.

What happened on the island was only the first thing. There was a second event that was related to the first, only this time it could not be kept from the prying minds of others. And even though Abby insisted otherwise, Olivia knew that it was all her fault.

It was the following Wednesday, and the whole sixth grade—all two classes—were on a field trip in New Orleans at some World War II history museum. At any rate, the classes were having lunch a few blocks away at Popeye's Louisiana Chicken on St Charles Street before heading on over in the afternoon for the Japanese half of the museum—they had spent the morning in the German half of the war display, and Abby was happily chirping at some of the girls about the schematics and the random, wanton destruction of German V2 rockets when Princess Julia arrived at her table, entourage in tow.

"What do you think you are doing?" The exaggerated, drawling tones of Julia's question caused Abby to pause mid-sentence and glance over at Julia. The Princess was standing there, looking very preppy in Abercrombie and Fitch, hand on hip, with four of her minions flanking her, their faces a mirror of Julia's disdain.

"Well, bless your heart," Abby called out, looking Julia up and down and calmly taking in her escort. "If it isn't our beloved princess. Her court in tow. Oh, Julia, would you care to learn more about the V2 rocket's habit of audibly clicking before silently falling to reign untold death and fiery horror upon those hapless Londoners who scrambled to take cover below?"

"I said," Julia repeated more emphatically, "What do you think you are doing? You don't sit here at this table. You don't sit at any table unless I approve of it."

"Now look here!" Olivia, who had been sitting next to Abby, began to stand up. "I don't think you realize just how annoying your royal highness act has become..." A firm and heavy hand pressed down on Olivia's shoulder, forcing her to sit back down heavily. She glanced back to see the hulking form of Balt Luster standing over her, a cruel smile playing at the corners of his lips.

"Oh yes," Julia continued. "I did anticipate your intervention, Miss Fist." She glanced back at Abby and grinned brazenly. "And contrary to Miss Rubideaux's intimations, I too pay attention to the historical presentations, and I understand the value of a strong and capable ally." She nodded at Balt, who seized Olivia by the torso and suddenly dragged her away from the table in a crushing bear-hug. Olivia yelped and struggled, but quickly ceased when she realized how strong Balt was. Her arms were pinned at her side, her feet dangled above the ground, and his clasping arms did not budge an inch. She could feel his hot breath on the back of her neck, and she shuddered in revulsion, ashamed that she had been so easily ambushed and subdued.

She opened her mouth to holler, "You are making a big mistake, Julia. I wouldn't mess with Abby. She's got superpowers that will bring all the gators of the bayou down upon you. That's right! I have witnessed it myself, and you are gonna wake the dragon and behold its wrath!" Olivia paused to breathe in the sudden silence that was the effect of her pronouncement. "You know what? On second thought, you just go right on ahead because I would love to see you get what's coming to you!"

Abby was frantically shaking her head, trying to stop Olivia from blurting out anything more. There was a heavy silence, broken by a few sniggers of the surrounding kids. Julia was observantly taking in every one of these details, and with one last triumphant look toward Abby, she turned and nodded to Stacy, one of her sycophantic minions. Olivia was just about to launch into another very public broo-haha when Stacy quickly stepped up and clamped her hand over Olivia's mouth, then two other girls moved in and quickly gagged her with a bright purple sash. Stacy yelped and glared dangerously back at

Olivia, who had bitten her in the brief struggle. It was the only proof that Olivia had not gone down quietly before her quick and efficient incapacitation.

"There now, see?" Julia purred and glided over to stand before Abby. "Oblivia, as usual, is oblivious, and her wild ramblings have been silenced. Thank god for that!" She turned and beamed at the crowd, many of whom were chuckling. She stepped back in front of Abby and flipped a stray strand of hair from her face. "Your champion cannot help you now." She snapped her fingers and plastic mustard and catsup bottles were quickly placed into her hands. She eyed Abby appraisingly, one eyebrow lifted in mock scorn. Abby could feel other girls move in behind her. She was trapped in her seat at the little round table.

As all of this transpired, the other kids had silently and almost instantly removed themselves from the nearby tables, and now Abby was alone, still seated and staring up at the face of Julia and her minions. She glanced around and could see the other children forming a ring around the tables. There were no teachers, no adults present. They were seated in a patio pavilion separated from the sidewalk and any passing pedestrians by a cement wall. As usual, Julia had picked her moment to strike well.

Julia stepped forward and raised the mustard bottle. She cocked her head to the side and smiled. "Hmm," she began. "It seems our little star has risen to find herself in company above her true station in life." She leaned in as hands behind Abby grabbed her arms and pulled her back tight against her chair. Another pair of hands firmly pressed down on her shoulders. "Wake the dragon?" Julia continued. "I think we'd all like to see that." Someone in the crowd snickered.

"But I do believe this little dragon has been acting like a hot dog—showing off and putting on airs. It has been so unlike you, Abby Jaybird!" Julia's smile widened unpleasantly into more of a snarl. "I just don't know what's gotten into you, hot dog."

A muffled tirade exploded from Olivia, words that cannot be repeated in decent company.

"I'm sorry, Oblivia? You were saying?" Julia glided over to the still gagged Olivia, who glared back at her. "Maybe we should start with you? You look like a hot dog, too. And every hot dog needs some dressing!"

Julia uncapped the mustard and squeezed a long, solid stream on to Olivia's head. There was laughter from some of Julia's minions, but most of the crowd looked on silently. Balt, who held the now-squirming Olivia tight, set his mouth into a grimace or maybe a smile? Hard to tell the difference.

Julia uncapped the catsup and glanced back at Abby, who sat perfectly still, pinned down by several arms, her eyes shooting darts back at their tormentor.

"Now, you know," Julia began, almost casually, "there will not be any adults for quite a bit. You see, Suzie, one of my oldest and dearest friends, is off," and here Julia paused to make finger quotes as best she could around her condiment bottles, "getting sick." Several more children laughed and nodded their heads knowingly.

"I'm afraid," Julia continued, drinking in the eager attention of the other children, who stood riveted in the large ring around the tables, "That poor Ms. Cottrell and that awful Miss Trudy are completely occupied attending to our sweet Suzie. She is such a peach! Did you know that she can vomit on command? Such a handy little talent, don't you think? Such a mess that will need to be cleaned up. It will take an awful lot of time, don't you think?"

"You think you know everything?" Olivia, who had worked her gag free suddenly interrupted. "You have no idea what you're dealing with, you..." Olivia squealed as Julia squirted the catsup bottle directly in her face.

"Shut up, you loathsome being." Julia barked, never turning her head from Abby's gaze. Olivia sputtered as the gag was quickly replaced.

Now it's true that Julia was a particularly clever girl, the type who always thinks of every contingency, particularly when she was carrying out her nefarious plans, which always ended up with her smelling like roses. What Julia could not have known, however, is that all the timing and planning in the world cannot account for the fact that Abby was only days, if not hours away from her dragon transformation. And as her minions silenced the protesting Olivia, and Julia stepped up to Abby, condiment bottles poised, she could not have anticipated what would happen next.

"Now," Julia cooed. "Miss Jaybird. Miss Plum Naked. What were some of those other names you came up with, Balt?" Julia glanced at the hulking figure of Balt Luster, whose snarl widened into a hideous grin.

"A.B.R." Balt said huskily. "All-Beaver-Review." Several more kids snickered at that. Julia turned back to Abby and smiled.

"That's right, All-Beaver-Review," She repeated slowly. "Not exactly a civilized or proper nick-name, Balt. But appropriate nonetheless. Well, I think this hot dog needs to come out of its bun." She nodded at two of her girls and then commanded harshly, "Strip her!"

The girls hesitated and the crowd was suddenly very silent. This was about to get either really good or really bad, depending on which side of the bullying spectrum you came down upon. Would it be entertaining or sickening to watch? A few of the kids with lesser stomachs, or more to the point, those with kinder, more humane dispositions began to inch away from the ring of onlookers, too alarmed at the prospect of the pending violation. Others wriggled in tighter, feral eagerness defining their demeanor.

"You heard me. Strip her." Julia repeated. But the girls still hesitated. "All right, not all the way, just down to her panties. There are children present. Sheesh!" Julia repositioned the mustard and catsup bottle in her hand for maximum squirting power as the girls, grinning stupidly, approached.

Now this whole time, Abby had remained perfectly still. Her eyes had never left the strutting form of Julia. She watched quietly as Julia attacked Olivia. Her breaths had become slower, and longer—a strange calm had taken over her entire being. Now her muscles, which had been rigid and tense, relaxed. She could feel the hard grip of her captors lessening in response. As Julia approached with her she-thugs, Abby closed her eyes. All of her power had retreated to deep within her, a small, white-hot ball of fire that pulsed inside of her but suddenly released toward the base of her skull. A tickling thrill shot down her spine, and she flexed her fingers and her toes.

As the first rough hands touched her shoulders and tugged at her blouse, the ball of fire exploded. Her body contorted into a rigid, flexing plank as hard as steel. The hands that had been holding her down flew away, the children sent sprawling around her. There was an initial shocked gasp from the crowd of onlookers, and a few girls began to scramble away as an ear-splitting shriek emerged from Abby's rigid form. It was an alien, metal-on-metal type of grinding sound that forced Julia and the others to drop down and clutch at their ears.

In an instant, Abby was released from her rigid convulsing state, and she sprang on top of her table. She glared down at Julia, who had fallen to her knees, terrified before her, and Abby contorted her body like a hissing cat, her back arching dramatically toward the sky as she emitted one more earth-rending, metal-bending screech.

Chaos ensued as the surrounding children screamed and began to scatter, pushing and thrashing their way around each other, knocking chairs over, sending food trays flying. With a quick look around, Abby froze briefly as she caught Olivia's eye. Olivia was sitting on top of Balt, who had been knocked over by the initial screech of power. She nodded at Abby, who smiled back, then leaped from the table, an impressive vault that traveled over fifteen feet before she landed, leapt again over the wall, then bounded away. Olivia thought she caught an iridescent flash of purple and green behind Abby's ears just before she leapt.

"That was so cool!" Olivia murmured and got up from the now audibly-freaking Balt.

"Did you see that? Did you see that? What the... Did you see that?" Balt was blubbering deliriously.

"I didn't see nothing," Olivia snapped back. "Don't wet yourself, Balthazar." She dusted off her pants, then walked over to Julia who remained on her knees, dazed, and staring at the tipped over table where Abby had been. The condiment bottles remained firmly gripped in her hands, yellow mustard and red catsup slowly dribbling from their spouts and on to Julia's lavender dress and bare legs. The other kids were screaming and running every which way. Some of them had gone back inside the restaurant. A crowd was beginning to gather nearby—strangers who had been passing on the street, other customers and restaurant employees. Olivia squatted down next to Julia and snorted.

"I told you so," she hissed into her ear.

The loud voice of Ms. Trudy could now be heard over the growing crowd. Her linebacker physique could be seen coming from the restaurant and pushing her way through the crowd.

Olivia turned back to Julia and quickly proclaimed, "Not one word of this, to anybody! D'ya hear? Not one word, or so help me we will come for you at night and chew your goddamned legs off! Not that you don't deserve it!" Olivia's words seemed to have very little effect as Julia continued to vacantly stare at the table. Ms. Trudy's booming voice was drawing closer.

Olivia clucked in disgust, "You're just a ditzy girl now, ain't ya, Princess? Gotta go." She ducked away and wove her way through the crowd, disappearing around the pavilion walls and down the street vaguely in the direction she had seen Abby go.

"Miss DeChamplain!" Coach Trudy's meaty hand clamped down on Julia's shoulder. "Do you want to explain what the devil is going on here?"

But Julia remained silent, her eyes still locked on the table. The table. Exactly where Abby had been just moments before, only now, turned on its side, where three large parallel scratches deeply gouged in the metal rim were all that remained to mark her passage. They looked to be left by something very powerful and with very sharp claws.

9

WHO LET THE DRAGON OUT OF THE BAG?

From the Audio transcripts of Dr. Joanna Kinsey
Chief Psychiatrist, CHNOLA Northshore Center,
New Orleans, LA

Excerpt of Audio File Transcript #AR10089-38

June 28, 2022

Subject: A. B. Rubideaux. Female. Age: 11

Transcript of recording begins: 10:07 A.M EST.

Kinsey: *So, this concept of the Fold—I must admit I'm highly skeptical.*

A.B.: *Your skepticism is simply your dependence on scientific process. You can't see how science has become your blind faith. Look to your study and knowledge of mythology. The Ancients buried their secrets in plain sight. They are simply cloaked in the form of a really good story.*

Kinsey: *So, I will find the truth in ancient Babylon, in the tales of Gilgamesh, and Tiamat?*

A.B.: *Or in religious metaphors. The Bible is filled with many examples. What do you think we are talking about when we ponder heaven or hell? They are constructs of our collective mind, and they are good examples of multiple dimensions within the Fold.*

Kinsey: *Those are fairly extreme examples. Are you saying that such dimensions exist because people believe in them?*

A.B.: *Yes, that's right. Hell will come to you and manifest if that is your constant meditation. There is no other way to explain the suffering on this planet. But, Heaven is possible, too.*

Kinsey: *But what if I believe in fairies? Does that mean that they exist, too? Can I make them manifest in this world here?*

A.B.: *Are you certain they are not already here? Or at least in another dimension, just next door to this one?*

Kinsey: *Maybe Lewis Carroll would think so.*

A.B.: *Precisely. And maybe you, too? Certainly, most children believe so. But they don't know any better, do they? You see? We are all Alice, in a certain sense. If you want to understand, you need to overcome your skepticism. After all, Tiamat, Heaven and Hell, or certain rabbit holes of the imagination… they are all multiple dimensions of reality and no small constructs to ponder without at least a modicum of proper seriousness…*

Kinsey: *Star Wars. Luke Skywalker's tale is the classic Hero's journey. Powerful and meaningful ripples in the pond.*

A.B.: *And those stories have been around since long before Gilgamesh. In our collective reality within the Fold we have lived and experienced these things over and over again. Do you remember when you asked me how old I was? This might be the better way to answer that. We have been called by many different names. But we are the same thing every time.*

Kinsey: *Hang on! Are we talking reincarnation? Multiple lives?*

A.B.: *Well, reincarnation is one way to make sense of it. The Hindus and the Celts certainly have tried. Tibetan lamas have made it into a rite of succession. But that's just an elaborate comfort to any ego that wants to claim immortality. No, that's not the point. How about this? For the scientist in you, a deeper study of DNA strands is not a bad way to get started, actually. That is a model and a pattern that will inform you. Or, if you prefer a more metaphorical landscape, you can study some of the folklore and spiritual practice of indigenous peoples of this planet—those who still live closer to the living spirit of the Fold and from whence I have come. From where I have always existed. The Ashaninca people of modern-day Peru, for instance, call me "Avireri," one of the Maninkari or "the Hidden Ones." (Giggling). Now those are brightly-colored and fluorescent serpents! "The Hidden Ones." Sounds so mysterious. Only I'm not so hidden now, am I? (Giggling). Here I am… It's all in the DNA, actually. Your studies of genetics are getting so close to unlocking the secrets behind our reality. And I am here now, talking to you.*

Kinsey: *Sorry A.B., but you've lost me. How is the study of folklore, or your choice of a dragon, or our understanding of time related to DNA?*

A.B.: *Well, shall we save our discussion of the cosmically conscious biosphere for another day? It was so much easier back in the times when the planet was lush and full of vegetation. It was easier to make the connections when nature was inform- ing us on a daily basis. (Long pause, tapping sound like a finger on the desk.) Ok, Let's try this: There are only four basic types of DNA, after all, and it is all playing out before us each and every day. But here is a thought: How did we get from the Garden of Paradise to salted caramel mocha frappaccinos at your corner Starbucks? (Laughter.) Ok, I do so love to digress… I shall try to focus on the concept of Time. (Giggling.) Ok—here goes: I have always existed right now, and I have never existed beyond that. I exist in the now, and that is always. I am… eternal—yes, that's the word that comes closest for you to understand. I exist everywhere and nowhere all at once. It has always been so. So, the question isn't how old am I, but more like "how" do I come to be here in your presence right now? Why are you perceiving me in this time and place? (Giggling.) Ooh, but that's a whole different question for another time. A better question, perhaps. But when we talk about "time" in the defocalized, non-linear sense, we have to redefine what we mean by awareness. And at this time, I am acutely aware that we are running out of time for this session of yours. (Laughing.)*

Kinsey: *Okay, but let me worry about the time in that sense. I am sure that you are aware that we have some spiritual traditions that come close to what you are talking about. At least as I understand it. You mentioned Tibetan lamas—We have teachers, masters… meditative practitioners who talk about higher consciousness, a transcendent state of mind that exists beyond time… what the Buddhists call Nirvana. Is that what you mean?*

A.B.: *Now, a Buddhist dragon would be a very nice dragon indeed. (Giggling.) Yes, you are getting closer… There's an infinite number of choices and a myriad of manifestations of the present for me and you. And each one contains all of the others. That is the "real" nature of time. I exist—you exist—we all exist in the Fold beyond this physical reality. The reasoning facilities of the frontal cortex of your brain won't allow you to process this. You can't perceive it, so it doesn't exist. (Giggling.) Oh, but it does exist, Joanna. You'll have to trust me on this one.*

Kinsey: *I don't see how any of that's possible, A.B..*

A.B.: *(Laughing.) Well, that's a "you" problem. And you've just proved my point.*

46 DAYS EARLIER: MAY 13, 2022

The trash bin to Abby's left was pretty ripe. Either something had crawled up in there and died, or the mix of a week's worth of food items had succumbed to rot and decay. Either way, Abby was wishing that she had picked a different hedge in another parking lot to make her bed in.

Earlier in the day, after she had run away from the confrontation with Julia at the lunch tables, she had zig-zagged her way through the streets of New Orleans, fleeing blindly with no real thought of a destination. She was in full flight response and had only one thought in her mind: to get as far away as she could. When her legs began to cramp up and her feet were sore enough to light a fire, she sighed with relief when she rounded the corner of a building and saw the Superdome looming in a large, empty parking lot. She liked the Superdome because that was where the Saints played football, and right about that moment she needed a saint in her life.

It had been no problem hopping over the low cement wall and walking up the ramp that led to the arena. The entire facility seemed deserted, but across the empty parking lot trees and shady green spots along the street wall beckoned—a welcome relief from a humid and hot summer day. When she found the hedge-lined wall, she saw that there was plenty of room to wriggle in behind and get completely out of sight. She had found that someone else had had a similar idea, for there were old blankets and large tied off plastic bags of what looked like trash and old clothing. There was a slight smell of body odor and urine. Cautiously, she had peered around the hidden encampment. It was surprisingly tidy, and all the rubbish was stacked in one area with a large clearing that was immaculate and free of debris. She had plopped down, too exhausted to investigate what lay beyond the dumpster. She listened carefully and not a soul nor even a small critter stirred. There was the humming of an air duct somewhere close by, and she could hear the cars going by on the elevated highway in the near distance. The droning noises were rhythmic and oddly soothing. They made her feel sleepy.

She leaned against the wall and stared at the hedge in front of her. She found that she could see the looming structure of the Superdome through the gaps in the hedge and across the vast parking lot, and she marveled at the size of the arena. She looked at the domed ceiling, and she noticed that in the late afternoon sky, the colors and edges of her sight were blurring and shifting around. There was an almost fractal quality to the light that shifted just above the dome where the roof met the sky. Purple, green, and deep indigo colors danced and contorted in the sky, blending in with the lines of the Superdome. Everything was starting to go fuzzy around the edges.

These were all symptoms of the change. Her skin tingled all over, and she flexed her fingers. The edges of her fingers looked blurry as well, and was she only imagining the nails of her fingers growing and sharpening into claws or was it really happening? She clenched her hands into fists and took a deep breath. The change was imminent. It would come before the night was over, and Abby would have to move on again and find somewhere isolated and private.

She took two more deep breaths and tried to think back to the events of the day—how she had run, blindly and in a panic—how she had nearly transformed right there on the patio of the restaurant in front of Julia and everyone! What had happened? Never had a change only gone half-way before. Somehow she had stopped it.

Two more deep breaths to quell the sudden rise of anger inside her chest. Did she really let out the dragon scream in Julia's face? She smiled at the sudden image and memory of Julia's shocked and horrified expression. Well, that mean, rich girl bitch deserved it if she wet her britches.

The humming air duct droned on. Somewhere in the distance a car horn honked. Abby curled up snuggly and closed her eyes.

It was almost dark when she opened them again. The wind had changed, and the smell of the dumpster was now nearly overwhelming. Ah yes, the dumpster. The homeless clearing, so tidy and hidden from view. She sniffed the air again, then realized that it wasn't the smell alone that had woken her. With a sudden start she whirled her head around and saw him.

A middle-aged man was squatting down at the edge of the clearing, smiling. His teeth, so white and brilliant were the first thing she saw in the twilight dusk. Then she saw the face—a kind face, dark brown, wrinkled and care-worn, but the wrinkles were the type of wrinkles that were made by smiling, from the large dimples to the crow's feet around his dark brown eyes, like the face would not have been complete without them. He squatted there, very still, his forearms resting across his thighs. Somewhere deep inside of Abby, something within her relaxed.

"I see you've found my summer home." His voice was deep and resonant, the southern drawl inflecting and drawing out his syllables. His smile widened, and his eyes disappeared into a fracturing vein of slitted wrinkles. "Only got a few more weeks before football season, and that's all she wrote. Pack up your troubles in an old kit bag and off we go."

Abby sat up and curled her feet under her, ready to spring away if needed. "It's smile, smile, smile," she said. "The old song. That's how it goes. My momma used to sing it for me."

"That's right!" The man hopped and then plopped his butt right on the ground and grabbed both his ankles, pulling them over his knees to sit Indian style. Well, he kind of looked more like a Buddha in a lotus flower position.

Abby studied the man more carefully now. He was African-American. His hair was immaculately braided into corn rows and hung down past his shoulders, streaks of grey at his temples and in the goatee beard around his mouth. He was wearing what once was a very nice suit—something you might wear to a wedding or if you worked in a fancy restaurant—but it was now a little frayed around the edges and badly in need of a wash. His pants weren't quite long enough, revealing the smooth, bare skin of his calves and around his ankles. He wasn't wearing any socks, and the man was incongruously wearing the dirtiest pair of red converse sneakers Abby had ever seen. One big toe stuck out of a flap that had come undone. His toenail was long, curved and yellow. Pedicures were not a top priority, apparently.

"Is this your home?" Abby asked politely. "I didn't mean to intrude, it's just… just that I didn't have nowhere else to go." She looked around the clearing briefly, then smiled. "It's quite nice. Like your very own sanctuary." She lifted up the blanket she had been lying on and began folding it neatly.

"Sanctuary. I like that." The man said and continued to smile. He gestured at Abby fussing over the blanket. "You don't need to pay that no never mind. I don't get many visitors. Intruders, yes. Now that's a different story. But visitors like you, young lady, no… we don't get too many around here."

"Intruders?" Abby asked, as a trickle of fear started tingling down her spine. She was suddenly aware of movement over by the dumpster. The man glanced that way, and his smile vanished.

"Oh yes," he said. "The predators come out at night. Of the two-legged variety. Mostly young punks and rump-chumps all hopped up on junk. Mindless monsters. No respect for territorial boundaries. Thieves mostly. And worse." He turned back to look at Abby, and his smile returned. There was a long, awkward silence.

He sucked in a long breath, then continued. "That's why folks like me sleep in the daytime. It's safer when the sun shines and there are more people out and about. But in the night, when the shadows deepen—that's when the monsters come out." He paused to smile again at the notable tension in the frame of the girl in front of him. "But don't you fret, now, it is my pleasure to meet you." The smile broadened on his lips, he raised his eyebrows and stuck out his hand.

"The pleasure is all mine. Much obliged," Abby replied quickly. She hesitated to ponder the wisdom of taking his hand into her own—she knew that the contact might lead—no, most definitely *would* lead to access into his mind and very being. Especially this close to the change, the dragon would surely come forth and sweep open wide the Folds within this man. Abby would not be able to stop it. The visions might very well overwhelm her. Still… it was also the best way to know right away if he was a normal person or some kind of psychotic nut-job.

She made up her mind in a moment and grasped his hand in a shake. "I don't know where my manners went!" She sputtered as she shook his hand vigorously—and that was precisely when the flood of images came jolting through her in an instant—wave after clairvoyant wave, blurry and non-distinct at first, like fractured warped slides in a kaleidoscope. Then they slowed down and took shape and form.

And the slide show began: Images flashed ephemerally in her mind, lingering just long enough for recognition before vanishing, only to be replaced by another. First, there appeared a brief scene of a slightly younger, cleaner version of the man hovering over a table in a crowded, fancy restaurant. Green-coated waiters with shiny gold buttons on their coats were bustling about. "Welcome to the Commanders Palace," the man was pronouncing, his smile beaming at a large group of seated people as he leaned in to pour a rich brown liquid from the kettle in his hand to their empty cups. "The House specialty—Duck Fat

Lattes!" He announced, then leaned down to a child beneath his arm, who was watching wide-eyed as the steaming, thick liquid filled her cup. He winked at her, then whispered, "Better than hot chocolate. Try it, you might like it!"

His smile lit up the room, and then the picture warped and bent, the smile still lingered, but now it was plastered across the face of a little boy—and A.B. knew instantly that it was the child form of this man, a much older memory. He was dressed in a crisply pressed blue suit, vaguely military in its cut with silver tassels gleaming on its shoulders and fancy silver stitching down its tapered front. There was music playing—some early 20th century jazzy bit of Americana—and the boy was dancing a soft shoe on top of a crate in the middle of the street. It looked like Bourbon Street in downtown New Orleans, and a large crowd had gathered. The boy jigged and ambled, slapping his feet down perfectly in time to the music. He was fluid and graceful, and the crowd stood mesmerized. The boy's smiling face was the cutest thing A.B. had ever seen…

Then the scene whipped away to a darkened room. A switching stick raised above the gloomy interior of a run-down brownstone apartment. "You like giving away your tips?" The voice of the woman who was holding the stick. Her face was barely visible in the light coming from the next room. She was thirty-something, but looking more worn for wear, her once pretty face ravaged by drink or something worse. She leered angrily, her eyes hard and black, darker than her face, and her very white teeth almost glowing in the gloom as she snarled. The stick descended and cracked against the boy's bare back. A.B. heard the whimper of the boy and recoiled as if she were being hit herself. She could see the glint of silver tassels on the suit jacket draped over a chair next to the cringing boy.

"You think that girl likes your little black ass?" The voice again, and the stick descending once, twice more, viciously. "What you gonna eat tonight now that she got your money? You think she worth the skin off your back?" And then a blur as the stick rose and fell again and again, the sound of it thwacking against the boy's flesh sickening A.B., who started to cry, murmuring for the woman to please, make it stop.

And then it was gone, and she saw the boy who was once again a man, sitting on the cobbled stone pavement of an alleyway, his back against a wall. She could see through his eyes, the swollen ankles around his feet. The needles that lay next to his feet. He sat, unmoving, watching a fly crawl across the toe of his shoe, but he was warm and comfortable, feeling the ripples of time roll over and through him, all peaceful and painless.

Then another blur of light and color. First there was an old woman, black and round-faced, smiling the same smile as the man--his mother? No, a grand-mother, much older but beloved and better known by the man. She stood in a beautiful white dress on a little hillock surrounded by swamp land, beneath a tree draped with the silvery green strands of Spanish moss. She turned her face and looked back, smiling. By some trick of the light, the moss strewn branches of the tree cast a shadow over her face—a criss-crossing pattern like a spider's web... something vague but instantly familiar suddenly washed over Abby's senses like a warm wave. The old woman raised her hand and waved, her eyes crinkling with the spark of some secret meaning. Then the image was gone.

Before Abby could even think, suddenly, there was a white man, big bel-lied, all pink around his jowly cheeks. He sputtered all flustered, pacing up and down in a pin-striped suit that might be two sizes too small. "I can't have it like this, Tree!" He stuttered and lifted his finger in admonishment. "You ain't n-n-never gonna come clean. Y-y-you just a sad old junkie. I can't have you w-w-working for me!" He reached over and ripped the pinned name tag from the man's coat collar. He held up the tag, which was clearly labelled "Old Town New Orleans – Garden District Tours," and in clear, elegant cursive script, the name "Tree" was penned across the front of the badge. "Look at you! Showing up like this? Y-y-you're an embarrassment. I've got no other choice, Tree. G-g-go get some help from someb-b-body else. I'm done with you." And then the man stomped away.

Then a blur of images—birds flitting in a park, a man playing a slide trom-bone, "Tree" ambling along an empty street at night in a light rain, his bright red converse sneakers weirdly out of place, a slight hitch in his step. Another blur. Then, a small crowd of onlookers and a tumultuous scene—the police pointing guns at him. Tree's head against the pavement in a pool of blood. In a flash, the image was gone, replaced by his face, close up, leaning in and looking directly at Abby beneath the orange lights of a large parking lot. He was holding a baseball bat, and then he winked and grinned before saying, "You know I would never hurt a fly. Just don't tell the hobgoblins that!" His beautiful smile lit up the dim twilight below laughing brown eyes.

And just like that, the slide show was over. Abby snapped her eyes open. The man was watching her intently, and she was still shaking his hand. She had no idea how long they had been doing that, and suddenly self-conscious, she pulled her hand back in to cross her arms and nervously rub her elbows.

"Normally I don't like touching people." She chuckled humorlessly, before adding, "Your name is Tree." It was a quiet statement, not a question.

The man laughed and ran both his hands through his hair. "Well, now, that's a name I haven't heard in quite a while. Most folks call me "Stump" around here. I'm afraid I'm just a shadow of my former self."

"Stump." Abby repeated. "I do believe I understand that."

"I bet you do," the man chuckled then his face suddenly grew somber. "You got to keep that under wraps, little lady. You got the gift of sight, terribly strong. Can't be going all willy-nilly."

Abby looked at him, startled and slightly alarmed. "Could you see what I was seeing?" She swallowed heavily and suddenly her mind was full of a hundred questions. She stammered. "I-I don't know how to keep it under wraps. C-could you see inside my mind? Do you..."

"Now, first things first," the man interrupted, sat back and smiled his beautiful smile. He stretched out his hand, "We didn't finish our introductions. You can call me Stump. May I have the pleasure of your acquaintance?"

Abby hesitated, looking intently at the face of the strange man, unsure for a few moments before she took his hand. She grasped it, waiting for the surge of expected images, and... Nothing happened. Slowly a smile spread across her lips, a wide grin to match that of the man, and she shook his hand firmly, but politely, and this time only once. "My name is Aurora Borealis Rubideaux. But most folks call me A.B. or Abby cuz that's a lot shorter." She released his hand and continued to grin at him.

Stump chuckled and patted his legs, "Miss Aurora Borealis Rubideaux, if that ain't a mouthful!"

"Yessir." Abby wiped her nose and glanced away.

"Well, Abby. It is my honor to make your acquaintance." He spoke formally and sat up straighter. Abby laughed suddenly, free and easy, rubbed her legs and sat up straighter, too.

"Welcome to my sanctuary," he continued as he gestured dramatically around the clearing. "My very own Superdome paradise in the beautiful city of New Orleans!" He pronounced New Orleans like "nahhhh-lens." Abby giggled and bowed dramatically with one hand behind her back.

Stump laughed and then continued, "And you are welcome to spend the night here. Please, have no fear. I shall protect you from the creatures of the night. Those hooligans and hobgoblins won't bother us in my... in our sanctuary." He said this last word with relish, pulled a baseball bat out of a large pile, patted it twice and smiled broadly once again.

"Stump?" Abby watched as he set the bat down next to him. "I think I would rather call you Tree." Stump tensed slightly, and Abby quickly added, "That is only if it's all right with you, of course."

"If it's all right with me," Stump repeated, almost wistfully. He glanced away from Abby and stared off into the distance for several moments. Abby glanced down as his hand absently fondled the baseball bat at his side, twisting it over and over. The sound of the wood rotating and thrumming against the ground was disconcertingly loud. Then he continued.

"My name once upon a time used to be Tree, but they took my permits, and they took my license, so now I don't do no more tours round the Garden District and what not." His eyes flicked back to pin Abby in her place. She tensed until the black dots of his pupils softened slightly, and the hint of a smile returned to his gaze. Abby realized she had been holding her breath and slowly, she remembered to breathe once again.

"Yes indeed, Miss Rubideaux," he continued. "They cut a man off cuz he likes to take a drink every now and then. Or occasionally appease his deeper demons." He absently scratched at his arm, and Abby imagined the track marks that must be hidden beneath the sleeve of his coat. Or at least she imagined they were still there and looked very much like they did on the TV that one time she stayed up with Henry to watch an episode of CSI. How long ago was that? Six months? A year? She was suddenly aware of the prolonged silence and snapped her eyes back to meet Stump's. He was watching her intently, but the kindness and the warmth had crept back into them.

He smiled before speaking again. "They cut me down, yessir. They surely did. With a lot of assistance from my own self, of course. That is usually the way of it. Nothing happens completely by itself. So, it's Stump now."

Abby found herself suddenly relaxed. She didn't know why or how, but she knew that she could trust this man. She couldn't bother to even explain it to anyone who might be concerned, but she just knew with an irrevocable certainty that this man was good to his core. A true ally. A friend. Baseball bats and dodgy junky habits and all. And more importantly, she needed friends right about now.

She suddenly thought of Olivia, left behind at the chicken restaurant, the chaos of her flight and a sudden pang of anxiety knotted in her stomach. She hoped that Olivia wasn't currently scouring the streets of New Orleans looking for her. Or even worse, that she was somehow in trouble because of her own actions.

She looked again into the eyes of Stump, and relaxed. Olivia would be fine. And Olivia would not stop until she found her. She suddenly had an itch behind her ear, and as she scratched it, she felt the course, dry scaling that had built up there. She was reminded that the "change" was imminent. And she would need to find a place of privacy soon.

"So, Stump. I need to ask you a few things." Abby took a deep breath and steeled herself before continuing. Stump sat patiently, like a Buddha, cross-legged and smiling. She looked directly in his eye. "Just then, a few moments back, when I first took your hand. Could you feel me in your mind?"

"Yes." His response was without hesitation. She flicked her glance away nervously but returned her gaze almost immediately. Stump was still smiling.

She continued, "How did you know what I was doing? I mean, I ain't never met nobody who could feel me like you did."

"Well now," Stump actually chuckled. "You never met my Granny Jane then, did ya?" He laughed again, his body shaking with mirth for several long moments before, at last, subsiding. "So, listen," and he was suddenly sober and solemn. "You got the second sight, and that ain't no big thing. Lots of folks have the gift. It tends to run in certain families. I know I got it from my momma, and she from her momma before her, and so on, and so on. But there is something else you want to tell me about yourself, isn't there? Not everything is what it seems. And I certainly know a little bit about that." He laughed again, and Abby laughed, too. There was something irresistibly genuine and charming about his manner.

Abby felt the itch behind her ears again, glanced down at the fingernails on her right hand and noticed the plaque build-up there, opaque and crusty, with claw-like tapering at the ends of her nails. It warped and changed back to normal right before her eyes. She quickly buried her hands in the folds of her dress. It was almost like the dragon was speaking to her directly. She decided in that moment to spill the whole can of beans. It was worth a shot, anyway.

"Well, yes, in fact," she began slowly, still holding his gaze. "I do have something more to tell you. I just don't know where to begin."

"Why don't you try at the beginning?"

"Well, gosh," Abby chuckled and rubbed her hands together. "If I knew where the beginning was, I guess that would be easy!" She paused and giggled again, until she noticed that Stump was patiently sitting across from her, waiting.

She took a big breath, and then it all rushed out at once. "I've got this dragon that lives inside of me, and I guess it's always been there, only I didn't really know it until I got sucked up into a giant tornado, and everybody was really worried about me, but I just couldn't explain to them clearly that I was fine—really fine and that in fact, everything was so beautiful and made perfect sense, only I couldn't explain it without sounding plum crazy, because while I was up in that tornado, which really wasn't a tornado but a state of mind—a kind of "dragon state of mind," and it was then that I realized that time isn't really what it seems to be and that you can be anywhere and everywhere all at once, and oh yeah! I almost forgot, when I get into my dragon mind, I can kind of see into people's minds—er, or more like I can see their lives kind of happening all at once, and it's like everything that happened to them in the past and whatever is the big thing happening in their lives right now and then everything else that will or might happen to them in their future because it's all really like a giant fold of cloth—the cloth of consciousness! And it's layer after layer that just contains everything about them, and when I go there I can feel the truth of it and know that it's no lie and that I'm not crazy at all but something else, that's really for sure, but I can't really tell them what it is because most folks are just scared or can't even understand what it is that I am experiencing cuz I guess you kind of really just have to be there to know what I mean. You know?"

Stump had been listening intently the whole time, the smile never leaving his face. When Abby finished, he leaned back and his smile widened. "So, you got a dragon inside you, hmm?"

Abby scrunched up her face and let out a deep breath, discouraged. "You think I'm a crazy person, don't you?"

"Hold on now," Stump chuckled and rocked forward to catch Abby's eye. "I say nothing of the sort." He paused and studied Abby's face for several, uncomfortable moments, and Abby got so self-conscious of his scrutiny that she had to snigger and turn away.

Stump finally spoke, "I don't see nothing crazy about you—inside or out. And believe me, I would know."

Abby turned back to face him and coyly smile, before venturing a little retort. "Crazy knows crazy, right?"

"Ha!" Stump exploded into laughter. "Now, you too young to be such a flirt!"

Abby laughed with him. As she finally regained her capacity for speech, she asked him more solemnly, "So, you don't find it odd that I have a dragon inside of me?"

Stump sobered up quickly, but his eyes still twinkled brightly. "Well now, I suppose there are stranger things on this earth. My Granny Jane used to talk to possum and squirrels—varmints of all type, actually. She had to set the rules straight about pilfering the walnut and pecan trees that grew in her yard. Sounds perfectly reasonable to me. So, if you got a dragon inside of you, I reckon there's a reason why. You ever think about that?"

"Yes, I have," Abby responded matter-of-factly. "I do believe there is a great purpose for me in this life, and for that matter in all of my other lives as well." Abby smiled at that, and Stump smiled back at her. She reached over and clasped his hand in her own. "I believe I'm here to help people. Make them whole and better than they think they can be."

"Yeah, sis," he said, and he squeezed her hand affectionately. "You got the picture. Right quick. Quicker than most who got the gift." He paused and seemed to be appraising her in a new light. After several weird moments, he spoke, "I think you're all right." He turned around and unzipped a canvas bag that was strapped over his shoulder. He began rummaging through it quickly, before producing a banana and a bag of sunflower seeds. He offered Abby the banana.

"Hungry?" He asked. Abby reached out and took the banana, which was slightly bruised on one end. Still yellow and green at the tips, just the way she liked them.

"Thank you," she said.

"Potassium," Stump announced. "An essential part of any young lady dragon's diet." He tore off the top of his bag of sunflower seeds and began cracking them, one by one. He produced a small, bright red plastic cup and used that to carefully and expertly spit out his seeds.

Abby peeled the banana and began to nibble on it. It was good, and her belly gurgled. She took a bigger bite, not realizing how hungry she had become. They ate in silence for a while, comfortable in each other's company. Only the cracking of Stump's seeds and the soft "Ptah!" of his seed spitting punctuated the night.

At length, Abby turned to study Stump's face for several moments. She could still see the child's face beneath the care-worn lines of the older man. The little boy dancer. The same smile. Then she thought of something that made her sit up in a jolt. Stump glanced up at her sudden movement.

"How did you do that?" She asked. "Just then, a while back. I took your hand and nothing happened. I couldn't feel or see anything. It was like you blocked me or screened me—and I don't mean to say that you were rude or unfriendly—it's just that there was like a shield between us, and I couldn't see any of your folds."

"My folds?" Stump laughed and put his bag of sunflower seeds away. He spit out one last shell before turning back to look at Abby. "Well, Miss Rubideaux," And here he paused and smiled down at her, "Abby. My "folds" are my own business. And what you seem to take for granted is that a man don't always want someone else to come in and stir up all of his skeletons." Suddenly his voice turned stern—still gentle, but stern. "Like I said, you got to learn how to keep that little trick of yours under wraps. For the sake of others and their right to privacy. But also, to protect yourself!"

"I'm sorry, Stump. I don't mean to do it. It...it just happens, and I can't stop it." She glanced down at the banana peel in her hand, looked around for a place to put it. Stump reached out his hand and took it, packing it away in his cup. She smiled in gratitude before continuing.

"And I got a whole bunch of questions. I ain't never met someone like you—someone who could see what I was seeing—someone who knew that I could see inside of them...their memories and their futures. All of their folds. How many folks like you are out there?"

"Oh, you'd be surprised. Quite a few." Stump said. "But we don't like to bring attention to ourselves. Least not in the usual sense. Most other folks get a might bit uncomfortable around things like this because they don't understand."

"Oh! I do so want to find more folks who do understand!" Abby stopped and suddenly flexed her fingers. She felt a surge of electric energy all tingly throughout her entire body. The change was coming—it needed to happen soon. She stood up and stretched out her legs and the kinks in her buttocks.

Stump watched her, stoically, waiting for her to settle down as Abby paced their little clearing nervously. She suddenly stopped in front of him, looked right at him, leaned her back against the wall and almost comically slid down to a sitting position: Plop!

A whisper of an idea was beginning to form in her head. It was kind of crazy, but as she glanced past Stump, through the hedge and up at the white roof of the Superdome, she saw the glimmering blur of purple, green and indigo light warping and distorting everything. It was crazy. But it was perfect. Nobody would even think about something like that!

Yes, little flyer. Yes. Perfect.

The dragon inside of her stirred in approval, and Abby snapped out of her reverie and focused once more on Stump, who still sat unmoving and patient in front of her.

"About those questions," Abby began through a slowly spreading grin. "They might need to wait till later. You and I have definitely got to talk! But I got one question I need to ask you right now."

"I'm all ears," Stump beamed back at her.

Abby pointed behind Stump and up at the roof of the Superdome. "What's the easiest way to get up there?"

So, the plan had been hatched, and Abby was all nervous with butterflies fluttering feverishly in her stomach, not just from the change that was electrically looming, but from the fact that another person was present with her so close to the change.

"It's too dangerous for you!" Abby was saying as they walked across the parking lot toward the main entrance of the dome. She scanned to the left and right—the lot was empty. They were walking quickly, but just a little too furtively for Abby's comfort. Anybody who might see them would know they were up to no good.

"You ain't gonna make it without a distraction. Plain and simple." Stump was breathing heavily under his words as he quickly shuffled along beside her with the awkward hitch in his gait. He suddenly pulled Abby to a stop and stroked the baseball bat that he was holding in his right hand. "There is always security around the main building. Ain't no big thing for you, but you can bet that they're gonna want to do their job and shoo off the crazy homeless black man with a baseball bat in his hands."

Abby objected, "It might take a bad turn… get ugly. You sure about that?" She gestured at the bat in his hand.

Stump leaned in closer to Abby, and she could smell the sunflower seeds still on his breath. The orange glow of the parking lot lights illuminated his head with a halo. "You know I would never hurt a fly. Just don't tell the hobgoblins that!" His beautiful smile lit up the dim twilight below laughing brown eyes.

Abby knew he was going to say that just before he said it because she had seen all of this before. Sure enough. She smiled back at him and nodded. "Let's do this."

"Yes ma'am!" Stump grinned and tossed the bat up, catching it with his other hand. "That's my girl."

"Soon to be your dragon!" Abby retorted and grinned. Stump guffawed, and they started toward the dome again, and as they drew in closer. Abby noticed the security cameras that Stump said would be there.

"Like I said," Stump was whispering now. "The cameras are all over the entrance gates and the reserved parking garages where the rich folks like to park. Most of 'em are aimed toward all those glass windows in the pretty shops by the main gate." He paused and pointed with the bat. "You go up that ramp, stick to the inner edges where it's darker. Main floor, you circle round to the back, and like I said, ain't no easy way up top! No ladders or catwalks… the Superdome is a modern wonder of the world. I don't know how they did it, or how they get up top without no ladders. You just gonna have to do…whatever it is you gonna do." He smiled at her. "Should be easy for a little dragon. And that roof is made of steel. Even Hurricane Katrina couldn't blow it off. You'll be fine. Up you go, like a little dragon lady to her little roost. Ain't nobody gonna pay you no never mind because all they gonna see is me, pacing up and down, gesticulating in front of all that pretty glass down below." He patted the bat in his hand. He looked left and right, and Abby could swear that he was enjoying this a whole lot more than she was.

He nodded, then took a few steps away before turning back to her. "You got five minutes before I get to working on them in earnest. All their attention is gonna be on me. That's five minutes for you to figure out how you gonna get up top. You think your little dragon bones up for that?" He reached over and patted her head.

"Right. I make the change and then I'm just gonna fly up there. Piece o' cake. Let's do this," Abby said more to convince herself than him. He grabbed her just as she was turning to go. Puzzled, she looked up into his kind and crinkled eyes, and he winked down at her.

"Don't you be falling or killing yourself, now," he said, still smiling. "I would never forgive myself." And with that, he turned and lurched away, twirling the baseball bat in his hand.

Abby stood and watched him go. As he walked out of the darkness of the parking lot and into the well-lit façade of the dome, he started whistling, a random tune that was oddly cheery and out of place. He started dragging the wooden bat along the ground, as he walked up the steps of the main ramp entrance, and it was loud as it thumped against each step and seemed to echo everywhere all over the place.

"That'll work, all right…" Abby muttered under her breath before breaking her gaze away and slinking off toward the garage ramps. She darted from shadow to shadow, reaching the first ramp. She paused to listen, and she could hear Stump singing now, something about a hole in his pocket or his bucket or some such nonsense. His baseball bat was punctuating his delivery with loud echoing "thunks."

She took one more look at the side of the dome which loomed above her now that she was so close. She glanced back down into the garage, then around the top walkway that surrounded the dome. Not a soul was around. Above her, and not more than 100 yards away was the highway overpass of the Pontchartrain Express. She could hear the cars and trucks whooshing by, but they seemed far away and out of sight. She took a deep breath, then walked quickly to the side of the dome. She had picked a spot where she couldn't see any security cameras, and the white walls of the Superdome were dimly lit. She was struck by how, in the night time, the entire structure looked like a giant spaceship.

She smiled, gaining a little more confidence, then flexed the fingers of both hands, rotating her shoulders back and forth to help herself relax.

"Well, ain't you a predictable little debbie-doo-right!" The voice came from a stone bench in the shadows near the garage ramp she had just emerged from. Abby whirled in an instant of panic before she saw the face that matched the familiarity of the voice. She relaxed as she watched her friend Olivia stand up from the bench and saunter over to her.

"Of all the places in downtown New Orleans," Olivia was smiling brightly as she came into the light, "how did I know you'd come to the Superdome?" Olivia stopped in front of Abby and snorted back a laugh.

"Gold and black forever, baby doll!" Abby grinned back at her, then both girls clutched hands and squealed,

"Go Saints!"

They laughed and embraced, and Abby kept parting Olivia's frizzy hair so she could get a better look at her. She was still a mess, with catsup and mustard stains all over her blouse and dried clumps still in her hair.

"Good lord!" Abby exclaimed. "What did the evil princess do to you? You such a mess!" Abby looked away suddenly embarrassed as she remembered Julia's assault with the condiment bottles just hours earlier. It seemed like days ago. "I'm sorry I didn't stop her in time, that snooty witch!"

Olivia lit up, all excited. "Well, don't you worry about that. The more important question is what *you* did to her!" Abby's best friend suddenly smiled wickedly and snort-snickered again. "If you could have seen the look on all their faces, especially Princess Julia's! When that ol' drill sergeant, Miss Trudy got a hold of her and grilled her like she was guilty of murder!" Olivia paused, and sighed in satisfaction at the delightful memory. Then she quickly turned back to stare right into Abby's eyes, and she slowly adopted an over-the-top, dignified air of solemnity.

"But what did you do back there, Abby?" She asked in wonder. "What really happened? I mean, it all happened so fast and that Godzilla screech you let out was enough to break everybody's ear drums. I mean, there's just no way to make heads or tails out of it… and it was pure chaos after you left."

Abby was suddenly not smiling anymore. "Tell me what happened after I left, Olivia."

"Well," Olivia licked her lips as if she were just warming up to her story. "I lit out after you right away, but I couldn't follow you cuz you was moving so fast. I only got a few blocks, and you were gone. I couldn't see which way you had turned. I had no idea, and nobody around me seemed to know anything.

So, I went back to Popeye's Chicken, and well, I tell you, it was like all hell had busted loose." Olivia smiled at her recollection and wiped her nose before continuing. "With Miss Trudy and the other teachers trying to maintain order, and they were barking out questions and ordering everyone about, and all the other kids was just screaming and yelling all at once like a pack of rabid dogs. It was a beautiful thing to behold. Especially ol' Balt, blubbering like a baby—I think you made him wet his pants, the coward. Truer colors were never revealed! But best of all was Princess Julia. She just sat there, still as a stone statue, all forlorn and thunderstruck. I think she was in shock. Miss Trudy had her by the shoulders, and she was shaking her, but Julia's head just snapped around like her neck was made of rubber." Olivia obliged Abby with her best imitation of a rubber-necked Julia. "I think it was the coolest day of my life!"

Olivia paused to leer like a loon, and it made Abby smile back at her. "How long did you stay? I mean what happened next?" Abby asked, her nervousness returning with renewed force. An overwhelming sense of regret rippled through her. She had been careless. The dragon was out of the bag, so to speak. And there might be no going back.

Olivia continued, breathless, "Well, the restaurant manager wasn't very happy—you did some serious damage to one of the tables, and then the police showed up, and I decided it was time for me to skedaddle. The last thing I saw was Miss Trudy lining up the kids and heading back to the bus. There were a lot of police round about there, and they was talking to just about anybody who might have seen anything. I wasn't gonna have some policeman interrogate me!" Olivia playfully punched Abby in the arm. "I guess the school didn't go back to the museum to see what them Japs were all about. In the end, I mean, might be a good thing, if you know what I mean. What was really looking like a long, dull day turned into the most amazing day of my life!"

Olivia was chuckling again, but Abby found that she herself had no more patience.

"So, wait a minute," Abby began trying to regain her composure. "What did you do? How'd you get home? Did you even try to get back home? I mean, you still got Julia's hot dog treatment all over you!"

"Are you kidding me?" Olivia almost looked offended. "I would not abandon you to the unknown perils of the city after night! I could see that things with Miss Trudy and the Police were not going to go very well. I slipped away before any of them would notice and came looking for you!" Olivia suddenly grabbed Abby's arm as she just remembered something else. "Oh, yeah. I kind o' need to tell you. It might be important. But just before I left, I heard one of them police asking Miss Trudy and some of them other kids about whether or not you had any weapons." Olivia paused as both she and Abby let their eyes go wide. "That's right, weapons! Like you was seriously carrying around some big ol knives or a machete." Olivia hacked the air with Kung Fu moves, slicing and slashing with gusto.

"I guess they was trying to figure out what happened," she finally continued in an almost comedic matter-of-fact voice. "Especially to that table you knocked over. You scuffed it up something good." And here Olivia paused and held up three bent fingers to make a dramatic clawing motion. "That was one hell of a scratch you left behind. Three marks like the sign of the tiger! Too bad it wasn't on Julia's face!"

"Don't say such a thing!" Abby suddenly turned away and looked down at her right hand. It was a normal looking hand with no claws or signs of the dragon. She was just then reminded of what she was about to do before Olivia popped up out of nowhere. She flexed her fingers and made a few fists before lifting her gaze back to Olivia and continuing.

"This ain't no laughing matter. I would never hurt nobody—not even Julia. But other folks—well most other folks, I mean. They can't know about this. They just can't! I'm serious about this…"

"Damn right it's serious!" Olivia interrupted. "You went all dragon mode in front of the whole class and half the population of the Garden District! Them police wanna talk to you."

Abby ignored her last remark, and yammered on, "No, no. That can't be right. I didn't make the change. Not complete, anyway." She grasped Olivia's arms again and looked straight into her eyes. "Tell me. Tell me if you saw anything!"

"Ow!" Olivia extricated her arms from Abby's fierce grasp. "Hold your horses, now. I bruise easily." She rubbed her arms and pouted.

"I'm sorry," Abby said, and she really was. "I just need to know what you saw. Please…" She gently reached for Olivia again and looked imploringly into her eyes.

"Okay," Olivia said a bit huffily. "No harm, no foul. I might have been exaggerating a bit." She smiled weakly, still rubbing her arms. "I didn't see no dragon wings or no claws. No breath of fire." She snorted again softly. "We just heard you screechin', and then the table got knocked over and everybody went flying like a sound grenade went off in the middle of the patio. Then you run off like you did, and there I was, covered in mustard sitting on top of Balt Luster, who was, by the way, bawling like a little baby. I didn't make that part up. And Julia? Well, she was really scared. I ain't never seen that look in her eyes before. I would die a thousand times or more just to see that again. It really was a beautiful thing to behold!"

"So," Abby began hesitantly, "so I... I didn't turn into a giant lizard--at least not what you could see?"

"Naw," Olivia replied. "And I'm a might bit disappointed, too. You told me that I could see the change. Only I thought it would be under different circumstances."

"Well," Abby smiled. "It's your lucky night!" She pointed up to the top of the dome. "I was just about to get a "dragon's eye" view of the roof of the Superdome. I've been waiting all day for the right moment. This is it!"

Olivia gasped and then squealed in delight. "For real? You gonna make the change right now?"

"Well, I was just about to when you so rudely interrupted me." Abby smiled, and nodded back at Olivia. "What happened earlier today," and she paused to shake out her hands, pop the kinks in her neck, and look up again at the top of the dome. She appraised it for several moments. "Well, let's just say you ain't seen nothin' yet!" She pointed at the bench where Olivia was first sitting. "Have a seat and watch the show. You are about to see what no other living human being this side of Mesopotamia has ever seen before!"

"Meso-potato-what?" Olivia laughed, then quickly she followed Abby's orders and scuttled over to the bench and sat down, her hands clasped expectantly before her.

Abby nodded once more, then turned and walked over to the side of the Superdome, turned around, placed her back against its smooth surface, then slowly allowed herself to slide down to a seated position. She closed her eyes and took a few deep breaths.

"Hey!" Olivia called over from her bench. "You ain't gonna wanna eat me or anything like that... once you go dragon mode, right?"

Abby opened one eye and smiled. "Don't be giving me any ideas, now." She closed her eye again and smiled, before taking a few more deep breaths.

"Relax. I only like fish. And I'm still me even after I make the change. Dinner is not the thing that is most often on my mind!"

Several seconds went by before Abby suddenly opened her eyes and perked up. "Oh! And if you see a Black homeless guy named Stump come by with a baseball bat? Don't worry, he's a friend."

"Okey-dokey," Olivia shrugged. She waited and watched for several moments as Abby closed her eyes and took several deep breaths. Gradually, Abby's breathing slowed, and she sat very still. Olivia realized that she was just as still and needed to take a breath, too.

Abby opened her eyes again and smiled. "You okay seeing me naked? I will need you to mind my dress. After. I mean after it happens. I'm not used to having somebody here to watch me."

"Don't you mind me." Olivia exploded into one of her trademark snorts." I got you covered." She watched as Abby closed her eyes and resumed taking deep breaths. "What now?" Olivia finally said after a few more minutes had passed.

"We wait." Abby said quietly, not opening her eyes. She remained still, and Olivia sat just as still, watching her in obedient silence as the evening grew darker and the purple twilight skies slowly turned to the indigo of deep night.

"I don't understand," Abby finally said. It had been over an hour and nothing had happened. She sat there, quietly, and opened her eyes. Olivia was slumped over on her side, laying across the bench seat. She yawned and sat up.

"Well that was about as exciting as watching the paint peel off the side of my grandaddy's barn." Olivia stood up and stretched.

Abby groaned and slowly pushed her way to her feet. "I don't ever have to wait like this. It usually happens right away, no fuss or bother. Snap!" Abby snapped her fingers. "And it's done. I'm flying." She sighed. "I just don't understand..." Her voice trailed off as she dusted off her dress.

"Well," Olivia offered, "Maybe it's like you said. You're just not used to having company when you make the change."

"Maybe so," Abby sighed again. "But I had all the signs. I could feel it. Like I always do. I should've made the change lickety-split. There's got to be some kind of explanation. I mean, I could have made the change back there when we were dealing with Julia..."

"You mean *attacked* by Julia," Olivia interjected.

"Right." Abby paused for a few moments to collect her thoughts. "But somehow, some way, I stopped it. I knew I couldn't go all the way." She turned, looked directly at Olivia and smiled. "And that is something I ain't never done before ..."

She was interrupted by the sound of a wooden bat hollowly thumping the concrete in the distance. Soon the girls could hear the voice of a man, singing. It was a nice, clear voice—a strong baritone.

"I got a hole in my pocket, and my money keeps on runnin' through!

I got a hole in my pocket, and my money keeps on runnin' through!

Can't see a silver dollar, but my baby darlin' wants them too!"

The voice grew louder, and sure enough, Stump rounded the corner, swinging his baseball bat like a cane and thumping the ground to punctuate each verse. He stopped when he saw the two girls, grinned his big grin, and side-stepped his way over like a dancer on his stage.

"Funny thing," he said as he came up beside them and spun around in a final flourish before halting to look both the girls over. "I sang my heart out and beat my bat upon the ground. There ain't a single security person in this facility. Not a one." He paused to look at Abby, then over at Olivia, then back to Abby again. "Ain't no dragons flying around here neither."

He smiled, and Abby smiled back at him. "Hi Stump!" She glanced nervously over at Olivia, but Olivia was grinning like she was the Cheshire Cat. "Umm, this is my friend, Olivia. My best friend. She found me here. Kind of. I mean, like she knew I'd be here. We're kind of special and connected that way."

She giggled and Olivia snorted and stuck out her hand. Stump took it very delicately in his own and smiled back at her.

"The pleasure is all mine," he said. Stump sniffed the air once, then twice more a bit loudly. Both Abby and Olivia glanced at each other awkwardly.

Stump glanced at Abby, grinned, then returned his gaze to Olivia. His face crinkled into hundreds of wrinkles in what literally was the crack of a smile, and he announced with utmost sincerity, "I like a girl that smells like mustard."

10

With a Little Help from My Friends

From the Audio transcripts of Dr. Joanna Kinsey
Chief Psychiatrist, CHNOLA Northshore Center,
New Orleans, LA

Excerpt of Audio File Transcript #AR10089-40

June 30, 2022

Subject: A. B. Rubideaux. Female. Age: 11

Transcript of recording begins: 10:02 AM EST.

A.B.: *You're not a very good scientist, you know.*

Kinsey: *A.B., I'd like to stay on track, here.*

A.B.: *You let your emotions cloud your empirical observations. Now, don't get me wrong—I think that's a wonderful thing! It's actually what makes you a superb therapist! Your ability to connect through empathy and an intuitive higher self. But just when I think you have finally come around—just when you are on the cusp of breaking through to an ascendant consciousness and a transcendent being, you slip back into the limitations of your training and procedural "best practices."*

Kinsey: *That's quite perceptive. Let me think about that. So, let's go back to the day Momma Bea took you out into the storm.*

A.B.: *See? You just did it again. The clinical psychiatrist's mask.*

Kinsey: *Well, I am sorry, A.B.. I guess that's just who I am. Old habits, I guess?*

A.B.: *(Snort.)*

Kinsey: *Tell me more about the tornado. What happened?*

A.B.: *Persistence and laser focus. Those qualities can bring you very far in this world. Yes. Let us continue!*

Kinsey: *By all means.*

A.B.: *Well, like I told you before. The tornado was just a collective perception for you mere mortals to behold. (Giggling.) The truth can't always be revealed just like that (A finger snaps). I flew with the dragons. And no, that is not just a metaphor. I flew into the void. Into a higher plane of existence. The voice came into my head, filled me with warmth and comfort, and my fear was replaced with euphoria. It was an invitation, and when I accepted, I was transformed. And then we flew in a prism of color and light. It only lasted a few moments. But it was eternal at the same time. I had never felt so... so present before.*

Kinsey: *You flew into a multi-dimensional space, yes? The "Fold" that you have talked about before?*

A.B.: *That is correct.*

Kinsey: *A.B., do you know that you were missing for nearly three days?*

A.B.: *Time is relative. And an illusion. Do you think you can better control the world if you break it down into minutes and seconds? It's all part of the separateness that humans have created. It is a flawed idea that only through objective and measurable means can we find comprehension. It is the source of our misery, and it will ultimately be humanity's undoing.*

Kinsey: *I think you've changed the subject again, A.B.. As much as I would love to revisit your remarkable insights into quantum theory and the non-local "Fold," could we please try to stay on track? I am trying to understand how a little girl gets sucked out of her mother's car by a monster tornado, disappears into the void for three days, then comes walking back down the driveway with not even a scratch on her body. And you are telling me that it wasn't an actual tornado but a multi-dimensional experience of euphoria that lasted only a few moments?*

A.B.: *Well, there... you see? I thought we had overcome the skeptical scientist thing, Joanna. I know we are getting closer to something significant because your heartbeat has suddenly accelerated. I think that acceleration and the sudden flush in your cheeks is caused by excitement. You are invested in this emotionally whether you want to be or not, Joanna. And that's not very clinical, now is it? Wait! Wait.*

Let me finish. (Deep breath.) Have you not been listening to anything I've said in all of our sessions? All of it is connected. The tornado. My disappearance. What happened at school. My capture and subsequent institutionalization. The fact that all of this has led to my now sitting here with you... again! These things are not just incidental.

Kinsey: *It's not a coincidence.*

A.B.: *That's right! Synchronicity has brought us together, right here, right now! In this moment. For a reason.*

Kinsey: *And that reason would be?*

A.B.: *That you need my help. And yes, I need yours, too.*

Kinsey: *I'm listening. Explain.*

A.B.: *You're going to help me save humanity.*

Kinsey: *From what?*

A. B.: From our imminent destruction. The futility, the fraudulence, and the baseless attempts by humankind to categorize, control, and ultimately to transcend nature. We, as a species, have severed the cord. And now we are drifting, alone, disconnected, and perilously close to causing the cataclysmic end of everything as we think we know it. That is the illusion. I am trying to tell you how to save yourself. You save yourself, and you can save the world. Like Gilgamesh. Frodo Baggins. Or Luke Skywalker. It's the same story being told over and over. What else are we here for?

Kinsey: *The Hero's journey?*

A.B.: *The only journey.*

45 DAYS EARLIER: MAY 16, 2022

Three days doesn't seem like such a long time to pass amongst the company of your friends. Unless you are homeless and living on the street. Then it seems like an eternity.

The day after Abby failed to transform into a dragon at the Superdome, Olivia decided to go home and take a shower—with a promise that she would be back the next day with a full report on the lay of the land. Abby was concerned about what had happened after the school lunch incident. So, after spending the morning with Abby and Stump, Olivia found a pay phone and made the call home. She didn't want to get into more trouble than she knew she was already in. And besides, she was tired of smelling like a condiment rack, and she was even more tired of how Stump kept sniffing the air then looking at her like he had half a mind to stick her between a couple of buns and take a bite out of her.

But actually, Olivia and Stump had hit it off splendidly--just like they were old friends, and the two of them spent more time with their heads together giggling like a couple of schoolgirls than just about anything else.

For her part, Abby was a bit removed from the levity of her friends. She was pensive and tense, trying to figure out why she couldn't make the change. Not completing her transformation had never happened to her before. It was always the same progression, the same sequence of physical, mental and emotional signs. She knew it and felt it like it were some kind of muscle that tingled and flexed. You know, like an athlete that missed her workout and then her body, and specifically her buttocks, would talk back to her in its own way. *Hey! Work me! Work me! Stretch me out!*

She looked down at her fingertips, flexed them, then rolled her neck to let out the tension and the kinks—the dragon signs were gone. Nothing to mark that the change was imminent. It's like she had lost or forgotten something important but couldn't remember what it was. Maybe what happened at the lunch tables with Julia and the rest had somehow unexpectedly altered the process. Maybe the unfamiliar concrete environment wasn't right—she needed trees, and water, the smell of wet earth and moss. The promise of fresh fish. Maybe she just got cold feet, and she couldn't go all the way with Olivia watching.

Olivia. When it was time for her to go, Abby had watched her head back down toward the city. She had half a mind to join her. She probably should join her. It had been over two days since she ran away from the mustard and catsup fight. Two days for Momma Bea to worry and fret. But something inside of her felt like it just wasn't time to go back yet. Maybe it was the dragon, rumbling deep inside of her, telling her to wait. Maybe she knew deep down that it would be far worse back at home. Something was happening there right now, and it wasn't any good! There was consternation brewing in the air, and Abby could feel it wrap around her like a second skin.

So, when Olivia left, she had looked over her shoulder one last time to look Abby in the eye. Olivia raised an eyebrow like she was asking: "You sure about this?" But Abby was resolute and just nodded once and shooed Olivia off with an irritating wave of her hands.

Abby watched her go until she rounded a corner three blocks away. Then Stump's hand on her shoulder squeezed gently, and it was time to go back to their little sanctuary and eat some lunch.

When they returned to Stump's camp behind the hedge, Stump pretty much gave her the space she needed. He limped around, then announced something about "supplies," and off he went, leaving her alone. But being alone maybe wasn't the best thing for her right now. Their little clearing at the far end of the Superdome's auxilliary lot C wasn't exactly a day in the Park. It turned out that Stump wasn't alone here, and there were in fact a considerable number of homeless camps nearby. But Stump was right about one thing: everyone seemed to do their sleeping in the daytime. She wondered then what that meant about the night time. Wasn't that when the monsters and hobgoblins came out?

Abby kept to herself inside Stump's camp, and Stump had told her that none of their neighbors would bother them during the day, but even so--it wasn't exactly a restful or relaxing resort. And the cars above on the Pontchartrain Expressway were a ceaseless whirr of sound. At first, Abby imagined it could be the ocean, but after half the day had gone by it just made her feel antsy. The construction site a few blocks away didn't help either. Construction workers had loud voices, and even louder equipment.

She also had an extreme need to relieve herself. Number one only, thank god! But it was a bit of a quandary to find out where. The other denizens in their camps below the expressway were either sleeping or looked like the kinds of folks that she ought to avoid interaction with. Eventually, she just followed her nose and found a small concrete water and power structure behind some dumpsters. There was no mistaking what the site was used for by people in the area, so she held her nose, glanced quickly around to make sure she was alone, and then with only the slightest feeling of guilt, she squatted and did her business.

Somewhere close to dusk, Stump returned. He had brought food. One-day-old pastries from a doughnut shop and hot dogs from a street vendor. Abby smiled to herself and thought about how appropriate that was. She was also ravenous and didn't care to stand on any sort of ceremony or sigh over wistful reflections. She chomped down two hot dogs in the blink of an eye, much to Stump's delight.

"Too bad Olivia ain't around right now." Stump had joked. "We could wring the mustard out of her hair." And so their meal together went. She offered him money, but he refused.

As dusk turned to night, they talked quietly, and Abby learned more and more about living on the streets, and how to survive. Stump explained how to choose your mark when panhandling, how to suss out dangerous people and, more importantly, why it was always the wiser course of action to give them a wide berth. She also learned a little more about Stump's youth, when he was a fairly renowned street performer. He talked a lot about singing and dancing. It was clearly a joy for him to reminisce about those days of entertaining.

But when it came to his family, he was fairly tight-lipped. He wasn't comfortable going down that particular road. Abby had a flash of the woman in the dusky room, her eyes glaring as the stick rose above the cowering little boy. She had a pretty good idea of why he was reluctant to talk about it. And after Stump's little speech about respecting folk's privacy, well, she thought it best to leave it alone and not bring the subject up. Maybe Stump would eventually talk to her about it, but he would do it on his terms.

They sat in silence for a long time, Abby glancing at Stump every now and then. He was studying her in silence and grinning. After a while, she had to ask why he kept staring at her.

"What?" She suddenly asked and giggled herself. "You keep staring at me like I've got something stuck on my face. Is it mustard?" Abby wiped her cheeks.

Stump, still smiling, shook his head and continued to stare at her. He finally hemmed and hawed before he spoke at last. "Mmm-mmm. My oh my." He leaned forward and reached out a hand like he wanted to touch her, but he was too shy and pulled it back. "I swear, I ain't seen a shining like yours for a long while. A long while."

Abby smiled and fiddled with the sleeves of her blouse. "What you mean by that? A shining?"

"It's your light… your aura," Stump said almost in a whisper. "You light up the dark like a lighthouse guiding in ships to keep 'em off the shoals. I seen it in you that very first night you came here. I could swear you was sent to me by the angels, and you were sent to me for a reason."

"You can see my light?"

"Burning up the night like a roman candle, yes indeed."

"Is it like you can see my… my soul-fire? Is it that kind of light?"

Stump's grin widened and he laughed. "Why sure. I've heard it called a soul-fire before. My Granny Jane called it that. Yes, ma'am. You got the brightest soul-fire I ever seen. Must be that dragon you got inside of you."

"But how can *you* see it? Why can't all these other folks in my life? How come you can see it?" Abby was earnest now, and her words were tumbling out now fast and all helter-skelter. "And just *what* is it exactly that you can see? You said there were lots of folks like you. How many? Where are they? Can you introduce them to me?"

"Hold your horses, now." Stump laughed and held up his hand. "One question at a time." He paused and smiled, watching Abby bite her tongue. "You chompin' at the bit. We got all night to lay it out for you."

"It's just that I feel like I'm drowning, Stump. I'm in deep waters, and they are pulling me down. I can't explain it."

"Well, now," Stump stroked his chin and continued. "Deep waters have currents. Sometimes they are hidden, but an experienced eye knows how to find them and avoid them if they are dangerous. But sometimes you need to ride those currents, let them take you where you are supposed to be taken. That can be scary, for sure, unless you know that you can always find control and come back to yourself."

"Yes, I want to have control!" Abby interrupted. "I want to be able to control the change, to control when and what I see… I wouldn't be so overwhelmed if I could see things coming before they got to me, or if I knew where it was going to take me before I got there!"

"All right. Let's see if we can establish who or what this is inside of you. There is a way to find a grounding—a foundation that is strong and secure—like a place where you can always get back to yourself. A place that is only for and about you." Stump paused and rubbed his hands together. "So, are you ready?"

Abby nodded and rubbed her hands together, too.

Stump laughed, then began again. "Why don't you start by telling me what happens when you touch other people."

Abby wrung her hands and looked back at Stump, miserable. "You mean like when I did what I did with you the other night? When we first met?"

"That's right. Let's start there." Stump sat up straighter and gently smiled, nodding his head, waiting for Abby to continue.

Abby relaxed, and then it all came flooding out. "Well first things first—I didn't do anything. I mean it wasn't me that started it or bid it come. It just happens whether I want it to or not. And that's when...that's when I feel the fold open up to me. I see things. I get glimpses of a person's life. Their memories. Their joys and sorrows. The things that happened to them in their past that made them what they are today. Sometimes they are terrible things. But sometimes it is beautiful. The things that occur that can shape and mold them...The choices they made. But, not always the choices they made in this life. Sometimes... sometimes I see what *could* have been—like if they had made a different choice or done something differently. And then I see them in their present, you know? How everything connects and comes together in the present moment, and it's like...like an explosion of possibilities, and only one thread is the real one, you know? The one convergence of probabilities that is true in this life, in this time we have together right now."

Abby paused to gather her breath, and Stump quietly asked, "Convergence? You learn them big words in school?"

"No, wait, wait!" Abby waved her hand dismissively. "Don't get me off track! Now, that's part of it too. It's like the words and ideas come to me through a direct download. A download from God. And that's how I know things that I know, why I see the things that I see. It's why most of the other kids think I'm a freak. I don't talk or think like them. But the download just comes to me and takes over! I can't help but see things about people's lives— things a decent person maybe ought not to see." And here Abby paused to glance at Stump guiltily. "But then there's people like Olivia. She doesn't judge or condemn me for the way I am. She celebrates it. And oh, Stump! I get so discombobulated. So easily distracted. I had something else I was trying to say!"

Abby paused to gather her breath and calm herself. Stump patiently waited until she composed herself and got back on track.

"It's not just the past and present," Abby began in almost a whisper. "But all of the future too! Especially for the folks I truly care about and know better—the ones I love, like Momma Bea or Olivia. I see them through the folds of time and follow each of the actions and consequences that each person can play out in an infinite number of ways, and it's mind boggling, because it all happens so fast—in a blur, and all at once—but I can track it and see it through to the various ends. I don't know how or why, but I can. And there are infinite possibilities, minor and extreme variations... some more powerful and recurring. And it's the ones that recur that are most interesting because I can start to see the patterns. In the patterns there are constants. More permanent things about a person—their character and their habits. Their core values. Things that aren't always taught but are just a part of their nature. You know? The way their energy flows, that's where their mind and body goes, more often than not. And it is so strong in some people—like Olivia. She is so solid and true! And then there are some that just have power, like what's in you."

Abby stopped, and they sat in silence for a while. At length, Stump spoke, his voice low but steady.

"First," he began, "this is not something that comes to you unbidden. It isn't something that is separate... It is very much a part of you—as much as your arm is part of your body or your fingers a part of your hand. So, that means that you can control it."

"Okay, but how? I mean, I don't know what or how I'm gonna do something until I'm already doing it!"

Stump held up his hand, before continuing. "In time. In time. You will learn how to control it, shape it, and become the master of it. Right now, without an extreme trigger from outside forces or circumstances—like what happened to you at lunch when them bullies and hooligans got a hold of ya— without something like that, your powers won't come forth."

Stump paused to let his words sink in. "Second," he began again, "in terms of what I can see—what folks like me can see—and there are quite a few of us—now that's what we call the second sight. You've got it in spades, from the look of ya! The second sight reveals the way a person's soul-fire can signify and show itself. Now, it ain't no "power" like what you called it, but it's a gift, or maybe more like natural skill that's handed down genetically. My momma had it, and her momma before her, and so on. I reckon your momma has it, too. Now, that skill means that you are open and exposed to… what did you call it? The Fold? I kind of like that… So, folks like us, we are open to the Fold and all of them signals and pictures you keep talking about—it's the world of spirit and imagination. Of other worlds. Other realities. Of what could be. Of what wants to be. Oh, yes, and there are some powerful things out there that want to be, yes indeed."

Stump stopped and suddenly rummaged through an old military style shoulder bag that was in a pile of sundries next to him. "But that's not all," he spoke as he continued to rifle through the contents of the bag. "No, ma'am. That's not everything, at all. Them other worlds. They are just as real as this one. Ah!" He exclaimed as he pulled from the bag what he was searching for.

The object appeared to be a claw or a tooth from some large animal, but it was blackened as if by weather and age. It hung from a leather cord like some sort of necklace.

"Now this," Stump continued, "belonged to my Granny Jane. It's a bear's claw, but it ain't like no bear claw from around here in these parts. That's because it comes from one of those other worlds."

He held it out to Abby. "Go ahead, take it. Feel it." Abby hesitated then took the claw into her hand. She caressed it between her finger and her thumb. It was cool and smooth like a stone. There was something vaguely familiar about it.

"There is power in an object," Stump intoned reverently. "Especially one that has travelled. Crossed over."

"Crossed over?" Abby asked, still studying the item, a tingly tickle of awe beginning to creep down her neck. An image of a jungle and a spider's web appeared in her mind.

"That's right. Travelled here from another world." Stump held up his hand before Abby could interrupt. "Now, I'm going to put this on you, around your neck." He gently took it from her hands and place it around her neck. It hung down lightly, cool against the skin of her sternum. "And it is from this point on going to be yours…"

Abby tensed and tried to take it off from her neck. "Stump, no… I couldn't. It's too valuable… it, it belongs to you, and it's from your family."

Stump grabbed her wrists to keep her from removing the precious necklace. "Now, listen here, I don't have no children of my own. And I ain't likely to start making them any time soon! Ha! I've been waiting for the right time—the right person to come along so I could pass it on. That would be you. I've kept it long enough." He placed a finger over Abby's lips and with his other hand he gently enclosed her fist around the claw. "Ain't no use protesting. It's already done."

They looked at each other for several moments until Stump smiled and spoke again. "Now, I'm going to tell you the story behind this object, and that way we will have made it your own. You will have the responsibility to care for it, and to carry it with you. Maybe add a few things of your own to its story, all in good time."

He sat back and smiled broadly, that same infectious grin that made Abby chortle herself. "So, first to the science of things!" Stump launched into his speech with renewed vigor. "A while back before my vagabond days, I had that bear claw carbon-dated by a friend of mine used to work over at the university. Anthropology department. He specialized in archeological digs. That claw tested no older than 100 years. A 100-year old claw, from an animal that has not existed on this planet for over 10,000 years!" Abby's eyes widened as Stump continued.

"Now, you may ask yourself: How can that be? Did this bear claw travel through time from our own historical past? Or did it come from another world, a world much like ours, but different? Maybe a world where such a bear still lives and has not become extinct. Either way," Stump paused for dramatic effect, "it's a marvelous thing."

Abby picked up the claw and studied it again. It was now warm in her fingers from the heat of her skin. Its polished surface seemed to almost glow.

"Second thing!" Stump resumed. "That bear claw was brought to me by my Granny Jane."

"Round face, white dress. She has your smile," Abby interjected.

"Yes, that would be the one. Now, you may ask, how did she come by such a thing?" And here Stump paused, looking off into space like he was seeing some other landscape beyond the Superdome's parking lot. His eyes got all watery, and several moments passed.

"Well," Abby grew impatient at stump's deliberate and dramatic reverie. "Go on! Answer the question for crying out loud!"

Stump finally snapped out of it and looked at Abby with a chuckle. "You gonna need to learn some patience, girl, mm-mmm! If you ever gonna control that dragon of yours, you will need to start with patience." He smiled, and Abby, still exasperated, shrugged and rolled her eyes.

"You know, my Granny Jane," Stump began like he was changing the subject. "She is not a part of this world, anymore."

"Is she dead now?" Abby asked.

Stump slowly nodded his head. "Some would say that. On the day she *died*," and here Stump made little quotation signs with his fingers around the word *died*, "she wandered off into the bayou. She gave me this necklace just before she left, and she had said that she was going to go back to her forest of the bear—where the claw had come from. She had a lover waiting there for her."

"You mean like heaven? The afterlife?" But as soon as she said it, Abby knew that was not the right question. With a sudden and alarming clarity, Abby knew that this bear claw had belonged to the Elder named Bo M'ba Nesh.

"Well, now, that's the thing," Stump was continuing. "That's what most people want to say she meant." Stump turned to look directly at Abby. "But if that's what she meant, then I think that's what she would have said. But she didn't use those words. She said what she said. And then she went away—she walked off into the bayou, and she just didn't come back. She disappeared."

"You mean she walked out there and she died." Abby didn't ask, it was a statement.

Stump shook his head and hemmed and hawed a little bit before replying. "Well, no, I mean she disappeared. They never found her. Her body anyway. Most folks think she went out there to die. That the swamp claimed her."

"But that's not what you think, is it?" Abby asked, a trickle of apprehension started creeping down her spine again. She could see the face of Stump's Granny Jane, standing there in her white dress. She was same woman as the elder who sat at her weaving loom, only the Granny Jane version did not have the spider web scars across her face.

Stump stared back at her, slowly smiling. "What I think... what I think is what I needed to tell you. We've come full circle, you see. This ain't just one big rambling perambulation of frivolousness. It's all related. To you and what you can do. To that foundation that will always bring you back to yourself."

Abby shook her head, confused, "I don't follow..."

"Yes, you do follow, or you will!" Stump was heated now with an odd zeal that had replaced his previous calm. "What I am trying to say is that Granny Jane didn't die. She crossed over. She travelled. She left this place for that place," and he pointed to the necklace around her neck. "Where this comes from. And all them pictures and them signs you see about other people and their lives? Well, those aren't just pictures or memories or possibilities for things that may or may not ever come to be. Those are real places, Abby. Other worlds—not just of the mind but actual physical places. All of them contained in the Fold, as you so aptly put it. And," Stump raised his finger to punctuate his point. "And, if you meditate and practice your gift of... activation—yes, that's what we will call it: Activation. And if you master this gift of activation, then you too can cross over—you can travel to those other worlds in this physical body. Like my Granny Jane."

Abby was stunned, her mind refusing to accommodate such an idea. "But... that... that's impossible..." Her voice faded away. She had already been travelling to those places, but Abby had thought that it had been only in her dreams. Dreams she could never quite remember.

What Stump was suggesting seemed... outrageous. Startling and outrageous. "That's impossible," Abby repeated again, barely a whisper.

Stump smiled and said smugly, "This from the girl who turns into a dragon." They looked at each other for a while—the one a superior grin pasted across his face, the other with her mind whirling. At length, Stump asked quietly,

"Have you ever wondered why it's a dragon that you called down from that tornado storm? Why is it a dragon, and not something else? Like, say, another person? Wouldn't that be easier for the rest of us? Easier for you?"

Abby shook her head, "I didn't call the dragon—she chose me, and I chose her. She already existed within me. Always has. I just didn't know it until we got together over a little storm. And it ain't about what's easy. It's about what it is. And sometimes what it is can't be explained. It is just plain hard."

Stump's smile widened. "Ah, and this you know with such conviction. Such certainty." Abby smiled back at him, and nodded, understanding slowly spreading. Stump continued, "It isn't always ours to ask why, but to simply know that something simply is. And you, my dear, most definitely *are*! And that is the foundation, the constant that you must always remember. No matter what world you may pass into, no matter what time—you are the constant, Abby. You are the one who always remains the same and true to herself."

Abby closed her eyes as Stump's words sunk in. He continued, "And the fact that you chose the dragon, or that the dragon chose you..."

"We chose each other!" Abby opened her eyes and corrected stump's narrative with a wicked smile.

"Right," Stump chuckled. "Well, that's the part that this world maybe still needs to figure out—what you need to figure out first! Worlds collide, and one only crosses over when there is deep and powerful purpose at hand." Stump nodded, more to himself than anything else. "Deep and powerful purpose, yessir!" He looked down to gaze directly back at Abby. "Yes, ma'am! Most people would say that there are no dragons in this world, and yet, here you are. You might accept it as completely normal. But for everyone else, you have come from another world."

"I'm beginning to understand," Abby said, still smiling. "You have taught me something, and you have helped me considerably, you silly old bear."

"I love Winnie the Pooh! How did you know?" Stump screamed into the night, and they both laughed riotously. "Let's continue this conversation later. Enough of the lessons for now. You have discovered what it means to be the constant one. The foundation. That is certainly enough for one night. I think it's time we should have another bite to eat and tell each other more stories."

"Oh, second breakfast? My favorite!"

"Right, whatever you just said," Stump laughed and shook his head, and started to put out their plates from their earlier hot dog feast. The plates were mostly clean, anyway.

And so the evening went. They dined on the day-old pastries that the coffee shops and bakeries always throw out (if you know where to find them), and Abby spent half the night talking about her many sojourns and adventures in the bayou swamp lands. Stump had not spent any time at all out in nature, which Abby found absolutely unpardonable for a native of New Orleans and the grandson of Granny Jane, so she right there and then made a promise to him that she would give him a personal tour of her favorite places. Stump proved to be an exemplary audience, politely asking for clarifications or expanded nuances of particular details. He was riveted by her stories and vivid descriptions. He laughed and hooted when Abby told him about Olivia's brief encounter with the gators, and he demanded that she tell the story all over again so that he could commit it to memory.

Before she even realized it, it was late in the evening, and heavy eyes beckoned for sleep. Stump told her not to worry. He would stand guard against the "hobgoblins and hooligans of the night."

So, feeling very unwashed and slightly sticky, she curled up on Stump's old blanket and fell asleep. She woke once in the night—some sound or commotion had caused her to stir—and she looked around in the dim light to find Stump standing, peering through the bushes, baseball bat in hand. He turned back to glance at her, smile and wink, before returning his attention to whatever lay beyond the bushes. Abby soon fell back to sleep, and the rest of the night passed without any incident.

Abby woke late in the morning to find Stump had been away and returned with plates of red beans and rice ("from the Mission," he had said.) Her growling stomach gratefully received the meal. It was still hot and surprisingly good.

Not much later, Stump dozed off to sleep, and Abby started feeling restless. A whole day and night had gone by, and there was still no word from Olivia. Her absence did not bode well, as far as Abby was concerned, and she had half a mind to find her way back to Houma before the deep doo-doo she was in got any deeper.

By mid-day, Abby's stomach was grumbling, she really wanted a shower, and even worse, she needed to go to the bathroom—number two this time. She thought about waking Stump, who was still out cold, snoring like a severely congested grizzly bear, but then she remembered that he had probably been up most of the night protecting her, and she thought better of the idea. So, driven mostly by hunger and the need to relieve herself, Abby quietly stepped around Stump and emerged from their little clearing.

She paused to assess her surroundings and found it quiet and mostly uneventful. There were a few older people nearby the dumpster—homeless by the look of them, but they weren't paying her no never-mind. She glanced up at the sky and could see dark clouds forming. There was a sniff of rain in the air. She decided it wisest to move right away or she was going to get wet. She headed south beneath the Expressway overpass and away from the Superdome. Traffic was light on the surrounding streets, and she turned down Claiborne Street, walked past a Home Depot, then double-backed to go inside.

Home Depots have toilets.

She found the bathroom and was shocked to see her reflection in the mirror. Her hair was a mess, her face streaked with dirt, her blouse soiled and rumpled, and she pretty much looked like the homeless child that she had become. She washed up, ran her fingers through her hair as a makeshift comb, and at last deemed herself presentable. As she left the Home Depot, the greeter person at the door, a middle-aged woman with gold-rimmed batwing glasses, eyed her suspiciously and said,

"Shouldn't you be in school, young lady?"

Abby returned her stare but had to smile, the woman's face was pinched so severely in disapproval as to be comical. She waved bye-bye as she walked through the glass exit doors, whistling the "Hole in my Bucket" song that Stump had relentlessly seared into her brain.

As she walked away, however, her chipper mood was replaced by a darker thought. Of course, she *should* be in school! She should also be home at night sleeping in her own bed with Momma Bea and mean old Henry watching Wheel of Fortune on the TV. And she could take a shower! A sweet, sweet shower.

She made up her mind right there and then. She would be home by dinner time tonight. She just needed to get to a phone and make the call. Momma Bea was no doubt worried sick! Abby was already in a heap of trouble. And the longer she went a-missing, the deeper in it she would be. Her lessons and meditations on the multiverse and crossing over like Granny Jane could wait for another time. She would go back to the Superdome parking lot and say goodbye—a temporary goodbye—to Stump, and thank him, of course. She paused and felt the truth of Stump inside of her. She just knew they would meet again and continue their conversations. But for today, she would wait until sundown for Olivia to come back.

If she came back. The more she thought about it, the more deeply disturbed Abby became. That Olivia had still not made an appearance could only be a disaster. She knew her friend, and she knew that Olivia was always a girl who kept her word. The only reason that she hadn't come back was because somebody or something had prevented her from coming.

Another loud grumble from her stomach brought her back to a more immediate concern: Food! She started walking faster now, leaning forward with her head down to counter the stiff wind that had kicked up. Rain for sure was coming. She glanced up to see a bus just pulling out of a stop a few blocks down the road. Some folks had just gotten off, a group of young professionals, and they were laughing and walking across the street into a Rally's. *Mmm. A Burger and a Shake.* Her step quickened and her stomach gurgled in response.

Standing at the counter, she reached in her pocket and found that she had less than 5 dollars. Momma Bea had given her more than enough for one lunch on the day of the museum trip. She hadn't been planning on a second meal. A quick survey of the lunch menu, and Abby could see that she needed to make a choice: She had enough money for a cheeseburger, or she could get fries and a vanilla shake. The young woman behind the counter looked at her like she was a little bug behind a magnifying glass.

"I'm not usually one to dawdle," Abby explained with a weak smile. The woman's expression did not change. *Not exactly hospitable*, Abby thought.

A few minutes later, Abby had a window table and was watching the rain drip against it, sucking sweet vanilla ice cream shake through an inadequately narrow straw. The choice was easy, actually. And she made sure that the woman saw her take extra catsup for her fries, her innocent smile as beguiling and charming as ever.

She glanced over by the bathroom door. A pay phone was on the wall, and that was a good thing. Now that everybody had their own cell phones, the coin-operated public phones were hard to find. She took out all of the change in her pocket: sixty-seven cents. Was that even enough to make a phone call to Houma? Was it cheaper to call at night? Abby had no idea. She wolfed down the last of her fries, grabbed her shake and headed out. Stump would know. And she needed to get back to him anyway. It wasn't nice to leave people without telling them where you were going or when you'd be back.

And that was the one thought that repeated in her brain as she strode with purpose, in a light rain, back toward the Superdome. *Don't leave folks without telling them where you were going or when you'd be back.* And that was exactly what she had done—to everybody.

"Is he like this all day?" Olivia asked quietly. She was squatting next to Stump, who was still out like a drunken walrus, snuffling and snoring in oblivious abandon.

Abby had just parted the hedge and whisked her way into their clearing, startled to see Olivia calmly waiting there. Her concern over Stump had been unfounded, apparently. Obviously, he did like to sleep in the daytime, like he said.

"All day, every day," Abby responded with a wry smile. She squatted down next to Olivia. They spoke softly over Stump's snoozing body. "He really is just a big harmless old bear."

"Yes, indeed," Olivia said. "You're lucky that he found you...or that you found him. I'm not sure which."

"Doesn't matter," Abby sighed. "We were meant to find each other. In this moment. This time and place. That is a truth I feel inside my very bones." She glanced over at Olivia, whose frizzy red hair was neatly pulled back with a hair comb. She was freshly scrubbed and radiant, in a Saint's jersey and matching gold and black sweat pants.

"Not fair," Abby intoned. "You've taken a bath and smell like coconuts. Me," and here Abby paused to take a dramatic whiff beneath her armpit. "I feel like a wet hound dog, and I smell like rotten eggs."

Olivia laughed, "Like one of them Chinese eggs been buried in cow shit for thousands of years."

"Aw, c'mon! Abby laughed despite herself. "I'm not that bad!" She pushed Olivia off of her haunches and on to her butt. Her friend had pulled her jersey up over her nose and was waving the air in front of her with dramatic intensity.

Stump snorted then grumbled something about duck fat lattes before rolling over and resuming his snoring. Both Abby and Olivia had to bite their hands to keep from laughing too loudly. In a few moments, they settled down and just stared at each other. Abby plopped on to her butt and took a deep breath. At least inside of her sanctuary it was warmer, and it was dry. She listened and could hear the rain tick against the leaves of the hedge and patter metallically off the nearby dumpster.

They both suddenly tried to speak at once, and Olivia waved her hand again and said, "Oh no, I insist. You first. Dragons before beauty!"

"Yeah, right." Abby drawled before sobering up. She looked long and hard at Olivia before starting in. "What took you so long? I've had like a billion butterflies in my stomach for the past day and a half! I thought you had been grounded or put in jail, maybe tied up somewhere because I know that only something like that would keep you from coming back to me."

"Well, you got that right!" Olivia exclaimed. "Believe me, I would have come back right away, but I couldn't." Olivia was suddenly very solemn, so serious that Abby felt her gut tighten like a corded knot.

"It's bad, A.B.. Real bad," Olivia continued. "I was practically grounded for life just as soon as I got home. And well, that was just about what I expected. But what's really bad is that you can't go back home—not for a while anyway."

And here Olivia reached across and squeezed Abby's arms. The knot in Abby's stomach got a lot tighter.

Olivia took a moment to gather herself before continuing. "I don't know how to say this, so I'm just gonna say it straight out. They've taken your momma and that old sour-faced Henry away. The police, I mean. They blocked off your driveway with that yellow tape like it was some kind of crime scene."

"They took Momma Bea away? What for? She ain't done nothing wrong!" Abby was suddenly angry and boiling up on the inside.

Olivia held up her hands and shushed Abby. "Now hang on! Hang on! I ain't even close to finished yet! Let me tell you what else I know." Olivia paused and bit her lip before continuing. "Them police... They were all over your neighborhood. And they weren't alone neither. There was these folks from the county and the state. Maybe even the FBI! Doctors and special investigator agents. They even came to my home and asked questions. Scared my momma half to death!"

Abby was suddenly very still, but her mind was racing. "What kind of questions were they asking?"

"I'm getting there." Olivia snapped, losing her patience. "I was about to tell you, sheesh! Can't a girl tell her story in her own way?" Olivia shrugged and stared back at Abby imploringly.

Abby waved her hand, half-way exacerbated herself. "Go on, then," Abby said trying to calm herself.

"The first thing, of course," Olivia continued matter-of-factly, "is that they was all looking for you! They wanted to know where you got your weapon..."

"I ain't got no weapon!" Abby interrupted, beside herself.

"Well, yeah," Olivia smirked and shrugged, "You gonna go downtown and tell them that? Tell them what really happened?" Olivia paused and waited, staring at Abby who just bit her lip and glanced away.

"I didn't think so!" Olivia resumed, leaning forward earnestly. "But listen! They was saying things like you assaulted Julia. You know, that it was you who attacked her. As if that is even close to what happened! But that's what they're saying and apparently that little witch, Julia is saying it's true. So now, you are officially some kind of fugitive. You might be a danger to others or even to yourself. Hang on!"

Olivia held up her hand as Abby gathered her breath to interrupt. "Let me finish, okay?" She glared back at Abby until her friend nodded for her to continue.

"Thank you. Now, that's not all. So, after they talked to just about everyone in your neighborhood, took away your momma and Henry, and put up that awful crime scene tape all around your house, I heard my momma talking to her friend. They said that your momma and Henry were arrested for criminal negligence and some kind of fraudulent activity over your adoption papers… and they also was saying that they could go to jail for reckless child endangerment—whatever the hell that means. And even worse. Back in school today, Balt Luster, that big cry-baby, he was all coming up to me like he ain't never been nothing but the best of friends, and he said that the police had also spoken to him and his family. He told me them county officials were telling his mom that your folks might be accomplished to your crime! That they helped you do it or forced you into doing it because they abused or molested you and did unspeakable things to make you into some sort of crazy child."

"Accomplice. It's an accomplice to the crime." Abby corrected Olivia, before continuing. "But that's just plum crazy. Those things might have happened to him—for sure they did! But nothing like that ever happened to me! Oh, Henry, he likes to drink and run around town doing god-knows-what, and he sometimes looks at me all creepy-like, but he never done anything to hurt me. And Momma Bea? Why, that's just full-on fabrication to say those things about her. She's the most decent human being I know!"

She paused to catch her breath and wring her hands. "Oh, Olivia, this is terrible. Just terrible." Abby scrambled to stand up. "I got to go talk to them. I got to get Momma Bea out of there…wherever it is that they got her. Oh Olivia! What am I gonna do?"

Olivia had stood up with her and was tugging on her arm to keep her from running out of their camp.

"Hold on now, young ladies." They both froze and turned back to see Stump had risen to a seated position and was fixing them with a glittering gaze. Apparently, he wasn't as asleep as the girls thought he was. "Don't be going all willy-nilly, you hear?" He beckoned for them to sit down, which they promptly did.

Stump cleared his throat before continuing, "Now, first things first. You!" And he pointed at Abby. "Stay seated and be quiet. You're not going anywhere just yet. And you!" He looked at Olivia, and he smiled to ease the tension in the air. "Little miss grounded. I got questions for you."

Both girls sat down. He waited a few moments to glance back and forth between the girls, who remained silent. Satisfied, Stump held Olivia's gaze and continued, "Now, about your story—that's all well and good. I believe everything that you said. A little girl goes missing, and well, that tends to get the attention of all kinds of folks, and you bet. County and state officials are gonna want to be involved. Especially around here in these days. And all those other things that you heard folks talking? Mostly nonsense and idle speculation. Folks like to gossip in the absence of facts. But I want to know something else, Miss Olivia Fist. You say you was grounded, that the police was everywhere and all over the place?" Olivia nodded.

Stump continued, "Then how you manage to make your way all the way back here from your home? Hmm? How did you get away without your folks and all them police knowing?"

Olivia slapped her knee and snorted. "You go on!" She laughed at Stump and turned to wink at Abby. "It's not like they put me under arrest. Lordy, I still had to get up and go to school today. In fact, it's even better than that! She reached into her pocket and pulled out a new iPhone. She held it up proudly for Abby and Stump to see. "My momma was so worried about my safety, that she gave me my very own, brand-spankin' new iPhone! It's Christmas come early! She said that I have to call or text her to let her know where I'm at all times." She paused and smiled conspiratorially. "But don't worry. I haven't used this phone for anything. I texted my mom once, so she thinks I'm still at school, so…"

"Shit howdy!" Stump suddenly sprang to his feet. He grabbed his baseball bat and grimaced. "They know that you're Abby's best friend, Olivia. Ain't no early Christmas gift reason for you to have that phone. They know that you would come looking for her, and …"

"And that you would lead them straight to me," Abby finished Stump's sentence for him.

As if it were a perfect punctuation to her sentence, the sound of several car doors shutting echoed across the parking lot. Abby peered through the hedge and could see blue and red lights flashing in reflection off the dumpster bin and the puddles of rain that had formed on the asphalt.

Stump turned to Abby and hoarsely shouted, "Abby, run!" He parted the hedge and stepped out into the parking lot. Abby grabbed her bag and with one glance at Olivia, she darted out the other way, hugging close to the wall.

"I'm sorry, A.B.!" Olivia cried. "I didn't know!"

Abby burst through the hedge, scratching her face in her haste. She took two steps and froze as men in suits in another car skidded to a stop next to the wall and piled out of the car. She turned to look back toward the dumpster, and she saw Stump, brandishing his baseball bat as three Sheriff deputies, guns pointed directly at him slowly approached, all business. A crowd of homeless onlookers had gathered behind them. It was exactly what she had seen in her earlier vision with Stump.

It was all happening in slow motion: Stump turning to look back at her, smiling, then turning back toward the approaching deputies. Stump taking one step toward them, then flinching as if to swing his bat.

"Stump, NO!!" Abby cried out just before the gunshot fired. Olivia screamed, and two more shots rang out in rapid succession. Abby watched as Stump fell, twisting toward the asphalt. His body landed soundlessly as the baseball bat struck the ground and woodenly thunked and drummed till it rolled to a stop. Horrified, Abby tried to move toward him just as hands came from behind to hold her fast.

Then there were more deputies, men in suits, a woman leading a shocked and tearful Olivia out from behind the hedge. A crowd of onlookers, the homeless denizens of the nearby camps, gathering to gawk and twitter. Somebody, a deputy, was barking out orders, telling everyone to stand back. Just stand back.

Struggling in the arms of an agent, Abby slowly began to wail as she stared at the unmoving form of Stump, the harmless old bear, his face turned back toward her, his chest was heaving in slow, labored breaths, his eyes dimming. The rain began to fall heavier now, and big drops pattered and bounced off his face. He smiled, the white of his teeth reflecting in the deep crimson blood that pooled around his head. And then he wasn't moving any more.

II

WARD OF THE STATE

AWAKENED

From the Audio transcripts of Dr. Joanna Kinsey
Chief Psychiatrist, CHNOLA Northshore Center,
New Orleans, LA

Excerpt of Audio File Transcript #AR10089-42

Jul 1, 2022

Subject: A. B. Rubideaux. Female. Age: 11

Transcript of recording begins: 9:56 AM EST.

Kinsey: *I have to admit something to you, A.B.. I've not been entirely honest with you.*

A.B.: *I could say that I'm not entirely surprised, but you know that already, don't you?*

Kinsey: *I'm serious. A.B.. Please, hear me out. I am always honest with you when we speak. The things we speak about are completely confidential. I would never betray your trust.*

A.B.: *I know that, Joanna.*

Kinsey: *What I haven't been honest about, completely, is the fact that I've kept some things away from you. I want to explain those things to you now, so hear me out. (Long pause.) I've run several tests, as you know. The results have come back, and it's very clear. You're not mentally ill. At least that is my determination after looking for all of the traditional, standard measurements for how we determine such a thing. Your brain is amazing and unique, yes. Your blood tests? Well I can't even imagine how that doesn't show up in your medical records—what little we could find any way.*

A.B.: *Momma Bea don't like doctors.*

Kinsey: *Well, that might very well be. Not surprising that you would never have had access or any reason to take these kinds of tests. But I have done them for you.*

And despite the chemical activity and signs of lesion or disruption that might, under usual circumstances, indicate a paranoid or schizophrenic personality, I have determined that there is no behavioral evidence of that. There are other things, however... things that we can't explain. There is no precedent for someone like you. It's not just your bloodwork and your CAT scans. Your charts are beyond anything I or anyone else has ever seen. You're a modern medical anomaly.

A.B.: *(Giggling.) I'm sorry, doctor. (More giggling.). (Singing.) I am the very model of a modern medical anomaly!*

Kinsey: *(Laughs, briefly.) Yes, and that's just it. I did that show in my middle school, many years ago, in a wealthy suburb of Alexandria, Virginia. But of course, how would you know that? You, I'm pretty sure, have never encountered Gilbert and Sullivan before. So, there you go, saying things and knowing things that you simply shouldn't know or have any inkling about. You have proven this to me again and again.*

A.B. *Do you mean to say, doctor, that you are coming to believe that I might be telling you the truth?*

Kinsey: *Well, that may be one of the reasons we've changed our venue today. But what I believe in this instant, is irrelevant. You have some very special visitors today. Folks that really want to talk to you.*

A.B.: *Those wouldn't happen to be the Men in Black characters that arrived in those very American cars with the government plates, would it? (Giggle.) I saw them earlier from my window. I watch, you know. Who comes in and out of the building. It helps to pass the time.*

Kinsey: *Well, I imagine so. And yes, our visitors do happen to be from the FBI.*

A.B.: *They're not going to poke me, are they? Stick needles in my arms or probe my various orifices? Extract tissue samples?*

Kinsey: *A.B., please. I'm going to be right here with you. I would never let them do anything like that to you.*

A.B.: Yeah, until they take me away. Which you know they will, doctor. Joanna. He has authority and a different set of rules. There is nothing you can do to stop him.

Kinsey: Not a chance, A.B.. They are doctors like me. They specialize in abnormal psychiatry. They are here at my request, in fact.

A.B.: (Long Silence.) I guess that part about confidentiality just went out the window, then. It's okay, Joanna.

Kinsey: A.B., I asked them to come here because they can help.

A. B.: Help who? You or me?

Kinsey: Well, both of us, I guess.

A. B.: I thought you understood by now.

Kinsey: I'm sorry?

A.B.: That you won't find any answers by talking to me or doing more tests on me. If you really want to discover what is going on, let me show you. (Long Pause.) All you have to do is take my hands, Joanna. We could start by talking to the very biosphere itself.

Kinsey: (Chuckling.) A.B., I am not a shaman. I don't know how to do that.

A.B.: Yes, you are. And yes, you do. You have approximately one hundred thousand billion cells in your human body--that's a hundred and twenty-five billion miles of DNA just inside of you alone! Your personal DNA strands are long enough to wrap around the earth five million times. All of it connected to the biosphere, and to the Fold. You are constantly interlinked to the biosphere. You are constantly talking to the multiverse.

Kinsey: Well, right about now, we are both interlinked with a government agency. Hold that thought, A.B.. I would like you to have this discussion with our friends from the FBI. Are you okay with that?

A.B.: *Oh, this should be fun! But, Joanna?*

Kinsey: *Yes?*

A.B.: *You should always remember one thing. (Long Silence.) These people are not your friends.*

38 DAYS EARLIER: MAY 24, 2022

You haven't really hit rock bottom until you spend a few nights in a detention center with two other girls—a severely unstable 15-year old crackhead and a pregnant kleptomaniac. The kleptomaniac may have been 12 or 13—trying very hard to act 16.

The past two days had been a blur for Abby. The deputies who drove her to the holding facility were stoic and tight-lipped. Neither one of them had been the one who shot Stump, and she was grateful for that.

Stump. After they took her to the squad car, she sat in the back staring out the window. He just lay there on the pavement, glassy-eyed and unmoving. It was the exact same image that flashed through her mind when she first shook his hand a few days before. It wasn't the kind of image she wanted to see again—all that blood, the rain falling down... and inexplicably, incongruently, Stump weirdly smiling. When the paramedics came and lifted him on a stretcher into the ambulance, she was relieved to see him taken out of her sight.

He was dead. They had shot and killed him for no good reason.

And then there was Olivia, who had been led away to another car, which was unmarked and driven by a lady in a suit. As the car pulled away, Olivia turned and slowly waved through the back window. Abby waved back, but found herself fighting back tears, suddenly overwhelmed by all of the shocking events and the uncertainties that lay ahead. She hadn't seen her friend since then. No word. Nothing. Not even about her family.

Her own car ride was uneventful. They checked her into a juvenile detention center somewhere in the Ninth Ward. It was late afternoon and she sat in the office for what seemed like hours while they "processed" her. A female guard came in and gave her a tray for dinner—some kind of meat casserole with powdery mashed potatoes and inedible, overboiled, and very sad green beans.

She spent the first night in a cell with the aforementioned girls. When she was first ushered into the room, a windowless 15 by 12-foot cell with institutional light green walls, two steel-framed bunk beds, and really bright fluorescent lights. The two girls were already inside.

"Don't even think about it, Lizzy," the hulking female guard who brought Abby into the room barked, as the crackhead had jumped up and snarled at Abby when they entered.

The guard pointed her stick at Lizzy, who smiled, muttered "Fresh meat," and sat back down on her bed.

"Who you bring in here now?" The other obviously pregnant girl drawled in a thick Cajun accent. She rubbed her extended belly and smiled at Abby and looked her up and down. "She not much more than skin and bones. You reckon I can eat her dinner if she don't want it?"

"Stow it, Ms. Germaine," The guard replied humorlessly. "Don't start in with any of your lip. You two just leave her be."

"Aw, Officer Mills, why you always do me like that?" The pregnant one teased, not taking her eyes off Abby. "You know I got two to feed?" She patted her belly and leered at Abby.

"Stow it." The officer replied evenly, jutting out her chin. She stared down Ms. Germaine, who pouted and returned to her bed. Then the officer turned to Abby.

"Pick your bed. Doesn't matter which. These two start any trouble," and she pointed with her stick at a camera above the door, "we're not far away." Then she pointed at a button on the wall next to the door. "You need to use the bathroom or need something for an emergency, you press that." She turned and glowered at the other two girls. "And that's just for emergencies, not foolish requests, Ms. Germaine." She turned back to Abby, and something like a smile flitted briefly across her face. "It will be lights out at ten PM, which is coming up soon. Meals at seven, 12, and six. But I don't expect you'll be here all that long."

As the guard turned to leave, Ms. Germaine piped up, "Why you say that, Deputy Mills? Why she so special? You got a special suite waiting for her? With a little Chicken Etouffee? Coffee and a nice omelette? Why don't I get a nice omelette? Why she so special, eh? Eh?"

The door closed behind the exiting deputy, and Ms. Germaine turned to Abby, "Why you so special, eh?"

"Omelette," the crackhead called Lizzie murmured.

Abby stood next to the door and silently regarded the girls. She still felt itchy and sticky from her two nights on the street, but she felt a might bit cleaner than the girls who now kept her company. They both wore drab, light brown institutional pants and blouses, and they looked unwashed and decidedly apathetic regarding their lack of hygiene.

"What you do to find your way in here?" The girl called Ms. Germaine asked.

"She's a real killer, this one. I think she's dangerous." Lizzy chimed in from her bed, then chuckled.

"Right, she's a killer all right." Ms. Germaine agreed with a smile. "Killer of spiders, flies, and cockroaches. That's your job while you in here with me and Lizzy. You got bug duty. But don't eat 'em. You give 'em to Lizzy over there." She smiled and held out her hand. "Eloise Germaine. Kleptomaniac and teenage catalogue bride."

Abby stared at her outstretched hand. She didn't take it. She looked up into Eloise's eyes. "Abby. Destroyer of restaurant property and recently detained vagabond." She glanced down at Eloise's outstretched hand. "I don't touch other people," Abby explained looking stoically into her eyes.

The girl called Lizzy whistled and slapped her thighs. Eloise brought her hand dramatically up to her hair and swept the bangs away from her forehead. "I see," She said. "Never know what you might catch." She smiled humorlessly and turned to retreat back to her bed and sat down.

Abby stood and stared at the two girls who wordlessly and sullenly stared back. She looked up at the two top bunk beds, then back down at the girls.

"Which one is mine?" Abby asked.

Lizzy sprang to her feet then clambered up to the top bunk of her bed. "Mine! This one's mine." She said and glared back at Abby breathing heavily.

Abby glanced around the cell, and her eyes fell on the security camera above the door. "They watch us all the time?" She asked. Eloise nodded her head. "Seems like an invasion of privacy to me."

Lizzy snorted in disdain, and Eloise laughed before speaking. "Where you think you at, girl? You expect Hilton Club points? Fresh sheets on your bed every day? I'll put a word in with the concierge."

Lizzy snorted again then proceeded to make inarticulate animal noises while bobbing her head up and down as she glared at Abby from her perch above. Abby decided to ignore her as she went to the bed below her and plopped down, reclining with her hands clasped behind her head. She was not comfortable, and the entire bed shook and squeaked as Lizzy continued her primal dance above.

Abby closed her eyes and tried to still the anxiety that coursed through her like a jillion jolts of electricity. Her mind was racing, and she couldn't latch on to any one thought. She thought of everything that had happened over the past few days: The incident at the restaurant; her escape to the Superdome; Olivia covered in mustard; her failed transformation into a dragon. Long, wonderful conversations with Stump.

Stump.

She tried not to linger on his lifeless form lying on the pavement. Instead, she thought of his dopey and infectious smile, the hitch in his gait as he walked along, humming the "Hole in My Pocket" tune. She thought of his childhood and his wonderful performances. His grandmother in her white dress standing beneath a bayou tree draped with Spanish moss. The forest woman whom she also knew as the spider elder named Bo M'Ba Nesh.

She was a traveler.

Unconsciously, Abby reached for the bear claw that was still hanging around her neck, beneath her blouse. They had taken away all of her other belongings, but somehow, they had missed this one. Maybe it was magically cloaked. Maybe it was meant to stay with her. She felt the smooth coolness of it, and her mind grew instantly calmer. She could hear Stump's smooth, deep voice: *You are the constant Abby. You are the one who always remains true to herself.*

That's right. Abby felt the calm return to herself, and she relaxed for the first time in hours.

True, Little Sister.

The dragon's voice rumbled up from somewhere deep inside of her. It had been silent for many days, now, and Abby was beginning to wonder if her connection to it had been severed. But it was soothing to feel the presence inside of her again. Her heart fire was rekindled, and she felt the cool bear claw lying against the skin of her chest, almost like a channel, a conduit to her soul—a connection to everything that lay beyond. It had been a while since she felt that heart fire, but now she realized that the flame was there all along. She just needed to think of it, and the dragon presence filled her being.

As she lay on the lumpy, hard bed in a detention cell somewhere in the Ninth Ward of New Orleans, she knew that the answer drifted, unbidden somewhere in her mind. She was connected to the entire cosmos and the multiverse, for crying out loud. Surely it was within her power to change her situation if she could only find the thread.

The lights shut off at ten PM exactly, without warning. Abby lay there for quite a while, her mind full of questions, too tumultuous for sleep. She was trying to summon the dragon, but it seemed the harder she tried, the further away from the dragon she got.

Other thoughts kept pressing in. Maybe Stump wasn't really gone? He looked dead, for sure, but even if he was dead in this world, maybe Abby would see him again in the Fold? Was it possible?

Seeing the image of Granny Jane had uncovered her memories of living among the *Sihanaka*, the Forest people—she was from the clan of the Spider. *Halabe*. These people were governed by a council of elders, which included Bo M'Ba Nesh. But such a revelation also brought forth a flood of questions: Was Bo M'Ba Nesh really the same person as Granny Jane? How did Abby visit with her before? Was it a real place? Was it locked away in the past or did it exist in the present, too? Could she "disappear" from this cell like Granny Jane? Just fade into the fold of another world, another dimension. How did she do that? Did it take years of practice? Would she need to move to some remote mountain top and live with Buddhist monks? Is it all in the mind or did she need to call the dragon? What was the dragon and where did it come from? Was she just going out of her mind?

Crazy. She was definitely just plum crazy. But maybe you need a little bit of crazy to travel through the Fold? Maybe there are others she could call—others who might be able to help her. Like Stump or Granny Jane. Like someone who was already a creature of the Fold. Another dragon like herself? How many were out there?

And then a face suddenly appeared in her mind, like the one on the spinning tree trunk a few weeks before. It was the face of a dragon.

Yes. Many. Soon. Good.

The dragon voice rumbled deep within again, startling her. The image of the dragon face lingered, then slipped away. She wondered why the voice came when she wasn't thinking about it. What was the point of deeper meditation and focus if the voice only came when it wanted to? And now she was seeing faces, too?

At any rate, the voice was with her now. It was almost like she was getting approval. She could sense that she was on the right track. Or maybe there was evidence all around her? People open to her in ways she was yet to discover. Someone like Fina Lee, her autistic classmate whose future was to become a famous writer. Maybe Abby needed someone like Fina Lee, who lived in her own special world—maybe she was in her own particular way closer to the multiverse, more accessible to the Fold. Abby would have to meet with her and talk about it.

First, Abby would have to get out of this prison cell.

She lay awake for a while longer, and thoughts of the dragon had lulled her into a new frame of mind. She was drawing nearer to a higher level of awareness; she was on the cusp of something bigger than anything she had known before. The Fold was wide, wide open, and she now knew that it was at least possible for her to go there, into the whole of the cosmos itself, traversing space and time. Well, maybe she would start somewhere closer to home first.

Sleep came fitfully after that, and after a few blurry dreams of Stump and Olivia paddling in a boat on the bayou, her dreams took a turn that would not build on her newfound confidence. In fact, in her dreams, she was lying in a dark, cold place, being pressed down. Was that Balt Luster nearby working at a table beneath a dull green light? She could hear the metallic clang of tools, hear him breathing heavily through his nose. What was he building? She couldn't quite move her head to get a good look, for she was paralyzed from the neck down and some sort of manic, demonic voice was whispering something dark and full of terror into her mind. No, wait… this wasn't her nightmare it came from somewhere else—from somebody else.

Lizzy. The girl on the bunk bed above her. Only, she wasn't in her bed anymore.

Abby's eyes flew open, and she was wide awake instantly. Lizzie was sitting on top of her, the girl's knees pressed heavily and painfully down on Abby's shoulders. Abby was pinned down, and when she struggled to rise up, Lizzy's legs clamped down harder, immobilizing her arms at her sides. That was when Abby noticed the emery board nail file clenched tightly in the girl's hand, pointed now inches from her face, Lizzy's face gruesome and grimacing above it in the gloomy dark.

"I could take your eyeballs out in a heartbeat, meat. Try that again, and I will!"

Abby let her body go slack, all resistance melted away in an instant. Lizzy smiled gleefully.

"What do you want?" Abby asked calmly even though she was nearly overwhelmed by the intensity of emotion and hostility that was pouring from the girl and through her dragon senses. The crackhead was an agitated whirl of conflicting emotions. Through the girl's bare knees pressing down on her shoulders, Abby could feel Lizzy's whole being raging through her, transmitting thoughts and feelings in a torrent of wild images and, above all, pain. It was immediately clear to Abby that the girl was not in control of herself—there was no evident reason or compassion in her being. She was a distraught wreck of a person who used anger and aggression to cover her deeper hurts. There were very dark corners in her memories, memories that now assaulted Abby without mercy. It was all Abby could do to shut out the barrage.

"I want you to cry," Lizzy spoke through clenched teeth. "I want you to suffer."

Abby breathed deeply, calming her instinct to fight back. She knew it wouldn't go well. Lizzy was a big, strong girl. And she was full of rage, a rage born from a much deeper hurt. A lifetime of hurt. And now she wanted to let that hurt out; she wanted to put it all on someone else. So, it was no surprise that Lizzy thought she could start right in on Abby once the adult supervision had left the room, once the room had gone dark.

Abby felt the rumbling presence of the dragon deep within herself. Through a flood of images coming from Lizzy—horrible things that had eaten at her life like a vicious monster that fed on her self-esteem and her dreams—Abby struggled to find something from Lizzy that remained in the light, something pure and full of love. Anything that still held out even just a sliver of hope.

The onslaught of images continued: "You're not worthy of this, you little slut!" A woman, Lizzie's mother, holding up a spatula covered in chocolate frosting, waving it in front of Lizzy's pouting face, drops splattering on her cheek... The image was gone in a flash as Abby dismissed it. No, she wanted something free from fear, free of anger and self-loathing.

Abby went deeper, sorting through a whirl of images, more voices: the curling smoke of a crack pipe, hypnotically writhing through the air below a ceiling light; a towel snapping painfully on her bare legs—the giggling of her female tormentors echoing through a gym locker room; her dad, sitting in the cab of a large rental truck, all of his things packed, staring through the window as he backed out the driveway. "Good riddance, you prick!" Her mother mutters next to her, as Lizzy wonders if she will ever see him again.

And then there was the single pluck of a violin string. A child Lizzy, maybe eight or nine years old, at her grandparents' summer house, on a beach in Carolina—a few weeks over summer break. Her grandfather was in the parlor, tuning his violin, smiling and beckoning to the young Lizzy.

"You want to make some music?" Her grandfather asked, beckoning her from the darkness near a stairwell. His hands were leathery and glowing translucent, like a sheath of old vellum paper—his veins clearly visible. Lizzy's hesitant footsteps. Her grandfather's kind face smiling, reassuring. "Come here child. You can touch it."

Then later, with grandfather's permission, alone in the parlor, polishing the wood of the violin with a soft cloth. The din of her family playing board games, laughing in another room somewhere on the other side of the house. And Lizzy was at her happiest time in her life.

YES! The awareness of this thrummed through Abby like one of the plucked violin strings. A flash, and Abby could see Lizzy, a not-so-distant future Lizzy, maybe in her thirties? But she was in a concert hall, playing the violin with other musicians on a stage nearby—Lizzy was the star of the group, playing a beautiful fusion of folksy, Smoky mountain, Celtic rhythms, and something jazzy with, danceable intensity. It was pure joy, and it was pure Lizzy. Unique and wild and wonderful. And it was almost real… No. It was real. More than just a possibility. It was a reality within the Fold, a reality that was within Lizzy's grasp if she just listened to her heart intelligence and followed her bliss.

Abby hadn't realized it, but she had closed her eyes and wandered off somewhere else, lost in the Fold. Now the weight and the pain of Lizzy's knees were making the feeling in both her arms go numb. She opened her eyes to see a now fuming Lizzy brandishing the emery board file dangerously close to her face.

"I swear I will cut them out of you, you smug little bitch!" Lizzy was whispering, hysterically.

The commotion had aroused Heloise from her bed. She was standing up now, pleading, "Don't you do it, Lizzy. Don't you do it!" She hurried over to the door and pressed the button repeatedly. It buzzed, and a red light filled the room.

Ignoring the commotion, Abby continued to look deeply into Lizzy's eyes. "I want to give you something," she said calmly.

"You what?" Lizzy snarled, her hand wavering.

"I'm going to give you something," Abby repeated.

"Yeah, I'm gonna take your left eyeball, actually. I'm taking it. You're not giving it to me!" Lizzy spoke now in a quiet voice, but the pressure in her legs eased up, and she sat back slightly.

"Don't do it!" Heloise squeaked from the doorway. "She's done it before! She's done it before! I know she has!"

Abby glanced over at her, then returned her gaze to Lizzy and smiled. "No, listen to me. I've got something else for you." Abby paused as she could see uncertainty settling in, Lizzy's angry resolve dissolving. "What I got for you… I need to tell you." Abby's voice was so calm, so... loving? At any rate, it was enough to completely throw Lizzy off her angry and hurtful intentions. The girl just sat there, perplexed, the file still poised upright in her hand.

"Yes, I think you know," Abby continued. We were connected back then, yes? We're still connected in our minds. Can you feel it?"

Lizzy stared down at her, wide-eyed, her bottom lip began to quiver.

"What are you talking about?" Heloise's voice from the dark.

Abby ignored it. "There's an old fiddle, a violin that belongs to your grandaddy. Yes?" Abby sat up slightly as Lizzy gasped and shrunk away from her. Abby's arm was now free, so she reached out, gently grabbed Lizzy around her wrist, and slowly lowered her weapon.

"It's still there, Lizzy. The fiddle. In the summer house. Right there where you used to polish it. Your grandaddy is waiting for you to come by and claim it. It's his gift to you. And listen to me, Lizzy!" Abby's voice remained low and quiet but had grown in its intensity. "I promise you. If you go back there and take that violin… if you put all of your heart and soul into learning how to play it—and it starts with your grandaddy. He will be your first teacher—if you do that, well, it's going to change your life. You're going to find your joy… your happiness. Do you understand? You know it's true. You're going to shine and find love in your life. And all of this... this shit! It's going to go away. I promise you! I promise!"

Lizzy stared back at Abby, her anger replaced by a look of wonder, maybe fear? "How... how do you know those things?" Lizzy asked. "How do you know my grandaddy? Have we met somewhere before?"

"No, no," Abby laughed warmly and sat up to grasp both of Lizzy's arms and squeeze them comfortingly. "It doesn't work like that. We've not met before today. It's just something that I can do, with others like you. I can help you find what you've lost. What you need to move forward, out of your fear, from your shadows—away from your pain."

"I've never told nobody about that fiddle." Lizzy was now staring at Abby in something akin to awe. She suddenly quirked her head to the side and smiled. "How did you do that? Get into my mind? You some kind of witch?"

"Ha!" Abby smiled back at her and felt her own heart-fire well from within and radiate out toward the girl. "Something like that, I guess. I'm still trying to figure it out."

"Cool..."

A loud commotion interrupted them outside the door. Footsteps and then voices. The lock sliding open. Lights suddenly came on in the room. Then Officer Mills was inside with two other male guards.

"Okay Ms. Lizzy." Officer Mills snapped. "That's it! Confinement for you!" The two other guards moved forward to subdue Lizzy. They took the emery board and roughly lifted her from the bed. They hauled her up and rather unceremoniously started heading outside the cell.

Lizzy went quietly, without resistance. She just stared at Abby as they dragged her away and down the hall.

Officer Mills was there in the doorway, looming over the girls like a fussing mother troll. She looked first at Abby, then Heloise, then back to Abby.

"You injured?" She asked. And Abby shook her head. "Then you okay in here? Abby nodded and the broad-shouldered guard breathed in, then out audibly. She looked again at Heloise, then back to Abby. "It's late," she said. "I'll want a report in the morning. We do not tolerate such disturbances. I will see about transferring you out of here. You don't belong here."

She nodded at Abby, then glanced again at Heloise, who remained uncharacteristically silent.

"Okay then," Officer Mills breathed heavily. "Lights out. Try to sleep. Breakfast at 0-seven hundred, sharp."

She turned around and left, the door closing behind her with a click as the latch slid fast.

Abby sat on her bed staring across at Heloise, who just stared back at her. Several moments went by with Heloise absently rubbing her protruding belly.

"What did you do?" the wide-eyed girl finally asked, barely a whisper. Abby did not answer.

And then the lights went out, and Abby lay back down to sort through her thoughts in the darkness. But her mind was far, far away from any darkness. She had burst into the light of her true gift and calling. She was connected to everyone and everything she encountered. Inextricably so. It was a humming thrum of energy and awareness just outside the perimeter of her physical body. And it connected her most inner core of being—her heart-fire and her soul-fire—to the infinite.

She was beginning to feel awakened.

Her mind would continue to race along, not settling down until breakfast came in the morning.

12

PATCHOULI AND CARY GRANT

From the Audio transcripts of Dr. Joanna Kinsey
Chief Psychiatrist, CHNOLA Northshore Center,
New Orleans, LA

Excerpt of Audio File Transcript #AR10089-42

July 3, 2022

Subject: A. B. Rubideaux. Female. Age: 12

Transcript of recording begins: 10:22 AM EST.

Kinsey: *So, what are we going to do about your mother?*

A.B.: *I'd rather not talk about my mother.*

Kinsey: *I'm sorry, A.B., but Beatriz has been asking about you. She wants you to come see her.*

A.B.: *Oh, that's fine. I thought you were talking about my biological mother.*

Kinsey: *Yes, you've told me before when we first started having these sessions that you have never met your biological mother. I am talking about the woman whom you refer to as "Momma Bea." I am sorry for the confusion. I only ask because there are no records of adoption, and that's the primary reason that Beatriz is now being held in custody. Well, that and the fact that her boyfriend, Henry Thierrey, turned her in.*

A.B.: *Yeah, I kind of figured that out. Boyfriend? I guess you have to call him something. Momma Bea was smart not to marry him. But boyfriend? Parasite might be more accurate.*

Kinsey: *Well, boyfriend or no, that's part of the reason you're here with me. Technically, neither he nor Beatriz are your legal guardians. They never filled out the paperwork. And we don't know who your biological parents are.*

A.B.: That makes two of us. But I don't need to know who they are. Momma Bea has always taken real good care of me. Don't need no legal guardian to be a good person. She shouldn't be in any trouble on account of me.

Kinsey: I agree with that, on many levels. But the law looks at things differently, A.B.. Do you have any idea why Henry would have turned her in and denied any relation at all to you?

A.B.: Why? Sometimes there ain't no why. He just a fly-sucking toad.

Kinsey: Well, you could help Beatriz by talking to the police about it. Mr. Thierrey has made some pretty stunning allegations.

A.B.: You have to go pretty deep to find anything "stunning" in Henry's mind. He likes to talk—a lot, but he never really says much of anything.

Kinsey: (Chuckling.) Well, that puts him in the company of lots of people I know! But that does not appear to be the case in this instance. I don't know if the substance of what he says is true, but these are things that may very well impact who has legal custody of you. It doesn't bode well for Beatriz. If you know something that he isn't telling—something that could help Beatriz, and quite frankly help you and your situation here—then you should tell them what you know. His statements have been very damaging, for both you and your Momma Bea.

A.B.: Damaging? Well, that's something Henry has always been good at—causing damage—especially to Momma Bea. So, how come it's only me and Momma Bea that's in trouble? What about Henry? Why ain't he the one answering all these questions?

Kinsey: His role in all of this will be part of the record as well. If they find anything that incriminates him, he will be held accountable.

A.B.: Well bless their hearts. Ain't that reassuring. The police are so helpful.

Kinsey: A.B., I want to make it clear: I don't think the police are your enemy here. You are a twelve-year old girl caught in a very unfortunate situation. If anything, *they want to find out the truth of your situation. The truth, A.B., which is nothing for you to be ashamed of.*

A.B.: *Shame ain't even close to how I feel about it, Joanna.*

Kinsey: *All right, then, you tell me. Let's start with Henry. You seem to have quite a bit of hostility directed at him. Has he ever harmed or mistreated you in any way?*

A.B.: *(Silence.)*

Kinsey: *Okay, let's go back to something else. (Papers turning.) I know you said earlier that you didn't want to talk about your true mother. Your biological mother.*

A.B.: *Momma Bea is the only mother I've ever had.*

Kinsey: *Yes, you've said so before. But why won't you talk about your biological mother, A.B.? This is not the first time this has come up. (Pause.) If I am to understand you and help you, A.B., maybe we can start talking about that now. The sheriff seems to think that there is a connection between Beatriz, Henry, and your birth mother. Do you know anything about that? About your birth mother before you were born?*

A.B.: *Still not going to talk about her. And I don't want to talk about not talking about her either.*

Kinsey: *Okay. That leaves us exactly where, then?*

A.B.: *I think this session is over, Doctor Kinsey. Joanna.*

39 DAYS EARLIER: MAY 24, 2022

The guard came with a breakfast tray and plopped it down. She barked out Abby's name and led Abby away. Apparently, breakfast was for Heloise only. Abby glanced back into the cell, just in time to see Heloise give a small wave of her hand before the door clanged shut between them. Abby lingered for a moment before the guard nudged her along. Abby knew without knowing exactly how that she would meet with Heloise and Lizzy again. There was now an inseverable connection between them. A cord of light and love that would tie them together forever.

Abby closed her eyes and smiled as the guard led her away. Heloise and Lizzy would forevermore be just a thought away.

The guard, a middle-aged African-American woman with the name "Deputy Tamika Thompson" on her badge, tried her best to remain stoically indifferent as she escorted Abby down the hall. At the guard's touch, Abby sensed a wave of images from the guard. The Fold was eager to open to her newfound awareness. Almost effortlessly, Abby shut it down before it could really begin. There was something there with the guard, a mother of three who spent a lot of time baking with her young children, and who had spent time when she was a child baking in the kitchen with her mother, and so it went on… A family legacy and tradition.

Mmm. Pecan pie.

Abby shut it down with barely a thought. A solid clamp that sealed off every memory, every pathway, every wrinkle in the Fold. Even one as tempting as pecan pie. Nothing was there. There was blessed silence, blessed normalcy as they walked down the hallway, the sound of their feet slapping the linoleum floor bouncing off the light green industrial walls of the government building. Abby's smile widened, happy at the discovery of her "shut off valve." The flood was there, oh yes, but she was no longer powerless as it threatened to overwhelm her.

She was gaining control. She was learning how to tap it only when she wanted to, and more importantly, to untap it when she didn't want it.

The guard had led her into a small office and motioned for her to sit at the small table in the center of the room. A few minutes later, she came back with a plate full of cookies and brownies and a glass of milk.

"Cookies," Abby said and smiled up at the guard. "I bet you make really good cookies, Deputy Thompson, if you put your mind to it."

Caught by surprise, the guard smiled, transforming her stern demeanor to another woman—well, the same woman, but one who didn't wear a uniform at home—the woman who was a mother and a daughter and a bit of a goofball who was quick to laughter and a witty comeback. The one who loved her children with the brightness of a billion suns. All of this Abby knew in an instant.

The woman continued to smile, and she paused before she left. "Why, yes. In fact, yes I do!" She said, beaming as she exited the room.

"I'm gonna try them! Some day!" Abby shouted at the closed door, and she smiled contentedly as she helped herself to the entire plate of cookies.

It wasn't long before "the Doctor" came in to introduce herself. An attractive woman of vaguely Scandinavian and Celtic ancestry, she was in her mid-forties but with the skin and hair of someone still in her twenties. Abby had never met Dr. Joanna Kinsey before, but she knew all of this instantly—her name, her age, her dietary preferences, and the fact that she took extraordinary care of herself, both physically and mentally (which was a secret source of vanity). She was very proud and confident of her acumen and insights that her clinical practice of psychiatry regularly afforded her. She was able to stretch and run them like a thoroughbred horse every day—Kinsey's image, not her own. She had a penchant for ancient folklore and mythology. She delighted at the hint of patchouli in the air. She had a rarely admitted indulgence in Gilbert and Sullivan light operas, old Cary Grant movies, as well as wild mushrooms and rare truffles: worth every penny.

Wait a second! Gilbert and Sullivan? What the heck is that? Another discovery. Abby could not only tap into other people's memories and possibilities, but she had access to their wisdom and knowledge, too. It was all there, laid out for her, hiding in plain sight. Especially to someone like Dr. Kinsey, whom Abby knew immediately would be a large figure in her life. She almost felt like slapping her forehead for not recognizing this earlier. She also felt just the slightest pang of guilt: She was beginning to understand the repercussions of Stump's warning about privacy and other people's minds. It wasn't ethical or remotely polite to poach thoughts, memories, and feelings from other people's minds, at least not without permission.

So, all of this came to her in a moment. As Dr. Kinsey came in holding a thick file and smiled brightly. Abby nearly choked on the last cookie on her plate. What was stunning to Abby was the fact that Dr. Kinsey's soul-fire, her personal aura, was among the brightest she had ever seen. She was an astral intergalactic force. Brighter than Stump's, maybe even rivaling Granny Jane's or Fina Lee's. And she didn't even know this about herself. How charming!

Abby returned her smile as the doctor extended her hand.

"Joanna Kinsey," the doctor introduced herself. "I'm a doctor, a psychiatrist to be precise. I'm here to take you out of this place. Is that all right?"

Abby took her hand and intentionally clamped down her "shut off valve." She had decided in the moment just before not to intrude into anyone's mind unless she was invited, or it was a necessity for her immediate survival.

"Absolutely," Abby said. "I'm not sure I'm completely adjusted to the need to ring a bell every time I want to relieve myself. It's not exactly normal now, is it?"

Kinsey laughed, and squeezed Abby's hand appreciatively. "No, I suppose it isn't at that." She replied. "Rather dehumanizing, actually. What shall I call you? This name here on your file has rather too many syllables in it, Ms. Rubideaux. I don't know quite what to make of it."

She was delightful. And right there, even with her valve firmly in place, Abby felt a strong confirmation that Dr Joanna Kinsey was going to play an integral role in her immediate life, and perhaps even throughout all of her future lives in the Fold.

Yes. Most definitely!

"A.B.," Abby answered. "Like the letters in the alphabet. Or Abby, if that's easier. Most folks call me Abby."

"Which do you prefer?" The doctor asked as she held the door open and beckoned for Abby to follow.

"A.B., I guess." Abby grinned as she swept by and the doctor fell into step beside her. "No one has ever really asked me that before."

"A.B. it is, then!" The doctor said as they walked down the hall and out into the sunshine and streaky clouds of a crisp late-summer morning, just after a rain in the city of New Orleans.

They walked across a driveway into a parking lot. A young man in blue jeans and a light brown suede leather jacket hopped out of a black sedan and opened up the backseat door.

Kinsey spoke first, "A.B., this is Michael. My driver extraordinaire. Michael, A.B.."

"Howdy!" Michael greeted them, smiled and brushed his curly brown hair out of his puppy-brown eyes. He opened the door wider and beckoned them inside. Abby thought he was absolutely beautiful.

Kinsey and Abby sat in the back for the ride, which Dr. Kinsey assured her would be a relatively short one.

"We can talk more freely when we reach my facility," Kinsey began. "But let's get to know each other a bit, okay?"

Abby almost blurted out that she already knew virtually everything she possibly could about Dr. Kinsey—and then some things that Kinsey couldn't possibly even know about herself—things that hadn't happened yet or might not ever happen.

"Okay," Abby settled on a single-word response somewhat reluctantly.

"How do you feel today, A.B.?" Dr. Kinsey asked, and several beats went by before she added. "You were the victim of a fairly traumatic assault, A.B.. It's completely understandable if you'd rather not talk right now."

Abby was surprised. "Assault? You mean back there with Lizzy? Aw, she didn't mean nothing by that. No harm, no foul."

"That's not supported by the video, A.B.. We have the entire incident recorded, with some audio. She attacked you. Threatened to carve your eyeballs out. Your other cellmate was genuinely frightened. And believe me, she doesn't frighten easily."

Abby didn't know how to respond to all of that. How could she explain that everything was going to be all right when others thought it was so bad?

Always speak truth from your heart.

Now, that might have been the dragon rumbling deep inside, or maybe it was the voice of Stump? Abby wasn't sure and felt a small tingling of panic well up, like she was back where she was days ago—overwhelmed and distinctly *not* in control.

She was trying to still her rising stress when she realized that Dr. Kinsey was speaking again.

"...Right? I mean it's okay to feel like you can brush it off, or even try to cover up what happened because you fear there may be repercussions." And here, the doctor paused to clasp Abby's arm. "But I want you to know that that girl will never get close to you again."

Always speak truth from your heart.

Abby took a deep breath, found her resolve and turned to face the doctor.

"Listen," she began, "it ain't like that. It ain't like that at all. Lizzy was a little mixed up back there... and... and well, she's been mixed up for quite a while, I guess. Her brain ain't quite right cuz of all the drugs she been snortin' and smokin' and lord knows what all. But I want to tell you. None of that is her fault. Not really. She's got a light inside of her that will burn bright someday.

Brighter than all of us, maybe. She just needed a place to hide… to… to convince herself that she could be strong. And who can blame her for her…" She paused to search for the right word. "Bravado," she finally said, pleased with herself. "But she'll find her way. We had a little talk. That's all. She's gonna be just fine."

Abby finished and smiled at Doctor Kinsey, whose left eyebrow had arched dramatically and who was staring so intently at Abby that all these little crinkles had popped out in the middle of her forehead like a tiny puckering mouth.

"Really," Abby chortled. "You just need to trust me on this one. She'll be fine."

"I see," Kinsey responded. "Maybe she will at that." Then they both leaned back and rode in silence for the next several minutes. Abby was fiddling with her gold cross necklace, which they had taken away from her at the facility, but Dr. Kinsey had given it back to her along with her backpack that had 47 cents in the outside pocket, a bruised banana in the main compartment along with her sweater from the day her class had all gone to the WWII museum. It seemed like years ago.

She glanced up at the rear-view mirror and discovered that their driver, Michael, was smiling at her. They made eye contact then both looked away, embarrassed.

"Just drive, Michael," said Dr Kinsey, who apparently didn't miss much.

Michael replied, "Yes, ma'am," still smiling.

After another moment, Dr. Kinsey turned to Abby and said very quietly, "Michael is amused because it's a very rare thing for him to see me at a loss for words." She winked and chuckled.

"Well, thank you for that kernel of truth contained in your jest, doctor." Abby said matter-of-factly. "I think we are going to like each other very much, indeed."

"Indeed?" The doctor's left eyebrow shot up again and Abby giggled. The doctor appraised her for a few more moments before continuing. "Well, Ms. Rubideaux. The world is full of surprises. There are things about you that no file could ever contain."

She held up her manilla folder and they both laughed.

A moment later, the car pulled up next to a complex of reddish-brown brick buildings. A sign on the wall said "Adolescent Behavioral Health Unit" with an address below it that read: 935 Calhoun Street.

"Welcome to the Children's Hospital of New Orleans Northshore Center!" Dr. Kinsey announced as the car came to a stop. They parked and got out of the car, Michael obligingly hustling around the back to hold her door open, still smiling.

Irrepressibly cute!

Abby stretched her legs and looked around. There were magnolia trees in bloom lining the other side of the street. The buildings themselves looked something like dilapidated factories from the last century, but they were still more appealing than the juvenile detention center she had just come from.

"Not much to look at, I know." Michael said in a mellifluous baritone.

"No, I guess not!" Kinsey said brightly. "Still, we call it home. Most of us refer to it as "CHNOLA." This is the Calhoun complex—part of the Northshore Center. It will be your home for a while until we can straighten out your family situation."

Family. A rush of thoughts filled her head. *Where was Momma Bea? Was she doing all right? Olivia. Was she in trouble, too? Even that old skinflint, Henry. And Stump.* She tried not to think about Stump.

It seemed that her whole world had been turned upside down and inside out. She reached out with her dragon senses, trying to probe the Fold, but it seemed the distance was just too great, or maybe she just didn't know how to get there and connect. She would try again later.

"Well," Abby said, shaking off her uneasiness and looking at the building in front of her. A breeze stirred in the Magnolia trees above her, somewhere nearby a martin bird chirped. A sign that there was at least a glimmer of something hopeful. She sighed, and stated flatly, "It's better than sleeping in a hedge next to a smelly old dumpster."

And with that they walked across the small plaza garden and entered the hospital. The martin was still chirping, Abby imagined the bird was speaking some bird language she couldn't quite understand. As they went through the front door, Abby glanced to her left at a wide, four-paned window. There were iron bars bolted across the face of glass—*Like a cage*, Abby thought.

Behind the bars, three children's faces stared back at her, listless and indifferent to her passing. Their round faces were colorless and pale, like the sky reflected off the glass above them. The martin chirped again, and Abby felt a slow shiver creep down her spine.

Be strong, little sister.

13

A MEETING IN A
FOREST BY A RIVER

Not even the rain has such small hands.

—*e. e. cummings*

SOMEWHERE IN NORTH AMERICA, 10,610 B.C.C. (OR THEREABOUTS)

Abby brushed her fingers along the giant fern fronds that flourished in the dappled light of the forest floor. The canopy above was thick, and the sounds of birds were everywhere. She walked easily, her bare feet brushing the ground without a sound.

A flash of white up ahead. The woman she knew as Granny Jane moved along the same path. Her white robe was easy to track through the dense green forest. She walked without fear. She walked with sureness and purpose. She was, in fact, humming, and Abby could catch snatches of the melody as it rippled in and out of ear shot—some trick of the forest, or maybe the wind. Abby knew that song—it was at once familiar yet strange. She closed her eyes. She could not quite place it, and it haunted her.

When Abby opened her eyes, the old woman had disappeared. Abby froze and intently watched the spot where she had last seen her. A single fern moved. All others were still around it. Without taking her eyes of the swaying frond, Abby hastened her steps and quickly arrived at the fern.

Nothing. The forest was still. She could not hear the humming tune. Only a few birds chirped above. Abby glanced down at the forest floor. The path she had been following was thick with pine needles and the moist mulch of decaying leaves. There were no tracks and the path seemed to have ended.

A brief moment of panic flooded through Abby's mind, which she quickly quelled by closing her eyes and taking a long, deep breath. Bo M'ba Nesh had taught her about the meditative and restorative powers of the breath.

Be still, little monkey. Breathe.

With the stillness, her awareness and perception sharpened. There were two birds perched above. A slight breeze rustled through the forest canopy. The scent of pine after a recent rain layered over the earthy scents of wet forest floor, decay, and fungi. Below everything, her own breathing anchored her, slow and steady. She sunk her toes into the ground where a patch of sun had warmed it.

Be still. Arms loose at her side.

There! A low snuffling sound up ahead and slightly off to the left. Abby snapped her eyes open and silently moved toward the sound. Parting fronds, stepping over the decaying trunk of a fallen tree, she drew closer and could hear rustling sounds and grunting—something big, something close, moving in the clearing just beyond the brush. Abby parted one last frond and then her heart skipped a beat.

The clearing was bathed in sunlight, revealing a rock outcropping consisting of several large boulders. But one of the boulders was moving. It took several moments for Abby to register what she was seeing: a huge cave bear, his brown fur streaked with gray along his backside, towered over Abby. Even standing on all fours, he was at least seven feet tall from paws to shoulders. He padded over to the boulders and rested his massive head in the lap of Granny Jane, who was sitting there, and she began scratching him between the ears and cooing to him like he was her very own little cub.

The bear moaned and shivered, clearly familiar with and enjoying the attention. Abby watched as Granny Jane—Stump's Granny Jane—grabbed both ears and raised her face to nuzzle against the nose of the bear. The bear moaned even louder in response. Abby couldn't move and finally remembered to start breathing again.

She felt a presence beside her and turned to see a much younger and lankier version of Stump standing next to her, smiling as he watched the bear and the woman interact. Stump looked like a dark brown Native American warrior, for he was shirtless and wearing only thick buckskin trousers. His torso was painted with a pattern of thick white and black swirls. Little red diamonds formed a dotted line across his forehead, and on his face, each cheek was adorned with a large spiral, one black and one white.

"Not much of a lover, is he?" Stump said softly. "I used to think there was some other reason why she spent so much time in the forest. I guess there is more than one kind of a love relationship, yes ma'am!"

Stump laughed and looked down at Abby and winked. Abby stared back at him, open mouthed.

"How... What..." she sputtered, recovering from the shock of seeing him in the flesh standing right beside her. "I saw you die. You were shot. How are we here?"

Stump chuckled and turned back to watch his grandmother rise and begin walking away with the bear at her side.

"Congratulations, Miss Aurora Borealis Rubideaux," he said brightly. "Welcome to the new world! You a traveler, now. A proper wanderer!" He pointed at the retreating figures of Granny Jane and the bear. "Shall we follow?"

Abby stepped quickly to keep up with Stump, who did not wait for her to answer. They jogged across the small clearing and then up the slight rise between the largest of the boulders.

"You chose to be here," Stump continued as Abby strode along beside him, "and you alone are in control." He paused and glanced down to smile at Abby. "I see you found your anchor."

Abby could smell the musky odor of the bear, who was only a few yards in front of them, Granny Jane's hand resting on its side. The two of them, beast and human, were in perfect sync—the long strides of Granny Jane matching the ambling gait of the bear. The old woman looked back at Abby and smiled.

"Stay as long as you want," she said. She turned back and led the bear up to the right and around a pine tree. They were following a small animal run, climbing a small, craggy hill. As they climbed, Abby could hear the growing sound of roaring water draw nearer.

"It doesn't matter how long you spend here," Granny Jane continued. "You won't lose any time back home—everything will be as you left it. It always is." She stopped and turned to look at Abby again, her smile widening as Abby stopped beside her.

"Or you could spend a lifetime here. Never go back," The old woman spoke and put her arm around Abby's shoulders. Stump drew up silently on her other side.

The odd company had crested the hill and stood looking down on a pristine river valley. A wide blue-green river tumbled down the ravine over many more boulders. The edges of the river were lined with smooth white shale and grey river rock. From their position, Abby could hear the water roaring below—the current was strong and brisk, and the spray from the water rushing over boulders reminded her of another river, somewhere far away, of small children with spider web cords criss-crossing their faces. It wasn't the same river at all, but Abby felt that somehow these places were connected.

"Go on now," Granny Jane spoke this time to the bear, and Abby watched as the bear ambled on, snuffling and snorting as he made his way down toward the river. The trio stood silently for some time, watching him go.

Abby took a deep breath and turned her gaze to follow the river downstream. She could see for miles, and the river made a wide, sweeping turn far below, disappearing behind a veil of mist into a high-walled, narrow gorge. It was truly one of the most beautiful places Abby had ever seen.

Stump and Granny Jane both chuckled, and Abby swung her gaze back to the bear, who was now splashing in the river. His moans and groans of pleasure could be heard above the roar of rushing water.

Abby reached up to grasp the bear claw necklace that hung around her neck. It was warm to her touch.

"The familiar and the strange," the old woman remarked, reaching over to stroke Abby's hand, her fingers lingering on the claw. "Sometimes the two exist together—well, more times than you might think!" She laughed, and Abby couldn't help but smile back at her.

"This belonged to you, didn't it?" Abby asked quietly. "In another time. Another place."

"All times and places are connected," Stump's rich baritone voice chimed in. "You have learned that by now."

Abby locked eyes with the older woman, who patted Abby's hand before speaking. "I'm hungry. That is one thing that never changes in all times and places." She laughed uproariously, and soon all three of them were laughing. The bear could still be heard chortling below at the river's edge.

"I have fish and wild turkey—fresh caught this morning," Stump finally said.

"What are we waiting for, then? Granny Jane perked up, and the three of them laughed and turned back to the forest.

But as they walked, Abby looked back, and her gaze lingered on the bear frolicking through the spray from the river. Was it just a trick of the light, or was there another figure emerging from the droplets of water?

Shimmering and ethereal, the figure emerged—a woman or creature from another plane. She was colorless and transparent but glowed with a powerful silvery light. Abby could see the rocks and the river through her wraithlike form. She was no specter, though, Abby decided on the spot. This was not a creature of the dark, but one that burned with the light of the stars. The figure was indeed strange and familiar as it stepped into the river and stroked the head of the bear. Even without color, Abby recognized the bearing and the shape at once. The headdress, the feathers, and the loose flowing robes. And now as the figure stroked the bear, the profile of a woman, ancient spiderweb scars visible all across her face.

Bo M'ba Nesh. I see you. Are you really here?

Abby's voice sounded in the infinite ether. The Elder from the Clan of the Spider turned and stared back at Abby. She waved, and her voice came through, clear and strong in Abby's head.

Always so many questions, little monkey. Little wanderer. Do you still not believe what you see before your own eyes?

Abby had stopped and was now fully turned back toward the river. She answered.

I do believe, Ancient One. I just don't know how I am here.

A hand gently pressed down on her shoulder and squeezed. Abby glanced over to see Granny Jane, whose gaze once more returned to the river. They both stood and watched the bear as the shimmering figure winked in and out of the light and the spray of the river. Then the wind changed, and the water spray was whipped away into nothing. The shimmering figure was gone.

"*How* is always the better question than *why*," Granny Jane said quietly. "You followed your breath, my dear. The mind is connected to your breath. The breath comes from within and without you. Follow the breath, and the mind can go anywhere. Everywhere and nowhere. You decide if the body comes along, too. It's as simple as following your breath."

"Huh," Abby responded. "Breathing… and that's supposed to be the easy part."

"Who said anything was going to be easy?" The old woman replied and laughed.

The bear groaned, lifted his head and bellowed. He turned and slowly walked away along the river's edge. It was a good time to catch some fish.

14

EVERYWHERE
IS NOWHERE

From the Audio transcripts of Dr. Joanna Kinsey
Chief Psychiatrist, CHNOLA Northshore Center,
New Orleans, LA

Excerpt of Audio File Transcript #AR10089-49

July 11, 2022

Subject: A. B. Rubideaux. Female. Age: 12

Transcript of recording begins: 9:37 AM EST.

Kinsey: *I understand that everything is connected. In order for me to document your experience of… of everything that has happened to you, I need to proceed in a certain order.*

A.B.: *You know that your dependence on order will be your ultimate undoing, doctor. Joanna.*

Kinsey: *(Sighing.) Okay, let's try this: Have you ever considered the possibility that none of this is real? I mean, in the sense of a quantifiable, objective reality, this is nothing more than an elaborate fantasy played out inside of your head? Or to put it simply, you are only dreaming of dragons?*

A.B: *(Giggling.) Oh, most assuredly so. Perchance to dream… none of this is possible without dreams. The only issue here is that what happens in my head, and hence in my dreams, is also happening in the Fold. They are connected, you know. And yes… I think you do know, Joanna. All of this is a manifestation. (Pause.) But I sense a note of skepticism creeping in here. One that I'm sure agent Novak would approve of. (Giggling.) He put you up to this, didn't he? You do realize, of course, that Special Agent Novak is a giant sphincter? That's an ass-hole by any other name.*

Kinsey: *A. B. Please. (Chuckle and long pause.) Do you really want to talk about Agent Novak?*

A.B.: *Not particularly. Any reference to him or just the mere mention of his name, especially if it's coming through his own lips, tends to take all of the air right out* *of the room. I thought you wanted me to describe, once again, the non-local or quantum nature of space and time that I experience during the change. We're kind of going all willy-nilly here, as a good friend of mine was fond of saying.*

Kinsey: *Absolutely. (Chuckling.) Willy-nilly. We can have a real field day. (Both laughing.) Please, go on.*

A.B.: *You're very good, doctor.*

Kinsey: *What do you mean?*

A.B.: *It's just that I've seen that look before, doctor. That smile that doesn't quite reach your eyes. You don't think anything I say is for real.*

Kinsey: *Now, A.B.. That I didn't say. I have told you this before: it doesn't matter what I think.*

A.B.: *It matters to me. And I think it matters to you that it matters to me. (Pause.) I'm not making this up, doctor. You know I'm not crazy. Can you just allow for one moment that the Fold is real? Every chaotic and beautiful wrinkle. Every wave of conscious thought and energy. It's more than just chemicals in your brain. It exists within but also beyond your empirical, objective reality. What is it you're so fond of saying?*

A.B. *and* **Kinsey** *together: "There is no objective point of view with an exclusive monopoly on reality!"*

(Laughing.)

Kinsey: *You know, on that much we do agree, and if it's real enough for you, then it's real enough for me. And for the record: I've never once said that the Fold isn't real. That it isn't possible. You've all but proven that much. It's just up to me to convince some other very important people of that. And I am trying to help you, A.B.. I am trying to understand. And if there's anything that I've learned from you—that you've taught me! Yes! It's that, in my heart, I believe you. It's only my head that remains to make sense of all this. So please, humor me and my insistence on an orderly process. Now, where were we?*

A.B.: You see? That's the doctor I like so much! Doc is being sincere. You really should stick with that, Joanna. (Giggling.) Where were we? Indeed.

45 DAYS EARLIER: MAY 27, 2022

There were no cave bears or fish to catch in the Adolescent Behavioral Health Unit at CHNOLA. The daily regimen of life here would depress most people. The doctors and nurses and staff that worked here all tried their best, despite knowing deep down that the facility was like a sad old shadow from another century—an energy sucker that drained the life and hope right out of the very air itself. The irony is that several of the kids who were institutionalized here were depressed before they went in. Didn't leave them much of a chance, the way Abby looked at it.

Still, this was where Abby chose to be. Was meant to be. A reunion with Stump and Granny Jane could wait. There was work to be done here.

There was no shortage of irony everywhere around her. Abby hadn't even known what irony was before the thought popped into her mind. But she was used to that by now. This knowledge and wisdom that just appeared from nowhere in particular.

Abby had begun to refer to it as *the download*. She had access to it whenever she focused on it. The world of spirit and the quantum field were one and the same, depending on which books you read. Abby didn't care to make any distinction or to insist that it might be one or the other. It was all just magnificently horrible and beautiful at the same time. She could continue breathing or she could just stop breathing. And it was up to her mind—her very being—to decide if she should dwell in the light or the dark. There wasn't one without the other, and while it was certainly wonderful to revel in the light, there was no need to fear the dark either. In fact, it was in the dark that things were often the most interesting.

Take the inhabitants of this fine CHNOLA facility, for example. By all ostensible and measurable standards, they were a sad mix of mentally ill, chemically imbalanced, mentally retarded, scarred and traumatized outliers—outcasts who had been shunned or put to the side by their families and society as a whole, by the rest of a world that simply didn't know what to do with them. And yet these outliers had depths that no one had plumbed. This was the irony.

Here at the hospital, for example, within the mind of a severely autistic boy named Will—a boy whose nanny would burn him with cigarettes because he wouldn't follow her directions—within that boy, whose world was about as bleak and mean-spirited as a particularly horrific plane of hell, Abby found a soul who delighted in the simple things that were all around him. The patches of blue sky that peeked from behind the clouds; the smell of cinnamon buns in the morning cafeteria; the warmth of his mother's hand when she held onto his. These were the daily scripts that ran endlessly through his mind. And all of the bad things—the heinous acts and callous apathy of the multifold of others—all the rest of humanity and a world that didn't see or didn't care— these things were instantly and unconditionally forgiven. They simply didn't matter to him. They were not important or worthy enough for him to dwell upon. How does the most experienced or illuminated human on the planet find wisdom like that?

Then there was Melody, the schizophrenic 12-year old who had been di- agnosed with a severe learning disability. She had been called stupid all of her life and had lived in a series of foster homes from the time she was a baby. They drugged her up and had her on a daily regimen of anti-depressants and stress inhibitors. She had every reason to be depressed and full of spit and venom at a world that had cast her aside, but instead, she found her way into the recre- ation room every day, where she sat and painted with water colors—beautiful pictures of flowers, animals, and the brick courtyard outside that Abby just marveled at, for their details were so intricate and full of a light and color that simply wasn't present in the dull, grey reality of the actual courtyard outside the window. When Abby had asked her about the beauty she expressed in the paintings, Melody had simply smiled and winked at her before replying,

"The barking flowerpots are horsing up spit. They know better. You only have to listen."

Abby knew that most folks would just dismiss that as crazy talk, but she didn't dare do it herself. Melody might very well have been on to something, and if she kept looking and listening and painting, well, she just might find more beauty and grace than anyone else in their "right mind."

Right mind indeed. It seemed to Abby that Melody and the score of others she met in the facility were closer to truth and actual purpose than most of the folks rambling around on the outside. All the *normal* folks. It was their secret here on the inside, though. One the rest of the world wasn't quite ready to discover.

So, while Olivia and Momma Bea would have been horrified by her current circumstances—living among the deranged and the chemically peculiar, Abby chose to experience it differently. With reverence and gratitude. Two feelings, by the way, which if you simply embraced and dwelled upon more often, just might lead you to remarkable physical and mental health. That would be a natural kind of intelligence that connects your body and your mind to a higher frequency—a healing frequency. Abby knew all of this and more, thanks to the download.

In such a state of mind, it was around her third day at the facility that Abby found herself waiting in Dr. Kinsey's office. And such a marvelous place it was, full of books and curious knick-knacks. The doctor was a collector of mementos—of things that told the stories of places she had been and people she had known. She placed her hands on all of the items to feel them and sense their energy. She had discovered recently that it wasn't just people but also objects that contained certain frequencies and memories—they told the story their past and of their meaning. If Abby held them and concentrated, she could access the information stored in them.

On one object in particular she let her fingers linger longer. It was a fist-sized wooden carving of a seated Buddha figure. He was curled into a ball, naked but for a small loin cloth, seated cross-legged and bent over so that his face pressed into his legs. His hands were covering his eyes. Abby caught her breath as she ran her fingers over the smooth wood of his back. It was so powerful!

She picked it up and held it in her hands. Immediately, feelings of sadness and heart-wrenching grief filled her. She knew in that instance that Dr. Kinsey had lost a child, that her husband, in his own broken state of grief had blamed her and had left her shortly after that. She knew that Dr. Kinsey still held on to a large portion of guilt and self-loathing regarding the death of her baby and the failure to hold on to her husband. This object, a gift from a dear friend, was intended as a token of solace and comfort, but ironically, served primarily as a daily reminder of her own suffering and daily penance.

The door opened and Dr. Kinsey stepped into the room. Abby quickly put the object down and turned to face Dr. Kinsey, absently wiping away a tear that trickled down her cheek. The doctor glanced down at the carving then quickly back at Abby. There were several awkward moments of silence before they both smiled.

Abby spoke, quietly reciting a line that filled her head unbidden. "And so the Buddha covers his eyes and weeps for all the suffering and sorrow that fills the world."

Abby sighed, and stared intently in the doctor's eyes. "I'm sorry for your loss, doctor," she said.

The doctor, clearly caught off guard, had frozen and placed her right hand over her heart. In her left hand she clutched a small briefcase. She stared back at Abby wordlessly. After several moments, she shook her head, literally snapping out of it, and smiled as she walked around behind her desk.

"So," she said carefully, "You are familiar with the writings of the Dhammapada?" The doctor sat down and beckoned Abby over to sit on the other side of her desk. Abby obliged and sat on a very comfortable armchair with red leather, rivet-seamed cushioning.

"I find great comfort in the teachings of Gautama Buddha," the doctor continued. "I'm no Buddhist, but I take the wisdom of others wherever I can find it. That was a gift to me from a good friend during a time of great pain in my life. It is my favorite thing in this office." The doctor paused and smiled genuinely back at Abby. She was in full control of her emotions now. "But you are free to pick it up and hold on to it as much as you want. It is meant to be touched."

"Thank you," Abby replied simply.

The door opened and Michael came into the room carrying a large tray. Abby watched him gracefully place it down between them. The tray contained two large glasses of sweet tea, a plate of small chocolate squares, and a tape recorder.

"Thank you, Michael," the doctor said, smiling up at him. "That will be all."

"Yes ma'am," Michael replied, smiling back. He glanced at Abby, flashed an even wider, dazzling smile, then turned and headed out, back straight, his blue-jeaned legs effortlessly and quietly striding, until he closed the door behind him.

Abby watched him the entire time, then sighed after he was gone and turned back to the doctor. "Could you have him bring me my breakfast every morning?" She asked hopefully. "Lunch and dinner, too? I do so like the way he walks."

"Ha!" The doctor nearly choked on her laugh. "You are a remarkable girl, Miss Rubideaux. But I'm afraid Michael is off limits for now. Wait a few years, please! Ah!" The doctor interrupted herself with the delightful discovery of the tray's contents. "I also take great comfort and pleasure in dark chocolate! Would you care for some? She slid the plate over toward Abby and also offered her a glass. "Sweet tea? Use the coaster please."

She handed the tea to Abby, who placed it on a white ceramic coaster that was decorated with a beautiful red and blue Celtic animal pattern. Abby took a piece of chocolate and watched as Dr. Kinsey picked up the recorder and placed it in front of her. The doctor opened her briefcase and rummaged around briefly before removing a small cassette tape, which she then popped into the recorder with a push of a button and a snap as the lid shut. She picked up her own glass of sweet tea, raised her glass toward Abby and took a sip.

"Abby," she began, "I've asked you to come here so that we could start having some sessions together. Well, maybe "sessions" is not the best word—more like conversations where I ask a lot of questions. I want to ask you about your experiences, your family, your friends, and school. About all the things that have been happening to you. You don't have to answer all of my questions, and we can stop at any time if you wish. I like to record our conversations so that I may listen to them later and take notes. No one else will have access to these tapes, for they are solely intended as a record of the clinical proceedings of my duties here as a psychiatric doctor—I would like to ask your consent before we begin. Is that alright with you?"

Abby, who was chewing on a particularly tasty morsel of dark chocolate, couldn't help but smile before responding. "Well, doc, that's a lot of words to ask for my permission to have a talk. This is where you're gonna do all your psycho-therapizing and start doctoring up my mind—determine whether or not I'm crazy as a loon, right? Sure, you have my permission... and really, you need to have some of this chocolate, too!" Abby and the doctor laughed as they both helped themselves to another piece.

"That's fine," Dr, Kinsey finally said, after groaning in delight over her chocolate and taking one more sip of tea. She cleared her throat and pressed play.

She spoke over the recorder in a very articulate and precise tone, "This is audio file number one, May 27, 2022. Dr. Joanna Kinsey interviewing Subject number AR10089: Miss Aurora Borealis Rubideaux. Female. Age eleven. Miss Rubideaux, are you aware that this conversation is being recorded?"

Abby remained silent, just grinning from ear to ear, completely and not-so-secretly entertained by the doctor's proceedings.

"Miss Rubideaux?" The doctor asked, smiling herself. "I will need a verbal response from you."

"Oh," Abby jerked herself upright and grinned back at Doctor Kinsey. "Yes, of course. By all means, I mean. Umm, are you gonna do that each and every time we talk together like this?"

"Yes, I'm afraid so."

"That is so cool!" Abby leaned forward and took another square of chocolate, popped it in her mouth, and sat back still grinning at Doctor Kinsey.

The doctor was chuckling now, quietly. A laugh that made Abby feel very nice and comfortable because she knew it wasn't fake or disingenuous.

"Okay," Doctor Kinsey continued, "Let's get started then." She glanced down at a sheaf of papers she had removed from a manila file.

"Okay," Abby said, a sliver of doubt suddenly prickling down her spine. "Where shall we begin?"

"Well," the doctor replied, looking up from her papers, "How about with your medical records?" She pulled out what looked like an official document. "You have a very interesting record, or lack of a record, I should say. "I've been meaning to talk with you sooner, but it took us a few days to compile any record of your life at all, actually. I wanted to ask you about your family, or the folks who claim to be your family. And maybe a few questions about your medical history and your school life. Is that okay?"

Now, as Abby sat there listening to the doctor, she realized in an instant that many of the things in her life were far from being normal—that she hadn't had any of the things that most kids had in terms of official papers and documents. That from the outside looking in, her life was a fraudulent and illegal web of lies. She had never been to a doctor. Never got any shots or vaccinations like all the other kids were required to. She had never been sick, so she didn't need any of those things. She had never been given a birth certificate from a real hospital—her birth mother had simply given her to Momma Bea before she went away, or just disappeared actually, from this world, anyway. She also knew, in that same moment, that none of the people who were making these inquiries, especially Doctor Joanna Kinsey, would hold her, an 11-year old girl, responsible for any of it. In fact, they would feel pity and remorse for a girl who had been crushed, rolled, and then reshaped by the tragic rolling pin of life. On top of that, she knew in that precise moment that Momma Bea and Henry were in a heap of trouble, for the world of human society would need an explanation, and the only explanation that made sense was that a couple of Cajun swamp rats were guilty of fraud, criminal negligence, reckless child endangerment and what, to all reasonable god-fearing people of the good state of Louisiana, appeared to be nothing short of the kidnapping of some other person's unfortunate baby.

She knew this and several other things all at once—that the dragon inside of her, who now guided and informed her with instant *downloads*—would be unbelievable and inconceivable unless she manifested it as proof of her claims. That the only way out of this pickle was for her to be absolutely truthful, sincere, and above all, patient.

You could just fly away, little sister. Iron bars cannot hold you.

The Voice inside of her plied gently. But Abby knew that she was at the beginning of a very important junction in her life. There was no more time to live her life anonymously and separately in the trees and the swamps of the bayou, as tempting as that was. It was time for her to introduce herself to the rest of humanity.

Yes. Yes. Yes. Yes. Now, who is the wise one?

She must be wise and discerning in the manner in which she proceeded. And her first order of business was to win Doctor Kinsey over. If she was ever going to be believed—and not doped up for the rest of her obviously crazy life like half the other patients in this facility—if Momma Bea were ever to avoid being placed in prison, or if friends like Olivia were to remain unharmed and above reproach in the nefarious dealings of a mad girl who claimed to be a dragon—then Doctor Kinsey was the key. She was Abby's main ally—the key figure in every wrinkle of the Fold that twisted and unfurled into the myriad of probabilities that would be the future.

Well, nothing like the present moment!

"Yes," Abby answered in what was only a beat after the doctor's question. "Of course. I want to tell you everything that I know. Fire away, doctor."

Doctor Kinsey regarded Abby for several moments. She spoke, at length, assuming the same clinical and precise tone as before.

"Very fine. Let' get to it, then. First things first." Kinsey paused before continuing. "And I feel I need to tell you that you might find some of these things very...distressing. Not everything about which I will ask you may have an explanation—at least not one you may be aware of. But I must ask you for the record despite my own misgivings."

"Well, shoot then!" Abby interrupted playfully. "You might find it more expeditious to be frank and terse in your line of questioning. No lengthy pre-ambles or apologies are necessary." Abby found herself imitating the doctor's clinical tone and giggled despite herself.

"I see," Dr. Kinsey regarded Abby for a few moments, took a sip of her sweet tea, then proceeded. "We've been to your home and have interviewed your parents, or guardians—I guess that's a better term. We asked them to provide us with your birth record and all medical documents. The man," and here the doctor checked her notes, "Henry Thierrey, was uncooperative and dismissive. Your mother, Beatriz Roy, was quite cooperative and provided us with your birth certificate. Unfortunately, the birth certificate proved to be a forgery. She was unable to present any medical records."

"Momma Bea don't believe in no doctors," Abby interjected. "And old *Henry*," Abby pronounced it the French way, "wouldn't agree to pay for those things anyway."

Doctor Kinsey continued, ignoring Abby's interruption. "We have also talked to the folks at your school, on the other hand, and they were in posses-sion of several vaccination records, all of which proved to be fake documents, poorly forged, and easily discoverable as such upon further inquiry."

"Well," Abby said, "You'd think that a state institution, like a public school would be more careful about these kinds of things. I can't speak for them, but the other part is pretty simple. Like I told you, Momma Bea don't like them doctors. She don't like the government either, and has no reason to start liking them now. She obtained those documents in order for me to go to school. They wouldn't let me in otherwise."

"Okay," Dr. Kinsey said, "But do you know how she obtained those doc-uments or if she made them herself?"

"You asking me as my doctor, or are you working for the police?" Abby asked, matter-of-factly.

"A.B., I assure you," the doctor began, slightly taken aback. "Everything we talk about in here is protected by doctor-patient privilege—it is protected and confidential. I do not work for the police. But your mother could be in serious trouble, and you may be the only one right now who can help her. I am only trying to understand how we got here. I want to advise you and help you, above all else."

Abby snorted, "C'mon now, I was only jibing. Pulling on your skirts just a bit. Okay, let me give it to you straight. I don't really know who, how, or where she got them documents from. It never occurred to me to ask. And that's the truth. I just know that she loves me, and she wanted me to go to school, so I could have a bit more of a normal life. Momma Bea is a good woman with a heart that is bigger than anyone else I know. She's a good Christian, too. Anyone that knows her well can tell you that. She never intended anything but the best for me."

"I don't doubt that," Doctor Kinsey replied, "Apart from the incident when you were a child—when you disappeared after the tornado—she has a very good reputation and no criminal record. And despite all the trouble she may have landed herself in—trouble that I am in no position to help her with, by the way, unless you can convince me and, more importantly, the authorities, otherwise—you may be happy to know that she was very distraught over you and full of questions, and she has demanded to be allowed to see you here. Demands which, for now, have been denied until the judge can make a ruling. So, at least in that regard, she appears to be sincere in her love and concern for you."

Doctor Kinsey stopped and ran her fingers through her hair, a gesture that Abby would come to recognize as a "tell" that the good doctor was anxious or under some kind of stress.

"Look," the doctor started over, "I'm getting off track here. Did you know that Beatriz and Henry were not married? That Henry Thierrey claims to have no relation to you even though the neighbors and the school believe he is your daddy?"

"Yeah. Henry, he's just her boyfriend. I guess they like to call each other "ma" and "pa," but they never really bothered to explain to anybody that they're not actually husband and wife. It don't really bother me or nobody else, I guess. Please don't call him my daddy." Abby rolled her eyes and made a gagging motion with her finger pointing to her mouth.

Kinsey paused here briefly, perusing her papers. "A.B.," she asked finally, "I need to ask this question, okay? Do you know if Beatriz Roy is your birth mother?"

"She is not," Abby replied succinctly, smiled and took a sip of her sweet tea.

Kinsey frowned, and several wrinkles creased her forehead, making her look much older. "Do you know how she came to be in possession of you?"

"Possession? That's an odd word." Abby chuckled. "Makes it sound like I'm some sort of contraband." She raised her hand and smiled sincerely before continuing, "Please, doctor, I'm just having fun. No slight intended. My momma—and that would be my real, biological birth momma—gave me to her when I was just a baby. I just call her *Momma* Bea cuz she raised me like she was my momma, and for all ostensible purposes, she is in fact just like a mother to me."

"I see," Doctor Kinsey went on. "Do you know where your birth mother is?"

"I might if I go looking for her," and here Abby paused, suddenly stunned by the thought that had never occurred to her before. *Could I really find my mother? Is she out there, somewhere in the Fold?*

Of course she is, little sister. She and many others.

The dragon's voice resonated within her, deeply. Abby shut it down, acutely aware that she wanted to pursue this line of thought when she was alone, later, in the dark… maybe when she went to bed.

"A.B., I want to run some tests," Dr. Kinsey proceeded, cocking her head slightly, never taking her eye from Abby. Abby knew instantly that Dr. Kinsey was both intrigued and concerned. She would be a terrible poker player. Abby was certain that she could read her without using her dragon powers. Probably win lots of money if she had a mind to.

Kinsey's voice made her refocus and avoid amusing distractions. "With these tests we could match up with existing DNA records that might trace us back to your mother, but we could also find out many other things about you."

"You won't find her," Abby said smiling again. "Test or no test, you won't."

"And why are you so certain of that?" Kinsey asked smiling as she took another chocolate and bit off a tiny corner for a nibble.

Abby answered quickly, "Because she is not of this world."

"Do you mean she has passed away?"

"Well, no," Abby scrunched up her face in thought. "At least not in the sense that you imply. She didn't die, if that's what you mean. She just didn't belong here, I guess. It wasn't her time to be here. She went out of this world, out of this time, back to her own world. It's a different time and place."

Kinsey was cocking her head again, and Abby giggled.

"Miss Rubideaux," Kinsey asked cautiously. "Do you believe your mother is from another world?"

"Oh, most assuredly! I guess that means that I come from another world, too. Oh, who's your daddy?" Abby suddenly barked a laugh and slapped her head.

Who is your daddy?

The dragon voice inside of her rumbled, and Abby was almost certain it was laughing.

"Oh now, that's not fair!" Abby exclaimed, her mind racing with a thousand sudden thoughts.

"What's not fair?" Doctor Kinsey asked, genuinely confused.

"I'm sorry, doctor," Abby suddenly turned to face the doctor and sobered up immediately. "But can we continue this another day, maybe tomorrow? You can't possibly imagine how enlightening this session has been, but I really need to process a few things by myself."

"Of...of course," the doctor stuttered, slightly startled and bemused.

"Oh, Doctor Kinsey, Joanna!" Abby was suddenly beside herself and literally hopping up and down with excitement. "Don't look so crestfallen. I will tell you everything. All of it! I can't wait to tell you everything, in fact. It's like you said, though. We should start from the very beginning...a very good place to start." Abby was giggling again.

"What?" Doctor Kinsey was now smiling, caught up in Abby's sudden exuberance. "What are you going to tell me?"

"Ah, well…" Abby suddenly stopped hopping up and down, sat down, and raised her eyebrow at Dr. Kinsey, who laughed in response. "I couldn't possibly tell you today."

"Why not?"

"Because you're not ready for it. You wouldn't believe me."

"Try me!" Dr. Kinsey smiled and crossed her arms. Abby knew immediately that Dr. Kinsey was skeptical and just doing her best to play along. She was really quite good at playing along because the largest part of her, the part that glowed and radiated like the biggest and brightest blue moon of an aura— the part that Abby could see right away the very first day they met—well, that part was genuine and real. And it was benign to its core. The very essence of an angel. But there was this little sliver of skepticism, like a shadow that hid itself under the cloak of rationality, which was currently overriding her better nature. That part of her didn't believe a word Abby was saying.

Humility is a good lesson.

Yes. Abby thought to herself. Especially for a Buddhist psychiatrist in need of a little reminder. You need to *be here now*, good doctor. The truth will set you free.

"Okay," Abby breathed out heavily, releasing all doubt and tension, then smiled. "You asked for it. I'll try to put it as clearly and as succinctly as I can. Are you ready?"

Dr. Kinsey nodded, still smiling, skeptical but genuinely intrigued.

Abby let it all out, barely pausing for breath between her sentences: "I'm in a hyper-accelerated state of conscious expansion—it's difficult to describe to you in only a few words, but I shall try my best to summarize for you the main points here today. We will then proceed to have several more sessions over several more days—but time isn't really relevant, actually, when I carefully and precisely spell out for you all of the details which shall slowly convince you of the meritorious claims contained within our conversations. It will be like sitting in with the Buddha. Or the master in his dialogues—I'm sure you appreciate the reference! But today, you get the bullet list! Just the highlights, so to speak. So here goes: I'm a dragon who has travelled through multiple dimensions of time and space. I have a gift to activate the higher consciousness of others and help all whom I meet. I am psychic and have the ability to see all that has gone before, all that is now, and all that may have been or in fact may be. I exist in a place beyond this dimension in multiple planes that defy what you understand through scientific or traditional religious means. I have been here before; I shall be here again. In fact, I have always been here—everywhere and nowhere, all at once, but for reasons that shall take some time to explain, and more importantly, time to convince you that you, Dr. Kinsey, shall play an integral part in the ultimate purpose of my being here now—oh yes!"

Abby paused as her eyes fell on the wooden Buddha figure on Dr. Kinsey's desk. Abby reached over and picked it up. She held it up and smiled at the doctor.

"Are you familiar with psychometry?" Abby abruptly switched topics. "All it took was one touch, and I knew immediately all about you."

Abby set the figure down and reached over the desk to grasp Dr. Kinsey's hand. Dr. Kinsey had placed both her hands upon the desktop and froze in place like a giant mannequin, one eyebrow arched, her face otherwise an inscrutable mask.

"And it's okay," Abby continued, her voice suddenly much softer. "It wasn't your fault, you know? About your little boy? You have to stop blaming yourself and move on. And your ex-husband? He don't really blame you for what happened either. There is forgiveness there, if you are open to it and ready to receive it."

Abby paused as Dr. Kinsey audibly gasped and stiffened. Abby let go her hand and smiled, holding eye contact as she could see Dr. Kinsey's skepticism replaced by incredulity and then the slow acceptance of a truth the doctor couldn't quite understand.

"That's right," Abby nodded and smiled wider. "Your favorite color is orange, but never to wear, only look at. You prefer wearing combinations of purple and green. I would give you a bottle of patchouli if I had one, for I know it is your favorite fragrance. You love Cary Grant movies and ancient folklore and mythology of any type. I know all of this about you and more. I know you will always be there for me. Every time. In all times. No matter what—you'll be there for me, and I for you. Always. Now, you may be skeptical right now, but you know it's true, but just not yet! Trust me, you will! You do! You have already! (Giggling.) And it's really quite clear to me now, and it's almost like the first time, but I'm sure this has all happened before and will happen again and, oh my goodness, is probably happening right now an infinite number of times all over...Most assuredly!"

Abby paused to catch her breath and to try not to giggle, because that would be inappropriate at this exact moment despite the comical look of consternation thinly covered by a professionally trained mask of objective indifference that was now plastered across Dr. Kinsey's very attractive face.

So, having paused for dramatic effect, Abby now announced in her best Discovery Channel voice: "In short, and with your help, I have manifested in this time and place in order to save humanity. From itself." (Less certain.) "I think." (Totally lacking confidence.) "Yes, just that. With your help, of course."

There was a silence that followed her pronouncement. Dr. Kinsey, was perhaps, rendered completely speechless. Oh well, Abby tried and the good doctor had asked for it. But it was very clear to Abby now, and forever, that everything was exactly as it should be, as it always was, and as it always will be.

Yeah. Right.

Abby spoke first, "I know. It seems a little bit manic. Crazy, right? But you'll come around." She stopped and slid the plate of remaining chocolates over toward herself. "Can I take these back to my room? The antioxidants will really help me sort through all of this, don't you think?"

15

INTO THE FOLD

AWAKENED

From the Audio transcripts of Dr. Joanna Kinsey
Chief Psychiatrist, CHNOLA Northshore Center,
New Orleans, LA

Excerpt of Audio File Transcript #AR10089-52

July 14, 2022

Subject: A. B. Rubideaux. Female. Age: 12

Transcript of recording begins: 7:32 AM EST.

Kinsey: *Dr. Joanna Kinsey dictating written notes from my personal records regarding subject number AR10089: Miss Aurora Borealis Rubideaux. Audio file number 52, July 14, 2022. Subject not present.*

(Long pause.)

Subject not present for our regularly scheduled session because she has gone missing after having been put under heavy sedation by order of FBI Special Agent Novak.

(Long Pause.)

A.B. She knew! She knew this would happen. Why didn't she do everything to avert this? Now she is helpless, on the run...lord knows where! All of this plays into Novak's hands. Transfer request to Groom Lake, Nevada facility has been submitted over my strident objections. A.B.'s actions—alleged actions—did not, in my opinion, warrant such an intervention. It has long been my view that A.B. is harmless; in fact, she is incapable of harming another living thing. Agent Novak feels otherwise. Agent Novak is a reckless, oblivious fool with little or no regard for the medical assessment of the subject... of A.B.. Nor does he have any regard for the subject's well-being. Agent Novak is a self-aggrandizing tool—what was it? Oh yes, a giant sphincter with severe self-esteem issues manifesting in his all-too-common, blatant abuse of authority, which inadequately strives to compensate for his slow and humbling realization that he is outwitted, outplayed, overmatched, and no longer in control... of anything. Oh A.B., I hope you know what you are doing!

(Long Pause.)

Strike preceding comments from the record. (Audible sigh.) None of us are in control. Of anything.

17 DAYS EARLIER: JUNE 27, 2022

A month went by, and Abby had met with Dr. Kinsey every other day or so, even on the weekends. The meetings were her favorite part of each day. Except when Agent Novak from the FBI showed up... but more on that in a moment.

Abby had settled into a routine at the CHNOLA facility. She was awakened every morning by a nurse or an orderly and escorted to the breakfast room for a very decent breakfast. Sometimes it was Michael who came to get her, and those were the best days. Abby found out that Michael played the guitar and sang David Bowie and Beatles songs, and sometimes he would entertain the children during their afternoon sessions, which usually provided free time for music or arts and crafts. It only made Abby love him even more, and she was almost certain that Michael was completely aware of her crush on him, and the fact that he didn't treat her any differently only made the crush deepen to the point where Abby flushed and palpitated any time she thought about him, like she had a hundred tiny electric fingers running up and down her spine and well, a few other places, too.

Her day continued with meetings in the late morning, usually, with Dr. Kinsey. On those days they didn't meet, Abby was free to roam the grounds, visit with other patients, sit in the garden, or read in the library. Then there was lunch followed by afternoon classes and art and music sessions—it wasn't quite like school, but it was pretty cool because all of the kids' schedules were tailored to their particular needs. Abby was dubbed a "low-flight risk" and a "rover" and could pretty much go wherever she wanted. She usually spent time with Melody in the art room, or read books in the library, or best of all, she would go with Michael on his rounds acting as his assistant.

On those occasions, she made it a point to "accidentally" brush up against him or grab his hand whenever an opportunity presented itself, you know, without seeming like some creepy stalker or a hopeless puppy dog begging for attention. She did this because Michael's mind and his pathways through the Fold were some of the most interesting and beautiful that she had ever seen. Michael was the closest thing to a highly evolved being that she had run into— for someone who wasn't a possessor of the gift like Stump or latently psychic like Dr. Kinsey, that is. There was not a single notion of violence or anger in his being. He was walking in a perpetual state of nearly unconditional love, which was amazing in and of itself. He was full of grace, to put it simply, and Abby was drawn to him like a bear cub to honey.

Abby was very careful not to "spy" on the particulars of his pathways through the Fold—she had decided to respect others and their privacy. But she could still get a general "read" on an individual and know their proclivities in a very general sense. She could also know their particular joys (Dr. Kinsey's penchant for ancient folklore and dark chocolate, for example) and whether they were dealing with certain traumas (The autistic boy, Winston, and the nanny who would burn him with cigarettes), and sometimes, she would receive unbidden a "download" of such a powerful and specific nature that it would literally floor her—like that time it happened with Fina Lee in the school hallway or with Lizzie and her granddaddy's fiddle—and at those times, she would need to sit down or take deep breaths. She was still learning how to control her powers.

It was during the long nights, after dinner and the television time—always Jeopardy followed by Wheel of Fortune—and Abby would eventually be banned from speaking up during Jeopardy because she always called out the right response even before the host was finished with his question, which the other inhabitants of the room found very annoying! Abby couldn't help it if her downloads made her an unbeatable trivia queen! At any rate, it was during the night, after all of the socializing and television, when Abby was alone in her room just lying in bed—that was the time she looked forward to the most.

Because that was the time when she could truly be everywhere and nowhere all at once.

What that meant, precisely, was that Abby was now open—wide open—to all the possibilities of the Fold. It was easier at night, when she was alone in the dark without distraction and the pressing invasive presence of other people, to let her mind just find nothingness, and then she would be off and out of her mind and actually find somethingness. She had become a wanderer. She was learning new things every day.

Like the fact that time wasn't a singular, localized phenomenon. In short, what that meant is that when she let herself immerse completely in the Fold, Abby could go anywhere in time. She could replay things that had already happened, for instance, or look into the probabilities of the future, because in the Fold, the current moment contained all moments in time, past, present, and future. This explained what she had already been experiencing with others when the visions came to her head containing their memories and their possibilities. Only they weren't just pictures in her mind. *They were real places in time.* Abby also had an inkling that she was able to travel to those places—physically—like Stump's grandma, Granny Jane. She had managed to travel only a few times, so the exact *how* of doing that remained yet to be discovered. Something to do with her breath and not actively thinking.

But in her mind, maybe Abby was also just a little bit afraid of what would happen to her if she traveled often. What would happen if she couldn't come back?

She also discovered that her birth mother was out there. Not really waiting, but present and radiant and beautiful. She existed simultaneous with Abby, who lay in her bed in CHNOLA on the North Shore of New Orleans on the planet earth in the year 2022. She knew that there were untold millions more just like her—beings who had evolved, who were existing within the Fold of spirit and potential physicality on this plane, in this time. Right now.

She knew that the Voice in her head wasn't her father—who by the way existed beyond time and space, like her mother, only it wasn't like he was a father in the biological sense. Her father was a divine being whose conscious manifestation went beyond any words to describe. The voice in her head however, belonged to her herself—or rather most of the time it was an extension of herself. But it also belonged to her brother, an entity whom she would simply refer to as "Enoch." Well, he was kind of like her brother. There was more than one entity that "talked" to her through her dragon voice, and each of those entities was a part of her being, too. They were inseparable. And everyone and everything was connected to the Fold, and within the Fold there most assuredly existed her brother, Enoch, whose dragon face had manifested in that oak tree on that day in the bayou not so long ago.

Enoch. He was her partner in crime and mischief and higher awareness throughout the countless millennia of their existence. Genetically speaking, he was the "double" in the double helix of her DNA. He was always there with her, if not completely present, then lurking, just beneath the surface. It was he who had invited her out into that storm when she was six years old. It was he who was the source of most of the "downloads" that she was receiving. It was he who had brought her back to this awakened state. And it was he whom she would most definitely have to talk to soon… if she was ever going to sort out the purpose for everything happening right now or that was about to happen a billion times over everywhere and nowhere all at once—whether she wanted it to or not.

But back to Abby's current predicament. She also knew that she could leave any time she wanted to. The facility could not hold her. No physical barrier could stop her. No government agency could compel her. No physical death would put an end to her. There was only transition. And becoming. But those things could wait. She was here for the people. It was humanity's time to make a transition. Humanity's time to evolve. And the people she knew and loved were the most important things right now.

She was here to be in the company and the presence of others. That was pretty much all there was to it. The purpose for any conscious life form that existed here or anywhere in the multiverse was made very clear and simple: We are here to be with others. All of them. Every single imperfect, discombobulated, stinking one. And she loved them all. Here and in all other possibilities of existence.

Quantum reality. Field theory. The oneness of spirit and the multiverse. Oh my. These humans were getting closer to understanding it. The mystical had merged with the latest scientific discoveries. It was time.

And it was the humans who needed her now. The planet was at a turning point. Olivia, Momma Bea, Doctor Kinsey, Lizzie, Fina Lee—even old Balt Luster and Princess Julia—she was here right now for all of them. Something needed to happen… something. She just wasn't quite sure what, exactly.

She needed to talk to her brother. For real. Not just the voice inside of her head.

You're too soft, little sister. There are other ways to solve this crisis of humanity.

"Not yet, big brother. Wait. We will talk soon." Abby giggled when she realized that she was talking out loud, in a room, in the dark.

Abby jumped up out her bed and padded over to the table. She clicked on the desk lamp and saw the guitar picks that Michael had given her. The ones she had decorated with Dr. Kinsey-inspired Celtic patterns.

Michael.

With Michael, she also knew something else. She knew that if she ever needed to get away from CHNOLA, Michael would be her ally, and he would help her. He would cover for her when it was time for her to go. That was the story played out multiple times in the myriad pathways of the Fold: Michael was a constant, like Dr. Kinsey.

Joanna.

Yes, the good doctor, whom Abby had by now spent countless mornings with chatting into a recording device, whose tapes no doubt Dr. Kinsey had spent endless hours pouring over and taking notes. Her diligence and commitment were admirable. More than that, Abby had never met anyone so willing to listen and be open to possibilities. Except for maybe Momma Bea, there was no one with more empathy and compassion. It made Abby smile to think of Dr. Kinsey's clinical mask of objectivity, which she wore so well, while all the while a roiling tumultuous passion of emotion and nearly uncontainable energy bubbled just beneath the surface. Her heart fire was just as bright as Abby's, and Dr. Kinsey, Joanna, didn't even know it.

Abby was crushed by the inevitability that one day, and that day was coming soon, she would have to betray Joanna's trust. She would have to leave the good doctor behind, and in so doing, Abby would place Joanna in a situation where her professional reputation would be left in shambles, desperately defending a case that no one else would believe. At least it would be that way for a long and painful while. Abby had searched the pathways to try and find a way forward where Joanna would be there, gladly, by her side, free and clear from the blame of others within the institution or the powers that be who worked for the ulterior and darker purposes of the government. But none of those existed in this world. Not yet.

And that was because of people like Agent Novak.

Agent Dmitri Novak. Yes, really. Dmitri. Like that shouldn't have been a warning sign to the powers that be within the FBI. Agent Novak was an uncomfortable, relentless shadow that had been spreading on the edges of Abby's awareness ever since she had begun her sessions with Dr. Kinsey, and ever since she had started going deeper within the Fold in her nightly sojourns, there he was, rearing his shiny bald pate in multiple pathways, demanding, cold-hearted, vicious in his tenacity to control and possess anything that would serve his greater, twisted purpose and misplaced loyalties to a State and a system that existed only for its own sake... But for Abby, his was a purpose that was no longer valid in this world or any world, for that matter. Agent Novak would find that out sooner or later.

Abby was just waiting for the trigger. For the moment of action to arrive. She knew that Agent Novak would enter the picture some day in the not-so-distant future, and when he did, well that would be when the proverbial shit would hit the fan. She would only have to wait a few more weeks. Until then, it would be daily sessions with Dr. Kinsey, art room discoveries with Melody, and as much time as possible anywhere near the vicinity of dreamy and delicious Michael. That couldn't be all that bad, right?

So, it was on a muggy and wet summer day on the first of July, one day after Abby celebrated her twelfth birthday (A cupcake and a candle with Michael serenading her with David Bowie songs), that Agent Novak finally arrived. It was a day that was beautiful in a streaky blue and gray after-a-rain kind of way; Abby was watching out the window when the black government-issued Ford sedans had pulled up. Then three figures, FBI agents, emerged from the cars, stereotypes in dark suits and dark glasses, Agent Novak's glistening bald head among them.

It wasn't much longer after that that Michael came to retrieve Abby for her morning session with Dr. Kinsey. Only they didn't go to her office like they usually did. This time, Michael led her to a larger conference room with video cameras in all four corners. He smiled slightly, sat her down, and was unusually quiet. He wasn't his usual, chatty self. He went to a side table and poured a glass of sweet tea, came back to set it down in front of Abby, and smile once again.

"The doctor will be in to see you soon," he said. "It's a different day today, isn't it?"

"No one day is quite the same as the one that came before it." Abby smiled back at him.

"You know what I mean, now, don't you?" His grin broadened to the dazzling smile that made Abby's heart flutter. Michael chuckled, then as he opened the door to leave, he sang in a quiet voice: "Ch-ch-ch-changes! Turn and face the strange, Changes!" He pointed at Abby, winked, then shut the door.

David Bowie songs always made her feel better. She was still smiling when Dr. Kinsey came into the room several moments later.

Kinsey was outwardly chipper and talkative as she bustled about the conference room. She kept running her hand through her hair as she went through some morning pleasantries—she was always genuinely happy to see Abby, and today was no different—but today, as she poured herself a glass of sweet tea and pulled out the tape recorder to begin their morning session, she was a bit strained in her eagerness, concealing a tension that lay beneath. Something was bothering her. Abby knew this immediately, and as she offered to top off Abby's iced tea, as Abby took back the glass and drank, she knew what it was. Special Agent Novak. He was waiting with his team in another office room, watching them on camera, waiting for the right moment to come in.

Dr. Kinsey turned on the recorder and began in the usual way. They were talking about several things: the interconnectedness of all things within the Fold, the need for being honest with each other, the results of the many tests the doctor had run, and so forth. It was a bit more scattered than usual, and the whole thing was just evasiveness. There was something else that was the real point of their discussion here today. Dr. Kinsey was, for the first time in Abby's experience with her, beating around the bush.

So, as Abby was listening and bandying back and forth in the usual way they had together, she decided to avail herself of one of the new tricks she had recently learned in her forays into the Fold.

Time wasn't linear, remember? All points in time existed simultaneously within each discrete moment of time, so Abby just decided to "roll the tape back," so to speak, and eavesdrop on the conversation Dr. Kinsey had been having with Agent Novak before she came into the room. It wasn't hard to do, as it had been a heated exchange and was still first and foremost in Dr. Kinsey's mind, which definitely helped to explain her distracted and scattered focus this morning.

So, while Abby talked and jousted in her usual manner, she multi-tasked her way through the previous half hour before the good doctor had come into her room. Now, as manipulations of the space-time continuum go, they don't really occur in standard time as we usually experience things, and Abby was able to comprehend everything that had happened in a matter of moments.

Feeling slightly guilty, Abby also knew that Kinsey would have no idea that she was doing it—in fact, as Abby listened to and answered her questions, she also ran back repeatedly a particular piece of the conversation between Dr. Kinsey and Agent Novak. It took her only moments to listen to and play back three times the following conversation, which actually lasted over two minutes at the time it took place, 24 minutes and 16 seconds before the current conversation she was having with Dr. Kinsey.

In that conversation, Dr. Kinsey and Agent Novak were in Dr. Kinsey's office. Joanna was seated behind her desk, arms folded somewhat defensively.

"I want to see her," Agent Novak was saying leaning in toward Dr. Kinsey, both hands placed territorially and aggressively on her desktop. His wedding ring was a large, ostentatious gold band with several diamonds inlaid. It constricted his finger and actually looked painful, like it was doing much more harm than simply cutting off his circulation.

"Today," he continued. "I want to sit in on today's session."

"Well, that can be arranged, of course," Dr. Kinsey replied, staring up at him from her seat behind the desk, somewhat annoyed by his posturing. *You are nothing but a thug, Agent Novak.* The doctor kept her opinions to herself, however, as the special agent from the FBI continued.

"If even only half of what you say in your report is true, then we're gonna want to bring her into the program," he released himself from his alpha ape position and strolled over to gaze out the window and down into the courtyard. "You understand, of course, that this isn't my decision alone. It comes from the very top. We're eager to see what she might be able to do for us."

Kinsey was immediately combative. "I understand what it is your superiors might want from A.B., but I'm here to tell you that I will officially object, for the record, to your interference in my ongoing therapy with Miss Rubideaux. We are at a critical junction. I've nearly broken through to a fuller understanding of what is going on in A.B.'s head. I fear that any disruption to her therapy right now may do irreparable harm."

"Jesus this is an ugly building!" Agent Novak interrupted her, still looking outside. "You must get a lot of wrist slitters around here. This place is pretty depressing." He turned and faced Kinsey, who had risen from her seat and now glowered back at Agent Novak. He smacked his lips and smiled without mirth.

"It doesn't matter what you think, doctor," he continued. "I already have the paperwork and the Justice department has already sent over the judge's release."

Kinsey was furious. "I'll challenge it. And this just isn't about what I think. There are any number of ethical and legal issues related to this matter. A.B. is still a minor, and she has rights. Furthermore, it's impossible in her current situation to get any legal guardian's consent."

"Two things," the special agent spat out. "One: She doesn't have any parents or legal guardians, so to speak. She's already a ward of the state. That's my domain. And two: She's no little girl. She's an extraordinary girl, in fact, a girl with access to the entire scope of human history through all time. A psychic phenomenon the likes of which we have never encountered before. Nothing that the Bureau represents or proposes to her would come as a shock to her system."

Dr. Kinsey was horrified at his callous cynicism. He was a cog in an enormous, indifferent bureaucracy. He could only see a tool—a weaponized possibility in Abby. He literally had no idea what Abby was all about—what she was here to do. She decided to make one more appeal, knowing that it would still, in all likelihood, fall on deaf ears.

"That may all be true," she began. "But you're overlooking a few things. Most significantly, that A.B. may very well decide to check out at any time. I truly believe she's only here because she chooses to be. What you propose will, in all likelihood, be met with a giggle and immediate dismissal. You're in way over your head, you know. Besides, A.B. probably already knows what you are up to. She's exhibited the ability to acquire knowledge and information remotely before. She's already ten moves ahead of you, Agent Novak."

"Precisely!" Agent Novak blurted out. "All the more reason to bring her in immediately. Transfer her to a high security facility." He held up his hand as Dr. Kinsey drew in her breath about to interject passionately. "Hold your horses, Dr. Kinsey! We're not prepared to go there yet. I'm a little bit ahead of myself. I assure you we'd much rather have her complicit and in full cooperation. Totally on board. So, what's the harm in asking her to come in? That's all I want to do today. Put a few cards on the table. See if she's game."

Kinsey regarded him for several moments before replying. "Be careful what game you play, special agent. She has cards you've never even seen." She paused to look through her files briefly. "Give me half an hour. I will find the right time to bring you in. I think I know our subject a bit better than you, Agent Novak. Trust me on this. I'll get her ready to meet you."

End tape. Roll it back. Repeat two times.

Our subject? Did Dr. Kinsey say that for Special Agent Novak's benefit, or did she truly see Abby only in this way?

Abby was now anxious to move forward and get this meeting over with. She now gave her full attention to Dr. Kinsey, who sat on the other side of the table from her. The doctor was finishing up an observation.

"So, there you go, saying things and knowing things that you simply shouldn't know or have any inkling about. You have proven this to me again and again."

Abby smiled, and tried to still the beating of her heart. Joanna had betrayed their confidence. Of course, Abby knew that she eventually would, but not because she wanted to. It was because she was bound by her duty. A misguided objectivity that refused to listen to the connections within her heart. Oh, and the fact that the FBI and Special Agent Novak had been pestering her since the beginning.

"Do you mean to say, doctor, that you are coming to believe that I might be telling you the truth?" Abby fell back into sarcastic mode, a game the doctor was very familiar with.

This time however, she didn't play along. The doctor replied, "Well, that may be one of the reasons we've changed our venue today. But what I believe in this instant, is irrelevant."

Ah. Here it comes. The rub—the true order of business. You've been dancing around it for a while, dear Joanna.

"You have some very special visitors today," she continued. "Folks that really want to talk to you."

Abby sighed inwardly. There was something sad about what was playing out in front of her. She spoke, "Those wouldn't happen to be the Men in Black characters that arrived in those very American cars with the government plates, would it?" She forced herself to laugh. She also pointed at the camera in the corner and raised her eyebrows with a wink. "I saw them earlier from my window. I watch, you know. Who comes in and out of the building. It helps to pass the time."

Kinsey seemed relieved. "Well, I imagine so. And yes, our visitors do happen to be from the FBI."

Abby was now fully engaged, and ready. Agent Novak wouldn't stand a chance. "They're not going to poke me, are they? Stick needles in my arms or probe my various orifices? Extract tissue samples?"

Kinsey laughed, a real chortle this time, just like old times. "A.B., please. I'm going to be right here with you. I would never let them do anything like that to you."

"Yeah, until they take me away," Abby replied looking Dr. Kinsey steadily in the eye. "Which you know they will, doctor. Joanna. He has authority and a different set of rules. There is nothing you can do to stop him."

Kinsey was unphased. "Not a chance, A.B. They are doctors like me. They specialize in abnormal psychiatry. And you are still my patient. Under my care. They are here at my request, in fact."

Abby sat staring back at Dr. Kinsey, who was running her hand through her hair once again. "I guess that part about confidentiality just went out the window, then."

Kinsey was now visibly distressed. "A.B., I asked them to come here because they can help."

Abby decided to see how deeply Joanna could deceive herself. She fired back, "Help who? You or me?"

"Well," Kinsey balked, then started again. "Both of us, I guess."

Joanna was decidedly less attractive when she was lying. Abby decided to apply a different tact—give Joanna another chance to overcome her stubborn denial of the facts that were all laid out in front of her. Facts that she still refused to acknowledge. "I thought you understood by now."

"I'm sorry?" Kinsey sat back and once again ran her hand through her hair.

Abby took a sip from her tea before continuing. "That you won't find any answers by talking to me or doing more tests on me. If you really want to discover what is going on, let me show you." She held out her hands to Dr. Kinsey. "All you have to do is take my hands, Joanna. We could start by talking to the very biosphere itself."

The doctor had to chuckle at that. Now both hands were running through her hair. "A.B., I am not a shaman. I don't know how to do that."

Abby withdrew her hands and calmly laid them palms down on the table between them. "Yes, you are. And yes, you do. You have approximately one hundred thousand billion cells in your human body—that's one hundred twenty-five billion miles of DNA just inside of you alone! Your personal DNA strands are long enough to wrap around the earth five million times. All of it connected to the biosphere, and to the Fold. You are constantly interlinked. You are constantly talking to the multiverse."

D r. Kinsey glanced up at the camera in the corner before responding, "Well, right about now, we are both interlinked with a government agency. Hold that thought, A.B.! I would like you to have this discussion with our friends from the FBI. Are you okay with that?"

Abby smiled from ear to ear, "Oh, this should be fun! But, Joanna?"

"Yes?" Kinsey had picked up a phone from the table in front of her and paused her finger before pressing down on the intercom button.

"You should always remember one thing," Abby paused lifted her glass to salute the camera in the corner. She was still smiling. "These people are not your friends."

"No, they are not," Dr. Kinsey muttered under her breath before punching the button on the phone. "Michael?" She spoke into the phone. "Bring them in, please."

She hung up the phone and turned to smile at Abby. "You know," she began quietly, "you don't need to answer any question you're not comfortable with. The same rules apply that you and I established at the very beginning of this process."

"Oh, I'm fully aware of that, Joanna." Abby lifted her glass and the doctor followed suit. They clinked their glasses together and took a drink. "Just relax," Abby continued. "I know what I'm doing. Sit back and enjoy the show."

Dr. Kinsey was about to speak but the door suddenly opened, and Special Agent Novak entered the room flanked by a younger man and a woman. The pair could have been twins in their dark suits, and Novak was Daddy Warbucks, a full head taller, chiseled and standing between them. Novak was smiling, a hideous contortion of his lips, and Abby was struck by the fact that in person, he was even more vile than she had thought.

The first thing that rolled over her was the enormity and the hostility of his very presence. He was emanating a dark and distorted frequency that screamed "danger" to anyone who had the good enough sense to pay attention to such things. His swarmy smile only served to make him a grim caricature of the conniving, self-righteous villain that he obviously played in virtually every pathway he wandered through the Fold. Here was a constant force, but one that was far from highly evolved. This was humanity's living nightmare. He was the blind, smug, entitled authority that thought he knew better than everyone else. He was oblivious. And it was because of people like him that the planet was precariously dangling on the precipice of disaster with our species so hellbent on destroying it.

"We finally meet, Miss Rubideaux!" His voice was deep. Maybe he was an opera singer in his non-special agent time.

Don Giovanni!

Abby had to muster all of her control not to start giggling right there on the spot. Oh, life was absurdly good, sometimes.

"A.B.," Dr. Kinsey stood to introduce them. "This is Special Agent Novak and his team. They're from the FBI's department of Special Behavioral Science. They're doctors, like me."

"Psychiatrists by any other name," Novak quipped. He nodded to his left and right. "This is Agent Browning and Agent Quick. They are here to assist me."

Abby glanced at the two younger agents who remained stiff and unsmiling. The man was petrified of Special Agent Novak. The woman was hostile and sullen. She clearly loathed the man that stood between them. Abby quickly surmised that this was the Special Agent Novak show, and that these two had more than once felt the lash of previous scoldings for stepping out of line. They were here just to observe and not actively participate in the proceedings.

Special Agent Novak regarded Abby with a slight cock of his head, still smiling. It made her shudder. "Do you mind if we join the proceedings?" he asked as they all sat down.

Abby glanced at Dr. Kinsey before replying, "It appears I don't really have a choice in the matter."

At that, Dr. Kinsey raised her eyebrows and slightly shook her head. Abby glanced at her, smiled, then returned her focus to Special Agent Novak, who was still smiling—well, leering, actually—and replying,

"Ah yes, choices. I've read some reports on what you have to say about the choices we all make. Very impressive. But no need to worry. This is a friendly visit, Miss Rubideaux. We are here at Dr. Kinsey's request."

"Well," Abby looked him in the eye. She recognized a liar and a bully when she saw one. "You have a funny definition of the words "friendly" and "request." And I can see where all of this is going. Look," and here Abby paused to reassess the situation. She decided to take advantage of her position and strike hard and fast. Novak needed to receive a message of who he was up against.

It was classic Sun Tzu and *The Art of War:* When sitting in the position of surprise and overwhelming force, attack and show no mercy.

She continued, "If you've truly read all of my reports, which I seriously doubt, actually, then you already know what I can do. So, let me make it clear and simple for you. I don't want this to go on much longer than it absolutely has to. My answer is no… to whatever it is that you propose and/or represent. And… Wait!" Abby held up her hand and motioned for Agent Novak to remain seated. He had started to rise from his seat. He eased himself begrudgingly back down.

"I want you to know," Abby resumed in a very clinical tone, "that I know why you are here and what you want. You want me to exhibit some of my abilities so you can report back to your grocery clerks and proceed with plans that involve me as an 'asset.' Well congratulations, I'm going to give you half of what you want, anyways. Just a taste of what you can never have. And the other half? The part where I consider joining your little operational team? Not going to happen. And yes, you are ready to dazzle me and show me all the reasons why I would be doing my country such a great service. But answer me this: If this is such a great country that is fighting the good fight, why then, if I do not agree to cooperate, are you more than willing to drop the friendly act and coerce me into cooperating through threats to my family, my unwilful detention, and unpleasant punishment towards my own person? Doesn't seem very *great* to me. Certainly not benign."

Special Agent Novak was smirking, and the other two agents remained expressionless. Dr. Kinsey was tight-lipped and wide-eyed. Apprehensive, you might say.

Novak scoffed and interjected, "Well, a little precocious, aren't we? You think you got it all figured out, do you?"

"Oh, more than that, Special Agent Novak," Abby purred. "I've already read the book, backwards and forwards and every which way. But I'm prepared to go off script. Maybe add a few new chapters. Chapters you won't like, Dmitri."

At the mention of his given name, Abby saw his nostrils flare, his jaw tense slightly. She was getting to him. She pressed her advantage, "Oh yes, Dmitri. A bit odd that your father, a Slovenian immigrant, would give his son a Russian name. An homage to his maternal Russian grandfather? Soviet occupation after the war was a bit of a mess, I know, but I'm sure that the current generation of the extended family wouldn't mind the mix in the gene pool. Don't worry, though, your family secrets are safe with me."

She glanced at Dr. Kinsey and winked. She looked back at Novak and continued, "But oh, the professional transgressions? I'm not sure those can be forgiven. I'm not just talking about all the procedural transgressions and the misrepresentations in your reports, but you know, Dmitri, that the little arrangement you have with the county health supervisor is something your superiors might be very interested in. When a mob enforcer engages in such activity it's called extortion, but I guess that some of you in the bureau just look at it as a perk that comes along with the job?" She paused and leaned in to make her point. "The fact that you have a badge don't make it right. In fact, it makes you worse than the criminals you like to put away for far less." Special Agent Novak was no longer smiling.

She turned to look at the male agent sitting to his left. He looked really uncomfortable. "And you, Agent Browning. Jeesh, why don't you grow a pair! I know all his shenanigans don't sit right with you. You've been there, witness to most of it, and what have you done about it? There's no code here that you must blindly adhere to. The department would come down on your side. Think it all the way through, man. You have more than enough evidence to make Dmitri here disappear from your life. What are you afraid of? And you!"

Abby turned to face the female agent and smile. "I think you should know, Special Agent Novak, that Agent Quick, here, would be very quick indeed to turn evidence on you. Oh yes, she would gladly slide right in to take your place. She has such ambition. In fact, she'd be really good at it—better than you, as I'm sure you're aware."

Abby paused and nodded at Agent Quick, then raised her fist and smiled. "Girl power!" she cried, before giggling. And then she looked back and forth between the two junior agents.

"You know," she continued, "the two of you really ought to get together more and compare notes. Other than the sheer brutish force of his presence, Dmitri here has nothing to derail either one of your careers. In fact, lots of other folks in the Bureau would be grateful if you ousted this self-aggrandizing, hypocritical prick!" She looked over at Special Agent Novak, "You're not very well liked. You do know that, don't you?"

Abby leaned back, satisfied, and took a sip of her iced tea. The other four people on the other side of the table sat in stunned silence for several moments.

Finally, Special Agent Novak snapped out of it. He gathered up and straightened his papers, filing them away into his briefcase.

"Well," he said. "I think we are done here for now." He clicked his briefcase shut, stood up, and the other two agents scrambled up after him. He pointed at the door, and Agent Quick stepped over to open it. Novak and Browning filed out of the room, and as Agent Quick closed the door, Abby was sure that she peeked back at her with something like a smile on her face.

In the quiet that followed, Dr. Kinsey remained seated and stared back incredulously at Abby, who was busy slurping down the last of her sweet tea.

"Do you think that was wise?" She finally asked.

Abby smiled back at her, "Oh he'll be back. And it won't be so easy next time."

"No, it won't. And when he comes back again, he'll be ready for you. You've just made a powerful enemy." Dr. Kinsey steepled her fingers together and regarded Abby solemnly. "I've dealt with men like Special Agent Novak all of my professional life. Call it an institutional hazard for a woman like me. Unfortunately, men like him still call the shots in our little corner of the world. And for a little girl like you with no proper papers or legal guardians? Well, suffice it to say that Special Agent Novak pretty much can do with you whatever he wants. He is given quite a bit of autonomy to run his department within the Bureau. And that means there are no checks and balances in place. He could make someone like you disappear into the program, and no one would know or care. He has the ability to follow through on threats."

Abby chortled, then responded, "You forget that I have you as my advocate! And you're very resourceful, Joanna. Oh, he's calculating and very thorough. But he's also overconfident. His hubris will be the chink in the armor that will bring the beast down. Trust me. As a dragon, I know all about such things!"

Dr. Kinsey just chuckled and shook her head. "Well, I imagine you would at that. But be careful, A.B.. A man like that will stop at nothing to get what he wants. He could take you in and there's not much I, or anybody else, could do to stop him."

"Don't underestimate yourself, Joanna." Abby smiled and nodded her head several times. "You are a warrior woman and a high priestess in all other times, including this one! And I want you to know that you have helped me find my way. It's what you have always done."

Abby looked long and intensely at Dr. Kinsey, who finally shrugged and asked, "What?"

"I want you to know," Abby began, "that I know you fought for me back there. That you tried to stand up for me against him. That no matter what happens in the weeks and days that lie ahead, you will always fight for me. You are my constant ally, in all the pathways that unfold. We're not done yet—the two of us together. And no matter how this particular chapter ends, or how you might find yourself in a predicament, I want you to know that I am always going to fight for you, too. Even if it seems like I've betrayed you or left you behind to be on your own, please know that I only did it because it was the best way forward. The only way. I will always count you as a friend."

"Okay," and it was Dr. Kinsey's turn to become solemn. "Now you're scaring me. What are you cooking up, A.B.?"

Abby pointed at the recorder and the cameras in the room. Dr. Kinsey pushed the stop button on the recorder, then pushed back her chair, opened a drawer and Abby heard a switch click.

"Okay, everything's off," Dr. Kinsey said. She looked back at Abby. "No one can see or hear us."

"I need to go talk to my brother," Abby said.

"You have a brother?" Asked Dr. Kinsey.

"Sure. Well, he is one of many that are among us. Always. He's just a thought away," Abby stopped and tapped her temple, smiling. "But I need to see him. Real time. I need to leave you soon."

"Could you just leave here anytime, then?" Dr. Kinsey hesitated, drumming her fingers on the desktop. "I mean, A.B., you've been here for... how long? A few months? I've never once seen, in all that time, any manifestation of these changes you've been describing. You're just a girl, A.B.. An amazing, brilliant and perhaps even supernatural girl with extraordinary psychic powers." Dr. Kinsey stopped to run her hand through her hair and smile. "But you have... I mean, in your mind? You have a sickness. And we are so close to breaking through. To understanding this elaborate fantasy that you've concocted."

Abby stilled the disappointment within herself. "You still don't believe everything I've said," she finally spoke, softly. "But that's okay. There are so many more things that I want to tell you. That I want to *show* you!"

Yes, show her.

The dragon rumbled deep within her. Abby slapped it down impatiently.

"No! We wait!" Abby snapped out loud. She glanced over at Joanna, who was regarding her somewhat skeptically.

"Sorry," Abby continued, slightly chagrined. "Look, a whole lot of things are about to happen around here. In the next few weeks, I want you to do something for me. Are you listening?"

"Yes," Dr. Kinsey answered calmly.

Abby took one moment to assess her companion, then decided that truth was the best option. It always was.

"Look," she began urgently, "I'm not kidding. Here's what's going to happen, and here's what I want you to do. "Over the next two weeks, you and I are going to meet like we have been doing. I enjoy our sessions immensely, as I know that you do, too." They smiled briefly at each other before Abby continued.

"Special Agent Novak will want to sit in on many of these sessions. You will let him without objection. He will, for the most part, behave himself. It's for Agent Quick, actually, that we do this. She is our ally, and she will help you and me before all of this is over. Novak is purely incidental. But we need her on the bureau's end. For later. When the government finally figures out that they can be the good guys."

She paused and reached over to grasp Joanna's hands. The doctor flinched slightly, and Abby was quick to assuage her anxiety.

"Joanna, relax. I promise I will never enter your mind without your permission or unless there is a life-threatening emergency." The doctor eased her tension, and Abby continued.

"Ok, now, this part is important. Pay very close attention." Abby squeezed her hands and the doctor smiled. "Yes, it's true that I could leave this facility whenever I want, but I'm not ready to do that. I still have things that I need to figure out. I like it here. And in the evenings, when I'm lying in bed, I am learning how to travel. How to go deeper into the Fold—and not just in my mind—physically, too. Yeah, that's right. And the other 'inmates' in this place?" and here Abby paused to cackle at her choice of words. "Well, believe it or not, it's one of the best places I've ever been to find out more about myself. There are others here connected to the Fold in ways that they can't even understand or that they are even aware of."

Abby paused to gather her thoughts. Dr. Kinsey was staring back at her intensely, the lines in her forehead all pinched together above the bridge of her nose. "But they are in it, almost unconditionally. It's a natural state for them to be there. Their brains are different, yes… and it's easier for them to access. I can help you write that groundbreaking paper that explains all of this, some day!" Abby and Dr. Kinsey both chuckled.

"But listen to me," Abby continued more earnestly. "There will come a day not so far from now when Agent Novak will make a decision. He will have decided, finally… duh! That there is no way to control me or have me join his team cooperatively. He will order his team, that nut-less yes man, Browning, actually, to sedate me. They're gonna try to transport me to another facility. I want you to let them do it. Oh, you can protest after the fact, make a real fuss over it—which for the most part, I am sure would be your genuine reaction! But don't try to stop them beforehand… just be somewhere else. Let them do it."

"But why, A.B.?" Dr. Kinsey was asking, "Why does it have to be like this?"

Abby grinned, but not from a genuine sense of pleasure. It was more a smile of resignation. "Because it's the best way forward. The only way, where you and Michael, and all of your staff come out of this okay, and where Special ass-sphincter Novak will have to take all of the blame. And don't worry, I'll be fine. Everything will be as it is meant to be."

"I don't know, A.B.. All of this just doesn't seem necessary. I have means at my disposal, protocols that I can follow…"

"No, Joanna," Abby interrupted her. "Trust me. This is the best way."

They looked at each other for quite a while. Dr. Kinsey finally nodded her head, squeezed Abby's hands, then smiled and pulled away to stand.

"Well," she said. "Ten AM tomorrow? My office. I have some chocolate from Austria that will be waiting for you."

"Mozart's balls?" Abby grinned.

"But of course!" And they both laughed.

Exactly two weeks went by before Agent Novak did what Abby said he would do. Dr. Kinsey had begun to wonder if everything that Abby purported to be able to see was just some part of a greater delusion—an elaborate, unprecedented self-deception. None of it was real. It was all just imagined—every last minutia of incredible detail.

But their sessions together seemed to prove otherwise. There was no question that Abby had incredible psychic abilities. She had demonstrated them again and again. Even with Special Agent Novak sitting in for several sessions, Abby didn't hold back. She, in fact, seemed to be quite expert at ignoring him.

And what Abby described in their sessions together...well, it was incredible.

Dr. Kinsey was sitting in her office late in the afternoon in the near dark of the day's end, reviewing the audio files—something which had become a nearly full-time vocation for her—when Michael came knocking. Well, it was a knock followed by him bursting into the room.

"You need to come with me now," Michael said.

Dr. Kinsey looked up from her desk and paused the recording, removing her head phones. Michael was shifting his weight from foot to foot, uncharacteristically grim in his demeanor.

"They're going to take her away," he announced. "She's been sedated and they're just waiting to fill out the paperwork for transport."

Dr. Kinsey shot up from her desk. "A.B.? Where is she now?"

Michael answered, breathlessly as they both scurried from her office and darted down the hall. "She's in the nurses' room, under sedation. They got her on a gurney, ready to go. Joanna," Michael pulled her to a stop as they rounded the corner to the reception lobby.

A small army of FBI agents were milling about, Special Agent Novak was talking to the receptionist at the desk, pointing down and gesticulating with emphasis. Dr. Kinsey only had a moment to take it all in before Michael spoke softly in her ear.

"Joanna, it's okay. She's in the room where she told me to place the flowers. I unlocked the window, like she told me to."

Dr. Kinsey turned to regard Michael, who was now smiling sheepishly, but then Special Agent Novak's booming voice filled the room.

"You're too late, doctor. She's mine, now. It's all but done. I'll just need your signature to release her."

"What?" Dr. Kinsey stared at her staff receptionist, Rona, who just shrugged and threw up her hands. She glanced around the lobby and saw a few other staff members and orderlies nervously glancing around as the FBI agents loomed over the exits and blocked the various doorways. She fixed her gaze on the smirking face of Special Agent Novak. He was holding out a clip board with the release form waiting for her to sign it.

"You know I'll fight you every step of the way," she said, resisting the urge to slap him.

"You know I don't care," he chuckled and turned the clipboard around and offered her a pen.

"She's gone!" Agent Browning suddenly shouted as he bounded down the stairwell and skidded into the room. "She's gone, sir," he repeated, panting heavily.

His pronouncement was followed by a few moments of suspended disbelief followed by an avalanche of action. Novak slammed the clipboard down on the receptionist desk then sprinted up the stairwell. He was followed by Agent Quick and Browning, then, with a glance at each other, Dr. Kinsey and Michael followed at full speed.

On the second floor they turned left and dashed down the hallway to the nurses' office. They came panting to a stop outside the door. Agent Novak was in the middle of the room staring stupidly at an open window. Melody, the schizophrenic 12-year old artist and the only other occupant in the room, was sitting up in her bed clapping. An empty gurney, the constraints broken as if by force, was directly across from her on the other side of the room.

Dr. Kinsey pushed her way into the room, Agent Quick and Browning stepping aside to allow her to pass. Melody stopped clapping and pointed at the window.

"She flew away," Melody said gleefully. "I will paint you a picture for your funeral parlor." She was bouncing excitedly up and down on her bed.

Dr. Kinsey sniffed the air. Something was off—there was a very strong and out-of-place odor—a musky, urine-like smell that was pungent and vaguely unpleasant. It smelled like snake, if snakes had a smell. Dr. Kinsey was reminded of the smell of a pet store next to the terraniums containing the various reptiles. She turned to gawk at Michael, who was smiling from ear to ear.

"I swear, sir," Agent Browning was explaining, "I was right outside the room the entire time. No one came in or out. There's no way she could get out. Then this nut job started clapping, and I came in."

"Roasted chestnuts," Melody announced solemnly.

Novak and Agent Quick had gone over to the window and were looking down. There was about a twenty-foot drop with no visible hand holds or leverage on the side of the building, which was flat and smooth red brick all the way down.

"That's a long drop," Agent Quick uttered. "Not likely."

"There's just no way, no way," Agent Browning repeated.

"Give me a perimeter around this building!" Novak snarled. "Make it two blocks! Now! She can't have gone very far."

Agents Quick and Browning snapped into action, and left the room talking into their devices.

"Oh, fly away, fly away! You won't catch her!" Melody was singing from her bed.

"Get this person out of here, now." Novak was glaring at Dr. Kinsey, fuming. "She's a witness, though. I want to talk to her later. Nobody touches anything in here!"

Michael moved over to Melody as Novak stormed out of the room. Michael and Melody left the room, both smiling. Dr. Kinsey touched his arm and asked quietly,

"What did you do?"

"Nothing she hadn't already known that I would do," Michael answered, still smiling. "She left something for you." He nodded over towards the end table where a fresh bouquet of flowers was standing in a vase.

Michael and Melody left the room, leaving Dr. Kinsey alone for the moment. She walked over to the flowers and saw the card attached. There was a big heart drawn the length of the card, and inside it in a precise, elegant hand were the following words written in purple ink:

Dear Joanna,

I'm only Dreaming of Dragons.

With Love,

A.B. (until next time!)

It was then that she noticed the small shiny object attached to the card. She plucked it from the little clip and held it up. It was a scale—reptilian or fish—about the length of her finger and twice as wide. She held it up to the light from the room, and it glimmered like the inside of a sea shell. There were sparkling tones of purple, maroon, and indigo contained within a sheen of green. It was beautiful.

Dr. Kinsey lifted it to her face and inhaled its scent: definitely a much stronger concentration of the musky aroma that had earlier filled the room.

She turned and gazed out the window. She could just see over the rooftops of the adjoining buildings. Twilight purples and streaks of orange and pink lit the western sky over lake Ponchartrain. The sun had just set, and evening was settling over the city of New Orleans.

Joanna breathed in the smells of the dusk. It was her favorite time of the day. Rain was on the way. And somewhere far away—she wasn't sure if it was real or imagined—she heard the faintest trace of a screeching, reptilian roar.

It was the sound of a dragon who was happy to be free.

16

⁂

OLD SCRATCH

AWAKENED

From the Audio transcripts of Dr. Joanna Kinsey
Chief Psychiatrist, CHNOLA Northshore Center,
New Orleans, LA

Excerpt of Audio File Transcript #AR10089-51

July 14, 2022

Subject: A. B. Rubideaux. Female. Age: 12

Transcript of recording begins: 10:48 AM EST.

Kinsey: *So, this brother of yours. Should I be worried? Am I ever going to meet him?*

A.B.: *Oh yes, my twin brother. Fraternal. Not identical. Far from identical—Enoch is less inclined to peaceful resolution of the mess humanity has created for itself than I am. Yes, I think you shall meet him. Eventually. But, no. I don't think you need to worry. You wouldn't be able to do anything about it anyway.*

Kinsey: *Do anything about what?*

A.B.: *About his solution to the current crisis we, and all the creatures of this planet, are currently experiencing. Oh, he and I are very different. I happen to have taken a liking to humans. To everything that humanity represents—to an unfulfilled promise that yet yearns to be free. A beautiful potential realized. He, and many others like him, feel differently.*

Kinsey: *How so?*

A.B.: *They are less patient. It's nothing personal, you know. It's just a question of efficiency. Unlike I, who have come here to help humanity ascend to higher consciousness, he and those who are of like minds, have taken a different approach. Well, it's really more of an ultimatum.*

Kinsey: *An ultimatum? What kind of ultimatum? And to whom?*

A.B.: *It's an ultimatum to humanity. One with a very simple message. "Evolve or be eradicated."*

LATER THAT SAME EVENING: JULY 14, 2022

I t felt good to stretch her wings. Just to be flying again. The movement of her wings, an effortless flapping, triggered responses throughout the muscles of her entire body. The cool, wet wind streamed over her. Yes, she was built for flying. She shivered in pleasure. She swooped and dropped suddenly, enjoying the rush and the sensation of her stomach dropping then rising up through the top of her head.

Better than any rollercoaster.

That was the little girl named Abby. The voice inside of the dragon. They were linked together, always, a connection that was electric and jolted down to each and every last neural synapse within her musculature. They were thought. They were emotion. They existed together, and they were one.

The dragon dove deeper, sweeping closer to the ground. She glided over bayou land, misty rain dancing and curling in the wake of her swift flight. She spread her awareness out over the very land beneath her and felt the warm patches of air hovering over the cooler water of the swamp below. She felt the sighing music of the trees, a spiderweb link of awareness that spread from roots through soil, up through trunks and then leaves, finally releasing into the very air itself. A murmur of eons, as old as the stone beneath the earth's crust. She felt the warm pulse of small mammals, mice and squirrels and rabbits in their burrows, hearts beating, life force thrumming. She felt the fish in the water, a concerted rhythm of impulse and cool flesh beneath glittering scales. That made her belly rumble.

Hunger.

But she resisted the temptation to dive into the waters. The fish and her meal could wait.

She caught an updraft of warmer air, rising off the oily slick of natural gas that was bubbling up from a sink hole within the swamp. She tucked her wings and spiraled and accelerated through space. Her senses reached further, spreading everywhere and nowhere all at once, nudging into the infinity of awareness through time and space that was the Fold.

Oh, she could fly forever, but first, there were unfinished things that needed to be done. For Abby.

The town of Houma appeared ahead, soft lights winking in the evening through the trees. The dragon turned and flew over a stand of trees in the bayou, hugging low, her belly almost brushing their tops.

There!

The small white house with forest green shutters occupied a clearing at the end of a cul-de-sac. The young girl with frizzy red hair was standing on the porch looking up, waiting. She turned and saw the dragon approaching.

Olivia.

The dragon dipped then pulled up, arresting the pace of her flight. She hovered briefly in the air, wings flapping once, then twice before lightly landing on the lawn in the front yard of the house.

A blast of warm air and a flurry of leaves brushed past Olivia, who stood gaping, hands on hips, with the biggest, goofiest grin anyone had ever seen plastered across her face.

"Well, I'll be a suck egg mule!" She pronounced, taking in the majestic spectacle. She was giddy, and she couldn't believe what just happened.

Well, don't stand there gawkin'! Get me something to cover up with!

The voice sounded telepathically, directly inside of Olivia's head.

"No way... This is so cool!" Olivia breathed out breathlessly.

Hello? I need a towel, or a bathrobe. A change of clothes? Anything? Go on!

"Oh, right," Olivia giggled then dashed inside the house. She came out just a moment later with a blanket in her arms, just in time to see a fourteen-foot tall dragon with purple and indigo scales, slowly spin, blur, then morph into the naked figure of a five-foot-two girl named A. B. Rubideaux.

Abby collapsed on the lawn and shuddered like a newborn pony. Olivia quickly moved forward and covered her with the blanket. Abby was shivering and covered in a sheen of sweat.

"Thanks," Abby breathed with a grateful smile.

"Well," Olivia responded, "That's not something you see every day." She helped Abby to her feet and after a few unsteady steps, guided her back up to the porch and into her home.

They walked past a small parquet floored entry way and into a cozy family room. "I got your message," Olivia smiled and tapped her temple. "Just like a download. Everything is prepared." She handed Olivia a bundle that was a change of clothes. "I think these will fit you. The bus ticket to New Orleans is in the right front pocket of the pants."

"Where's your mom and her new boyfriend?" Abby asked taking the clothes.

"They went out," Olivia clucked, "On a Wednesday night. Yeah, like that has ever happened before. We are alone." Olivia paused to regard her friend with something like joyful amazement on her face.

"How are you doing all of this, Abby?" she asked. "I mean there I am sitting in the parlor doing my math lessons and WHOOMF! There you are inside of my head, giving me instructions!"

Abby chuckled and spoke over her shoulder as she passed into the bathroom, "Call it a trick of the dragon trade." She smiled and ducked behind the door to change into the clothes.

"All right," Olivia said, pacing the room like a cat in heat. "I'll buy that. But tell me this: You could go anywhere. Do anything you want. Why come back here to see me? Why not just go directly to New Orleans?"

"First of all," Abby called from the bathroom. She poked her head out from behind the door. "I missed you." She popped back out of sight but continued talking. "You are my best friend. And I need your help. I can't do all of this alone. I'm still finding my way."

Abby walked out of the bathroom in a pair of blue jeans and a Saints tee shirt. She was pulling a green knit sweater on around her shoulders. She paused to grin at Olivia as she buttoned up the sweater.

"Really?" she said. "Sponge Bob underpants with matching socks?" She looked down at her feet and wiggled her toes. Sponge Bob and Patrick grinned up at them.

"Hey!" Olivia laughed. "I've outgrown them, and you're more petite than me. They fit you okay, right?"

"No complaints," Abby smiled and the two girls high-fived each other. "And second of all, to finish answering your question, I can't just go flying around in a city like New Orleans. It would raise a few eyebrows, to say the least. Plus, I'd rather wear your clothes than bust into a thrift shop or steal them from some homeless person, which I would have to do if I went there directly."

"Yeah, totally," Olivia snickered. "Your like the Terminator when you arrive here, butt naked only not nearly so pissed off."

"Oh, I'm pissed off, alright," Abby said. "I just wear it well. And I have a mission. I need to meet my brother, Enoch. I know, I know!" Abby held up her hand to placate Olivia. "Until a few days ago, I didn't know about him either. Well, actually, I didn't remember him, that he actually existed. But he's been there in my mind the whole time, kind of lurking. Toying with me, actually. That's closer to the truth."

She blew a stray bang out of her face and sighed, turning to face Olivia. "So, it's not like I've been holding out on you. I would've told you about him, but since the last time we've met, so much has happened! I've unlocked so much! I can do so much more, Olivia! It's truly incredible."

"Well, I'm happy now," Olivia replied, smiling. "I've seen you in dragon form. It's real." Olivia walked into the kitchen, still talking and Abby could hear the refrigerator door open and close. "Now I can die and go to heaven, I guess. What more is there to do in this life?" Olivia came out with two Snickers bars and handed one to Abby. "Hungry?"

"Oh, yes!" Abby took the chocolate and immediately went to work on it with several quick nibbles. Between smacks of chocolatey caramel, she continued. "You ain't nearly done with this life, my friend!" Abby said and waggled her snickers bar at Olivia. "We've got plans for you. You signed up a long time ago, whether you knew it or not. You're on board."

"On board for what, exactly?" Olivia had wolfed down her chocolate, and she now crumpled up her wrapper and tossed it squarely off of Abby's forehead. "Yes!!" Olivia bent over and pumped her fists like she had just made the game-winning shot.

Unphased, Abby took another bite of her candy bar, savored it for a few moments, then replied nonchalantly, "Oh nothing much. We're just here to save humanity."

"Of course. All in a day's work. I'm in." Olivia grinned. "What are we saving them from?" Olivia rocked back on her heels and held her head up higher. All she needed was some suspenders to grab on to and her look of smugness would be complete.

"From themselves," Abby said slowly. "I think. But it might be more complicated. Most of them, I think, just aren't ready for the download. I need to help them first."

"O-o-o-kay," Olivia said, grabbing her backpack. "Can we be a little more specific? What's the plan?"

"There is no plan. I need to think it through a little more." Abby said, suddenly feeling rather dismal. She collapsed on the couch and hugged her shoulders, rubbing the tops of her arms and taking deep breaths. She really had to resist the urge to take a nap.

"And this brother character of yours?" Olivia asked. "What's he got to do with it?"

Abby looked up at Olivia and sighed. "Oh yes. Enoch. Well, that's the first order of business. I need to talk to him. He's the missing link. Things are happening out there, all across the Fold. I just hope I'm not too late."

"The Fold?" Olivia asked, scrunching her face in the very picture of perplexity.

Abby glanced at her and chuckled. "Gosh, I missed you. Yeah, the Fold. I will tell you all about it sometime, when we've got a whole week or something. For now, it's something I've got to do on my own. You've done enough, Olivia. You're the best friend, ever."

"Hang on," Olivia quipped. She reached out her hand, Abby took it, and she pulled her up from the couch. "That sounds suspiciously like another long goodbye. Nuh-uh. Nope. Not this time." Olivia was shaking her head. "Last time I left you, you were sitting in the back of a police car, and Stump was shot dead. And then what? How many months go by without a word? Without any information at all? Nobody knew nothing about where you were or what had happened. Nobody knew nothing at school. Nobody would talk about it. My momma wouldn't let me go down to talk to the sheriff or the county people. Nope, this time you're talking to me. If I'm gonna be your full partner in crime, then there will be no secrets between us. Your bus leaves in about thirty minutes. I'm walking you there, and you're gonna explain a few more things to me. Deal?"

Abby grinned. "Deal!"

Abby stood, nearly breathless, staring across into the face of her best friend, Olivia. It was a few minutes before eight PM and they were at the bus station. The driver had started up the engine.

"Okay," Abby said, taking the backpack from Olivia. "You know what to do."

"Tomorrow morning," Olivia stated, "shortly after dawn. I am to meet you at the boat landing with spare sets of clothing and a sleeping bag. Some non-perishable food. Camping supplies. I know. We're setting up your new home on Gator Island."

"It's Old Man Willow Island," Abby laughed.

"Nope!" Olivia stuck her chin out and huffed. "It will always be Gator Island for me."

"Have it your way, then." Abby breathed heavily and glanced over at the bus. She hoisted her bag on to her shoulder. "The plan remains the same."

Abby and Olivia had walked briskly from Olivia's home to the bus station of downtown Houma. It was about a 15-minute walk at the pace they had set. Abby was so pumped up, that she couldn't go any slower. Along the way, she had tried to explain everything that had happened since she and Olivia had last parted ways. Her experience in the detention center, the last few months with Dr. Kinsey in the CHNOLA facility; her breakthroughs in the evenings there where she had been honing her dragon and wanderer skills.

She didn't go too deeply into the nuances of the Fold—quantum theory, the ability to be everywhere and nowhere all at once—intergalactic, multi-dimensional consciousness was not something that Olivia would truly comprehend. But she was able to tell Olivia a few things that she could understand. That Abby was advancing and discovering new things about her abilities and the truer nature of the cosmos. She could now acquire knowledge and experience through her dragon "downloads." And the downloads were in her control—not just random waves that rolled over and through her from out of the blue. She could communicate telepathically—hence, her sudden appearance in Olivia's mind when she assumed dragon form and flew from New Orleans to Houma. She no longer needed to touch someone to have access to their memories and experiences—that could occur remotely. But she told her she would never do that to somebody without their permission. Something about Stump's "traveler's honor."

Oh yes, and she showed Olivia the bear claw that Stump had given her and explained where it had come from and what that meant about travelling to other dimensions and other realities. She mentioned Granny Jane, Bo M'Ba Nesh, and her brother, Enoch, and her birth mother—all of whom were wanderers that had the ability to move between worlds through space and time. That the dreams and possibilities contained within each person's conscious mind where not just thoughts or memories; they were real, tangible places and it was possible to physically travel there—Inside the Fold.

Abby had also explained to her the plan—sort of plan, anyway—and one which Abby had been concocting on the fly as they walked toward the bus stop. Abby needed to meet her brother and find out a few things. He was calling to her. Reaching across the folds of time and space to finally be here with her physically in this time and place. After that meeting, she would rendezvous with Olivia and retreat to their little secret island in the lake upon the bayou. It was the only place that Abby felt no one would be able to find them, and she needed a base of operations as well as some time to figure out what she needed to do. The island was the place she felt most comfortable. Hence the clothing, sleeping bag, food, and supplies that Olivia had agreed to gather.

Olivia now walked over to the sidewalk next to the bus that Abby was about to board and smiled her goofy grin back at Abby.

"You sure about this?" Olivia asked, half teasing. "I could come with you. You need me, dragon girl."

"Yes, I do need you," Abby responded and gave Olivia a hug. "But not with me now." She pulled away slightly, so Olivia could see her face and look into her eyes. "I need you to do one more thing. And that can only be done here, behind the scenes, quietly. I need you to find out where they're keeping Momma Bea. I know they're not back at the house. She's in custody somewhere. And Henry…" Abby stopped, closed her eyes, and pinched up her brow in concentration. "Well he's just gone. Something's happened, Olivia, and no matter how hard I try, I can't find either one of them. They are shielded… invisible to me. I can't access her remotely. Like I did with you. I can't find the connection. So, I need you to get a message from me to Momma Bea, okay? Tell her that I'm fine, and everything will be okay. She's not to worry. We will see each other again. Tell her that's my promise! And…and that I'm still her sweet peaches!"

Olivia turned and glanced at the bus driver, who had come down the steps and leaned out the door, tapping his wristwatch.

"Oh Abby," she said hurriedly, "Your bus is about to leave. I'll take care of that and everything else. Don't you fret, now. I'll see you tomorrow morning at the crack!"

Abby smiled. "At the crack," she repeated. And she turned to climb on the bus.

"I mean ten AM would be a more civil hour!" Olivia called after her as she stepped up into the bus. "It's not like we got any cows to milk, or anything like that." She laughed, and she could see Abby smiling through the window of the bus. She watched as the bus hissed, the door dipped and shut, and then it slowly pulled away. Abby was waving through the window, and it reminded Olivia of the last time they had said goodbye with a wave through a window, only this time nobody had just been shot and killed. This time they were secret agent travelers through space and time, and they were on a mission. Olivia turned and started walking back home.

"I'm gonna need an outfit," she said softly to herself. "Just like Scarlett Johansson. Black Widow or the Wasp? Body tights. Sweet."

Abby walked slowly through the Garden District of New Orleans. It was late in the evening, maybe around 11 PM. She had passed a few other people on the streets, but they didn't pay any attention to a twelve-year old girl with a backpack. Ever since the bus ride, she had been fully tapped into the Fold, not really thinking any thoughts, not really grounded physically to this or any other world. The sidewalk she was currently walking on seemed immaterial and temporary, like she could just disappear through it at any moment. Her footsteps made no sound as she moved along like a cat. She felt like she was flickering in and out of space, like a hologram beam that was slightly distorted—one moment here, gone the next, then back again. She was just following a certain frequency, a vibration that was leading to her brother, who was reaching out to her.

Enoch.

She called out with her mind.

Have you come to fly, little sister?

His response was almost immediate. Abby stopped and turned to face the Victorian style house that was on her left. It was massive, with tower-like turrets flanking each end of the house, and gabled peaks above a three-storied frame. This was a multi-million-dollar mansion.

Abby felt a trickle of perspiration run down the small of her back, even though the evening was cool and crisp. She peered into the walkway that divided the front yard beyond a wrought iron gate. A figure was gliding down the stairs of the front porch, walking toward her. There was light emanating from an open door beyond, and wisps of fog or smoke seemed to whirl around in colorful puffs as, before Abby knew it—and maybe it was done by some trick—the figure suddenly stood just before her, peering through the gate.

He was a handsome young man—not much more than an adolescent—standing in an immaculate Victorian-era green suit embroidered, by all appearances, with golden and red thread. He wore a matching top hat and carried a long black cane with a golden dragon on its top. He had the same dark curly locks of hair as Abby, and the same piercing green eyes, but his skin was paler.

"Oh, good evening, Aurora!" His voice was mellifluous and rich, a silky baritone that sounded much older than the boy looked. "My little sister has found her way back to me!" He smiled and reached over to pull open the gate.

Abby stepped in, and studied her brother as, now that she stood in his physical presence, a wave of memories and information rippled through the fold and converged in this present moment, standing at a gate, before a beautiful mansion in the Garden District of New Orleans. She knew him. Oh yes, and very well, for they had been together before—countless times. And all through time. Inseparable. She was the *Yin* to his *Yang*.

"Enoch," she said with a genuine smile. "You know it's the 21st century. Your only about 150 years off with your wardrobe."

"Ah, my dear!" Enoch stamped his cane and twirled around once very gracefully. His frock coat whipped and snapped in the wind. "Certain things never go out of style. And these times are starved for good taste. You wait and see. What do they call it now? A meme? I'll slowly let the idea ripple and bubble just below the surface. And before you know it, it's on all the people's iPhones! All the designers and the couture shops will be filling up their fashion runways and their exclusive shop windows with my vintage collection. It will catch like wildfire. I'll bring this style back in no time. No time at all. All the young men will be begging for the look. It's inevitable!" He laughed as he closed the gate and beckoned her inside. "Won't you please come in. I've been expecting you."

"You've been in my mind for quite a while, not declaring yourself. Hiding." Abby said as she walked alongside him, up the steps, across the porch and through the mansion's open front door. "Pretty sneaky."

"Oh, you've got to have a little fun, sis!" Enoch said as he entered behind her. A pair of young serving girls dressed in tight black evening dresses approached. They were beautiful and exotic. Middle Eastern? The first one took Enoch's coat, hat, and walking cane and whisked away. The second was carrying a tray upon which sat a large silver bowl filled with truffles. She swooped in and offered them, and Enoch said "Ooh," and reached down to grab several and pop them in his mouth. Abby shook her head no, and the girl spun away down a side hall.

"Won't you come into my parlor?" Enoch said in a garbled voice full of truffles. He smiled, revealing thick red fluid and bits of chocolate clinging to his teeth.

Abby glanced around. The entryway was massive, with side hallways leading off left and right. The serving girls had gone down to the left in what appeared to be the kitchen. Straight ahead was a foyer with a massive spiral staircase leading up. The floor was white, gold-veined marble, but everything else was carved, dark mahogany wood and intricately detailed: the walls, beamed ceiling, and the railing of the stairs—everything was carved in the precise and exact detail of a woodland motif. There were trees and fern leaves, and woodland creatures scampering. There were Celtic motifs and corded knots blended into the woodland scenes. It was masterful work and one of the most beautiful things Abby had ever seen. A giant golden chandelier hung in the center of the foyer and as they passed beneath it, Abby could see the burning flames of natural gas that lit each tapered sconce. The carved etchings and figures within the chandelier matched the woodland motif of the walls and ceiling.

Enoch lightly flitted up the stairwell to the first landing and continued straight down a wide central hallway, Abby following closely. He was rambling as he went.

"You know, it's not my fault you picked a young Cajun girl from rural Louisiana. Really! I mean, living in a swamp with no access to Wi-Fi or computers. It's a wonder you've awakened at all."

He glided into a side room, pushing open gold-gilded mahogany doors and sweeping into a very grand parlor. The room was magnificent, with the same dark wood, but the walls were hung with rich red and golden tapestries and filled with gilt-leafed 18th century French furniture. Everything was splendidly ornate and immaculate.

Enoch swept into a large red-cushioned, high-backed chair, and gestured for Abby to sit in the companion chair next to him. A fire crackled in the hearth opposite the chairs.

"You could have anything you want here, you know," Enoch was continuing as he motioned to the luxury around him. "We are like gods, still. That much hasn't changed. But oh, the accoutrements! The playthings at our disposal." He paused as yet another serving girl, similarly clad in the elegant black evening dress, came in with a fine silver and porcelain coffee service and set it down on the table between them.

"That will be all, Shala. Thank you." Enoch said as he reached over and began to pour. The servant smiled widely at Abby, curtsied, and left the room as silently as she came in.

"You've changed quite a bit, brother." Abby smiled as she watched him pour the coffee.

Enoch paused to regard Abby as he set a coffee down between them. "You need to live a little, Aurora."

"A.B., actually," Abby interrupted. "I go by A.B., now. That name has been co-opted by a Disney princess."

"And a princess you should be!" Enoch laughed as he sipped his coffee. He gestured to the cup beside Abby, and she picked it up to sip. It was hot, creamy, and delicious.

"Look around here," he continued. "Why not avail yourself of the many fruits? There's no harm in it. In fact, it's the quickest way to earn respect in this material world of consumerism and privately-owned capital assets." Enoch leaned in conspiratorially and continued in a hushed tone.

"You could make a killing as a day trader. Or have you considered playing the ponies? With our gifts? There is wealth and power unimaginable, all at your fingertips. We could indeed become just like the kings and queens of old."

"That's not why we're here, brother." Abby responded drily. "You should know this better than any of us."

"Oh right, dare I forget that father might banish me once again before I succumb to the sins of humanity?"

"It wasn't a banishment," Abby replied. She could remember everything, now. "It was a reward for your purity and compassion."

"It was unspeakably harsh and cruel!" Enoch clipped. "Just when things were getting interesting, he took me away and had the audacity to call it 'protection.' Well," and here Abby watched her brother as he stared into the roaring fireplace and drifted somewhere else, momentarily.

"This time," he suddenly came to life, "things are going to be different. I've been promoted, you know. Given autonomy to deal with humanity as I see fit. And as you know, humanity is not fit."

"Nonsense!" Abby blurted. "They are as fit as anyone else who has ever existed. And what would you know about it? You've hardly spent any time among them—you've never really bothered to. But I have. I know them. They are flawed and a bit fickle. That's true. You know they are so very young. But they have promise. Amazing promise to be better… to go beyond anything else that has come before!"

"That's if they don't burn down the entire planet first." Enoch spoke with a grim smile on his lips. "Or break through this illusion called earth to run amok causing untoward destruction in all the wrinkles of time and space. The problem with you, dear sister, is that you love, unconditionally. You have a soft spot for them, and it muddles your perception." He paused to sip his coffee and to sigh appreciatively.

"We cannot stand by idly," he continued waving his hand in front of him, "and watch the disaster unfold any longer, just for the sake of the few who may be worthy when so many remain so undisciplined and so… so uncivilized. They are so deliciously dangerous."

Enoch paused to pull out a remote controller from a side table and point it at the wall. As he pushed buttons, the walls started rolling down to reveal a vast bank of television and video screens. The entire wall was covered with them, images flashing in silence. Abby could see several news channels: CNN, Fox, Al Jazeera, BBC and countless others. There were History channels and Discovery, You Tube videos, stations and broadcasts from all across the planet—Enoch pressed another button and then there was audio, and the room erupted into a cacophony of sound and image.

"You see?" Enoch nearly shouted above the maddening din. He pressed a button and the screens went silent. He continued in a softer voice, "They have bridged the gap with their technology. Literally, like us, they can go anywhere and see anything they want. Oh yes, they are clever. But they are so reckless. Their cell phones, laptops, and devices now rule them. They are slaves of a wireless addiction, an algorithm that is insidiously present in every aspect of their lives. In their cars, their bank accounts, their jewelry and wrist watches. It's going to kill them, actually. Make them so sick, and they won't even re-alize it. It is a very slow poison, you know? As every second of every day they are obsessively, compulsively checking and monitoring all of the useless and extraneous elements of their insignificant and meaningless little lives. All of this to such a degree that their beloved possessions now own them. What to do? What to do?" And here Enoch turned his gaze away from the screens and smiled at Abby.

"They are like children," Enoch said, "playing with fire, and they do not understand how close they are to the very brink of destruction."

"So doomy and gloomy, dear brother." Abby quipped and placed a hand reassuringly on top of her brother's. "They just need more time. We must trust that they will find their way, eventually. A little more faith, dear brother. And time. We have plenty of that."

Enoch smiled and brought his other hand on top of Abby's, which he patted like a child's. "There, there. Ever the mother hen guiding and protecting her wayward chicks. But you need to know something else." Enoch released her hand and suddenly stood. He began pacing the room and continued speaking.

"Things are coming to a bit of a head, I'm afraid. Human scientific advances and new technologies have outpaced their social, political, cultural, and spiritual growth. They are so close to breaking through, as a collective species, into the higher frequencies and dimensions that transcend space and time. Your "Fold," I believe you call it? No matter. The point is this. They are not ready. Their consciousness has not ascended. They have access to a tool that will enable them to destroy the very fabric of reality. They must be stopped."

"No," Abby said in growing alarm. "You couldn't be further from the truth. They are ready. Many of them have already begun to make the transition. There is no other way to make the transition other than through higher love and expanded consciousness."

"That may be true for the few," Enoch said, turning away to once again gaze at the wall of TVs. "But we're not concerned about the few. It's the many that worry us. The unruly mob. What? We just clap our hands and *Voila*! Instant cosmic consciousness? No, my dear sister. It doesn't work that way. We have reached a pivotal point with humanity. They may very well have found a way to access the veil and break through the Fold without ascension. Without deeper awareness. And I tell you, sister," Enoch turned to regard Abby with something akin to a sadness in his eyes. "I'm not alone in my thinking. We cannot allow such a thing to happen, like it's happened before. An intelligent, sentient species riding through the ripples of space and time without compassion, without constraint of it's more primitive and territorial impulses would be a disaster. One we cannot allow. There must be an intervention."

"Well then, Yes! We teach them!" Abby cried. "Why can't we show them the way?"

"We have tried, Aurora. For 100,000 years, we have tried." Enoch stepped over to Abby and took her shoulders in his hands and rubbed her softly. "And in this world, at this time, humanity has taken a turn that contains too many variables—too many uncertainties. Their pathways forward end in misery, destruction, and waste."

"Not all of them," Abby pleaded. "I've seen a way forward. You said that there must be an intervention! Well why not take them down the right path. Why not show them another way forward—one in which they can join us truly as companions and equals?"

"That way is not likely," Enoch said, shaking his head. "You know it to be true. Can you guarantee such an outcome? The universal trigger event has been there for the taking, for eons. But they are too wild, too foolish. Too blind and selfish to see it! Wayward children who refuse to control their impulses." He spied a silver dish on a shelf along the wall, walked over and popped two more chocolate truffles into his mouth.

"And that is understandable." He said with another grin, as he popped in a few more. "There are multifold reasons to wander astray."

Abby shook her head in disapproval. "I'm beginning to understand why father removed you the first time. You're like a childish imp yourself. What kind of example would you set for them?"

Enoch whirled around playfully, laughing. He stopped to look back at Abby and spoke, "You know as well as I that we choose the forms that they only want to manifest themselves. You've chosen a little girl's dragon. I'm a venture capitalist. Who's the one who has come to this time and place off by a few millennia, hmm?"

Abby crossed her arms and stared daggers back at Enoch. He laughed, a long throaty indulgence that eventually made Abby smile despite herself.

"Look," he finally said. "You and I don't disagree. Yes, the time for intervention has come. But they must choose their own destiny. I'm only here to give them what they want. One by one. It must start one by one. And one way or another, this world will end."

A chill tingled down Abby's spine. "What have you done, Enoch?"

"Nothing that humanity isn't already asking for," he replied with a cocksure grin. "There are so many delightful depths. Such possibilities of imagination."

Abby reached out into the Fold, blasted through Enoch's protective shield—and yes, it was he who had been blocking her access to family, to the ones whom she loved. Maybe he let her burst through, it didn't matter. She was in now. First there was Stump, the foolish cavalier, brazenly brandishing his baseball bat. Then a visceral, overwhelming sense of hate and fear, a rage beyond rationality that emanated from the sheriff's deputy who pulled the trigger of his gun, again and again. Stump falling, knowing that this was how it must end.

Momma Bea.

She came next, and Abby reached out to her. She was still alive, in this world, only she was broken and defeated. She was dressed in the orange overalls of a prison inmate, slumped against the wall of her cell. She was sobbing, weirdly relishing the waves of revulsion and self-loathing that rolled through her. It was the only part of her mind that she could still cling too, through the haze of medications and sedatives that the doctors had forcefully given to her. She sat in solitary confinement, watching the cockroaches scamper over the tray of food that lay, untouched, near the slot of the door of her cell.

Tears welled up in Abby's eyes. It was so wrong. So unnecessary. It didn't have to be that way for Momma Bea.

Then a scream of terror tore through her. In an instant, she was in a dark chamber, a cavern of some sort? Henry was there, on his back, squirming and screaming. In the dim light of a nearby flashlight, Abby could see the expression of total and complete horror that had clenched Henry's face into a spasm of terror. His screams, it seemed, would never end, as his panic and fear were about to burst his heart.

Abby snapped back to Enoch's parlor. Enoch had returned to his chair and was coolly regarding her, sipping his coffee. He looked impish and unflappable in his frilly and laced silk shirt.

"Why?" She asked trembling, as she sank back down into her own chair. "Why does it have to be like that?"

"Oh, it's nothing that I dream up, my dear." He sipped his coffee again. "I assure you; these are only things that they bring upon themselves. I merely expedite the process."

"But Enoch..." Abby struggled to find the words. "You've made a choice, too. You've chosen evil. Or something way beyond morality. You have chosen the Devil."

"Old Scratch himself!" Enoch announced with his most charming smile. For a moment, Abby was sure that a pair of faun-like horns popped from his head, that his smile revealed a bestial glimpse of tusks in a jaw that protruded demonically forward. But then it was gone, and the Victorian image of the Devil himself was her brother, sitting in his chair, smiling and sipping his coffee.

"I am not immoral, dear sister," he slowly continued. "Amoral? Perhaps. But none of these things are of my choosing. I, like you, simply manifest in the image of their imagination. Their fancy. I am only giving them what they want."

"It doesn't make it right." Abby was horrified by this new aspect of her brother. Well, maybe not so new... but new to her since the last time they were together.

"Right has nothing to do with it," he went on. "Consider me nothing more than a cosmic bureaucrat. Just a low-level official who is here to enforce a right of easement on a driveway that the neighbors no longer wish to share."

"And what is that supposed to mean?" Abby asked, dreading the answer, but already knowing it because this had happened before. She knew what he would say before he even said it.

"The super-highway to enlightenment must still be built," he announced proudly. "Work proceeds as planned. The body of the multiverse must be respected and protected. What humanity chooses to do with itself is of no concern to me, actually. Until they threaten to bring destruction upon us all. And make no mistake! The cosmic biosphere goes on, and it will heal itself. Humanity is a malignant tumor. And the simplest solution is to eradicate the cancer."

He paused to raise his cup before draining the last of it. "In other words," he said, fixing Abby with his bright, green eyes, "Humanity has received an ultimatum: Evolve or be eradicated." His smile spread wider across his face. "There is no more effective way to proceed with that than to leave them to their own devices."

Abby closed her eyes and allowed herself to go lax. All the tensions and constrictions that her conversation with her brother had produced could just go away now. Please? She took a deep breath and concentrated. On nothing. Which is something that she had become quite good at doing.

She reached across the Fold and scoured the pathways forward. Most of them were dark and filled with images of destruction: Nuclear explosions; global warming that was strangling and ravishing a dying planet; hordes of humanity suffering in desperate conditions. Untold suffering and misery. And suddenly, brilliantly clear and in focus, she was standing in Joanna's office. The good doctor was holding the wooden carving of the Buddha in her hands, and she was crying, her shoulders slowly shaking in huge, wracking sobs. Abby had to control every impulse in her being not to reach out and comfort her—let her know that everything would be alright.

No! There is another way!

Abby wrenched herself away from Doctor Kinsey's office and threw herself back into the Fold. There were still a few pathways that were pristine and clear. Pathways that were filled with lush greenery, clear flowing water and gardens. An invisible balance of technology and a thriving biosphere, one where humanity assisted and nurtured the entire planet. One where all of humanity lived together in peace. One where the most evolved among them streaked benignly and without limit across the Fold. Into everywhere and nowhere all at once. Higher planes of reality. Ascension. It was still a possibility. And Enoch knew it.

Abby opened her eyes. She stared back at the smiling face of her brother.

Ah, are you ready to fly, little sister?

His voice sounded deep within her. It was telepathic, his smiling lips never moved.

"Yes," Abby answered aloud. "I am. And you should join me, brother. Nothing is written within the infinity of our fates. There is more than one way forward. Do not confuse your lack of patience with efficiency. Or with the will of the multiverse! Humanity has only scratched the surface. The future lies open to be embraced. Who's to say how it shall end, in this life or in another?"

"Oh, very well." Enoch chuckled, and poured himself some more coffee. "It's just much more fun to do it my way. Don't be so serious, sister. You need to relax: Delight in petty wickedness spares one a great many evil deeds."

"Do you think it's 'fun' what happened to Henry Thierrey?" Abby asked, slightly annoyed. "He was no good person, but he didn't deserve that."

"That," Enoch articulated carefully, "was entirely of his own creation. The man was a bit of a superstitious idiot. Fancied himself a genius of geometry and physics. The monsters that devoured him came purely from his own diseased and paranoid brain. It amuses me to no end how far a human being can go with self-delusion." Enoch was chuckling again, entertaining himself with his macabre little vision.

Abby spoke, staring into the crackling flames of the hearth. "You forget, brother, that this has always been more than just a game for me. We have divine purpose. And we are here for the sake of others. Not to stoke their fears and accelerate their faults. But you are always playing. Finding ways to amuse yourself, often at the expense of others. It is your weakness."

"Oh, dear sister!" Enoch leaned forward and smiled again, very charming in his earnestness. "And your weakness is that you love too easily. You shall feel the burn of love's disappointment once again, I fear."

"Oh, a thousand times over, I should think." Abby smiled, then quoted: "Wholly to be a fool while spring is in the air! My blood approves. And kisses are a better fate than wisdom, brother, I do swear by all flowers, don't cry..."

Enoch grasped her hand and chuckled one more time. "We shall see," he said. "But know this, dear sister, when I play, I always win."

Not this time, big brother.

Abby's voice sounded telepathically within Enoch's head. She held out her cup for more coffee, and Enoch, still chuckling, happily obliged her and filled it to the rim.

EPILOGUE

"FILL THE CRACKS"

July 15, 2022 – Houma, Louisiana

"I never seen nothin' like it," the young deputy was talking even before Sheriff Hibbard could step out of the car. Boots crunched on the gravel driveway as the pair of officers walked toward the dilapidated old wooden house. Bulging horizontal slats covered in worm-sign and moss adorned the exterior of the house. The sagging wood shingle roof looked like it could cave in at any moment. Wood rot and neglect. The encroaching swamp was about to claim another home, and the sheriff was wondering yet again why folks insisted on building with wood out here in the dank miasma of the bayou.

Two other deputies waited on the front porch, solemnly staring back at the approaching pair, hands on hips, fingers touching pistols. Another civilian man stood fidgeting next to them, nervous, like a buck rabbit sniffing out the distant baying of the hounds. The porch floor creaked and moaned under his shifting weight. The Sheriff took all of this in as they walked by an old Ford F-150 truck parked next to the garage, and closer to the house, two squad cars sat, their blue and red lights flashing silently in the balmy misty night.

Good. Sheriff Hibbard ruefully reflected. *I hope they came through the streets of Houma on silent mode as well. No need to wake the good people of the bayou at godforsaken two in the morning.* He glanced over at the wildly gesticulating young deputy beside him, who was still yammering. The Sheriff glanced down at the officer's name tag: *Martin. Well, Deputy Martin, I hope you know how to come in silent and clean. You're starting to get on my nerves.*

"We ain't touched nothin' either," deputy Martin was breathily and relentlessly prattling along. "Wanted to leave it just like we found it, so you could see for yourself. All pristine like."

"Thanks for that, Deputy... Martin, is it? I'm glad to see your training hasn't completely abandoned you." Sheriff Hibbard spat out a wad of phlegm and grimaced unhappily. He nodded toward the civilian. "Who's that? He looks familiar."

"That's the neighbor. Jacques Boutin. "Oh yeah, we know him. Busted for meth a while back—and a bit of a drinker, been in and out of the tank a few times on Friday nights. He's the one who found the body inside. Boy, he's got a story to tell as well. Lord a'mighty... I never seen nothin' like it in all my days. All my days." Deputy Martin shook his head and stepped aside as they reached the porch stairs.

"What've you got for me, Billy?" Sheriff Hibbard noisily creaked up the porch stairs and one of the deputies stood aside to let him pass.

"Well, Sheriff. I think it best for you to see for yourself." The deputy named "Billy" handed the Sheriff a flashlight. "Don't bother trying to find a light switch. You'll soon see why."

Sheriff Hibbard took the flashlight and assessed the faces staring back at him. The two officers' jaw lines clinched, grim and tight. The neighbor man, Jacques, all skittish and wild-eyed, but incongruently amused. He was a wiry man, about fifty—salt-and-pepper hair trimmed short in a buzz cut. He was sallow-faced and leathery-skinned, with a blotchy red nose. Looked like a tweaker. Definitely a drinker. He stood there shifting left and right, wringing a worn and greasy yellow baseball cap in his hands. He tittered and was about to speak, but the Sheriff cut him off in a stern tone.

"Pull yourself together, Monsieur Boutin. I'll get to you in a moment."

The Sheriff flicked on the flashlight and examined the door frame. It was open, but it looked like the door had been forced in, and there were bits of dusty debris on the floor where it had been pushed inward. He shined the light above the door frame, then down and all around, where it looked like a plaster wall had been covering the door frame from the inside. He had to stoop lower to pass inside, Deputy Billy right behind him.

A sweep of the interior of the house revealed an astounding thing—the entire room had been covered, in a rather slap-dashed way, with some sort of clay or plaster. All of the edges of the room were gone, and it was like stepping inside a giant egg, for the interior of the room was completely oval from ceiling to floor. There was no furniture inside the room, but there were large round balls of plaster dotted here and there, and on the far side of the room a body was lying prone beneath a large section of the plaster wall that had begun to peel away and tear down toward the floor. Sheriff Hibbard shined his light on the crumbling section of the plaster and could see the corner of the room where the exposed walls met. The plaster was being held in place by chicken wire and wads of newspaper stacked between the plaster and the original house's wall. At the rim of the crumbling plaster there was the edge of a picture frame just showing, still hanging on the wall beneath the plaster coating.

The Sheriff walked carefully toward the body as Deputy Billy's light turned on behind him and arced around the makeshift chamber. "Jesus, it's like walking into the womb," the sheriff mumbled as he glanced around at the interior of the oval-shaped cocoon. He stepped over a large plaster ball, and continued toward the body, then he stopped and shined his light on the face.

It was a man, forty something, lying on his back and wearing soiled blue jean overalls over a bare chest. He was stocky, with a bit of a beer belly and his obviously dyed brown hair was cut mullet-style like something straight out of nineteen-seventy-seven. His left hand was clutched tightly by his chest, and his right arm was thrown back awkwardly behind him. In that hand he clutched a mason's spatula, still covered in plaster. His entire body was covered in specks and flecks of it as well. He had definitely been busy working the plaster.

Next to this hand was a busted open ball of clay with another smaller spatula lying amidst the crumbles. Sheriff Hibbard fixed his torch on the man's face, his expression contorted and pinched in a silent scream of terror, mouth gaping open, revealing a set of nasty rotten teeth. His brown eyes were open, their empty, glassy stare locked terrified and uncomprehending on the crumbling wall above him.

"That's Henry Thierrey, the deceased." Deputy Billy spoke up softly behind. "No sign of external wounds or foul play." He paused to look down at his phone, thumb awkwardly scrolling down an open file. "He's got a criminal record—petty theft, disorderly conduct. No felonies or history of violence. Busted for drugs a few times, but he and his girlfriend were recently involved in a case of fraud and reckless child endangerment. He managed to claim his ignorance. His girlfriend, one Beatriz Roy took the fall. She's in Angola doing time right now. The child is a ward of the state in CHNOLA. He has no other family or associates."

"That's good," the Sheriff muttered. "Gives us a place to start. I want to talk to them both."

"Yessir! Already on it." The deputy shined his light on the spatula in the dead man's hand. "That would explain the chamber. According to the neighbor, he'd been at it for days. It's plaster of Paris, the cheap stuff you can buy down at Home Depot. There are boxes and boxes of it in the garage, and in the bedroom, you'll find most of the furniture from this room piled up every which way. You can't get into the bedroom, cuz he covered up the door…" He pointed to the left side of the chamber. "But we could see into the bedroom through the window outside."

He paused and flashed his light around the freshly plastered room. "Now in here, in what we think is the living room, he covered up everything in here including the windows to make this… this… egg chamber. But we were able to get in through the back of the house. It's only this room where he built the chamber. The rest of the house is normal, 'cept for the broken furniture and stuff."

"Egg chamber," Sheriff Hibbard echoed wryly and snorted. "I like that." He reached up and touched the plastered ceiling. It was dry and hard. He could see swirly patterns hardened into the surface where Henry had applied the coating.

"Yeah, I'd say that's been set for at least 24 hours," Deputy Billy continued as he walked over to a large sloppily made mound of plaster. "What he couldn't move, he covered up in big round balls of plaster." He nudged the mound with his boot and it didn't budge. "Hard as a rock." He squatted down and scratched at the base of the plaster boulder. "I think this is the flat screen TV and stereo system—the whole wall unit been broken down into a pile. Some of it's in the other room. Along with a big roll of chicken wire."

He shined his light to the middle of the room on another large mound that was partially split open. "That's a wheelbarrow, minus the wheels and the wooden frame and handles. You'll find those parts in the other room as well. It's all in a heap next to the furniture. This is just the basin, which he appears to have used to mix the plaster before he covered the whole thing up inside this chamber. Wheelbarrow included. There's also about a dozen mixing bowls of the stuff in the kitchen, too. Mr. Thierrey certainly been busy. The neighbor man can tell you more."

The sheriff crouched down to get a closer look at the body. The tell-tale clenching signs of rigor mortis had already begun to set in. He studied the hand with the spatula and the broken-up ball nearby. He pulled out a latex glove, snapped it over his left hand, and picked up the other spatula, sniffed it, then let it drop with a dull clink.

"What were you up to, Henry Thierrey?" The Sheriff half muttered to himself as he gazed around at the inexplicable scene around him. His latex covered fingers thrummed a vibrato rhythm on his knee. With a groan, he stood up and turned to the deputy. "Looks like a cardiac arrest. No sign of a struggle. Cause of death? Petrification. This man died terrified, by the look of him. Let's get the coroner in here pronto."

He reached down to pick up a paper-wrapped object that caught his eye. He unwrapped the object for scrutiny: a liberty-head dollar pinched between his fingers. "Don't see one of these every day."

"Well I'll be..." Deputy "Billy" leaned in with his flashlight and tilted his head, inspecting the coin more closely. "Nineteen twenty-one," the deputy declared reading the faded date engraved on the coin.

The Sheriff flipped over the paper that the coin had been wrapped in and clucked his tongue. In tiny red-painted brush strokes he could just make out the words that had been carefully written across the wrinkled paper:

They are coming. Very soon now.
Got to fill all the cracks before it's too late...

"What does it mean?" The deputy muttered looking over the sheriff's shoulder. The sheriff turned and handed it over to him.

"Put that into evidence," the Sheriff said. "And get that light out of my face. I'm gonna break my neck in here." The sheriff waved the deputy away and stooping low, headed for the door. "Better get the county CSI down here.

I don't want the State or the Feds getting' in here just yet. We're keeping this one in the Department, Billy. You understand?" The Sheriff stopped and waited for the deputy to catch up to him. He pushed the flashlight of the deputy down toward the floor and smiled grimly. He clapped the deputy on his back, which left a nice dusty hand print of plaster on his green uniform jacket. "See if we can find anything more of the unusual variety." He pointed to the coin and paper that Deputy Billy had dropped into a plastic baggy clutched between his fingers.

"Yes, indeed." The Sheriff quickly peeled the latex glove from his hand. "Let's see if we can put the pieces of this puzzle together."

He took a step before stopping short and turning back to the deputy, who nearly plowed into him. "I don't want any of you clowns disturbing evidence, you hear me? No trinkets or souvenirs for show and tell with the little wife and friends. This is big, Billy. We're gonna do everything by the book."

The deputy nodded, "Yessir." He pointed at the door. Jacques Boutin was standing in the frame of the door, leering.

"Ain't no book for the likes of what happened here. No sir!" Boutin's thick Cajun accent fell flat against the plastered chamber walls.

The man was still skittish, twitching from left to right and still wringing that greasy old baseball cap in his hands. But now his eyes glowed with a feverish light. Was he spooked or relishing the moment? The sheriff couldn't tell and just stood there gaping as the man burst into a stream of high-pitched Cajun French, a garbled tangle of words that the Sheriff could hardly make heads or tails of.

Holding up his hand, Sheriff Hibbard barked out an order, "Put a lid on it, Monsieur Boutin!" The man audibly clamped his mouth shut. Then leaned back his head and laughed hysterically.

The other deputies suddenly loomed up behind Boutin and pulled him from the door. They dragged him backwards on to the porch and held him fast as the Sheriff emerged from the house.

"Sorry, sheriff... he just came to like a bolt from the blue and we couldn't stop him..." The deputy named Martin stammered. Jacques Boutin continued to giggle and just hung limp between the deputies.

"You see him build that wall?" Boutin began, smiling wildly at the sheriff. "No, no... not just a wall. It's a...a barrier." Boutin was cackling again now, his body shaking and convulsing. "Henry say they gonna come through the cracks… He say they gonna come any time soon. He say he got to fill the cracks. He make everything smooth." Boutin paused and struggled against the deputies, who still held him, to bring his hands together. He formed a large oval with his hands in the air between them.

"Like *le oeuf,* the… egg." Boutin chortled again. Then he let himself go limp again before suddenly standing erect, arching his back and howling with laughter.

"Get that man under control!" The sheriff snapped, and the two deputies roughly dragged him, struggling, down the porch steps and on to the gravel driveway. They flung him to his knees and wrenched his arms behind him. One deputy pressed his night club against the back of Boutin's neck as the other one hand-cuffed him.

Jacques Boutin continued to chuckle, but now his laughter subsided as he spat out a gob of blood and then spoke. "Don't make no difference what you gonna do to me. They gonna come for us all, and when they do, ain't nothing we gonna do no way, no how!" He suddenly let himself go limp and just chuckled, staring down at the gravel, spitting out more blood.

"What's he talking about, sheriff?" The deputy with the night stick asked. The other deputies shifted uncomfortably, staring at each other, uncertainty painted across their faces.

Sheriff Hibbard strode over to Boutin and crouched down in front of him. He waited until the man, stopped chuckling and lifted his head to look him in the eye.

"You go on now," the sheriff intoned calmly. "You say what you want to say."

Boutin held the sheriff's gaze, and slowly the mad smile slipped away from his lips. He softly spat more blood down on the gravel before he spoke again.

"Ol' Henry… He gonna make himself inside the egg. Everything smooth. Cuz that's how they come for you. Through the edges. Through the cracks. Henry, though, he say he smarter than all of them. He gonna make it so there's not even one single line. Everything gonna be smooth, *le grand oeuf!*" Jacques paused dramatically, his gaze drifting afar, as if searching for some lost reverie.

"Who?" The sheriff impatiently snapped him out of it. "Who is going to come through the cracks, Jacques? What was Henry afraid of?"

Jacques brought his eyes back down to meet the sheriff's, focused, then slowly rolled his shoulders back. With great deliberation, he scrunched up his right shoulder and then carefully wiped the bloody spittle from his chin against his shirt.

He smiled again, then spoke more slowly now, with less of an accent. "*What, Monsieur* Sheriff, not who. What. And whatever was coming, it was coming though the edges and the cracks. He said this repeatedly. He was very clear." Jacques stared back at the sheriff impassively, all traces of his earlier hysterics gone.

"None of this makes any sense, Jacques." The sheriff shook his head and waited.

A slow smile spread across Boutin's face. "If it makes you feel better, you can say that Henry was crazy. *Hystérique.* All hot wires in his head. *Hystérique,* and three days ago he come to my house. He warned me to stay away from the edges, to eliminate all the lines... all the angles. He told me to fill the cracks, or they would come for me, too. Then he took my tools and drove off in his truck with all of my things."

"Sounds like some paranoid, tweaker-addled bullshit to me." Deputy Billy suddenly chimed in. "Goddamned egg... Why's it got to be in the shape of an egg, of all things?"

Jacques fell into a fit of sniggering again, and it was several moments before he was able to look the sheriff in the eye and speak again. "An egg, a circle. The key, Monsieur Sheriff, the key is no edges. No lines. It is a question of... of *géométrie*, perhaps." Boutin gasped as if holding back another outburst. "Henry was always talking about *géométrie* and numbers and the like. But his little egg, in the end? It did not protect him, no? He could not fill the cracks. They still come through the edges, and they still find him there."

There was a long moment of awkward silence among Jacques Boutin, the Sheriff and the deputies before young Deputy Martin blurted out in earnest. "Why we got to fill the cracks, Sheriff?"

Sheriff Hibbard stood, hands on hips, and stared back at the young deputy's solemn face, then he turned to walk back to his patrol car. The gravel crunched beneath his feet. None of it made any sense at all. There certainly were a lot more questions, and he had no answers. It was going to be a long night.

As if to remind him of how crazy all of this was, behind him, slowly, like a rolling wave, Jacques Boutin's laughter bubbled up, and then it erupted, loud, frenetic, and relentless.

ABOUT THE AUTHOR

K. G. Duncan lives with his wife, Xiao Qing, a dog and two feral cats in Los Angeles beneath the foothills of the San Gabriel mountains. He grew up in a musical theater family and has a B.A. degree in Linguistics and Philosophy and an M.Ed in Education, both from UCLA. He lived in and travelled extensively throughout China and is recently retired from UCLA Extension's American Language Center, where he taught English and developed curriculum for international students for over 28 years. He is currently the Executive Producer and Program Director for the John Raitt Awards for Youth (the JRAYs), a non-profit organization that celebrates and awards outstanding student achievements in high school musical theater throughout Los Angeles, Orange, Riverside Counties and the Inland Empire.

This is K.G. Duncan's debut novel. Check out some of his other projects at Underthesunpress.com ● facebook.com/kgd.underthesun

Made in the USA
Coppell, TX
17 November 2022